THE LAST ENCHANTMENT

ALSO BY NEVILLE DAWES

In Sepia
Prolegomena to Caribbean Literature
Interim

NEVILLE DAWES

THE LAST ENCHANTMENT

PEEPAL TREE

First published in Great Britain in 1960
by MacGibbon and Kee
This new edition published in 2009
Peepal Tree Press Ltd
17 King's Avenue
Leeds LS6 1QS
England

ISBN13: 978 1 84523 029 6

Supported by
ARTS COUNCIL
ENGLAND

FOR CHOCHOO

CONTENTS

INTRODUCTION

KWAME DAWES

'The impertinent pen, the sensual stare, the tenuous talent'
– 'An Epitaph', Neville Dawes

It is tempting to read *The Last Enchantment* as an account of Neville Dawes's own biography. The temptation is prompted by the novel's plot line, which covers much of the territory of my father's life in his twenties. Ramsay Tull's father dies when he is roughly at the same age as Neville Dawes was when his father died, and though Alphonso Tull is, in terms of biographical facts and, I think, temperament, quite different from Augustus Dawes, one can't help but read the aspirations Alphonso Tull has for his children as being based on those that Augustus Dawes, a missionary to Nigeria, himself a 'stern uncompromising Christian' (p.32), had for his four children.

Allowing such biographical temptations to take root might be entertaining, but it runs counter to the considerable efforts that Neville Dawes makes to ensure that we do not confuse the novel's protagonist with the author. However, it is safe to say that Ramsay Tull's journey, which broadly suggests his own between the ages of twenty and twenty-seven, allows Neville Dawes to explore from a critical distance many of the ideological, psychological and emotional preoccupations that consumed him for most of his younger years.

Tull is a black lower-middle-class man who aspires towards the middle class proper through education. He is a smart man with strong political views who gets a scholarship to study at Oxford University. He returns to Jamaica with his political ambitions still intact – along with his desire to connect with a woman. But Jamaica is not kind to Tull. The novel ends with his mental and emotional breakdown. He flees to his ancestral village where he tries to recover from his disenchantment with the race and class problems of his society.

Unlike Neville Dawes, though, Ramsay Tull is not a writer

(though a couple of episodes are presented as stories written by Tull). Neville Dawes was an ambitious poet when he was a teenager and that ambition grew while he was at Oxford. Also unlike Ramsay Tull, my father was an exceptional cricketer (a blue at Oxford). It may be more useful (and perhaps, his intention) to read Ramsay as a foil for my father's exploration of his own preoccupations. However, having said this, it is clear that my father does not extract himself completely from the novel. He appears, for instance, in the character of the young seventeen year old who appears in the first-person narration that is dropped in without warning or ceremony throughout the middle of the novel. Here Neville Dawes appears to be experimenting with the idea of the author figure as part of the narrative. These appearances are cameos that allow Dawes to study his other characters with greater care.

The anonymous first-person narrator was, like my father, born in Nigeria. He is a poet. He is a cricketer. He is a loner. He is, though, fascinated by Ramsay Tull and Mabel Tull. He is drawn into their world as an observer. His tone and manner is less angst-ridden than Ramsay Tull's. The world comes to him and he welcomes it with pleasure and without any great emotional turbulence. An appealing way to read these two characters, would be to see them as alter egos wrestling with modes of being in the face of the political and social realities Dawes is writing about. The first-person narrator exists without dogma and seems to find in himself an enviable ability to disconnect from the political preoccupations that consume Tull. Dawes himself was never such an apolitical figure, but one who, like Tull wrestled, with trying to turn ideology into action. Lurking behind these two contrasting characters is, I think, Dawes's interest in the effect of political engagement or lack thereof on the individual. The first-person narrator is a writer, a pure observer, whereas Tull is one who wants to act. The writer envies the activist, even though the activist ends up confused and broken at the end of the work. I think it is safe to see Dawes caught somewhere between these poles.

The interplay between Ramsay Tull and 'I', foregrounding the relationship between autobiography and fiction, speaks to Dawes's willingness to experiment with the novel form, an aspect of *The Last Enchantment* that appears to have been overlooked at the time of its original publication. For the first readers of the novel there was the goad to play the game of matching characters with actual figures in Jamaican life, a game that bothered many people in Jamaica. Some people felt attacked by Dawes and others felt misunderstood. Today's reader will probably be less interested in this guessing game than in looking at how Dawes went about trying to realise his commitment to making this work as true a reflection of Jamaican society in the ten years after the Second World War as possible.

These were critical years: years that saw the introduction of universal suffrage; the emergence of mass political parties with nationalist/independence agendas; and a degree of internal self-government, though short of the formal political independence that came in 1962. They represent years in which Jamaica was beginning to define and understand itself.

On the surface, *The Last Enchantment* relates to a period of relative innocence in Jamaica's recent history, but a careful reading reveals that it offers a detailed and sophisticated examination of the complexity of the Jamaican social matrix in which are present all the lineaments of future developments. What the novel has to say about the nature of political aspirations, social change and the country's continuing turbulence seems eerily prescient. The cynicism and disillusion with which the novel ends helps us to understand the politics and social mores of the 1960s, and the upheaval and idealism of the 1970s. Indeed, in the 1970s, Neville Dawes would have observed that perhaps the great revolution that was prophesied, seemingly foolishly and romantically by Edgar Bailey, was on the verge of happening. Yet, as the novel reveals, any such revolution would be a vexed and unsettling one given the attachments to the status quo of some sections of Jamaican society and the deeply entrenched and personalised fissures in the population's political loyalties. Thus the novel also helps to explain the movement towards political conservatism in the 1980s that was, significantly, yoked to a move towards libertarian hedonism in popular culture during that same period. From the austerity of the 1970s, to the party world of dancehall in the 1980s: Restoration Jamaica. Dawes's novel also helps us to understand the nature and sources of political violence and thuggery, and most importantly, the character of the Jamaican politician – not only the elite group of Jamaican politicians, but the working-class politician, the aspiring middle-class politician, the educated politician.

But if this is a political novel, it is only in the sense of it being about the human experience of politics rather than an exploration of political ideology. In *The Last Enchantment*, people want to believe that change can come to the society – that a social revolution is possible. But politicians succumb to the pragmatics of daily existence; they become corrupt or, in some cases, they fail beautifully. If the novel as a whole has a political position, it appears to be a warning not to trust Jamaica's middle class, the most unreliable, hypocritical and uncertain class in the society. All the novel's central characters belong to this class. If one was to miss the elements of irony in the tone of the novel one would think that none is redeemable. One must question, though, whether this is the novel's ultimate position. There is real satirical anger over the play-acting and corruption, but the novel does not, I think, rule out the possibility of the growth of an enlightened and self-aware middle class. Ramsay Tull's persistent efforts to find himself suggest this potential.

In many ways, the elements of vituperativeness in Dawes's critique of the middle class grow out of his own frustration with himself and with the impact of colonialism on the mind of educated Jamaicans. My father knew he belonged to the middle class and the novel shows that he was acutely aware of the contradictions inherent in his life and his cultural and aesthetic sensibility. He complained often that the reason he left Jamaica to head to Ghana at the age of twenty-five – Ramsay Tull's age at his breakdown over his political disillusionment – was that he could not trust the middle class and found them a dull and hypocritical lot. Nonetheless, it is clear that Dawes saw the middle class as playing an essential role in the new Jamaica, particularly if it could reach a developed state of self-awareness. He saw the middle class, at least during the years in which the novel is set, as powerfully motivated by a sense of national pride. Where his critique of this class was most reasoned was in seeing that whilst it was beginning to reject the prejudices and inherent self-loathing fostered by colonialism, what was often lacking was an understanding of Jamaican history that recognised and celebrated the role of Africa in its making.

With respect to this critique, my father put his principles into practice when he took his first wife and child to Ghana in 1955, where he lived, with an interlude in Guyana, for the next fifteen years. During those years, he divorced his first wife (a gifted artist in her own right who would later go on to have an illustrious career as a theatre director; she returned to Jamaica after only two years in Ghana), married a Ghanaian woman, my mother, and became a part of a new idealism that he admired and perhaps envied.[1] By the time he wrote *The Last Enchantment*, he had been in Ghana for a number of years, and it is clear that the views he already held about Jamaica and Jamaican attitudes to race had been reinforced by his years in Africa. His portrayal of the Prince in the novel is consistent with his view that in general Africans understood themselves more fully, were less bothered by comparisons with the culture of the white colonial establishment than were Jamaicans, and had a clearer understanding of their social roles. But Neville Dawes knew Jamaica best. And the world he describes in *The Last Enchantment* is fascinating for its accuracy and consistency with contemporary Jamaica. And for this same reason, it is a disturbing work.

Two years ago, an old friend of my father, Harry Drayton, who knew him quite well during his Oxford days, sent me some of their correspondence of that time. Apart from the eerie experience of reading my father's work when he was so young that he was still trying to work out his future, I was fascinated by their correspondence about *The Last Enchantment*. On a visit to London, my father had brought with him the only two copies of the novel he had (one was a carbon copy of the original). One copy was with a publisher when he wrote to Drayton to tell him about the work and to seek some advice about its structure and themes. It is clear that Harry was *simpatico* with my father in terms of politics, and the core of their dialogue surrounded the tough question of whether art could advance the cause of the revolution.

My father wrote page after page outlining the plot of the novel and essentially created for Drayton a digested version. He wondered about the extent to which a work, honest in its exploration of human experience, could at the same time advance a political agenda. It was clear to me that my father did not think the work had succeeded in this – and it doesn't, because he allowed the story to follow its logical trajectory. He was not sure whether his cynicism and uncertainty about dogma was what was undermining his political agenda, or whether there was something even more fundamental at work. In his discussion of the novel, my father reflected on the position of the West Indian writer as it pertained to matters of authenticity and voice. He thought he knew what a genuinely revolutionary work would look like, and he understood that it would have to come from a working-class artist. Here, Dawes did not mean an artist who sympathised with working-class values. He knew that what he had written was a close exploration of middle-class Jamaica but he felt that his own ambivalent relationship with that part of Jamaican society did not equip him to write the kind of book that was still to be written – a book that came from outside the colonised social and aesthetic values of the middle class. One can hear him arguing with himself in the conversation between Mrs. Phillips and Ramsay Tull when the latter goes to visit her in her splendid home in the hills:

> 'The real danger about our artistic awakening is that it's too closely linked to a political awakening. I am afraid that when the political enthusiasm dies the artists will either have to start all over again or die, too. It isn't that they can't observe or are writing political tracts. They have feeling all right, but it's political feeling. Don't you follow?'
>
> 'But they will have important historical value,' Ramsay said. It was an adequate phrase which avoided passing judgment.
>
> 'Of course, they will have, as you suggest, important historical value.' Ramsay was flattered, as she intended he should be, because she had repeated the phrase he used. 'But what is going to happen to them personally?...' (p.170)

In a letter to Harry Drayton, he observed that he was not the one to write that great West Indian novel. He felt that he, like most of his contemporaries who had travelled to the UK to be educated and become writers, had somehow become co-opted into the colonial values of the middle class. He prophesied that some small boy in Western Kingston, some poor ghetto youth, was going to write that work free of the mental and emotional shackles of colonialism and all that it represented.

It was as a logical fulfilment of that prophecy that my father connected so immediately with the art of Bob Marley and saw its importance. For years after the release of 'Natty Dread', my father would talk about the importance of that single. This makes sense. Bob Marley was doing two very important things as an artist in that song. First he was invoking Africa and the memory of slavery. 'Home', for Marley, resided in Africa and the gap between the Jamaican natty dread and that home was the gap of identity that haunted many of the characters in Dawes's novel:

> Oh, Natty, Natty,
> Natty 21,000 miles away from home, yeah!
> Oh, Natty, Natty,
> And that's a long way
> For Natty to be from home

By 1975, Neville Dawes had lived in Ghana for fifteen years and his views on the importance of a pan-African sensibility to an understanding of Jamaican society had grown stronger. But he also saw that Bob Marley was doing something else of critical importance. He was naming the landscape of his country with intimacy and in particular in a voice that was not affected by the manners and codes of a colonial education. In 'Natty Dread', Marley sings of walking through the streets of Trench Town – an act of ownership and assurance in the poetic possibilities of that landscape. This would have appealed to Dawes whose novel is as much about the physical world of Kingston, as it is about the people living in that world. But what Marley had that my father thought was needed above everything else was a voice shaped by the folk sensibility of Jamaican culture. Marley was as close to being the artist of indigenous genius as we had got. Judged in the light of the various theories of art explored in the novel, Marley's importance is clear. Unlike the nationalist poet Stephen Strachan who 'Madonna' Phillips (a curious 'black-face' parody of Edna Manley) declares as not having his own 'séance table', Marley unquestionably had his own table:

The artist, surely, is something like a medium with a séance table; the mediocre artist borrows somebody else's table but the great artist builds his own. Stephen has no personal seance table, if you see what I mean. Take away the progressive movement, so that we hear only the Whitman phraseology and not the new urgent Jamaican voice that is striking a new chord today... (p.170)

Marley had that 'new urgent Jamaican voice that is striking a new chord'. Whether Neville Dawes agreed fully with Madonna's views is unclear, but Ramsay seems to have no quarrel with it, although he is irritated by other things about her. Strachan, along with the middle-class theatre people and the artists who go off on a retreat to develop their art, represents a level of mediocrity and mimicry in West Indian art (including, as he sometimes saw it, his own work) that Dawes cuts to shreds in the novel. He is acknowledging, in his own text, that he does not yet have an effective model for the revolutionary artist to rest his hope in. I am sure he saw Marley as the small boy come of age.

But I think that the Marxist in my father made him harder on his novel than it deserves. It is easy to describe the novel as a political novel, but such a definition is unfairly limiting. The work is very engaged with and interested in politics, but the exploration of issues of identity and place, and the complexity of ideas of home are its dominant themes. We know this from the novel's ending. We know this because it seems to abandon the political trajectory without announcement or fanfare (Capleton dies a painful death and Edgar Bailey leaves politics), and then it ends with what can only be described as a prose poem about home – a poem about return that declares the 'narrator's' embrace of Jamaica. This is not Ramsay Tull speaking, here. This is the first-person narrator whose basic biography is significantly close to that of my father.

As suggested above, the passages of 'I' narration – three of them – that appear without warning throughout the book, represent an experimental strategy in narration that begs for attention.[2] Each of these passages comments on the central character, Ramsay Tull, but mostly they serve as an opportunity for Dawes to explore lyrically the milieu in which the work is set. We are led to trust this narrator. When he says that Tull is not a genuine communist, we trust the judgment. And we do this because the 'I' narrator does not see himself as a genuine communist, either. Instead he sees himself as an artist, as a writer, as a poet.

I am fascinated by this poet because in many ways he stands as an apologist for my father who once explained that he turned from poetry to prose because he had outgrown the former. The narrator is thus an alter ego for Dawes the politically engaged, who will eventually cast himself as a novelist seeking to find the language that will allow him to write socialist literature. The poet is a beautifully engaging figure. He is drawn into jazz and defined by jazz. He is something of a romantic. He is clever, and yet filled with irony. He is fearless and cynical, and is not cut through with the kinds of self-doubt and uncertainty that we see in Tull. And it is this man who finds a way to end the novel from a place of hope:

> I lay on my back in the little coffee-grove behind Chen's shop. Midday, and the mastering sun strong on this hillside village, lazy as the flicked leaves, the drift clouds and the sleepy dogs. It was August and the pimento perfume came to me on a light breeze. I could hear the children singing on their way home from the river. Mount Horesh. I remembered, with a sweet feeling in my stomach, that at night, 'Over there,' the story-teller would say, 'at the lights of Runaway Bay, the fishermen and the slaves' duppies in white baptismal dress.'
>
> I was a god again, drunk on the mead of the land, and massive with the sun chanting in my veins. And so, flooded with the bright clarity of my acceptance, I held this lovely wayward island, starkly, in my arms. (p.330)

Anyone who knows Dawes's poetry will recognise this passage quite easily. It is a barely 'prosified' version of his poem 'Accept-ance', which, from all sources, I understand to have been part of a sequence of poems he called 'Portrait of a Village'.[3]

> I praise the glorious summers of pimento
> sun-purple, riper than the wet red clay-smell
> of my youth by cornlight and river-run
> as, dog and I, we screamed the small green hill
> and the salt smooth wind from the leaping sea
> sang in the yellow sunflower.

I praise the dumb scared child I was
in coffee-groves and the barbecues of graves
smelling of ghosts' old country flesh, laid
by my father for his tribe (fictitious as angels):
a small alone boy riding to harvest hymns
in the green of the day as the shackle-bell tongued
on the churchy hill-top.
…
I praise all this
returning to a shower of mango-blossom –
the creaking village, the old eyes, the graves, the sun's kiss
and, lonely as ever, as the bare cedars,
I walk by the stream (where boys still plash,
dusking and falling in the star-apple sunset)
and find her there, ancient as the lost lands,
bandannaed and grey and calling:
then I read the monumental legend of her love
and grasp her wrinkled hands.

For much of Dawes's work, this rural setting and the apparent grace of return remains a constant touchstone – a place of both rootedness and possibility that appears to exist despite and beyond the unsettling world of progress, of education, of so-called enlightenment, and even of dogma. While much of this could be understood as pure nostalgia – a romanticising of the past – it is clear in *The Last Enchantment* that Ramsay Tull, like Dawes, is in search of some kind of authenticity – an indigenous sensibility untarnished by the dictates of colonialism or indeed beyond or not sufficiently expressed by the class consciousness of Marxism. I think Neville Dawes (as author through his 'I' narrator and, to a lesser extent, through Tull, who is shown as having the instinct to seek out a place of self-renewal when he flees to the country) found there a space where Africanness is located, where memory of a slave past is well understood, where beauty is constant and where innocence remains intact. The 'wrinkled hands' represent that historical memory of belonging – a quality that departure and education has threatened.

If Neville Dawes knew that he couldn't speak in the authentic voice of the boy from West Kingston, he was clearly looking for ways out of the Anglicized colonial aesthetic. Kamau Brathwaite recognises this in his 'Jazz and the West Indian Novel'[4] where he mentions *The Last Enchantment* rather briefly as a work that reveals the author's interest in jazz as an aesthetic, but as one that does not fully realise its use. Perhaps it would be more accurate to say that *The Last Enchantment* did not offer Brathwaite the kind of example that would suit his sometimes formulaic application of a 'jazz aesthetic' to West Indian literature. While Brathwaite acknowledges that at the end of the novel, Dawes's introduction of the Anancy story represents a type of improvisational gesture that suggests a jazz-inspired technique, he argues that it falls short as a genuine jazz trope because it is not organic to the larger structure of the work. With hindsight, it is possible to see rather more clearly that this is not a failure of realisation, because a jazz aesthetic is just *one* of the elements in a novel that is consciously in dialogue with itself. Brathwaite also uses Dawes's novel to point out that much of West Indian fiction at that time was being written by writers who were by then too distant from the folk sensibilities of their cultures to turn the employment of a jazz aesthetic into something authentic and almost indigenous (as in a sense ska musicians such as Don Drummond were doing in Jamaica). In making his point, Brathwaite recognises that even his employment of jazz represents a problematic act given the implications of appropriating an art form indigenous to another culture (where the nature of jazz is located in its position as a genuinely American *and* Black aesthetic), but argues on the basis of history (the common African and slavery heritage of the West Indian and the African American) and on his personal experience as a teenager and young adult in Barbados of discovering jazz in a visceral way and as a key part of the shaping of his imagination and his art, for a genuine relational affinity.

The same, of course, could be said for Dawes, as Brathwaite himself would have known. Dawes was a jazz pianist in his youth and far more than a casual fan of jazz all his life. The presence of jazz in the novel is therefore not casual. It is not merely part of the background ambience or setting for the work, but a conscious element in the dialogic nature of the work, present because of the political and cultural meanings of jazz music in the mid-twentieth century. A reader could find great reward and insight studying

19

the jazz references that permeate this work. For Neville Dawes, jazz had a sensibility that was racially pertinent and, in its bebop form, revolutionary. As such it could be used to signal a break from an English, colonial aesthetic. Yet far from being a folk form, bebop was a music of urban modernism (and we need to remember that at the time both Dawes and Brathwaite turned to jazz, reggae had not yet emerged as the form in which words and music had become inspired equal partners). On the other hand, Neville Dawes was convinced of and attracted by jazz's mutability, its capacity to offer a series of aesthetic principles that could adapt to different cultures and to different art forms beyond music. He would have been fully aware of Cuban, Brazilian, South African and West African forms of jazz emerging around the world. The use of the occasional first-person voice (as the solo break), the play with autobiography and fiction (in a way that relates to the way jazz states a melody and then improvises on its chord changes), and the poetic stretch at the end of the novel (jazz's penchant for quotation), all constitute elements of this jazz sensibility in the work. Beyond the anti-colonial aesthetic of jazz form, by dropping in the Anancy story at the end of the work, Dawes was celebrating an African sensibility as part of the resolution of colonialism. By this time, from the perspective of the Ghanaian years, he had seen for himself West African culture's genius in somehow surviving and thriving despite the Middle Passage and the horrors of slavery and colonialism. As a Jamaican he knew that this Africanness did not have to be borrowed or invented but existed as an elemental part of the Jamaican culture.

It was this quality of the novel that made some other contemporary critics uncomfortable. V.S. Naipaul, for instance, whilst praising the novel for 'an occasional brilliant turn of phrase', quarrelled with it because he saw it as a racialist work – a work overly preoccupied with matters of race – specifically, the Negro race.[5] Naipaul's criticism reflects both a panicky discomfort with race as a concept (which is ironic since Naipaul's own experience at Oxford was marked by his anxieties about the racism he experienced) and his alarmed response as an Indian Trinidadian to what he describes in *The Middle Passage* (1961) as 'the long delayed Spartacan revolt... the closing of accounts this side of the middle passage', but which he evidently saw as the expression of a Black pathology.[6] Clearly Naipaul's problems with the novel had less to do with its qualities than to do with his own racial preoccupations, but his complaint is important if only to help us begin to explore what Dawes *does* say about race in the work, because in this area, as in others, the novel still has a great deal of relevance.

The novel's narrative regularly challenges the almost desperate desire of so many of its characters of influence to assert the myth of racial equality in Jamaican society. Characters like Cyril Hanson and Raymond Phillips are adamant that the existing models of racialism – particularly those formulated in America – have no relevance in Jamaica. Dr. Phillips berates Tull for even suggesting that race is a significant issue in Jamaican society. For him, those days have passed. The novel, though, is full of passages that set out to show that this view is wrong and an expression of the ideological mystifications of the Jamaican middle class. Tull's internal struggle revolves around confronting the myth with his experience of race, both inside and outside Jamaica. At first, Ramsay is inclined to reject the relevance of race because the argument for its significance comes from his deeply conservative father, and in a form that is eminently rejectable. Ramsay's father, who dies at the beginning of the novel, makes it clear to Ramsay that race is elemental to the Jamaican experience:

> 'Yo' grandfather born in slavery,' Alphonso told Ramsay. 'He was six years old at 'Mancipation. You mus' never forget, after all your education, that your grandfather was a slave. But all the same, same place here in Orange Town everyone of his children get a' education an' learn a trade an' turn out good. Tek your Uncle Boysie now, for instance, in Cuba. They was never a better carpenter in Orange Town. Is he built Tabernacle Church, you know...' (p.32)

Whilst Alphonso Tull's working-class background lends credibility to his views, his attitudes to race are rooted in the ideas of Booker T. Washington and Dr. Aggrey. Washington's narrative is one that allows the Negro to recognise his slave past, but treats it as inspiration to rise out of slavery and become better than that slave past allowed. Alphonso is not asking his son to be proud of his grandfather, but of being proud of how far they have come.

Now, Ramsay needs to know his place and be satisfied in it (an argument endemic to the class structure of colonial society). At first, Ramsay does not want to embrace these ideas in any form, he wants to embrace a more heroic and noble past, but is haunted by the question of whether he can shake those limitations that he feels he may have inherited from his father. In this respect the novel helps us to understand why the elder Tull's conservative views are deeply important to Jamaican society.

Dawes's commentary on race is most telling in the sequence of ironic vignettes in the middle of the novel, entitled 'JAMAICA 293' (the significance of the title is in the ten score and 93 years between the founding of the English colony of Jamaica in 1655 and 1948 when Ramsay Tull – and Neville Dawes – left Jamaica to go to England).[7] They are four short narratives, two of which feature contemporary working-class black people. The sequence begins with a short history of colonialism, one in which Henry Morgan and Britannia rule 'shapely mulatto women kept by the yonge 'Squires for a certain Use' (p.181). The other figures include a young 'scuffler' who steals mangoes for a living, an educated black man who returns from England and suddenly, in the middle of the street, begins to laugh in a way not expected from respectable black people – a liberating laugh, and there is also the insurrectionist Baptist, Sam Sharpe, the leader of the 1831 revolt, who 'came riding over the hills of Westmoreland on a white horse with a bible and a mouth of eloquence so they hanged him for his slavery in Montego Bay. And he will always ride those hills on a white stallion.' Sharpe will haunt the country and Dawes's own imagination for years, most notably in his poem 'Daddy Sharpe'[8] that celebrates this rebel – a piece that may have played some part in the elevation of Sharpe into an official National Hero. Then there is George Headley, the great crick-eter, whose cool triumph in the game is, for Dawes, extremely significant. This short passage is one of the most important pieces of cricket prose in our literature. The relish is there. The game unfolds with quiet intensity. It is the romantic moment – the instant in which a working-class man outclasses the world with sheer brilliance. He is the model of greatness. But even this greatness is undermined. There are other such sporting figures in the novel. The greatest googly bowler in the island goes blind and is reduced to working as a servant at the Kingston Club. Acceptance into the upper classes is virtually impossible even for the talented and the gifted. But George Headley has no such aspirations. His one interest is to carry the team, to be a gladiator on the field and, in many ways, Dawes uses him as a figure of myth – a model of achievement that is illusive but that remains central to the aspirations of the working class.

Finally, there is a working-class woman whose life story of suffering, of living and hustling in the squalor of the Dungle, becomes another symbol of the society. The sequence expresses a tragic sense of despair in response to the lie of racial equality.

These 'vignettes' are unapologetically about the politics of colonialism and the way they intersect with matters of race. But more than that, Dawes presents them as variations (or *vershans*) on a theme that constitutes the necessary backdrop to this novel. If Tull is struggling with the implications of race, and others, in the face of the evidence, are denying that the racial question is endemic to the society, the explanations for their positions, Dawes argues, must be sought in the Jamaican historical experience. Apart from the British soldiers, who have long left Up Park Camp, the world that Dawes describes in these cutting vignettes would be all too easily recognised by a reader of current Jamaican fiction.

Beyond what it shows us about a key period of Jamaica's recent history, *The Last Enchantment* remains profoundly readable because Dawes's characters are very well drawn and their fate is important to us: Edgar Bailey's ambition, Mona Freeman's quest to find a purpose for her life and to shake off her bad reputation, Ramsay Tull's attempt to find significance in his life after his return to Jamaica, Mrs. Hanson's struggles with aging, her complicated ambitions and inability to come to terms with the reality of race, and so on. Even a less attractive character such as Cyril Hanson is drawn with a care for detail and a complete commitment to the logic of his views. His open, cool betrayal of Ramsay Tull is one of the most arresting moments in the novel, and even though the novel is marked by a detached sense of irony and an edge of satire about the nature of middle-class life, we are never able to feel that Tull has found a real alternative to that life.

At best he can mock it, though ultimately it is that lifestyle that drives him to breakdown. Describing the wedding between Cyril Hanson and Patricia Phillips, the daughter of the country's premier, the novel tells us:

> The reception was on the lawn of the Phillips' house and 'Sylvia Surrey', reporting the 'wedding of the year' in her daily society column, wrote an inspired description of the richness and quantity of the food and drink consumed… (p. 323)

What Dawes captures here is the self-important tone of those who want to grant this class an elevated status, and the lack of scale and absence of irony that allows this class to take itself so seriously.

Ultimately, Dawes has exactly what Mrs. Phillips says Strachan does not have. He has technical skill as a writer. The prose is at times quite beautiful in its lyricism, but its general quality is one of economy and precision. There is a constant liveliness and energy in its treatment of characters, even those not going to be terribly important to the work. He relishes the challenge of painting a picture for the reader:

> The door opened and an enormous ebony-coloured man, wearing a duffle-coat, came in with the wind. He was built like a heavyweight boxer but his head was very small. He had been drinking and was not accustomed to being drunk so he was trying to look profound. He had the aggressiveness of an unintelligent man who is trying to become a well-known personality and the childishness of a powerful body that is temporarily paralysed by alcohol. He gurgled when he laughed and when he sang it sounded like a *tremolo* laugh (and he sang often during the evening; he had a powerful baritone which he said could break wine glasses or something). (p.240)

These details establish both the uniqueness of the character and more general psychological observations. They carry the man into our consciousness. Dawes brings this same sense of idiosyncratic detail to the dialogue where his use of dialect brings to mind the work of Zora Neale Hurston, sharing with her the gift of being able to capture the continuum of, respectively, African American and Jamaican speech with a linguist's care for detail. Dawes's Jamaicans speak the language of a modern city. Absent are the Americanisms of Roger Mais or the sometimes clunky clichés that Vic Reid sometimes comes up with in presenting rural speech. Dawes comes to the language of his characters like a skilled stand-up comic comes to his jokes; for him, the exact phrase is crucial to the effectiveness of the joke. Above all, his characters are defined by their language and by the timing of their remarks. We can see this in the scene describing Ramsay Tull's leave-taking when his work colleagues board the ship to see him off to England:

> 'All set?' Alf-Gordon asked. He put his hand round Sweetness' shoulder. 'You going to leave Sweetness with me?'
> 'Cho, you doan have a chance,' Bertram said. 'Him will her to me long ago.'
> She sighed and looked serious.
> 'How all of you leave the office at the same time?' Ramsay asked.
> 'We going back right away,' Alf-Gordon said. 'I jus' borrowed Mr Sweeney's car for five minutes.'
> 'The bar open, Alf,' Donald Stevenson said. 'Come let's have a quick one for the water,' Alf-Gordon said. 'Come nuh, Sweetness! You doan touch the strong?'
> In the bar Alf-Gordon said, 'You know, I want you to do something for me when you go to Paris. When you go to Paris' (he lowered his voice so that Sweetness wouldn't hear), 'I want you to catch a nice piece for me, in Pigalle.'
> 'How you –'
> 'In Pigalle,' Alf-Gordon said. 'Remember the name, Pigalle.'
> 'How long you going for?' Bertram asked.
> 'I don't know. I mightn't come back,' Ramsay said, with the new irresponsibility: then he saw her eyes. 'No, I'm joking. Three years.'
> 'By that time you just get a fine accent,' Bertram said and added, half to himself, 'Cup o' tie and a sloice o' kyke.' Bertram knew a lot of English soldiers (pp.178).

The gentle witticism with which the passage ends reminds us of the early Naipaul. It is a wit that I associate fully with my father who was known for engaging his friends and enemies alike in bouts of merciless ribbing and repartee. His jokes were littered with puns and a rich stock of Shakespearean allusions and Jamaicanisms. Note the cutting humour when he describes the work of one of the high-ranking ministers of the new government:

> French depended exclusively on a young civil servant, a gradu-
> ate of the London School of Economics, who was an expert on
> graphs. (p.252)

Elsewhere the critical voice is not hidden behind character. We get an early taste of it when the authorial voice attacks the 'stupid welfare workers', 'governors' wives' and 'unscrupulous novelists' for perpetuating the 'mistaken idea about perfect racial harmony' in Jamaica (p.51). The cultural establishment of Jamaica is treated with as much ridicule as the philistine middle class. In many ways, for Dawes, they are one and the same. Note the sharp irony in his description of the new national festival, which the narrator describes earlier as a 'great success'. The poet Strachan's poem is called 'Jamaica, whither?' (That the unintentional pun is missed by the poet and the organisers because of their penchant for archaism is, for Dawes, part of the joke.)

> The picture of Jamaica which emerged from the Festival
> was that of a country peopled entirely by politicians and various
> grades of intellectuals. The ordinary worker was hard to find
> during the Festival. Sometimes you saw him nailing a platform
> or running an electric wire, and, once, during an important
> rendering of a Chopin prelude in the Institute Lecture Hall he
> was heard hammering on empty oil drums in a backyard in the
> nearby lane – but, on the whole, he showed very little interest
> in the Festival. Mrs Phillips said this was a pity because the
> Jamaican worker is 'so picturesque'. (p.255)

And virtually an entire chapter is spent in a relentless assault on the pretentiousness of a group of middle-class artists on an absurdly hopeless arts retreat in the hills. Ramsay Tull is caught in the middle of all of this, and his emotional disease is his sense of privilege at being included, even though he is disgusted with the mediocrity of the enterprise. Indeed it is Dawes's ability to allow his central character to remain vulnerable and critical at the same time that makes this work a sophisticated study of Jamaican society.

I have suggested the importance of both the Anancy story and the lyrical prose poem of return that end *The Last Enchantment* as keys for reading the novel. The former has been found mysterious. The story has had many incarnations and is usually called 'The Tar Baby' and the key moment in it is when Anancy or Brer Rabbit attacks the tar baby and ends up stuck to the creature. It is an ignominious end for the anti-hero, who is a bully of sorts. But in this version of the tale, it is hard to tell who the real victim is. Anancy has very little control over the circumstances of his life. Indeed, he seems embarked on a picaresque adventure in which he keeps reacting in the same way to the same thing that keeps happening to him, and never seems to learn anything. Until he faces the tar baby, one could see the tale as a Sisyphean journey of pure futility. The deception, of course, is that things seem to change. The characters change, the action changes, and the setting changes, but the fundamental plot remains the same. Thus narrative as a reflection of progress becomes an illusion. More than that, the central character remains completely incapable of controlling his fate. His march has taken him from a 'juk' by 'ping-wing' to having a fish. He has done well for himself without doing very much. He meets his match with the tar baby who won't speak, and simply captures Anancy by his silence. This is the message reinforced by the proverbial phrase that ends the narrative: 'Who say no, do no harm/ Amen to glory/ Cananana Poh.' The proverb 'who say no, do no harm' speaks well to the value of silence and the value of self-control, and the riddling last words mean:'That's all I have to say'.[9] Anancy might have ended his problems sooner with silence, but he does not.

Dawes, then, chooses to end the novel with a certain existential absurdity that speaks to the futility of the machinations of man. In many ways, all the tricksters of the novel are either exposed or find themselves unable to achieve what they might want. More than that, the story seems to argue the pointlessness of the political games that drive the work forward; it is not the political goal that is pointless, but the play-acting that passes as politics. At the end of the work, it is the poet who stands at home in St. Ann and imagines himself cradling 'this lovely wayward island' in his arms. This is a West Indian novel, indeed, and a profoundly Jamaican novel – one that will continue to resonate with meaning for anyone interested in understanding this wayward and lovely island.

Footnotes

1. This background to my father's life in Ghana is more fully explored in *A Far Cry from Plymouth Rock* (Peepal Tree Press, 2007).
2. It's interesting to note that George Lamming does something similar in his contemporary *Season of Adventure* (1960) where, again without warning, an authorial 'I' breaks into the narrative texture and makes a self-critical statement about his failure to take responsibility for the real Powells of the world.
3. Originally broadcast as part of the B.B.C. *Caribbean Voices* Programme, Script 893, 15.11.1953. Forthcoming in *Fugue and Other Writings*, Peepal Tree Press, 2009.
4. Originally published in *Bim* 11, Jan-June 1967; *Bim* 12, July-Dec, 1967 and *Bim* 13, Jan-June 1968, and in *Roots*, 1993.
5. Quoted by Patrick French in *The World Is What It Is* (Picador, 2008), p. 193. It is not entirely clear whether the source is a review in the *New Statesman* or private correspondence.
6. *The Middle Passage* (London, 1962, Penguin ed.), p. 201.
7. Thanks to Hannah Bannister of Peepal Tree Press for pointing this out – an explanation that had eluded me.
8. 'Sam Sharpe', first published in *From Our Yard: Jamaican Poetry Since Independence* (ed. Mordecai, Institute of Jamaica Publications, 1987), p. 65; forthcoming in *Fugue and Other Writings*.
9. Thanks to Helen and Mervyn Morris and Marjorie Whylie for putting me on the track of what this phrase might mean. Mervyn pointed out that in Cassidy and Le Page's *Dictionary of Jamaican English* 'canana' directs us to 'kanana':

     kanana sb or adj dial; abbr or by-form of next. A word indicating that there has been nothing said, or no answer given when one was expected... Used both declaratively and interrogatively...

     kananapo ... sb, adj, or adv dial; var of *karanapo*.
     1. A marked silence; a failure to answer a question asked; as an adj, silent; as an adv, silently. ...

     karanapo ... sb dial; cf Twi [words meaning] silent, absolutely still, perfectly quiet.

     Mervyn Morris's guess is that in *The Last Enchantment* there is an 'a' added to what should really have been 'Cananna Poh' and Marjorie Whylie confirms that the phrase means 'There's nothing else to say'.

PART ONE

BLOOD AND POINSETTIAS

'*Amicus Plato*, my father would say, construing the words to my uncle Toby, as he went along, *Amicus Plato*; that is DINAH was my aunt – *sed magis amica veritas* – but TRUTH is my sister.'

Laurence Sterne, *Tristram Shandy*

I

Late November in Kingston, with a firm promise of December's poinsettias. In the morning a cold breeze whirled the dust in the dry area, once a garden, in the front yard of the Tulls' house on St James' Road. Even downtown Kingston was cooling off for Christmas. The traffic on St James' Road, unaware of the dead body in the small back room of the house, continued to run smoothly, the cars changing gear down at the sharp gradient some distance from the front gate.

Ramsay Tull sat on the verandah in a wooden armchair from which the red paint was stripping. He was reading an obituary notice in the *Daily Gleaner*. It was the first time that he had seen his name in a newspaper.

> TULL – Alphonso. Died 26/11/46 leaving wife, Alice; sons, Bobsie and Ramsay; daughters, Madge (Mrs. Ray Turner), Rosalie (Mrs. Martin Lowe) and Mabel, to mourn their loss. Funeral leaves 12, St. James' Road at 4.30 p.m. today, thence to May Pen Cemetery.
>
> R.I.P.

Ramsay Tull was nineteen, with a large domed forehead and the ebony colouring of his mother. His father's death had a curious effect on him – he was only numb from his mother's weeping and felt no grief. Yet he had loved his father and remembered him now in the afternoons and evenings of a village in the country.

The afternoons at Orange Town, a small village perched on a hillside in St Ann, had been quiet with brilliant sunlight through the leaves as the land rested. Even the voices that called or sang were lazy and sleepy. Ramsay remembered the green afternoons and the purple evenings.

Alphonso Tull, who in the strange course of his life had been a shoemaker, a tailor, a labourer in Panama and finally a small landed proprietor with eighty acres in banana and pimento, had been determined to educate his children as good Christians. He had failed. A stern uncompromising Christian, he was deeply disappointed at the way in which his four younger children – Rosalie was the eldest – had grown up, godless and gay, in the frivolity of the city. He wanted to save Ramsay. His philosophy, incoherent and distorted, was that of a hard-working negro prospering by white man's grace in a white man's world. His heroes were Booker T. Washington and Dr Aggrey, and he tried to make Ramsay, barely nine, read *Up From Slavery*. Ramsay never read the book and came to hate the sight of its grey moth-eaten cover.

'Yo' grandfather born in slavery,' Alphonso told Ramsay. 'He was six years old at 'Mancipation. You mus' never forget, after all your education, that your grandfather was a slave. But all the same, same place here in Orange Town everyone of his children get a' education an' learn a trade an' turn out good. Tek your Uncle Boysie now, for instance, in Cuba. They was never a better carpenter in Orange Town. Is he built Tabernacle Church, you know....'

Ramsay would think (as Marcus, the yard-boy, had taught him), 'Why this ole man doan shut him mouth an' mek me go see if the springe dem catch?'

'Yes, Papa,' he would say.

'You must always show respec' to white people, though, mi son. Is dem rule the world, you know. You never see a naygah can do anything except a white man teach him. But doan mek nobody cuss you call you naygah. I hear say your Uncle Boysie shoot a white man in Cuba, nearly kill him for him cuss him, call him "naygah". One day black people will rule, though. We only has to show respec' and carry ourselves decent an' study everything a white man can do!'

Alphonso Tull talked like this endlessly – as they rode to ground on Saturday morning, as they walked back from service on Sundays, as they sat together late at night eating, as equals, large quantities of sugar-cane and mangoes.

Ramsay's main interest in Orange Town – where he lived till he was ten – had been setting springes to catch grass-quits, walking barefoot through the hot barbecues of drying pimento and listening to the indecencies that Marcus carefully taught him. Marcus showed him how to make vulgar signs with his fingers at the girls at school and Ramsay never forgot the beating he received for making a sign, absentmindedly, at fat Miss Bennet, the assistant teacher. Ramsay at that time wasn't at all interested in white people. The only white people he had ever spoken to were Busha Grant and the Baptist parson.

Ramsay threw the *Gleaner* on the floor, went to the back verandah and leaned over the railing smoking a cigarette. The morning mourners had gone and the house was quiet. He went to look, for the last time, at his father's body laid out for burial. The room narrow and gloomy, the grey curtains drawn, the small table with a few dusty books, the large white sheet, the strong smell of antiseptic. His father's face was clean-shaven and ashen in death, the skin taut around the large beaked nose. And though the eyes were closed there was no repose about the face – it struggled, as it had done in life, in the deep wrinkles of the upper lip.

Ramsay was startled by a sudden commotion in his mother's room on the other side of the house. He could hear Bobsie's thick guttural voice and the pleading whispers of his mother. Bobsie was drunk, and Ramsay stood beside his father's body feeling himself in another cool peaceful world where the indecency of Bobsie's being drunk on such a day had no relation to the fact of that dead body.

Mabel, his sister, poked her head into the room and said, 'Ramsay, Aunt Alice call you!' Mabel always referred to her mother as 'Aunt Alice'; it was one of her affectations.

'It's a disgrace, Bobsie,' Mrs Tull was saying. 'You doan have not a respect for your dead father! See your brother here, Ramsay – stink of rum. In my bitter sorrow today this boy drunk!'

She rested her large kimonoed body gently on the yellow and purple quilt and pillows, and dabbed her forehead with a hand-

33

kerchief soaked in bay rum. The room reeked of bay rum mingled with the slight diffuse sweetness of talcum powder.

'Choh, Bobsie, man,' Ramsay said in an undertone to his brother, who sat on a low stool near the dressing table whistling tunelessly through his front teeth and watching his mother, 'Choh, Bobsie, man, is a dyam disgrace!'

Mrs Tull sat up abruptly and hissed at Ramsay, 'Doan use any bad word in this house!' She was near hysteria. The room was suddenly quiet, except for Bobsie's whistling and Mrs Tull's asthmatic sobbing. Then the sound of a Blues drifted into the stillness. Mabel, who was leaning through the window, wiggled her large rotund buttocks to the rhythm of the music. She walked across the room and stood in front of Bobsie with her arms akimbo.

'You are a wutliss ole drunkard, Bobsie,' she said. 'I shame to be your sister!' Her finely-moulded lips curled and her nostrils quivered disgustedly at the acrid smell of rum which came from Bobsie. He thought slowly and deliberately. Then he spoke quickly, looking at the floor, spitting the words out.

'You, Miss Mabel, doan come to me with none of your facety chat. What are you? You jus' turn prostitute now.' Then he raised his head, pushing his chin at her. 'Every young boy in Vineyard Town do it with you already!'

The remark stung her. She searched through the wardrobe, the dressing table drawers, till she found a pair of scissors. Ramsay was only just able to grab hold of her as she rushed at Bobsie. Bobsie got up with exaggerated unconcern and walked out. He looked very much like his father, particularly in the way he ducked his head stepping down each stair.

When he had gone Mabel sat beside her mother, both staring at the wall in a pantomime of deep breathing and sobbing. Ramsay found it less painful to think that his father had merely gone away for a while and wasn't really dead. Still crying, Mabel put her arm around her mother's shoulder.

'Mama, is a wutliss lie what Bobsie say, you hear, is a wutliss lie!' she said.

The afternoon of the funeral began with polished serenity. Bright sunlight glistened on the long line of cars in St James' Road. The two grey horses that pulled the hearse were plump and sleek. As people gathered, the impression was one of shifting masses of black and white, like a linocut, in the old shrunken smooth black suits of the men and the white dresses of the women.

Although the Tulls were Anglicans they had asked the Rev. James Smith, the only relative in the ministry, to do the laas' for Maas Alphonso. The Rev. James Smith was a pastor in the First Church of Christ's Holiness in Allman Town. He conducted the service in an individual way, being careful not to offend people of other denominations. He read the usual passages from Corinthians and Revelation but he prayed *ex tempore* because many of the mourners were Baptists, relatives of the Tulls who had travelled over from Orange Town that morning.

It was during the prayer that Bobsie came in. His arrival was heralded by a wave of murmuring which began in the street and finally overwhelmed the Rev. James Smith's prayer. Bobsie was completely drunk. He alternated between swearing and trying to remember the words of a hymn. He could hardly walk. As he staggered into the room Ramsay tried to persuade him to go back outside. What followed was almost a fight between Bobsie and Ramsay. Bobsie's language was filthy in the extreme, but it was clear he knew he was at his father's funeral.

The Rev. James Smith continued to pray but he could not be heard above the noise. Then, one of the men from Orange Town decided to 'raise' a hymn and drown Bobsie's swearing. The man was a Baptist and the only hymn he could think of at that moment was 'Blest be the tide that binds', which is not a funeral hymn. There were no Baptist hymnals available, so at the end of each line he shouted the words of the next line.

> (BlestBE the tide that binds)
> Bless bee-ee: da tie-ad: dat bine
> (OurheartsinChristianlove)
> O ha-ats: een Chree-e: stan love)
> (Thefellowship of kindredmind)
> Tha fell-ow sheee-eep: of kee-en: dradmine
> (Is liketo that above)
> Ease li-ike: to tha-at a-BOVE.

By the time they had finished the second verse Ramsay had succeeded in putting Bobsie to bed. The Rev. James Smith continued his prayer, while Mrs Tull, Madge, Rosalie and Mabel wept in shame.

After the funeral nine cousins returned to the house to spend the night there. They sat in formal grief in the sitting room and remembered Alphonso Tull. Mrs Tull, Madge and Rosalie, and their husbands and Ramsay were there.

'Excuse me, Aunt Alice, but Mass Alphonse die of the same old complaint?' Miss Rhona Tull asked in her schoolteacher's voice. She was very black and her short hair had been losing its 'straightening' all afternoon. Alphonso Tull had had no 'old complaint'. Miss Rhona was merely being inquisitive and fast.

'You know up to Tuesday, Miss Rhona, Maas Alphonso was hearty as you or me,' Mrs Tull said. She was calmer now though she still dabbed her forehead with bay rum. 'Tuesday night him tek in an' today Thursday him gone. Gawd move in a mysterious way, Miss Rhona.'

There was a murmur of assent and reverence from the country cousins, and an old woman, Alphonso Tull's aunt, said 'Amen'.

'I remember what a shining light him was in Orange Town village, Miss Alice. Since unu come town not a day pass without we speak of Maas Alphonse.'

They went on remembering. Ray Turner, Madge's husband, slipped away to the dining room. A moment later he returned and called Martin Rowe, Rosalie's husband.

The country cousins talked about the goodness of Maas Alphonso, and the hard life in the village, of deaths, Miss Prissy have a stroke laas' month, an' drought nearly kill we in August, you coulda ongle get a trickle of water from river an', you know, Miss Alice, how river water did sweet, well, since August it just lose it taste.

A man who sat on the floor near the verandah began humming Maas Alphonso's favourite hymn, 'At even ere the sun was set'. They sang it softly, in smooth harmony. Madge and Rosalie cried. During the singing Ray Turner came in and whispered to Ramsay. Then he too went into the dining room.

When Ramsay left, Sister Vashtie said, 'What a big young man Maas Ramsay turn since him go to college, eh, Miss Alice?'

'Him have good head,' another cousin said. 'What a way him use to write jus' like a copy-book. Him going study for anything, Miss Alice?'

Ray and Martin sat at the dining table. They had an open bottle of Three Dagger Rum in front of them. With them was Mabel.

'Ramsay boy,' Martin said, 'you better take some of the stuff. Set your mind at rest, man.' He poured rum into a glass and set it in the centre of the table. 'For the ole man,' he said.

Mabel fetched two bottles of ginger ale from the ice-box and they sat drinking, silent and indrawn. Mabel could hold her rum like any man. She was twenty-two, buxom and wild. Her aggressive body with its pouting breasts was a challenge to every man who saw her. And when she walked, her shoulders thrown back, striding, with the wind blowing her skirt sheer against her legs, she was like a study by Delacroix. There was no dissipation known in Kingston that Mabel had not indulged in. She had been going with men for years, had had two abortions and wanted to be a nurse. She sat with her chin resting on the table, eyes closed, arms stretched at full length and her fingers tightly clasped. The shadows from the bottles and glasses made patterns like scars on her cheek.

Martin ran his fingers gently up her arms and said, 'Wake up, chile! Day light!' Mabel started, opened her eyes and leaned back, stretching. Then she laughed. It was a deep rich fruity sound, a sweet laugh. She was in love with Martin. Ramsay thought you could forgive Mabel anything because of her laugh. He tried, getting drunker, to feel more bereaved but he could think only of Bobsie and the smell of antiseptic in the small back room.

The country cousins had settled themselves to sleep on the sofas and chairs in the sitting room. Madge and Rosalie put their mother to bed and then went into the dining room.

'But Father Divine,' Rosalie said in horror when she saw the empty rum bottle, 'is drink unu sit down in here drinking?'

'We just having a drink for the ole man,' Martin said. 'Is good luck for everybody and will rest his soul in peace.'

'Come, Ray, I'm going home,' Madge said, her voice breaking.

Mabel got up and smoothed her hair. She said, 'Rosie, I'm coming to sleep at your place. I could never sleep here tonight!'

37

They left Ramsay alone at the table. Presently Bobsie came in to drink water. He had slept for six hours, was stale with rum and his lips were swollen.

'They put away the ole man well?' he asked Ramsay, not looking at him but drawing circles in a pool of water on the table. Ramsay grunted and they were silent again.

'You been drinking this coloured rum, man?' Bobsie said. 'You going to stink of it tomorrow. The best thing you better do is buy two paradise plums and a nutmeg in the morning and chew them up together. That way nobody will smell the stale rum on you.'

Ramsay gave him a cigarette and he got up and shuffled off to bed.

Hanging on the wall above the china closet was an old framed photograph, full length, of Alphonso Tull. He was dressed in the Edwardian fashion – a round loose detachable collar, a long jacket cut square and reaching below the knees. He had flicked back the right side of the jacket and had rested his right hand proudly on his hip, revealing braces and a large belt buckle. His left hand rested easily on a chair and his wide moustache drooped in a slight smile. Ramsay had looked at this photograph almost every day of his life and tonight it had no more significance than the words, 'This man is dead'. But he remembered, inconsequentially, 'in a white world, respect'.

He went into the bedroom where Bobsie was asleep and snoring. He turned on the reading lamp he had made from an old biscuit tin and tried to read one of Horace's *Odes*. The words only danced on the page. He turned the light out and in a moment was floating to sleep and trying to remember what it was that Bobsie had said he should buy next morning.

★   ★   ★

Mona Freeman, a heavily-built girl of twenty-three with Indian features and long hair, sat in front of a roller-top desk in the outer room of the Resident Magistrate's office in Kingston, keeping her short-skirted fleshy legs tightly crossed. She was filling in forms. All the six other temporary clerks in the office were filling in forms, except Bertram Shaw who was at the grating chatting to a plainclothes policeman known as Power. The six male clerks, with the Civil Service decoration of clean white face-towels draped gently over the left shoulder, were writing steadily and at the same time discussing their amorous adventures. Bertram Shaw, short, round and twenty-two, had been famous at school as a soccer player and as a user of extremely indecent language in all kinds of company. He was trying to persuade Power to buy him an illegal lottery ticket (called Peaka Peow) on the basis of a dream he had had the night before.

Occasionally a uniformed constable came from the inner office occupied by the Clerk of the Courts and handed papers to the Deputy Clerk who sat facing the window with his back to the other clerks. The room had a damp disinfected smell and a slight mustiness from the stacks of old paper piled against the walls.

Ramsay was writing out charges for Indecent Language. He arranged the carbons carefully for there had to be six copies.

'… on the 8th day of October in the year of our Lord One
Thousand Nine Hundred and Forty-six did unlawfully use
and utter the following Indecent Language, to wit …
Contrary to Section …'

Myrtle, the maid who cleaned the office and served the clerks with large glasses of iced water, came in through the side door near the grating. Alf-Gordon, who had already spent three years in the Courts Office mysteriously without either promotion or increment, took off his spectacles and beckoned Myrtle.

'Myrtle, please bring me a glass of ice-water,' Alf-Gordon said.

'Ice-water not ready yet, Mr Gordon,' Myrtle said. She was about thirty-five, rather tall, and a zealous Seventh Day Adventist though she worked every other Saturday. She spoke with a clipped, genteel accent.

'Listen Myrtle, mi dear,' Alf-Gordon pleaded, 'I get tank up with rum laas' night. Thirsty killing me!'

'I doesn't serve ice-water before ten o'clock, please,' Myrtle said, on her dignity.

'It must be that bow-leg man you keeping make you stay so,' Alf-Gordon said putting on his spectacles with a flourish. All the clerks, except Mona Freeman and the Deputy Clerk, laughed.

'You just leave him out, Missa Alf-Gordon,' Myrtle said, without anger. 'Him trouble you? Even though you see him there hordinary so, him understand himself!'

Bertram Shaw guffawed loudly and the Deputy Clerk told him to shut up.

The telephone rang. The call was for Mona Freeman and she swung across the room to take it. All the clerks stopped what they were doing to watch Mona walk across the room. Alf-Gordon cleared his throat significantly. She put her lips very close to the mouthpiece and spoke so softly that Ramsay, whose desk was nearest the telephone, could not hear what she was saying. So Alf-Gordon tiptoed across the room, stood behind Mona and mimicked the Clerk of Courts exactly. 'Miss Freeman, will you please stop making love on the telephone!' Mona waved her hand at him in mock annoyance.

'Why you come back today?' Alf-Gordon asked Ramsay. 'If it was me I'd take two weeks off.'

'I'm all right,' Ramsay said. 'Anyway I don't have anything to do at home.'

'You could go to Bournemouth an' have a swim every day,' Alf-Gordon said. 'By the way, Capleton appearing in No. 1 Court this morning, you know.' Capleton was the leader of the left-wing People's Progressive League. 'They going swing him this time,' Alf-Gordon added tauntingly.

'Who is defending him?' Ramsay asked.

'Fernandez defending and Crown Counsel prosecuting. They going swing him just the same. If they don't catch him on "inciting to riot" they'll have him with the Emergency Regulations. Communism is foolishness.'

'The Russians have won the war, though,' Ramsay said, watching the satisfied smirk on Alf-Gordon's face. This same daily argument was beginning to annoy Ramsay. It wasn't even an argument but a series of statements and counter-statements.

'What does that prove?' Alf-Gordon asked thumping the top of the desk. 'Hitler might have been winning the war. It doan prove anything. Anyway they're going to swing Capleton for hard labour and he'll be breaking rock-stone at Rockfort quarry.'

The Courts Building began to hum at ten o'clock with the

voices of policemen, solicitors' touts, litigants, a few whores, and many casual spectators. Lawyers drifted lazily through the office asking for their cases to be called early. Alf-Gordon chatted affably with all of them. He was a drinking companion of most of the younger solicitors and sometimes prosecuted in the Petty Sessions Court. A few minutes before ten o'clock an ageing paunchy Justice of the Peace shuffled into the office.

'Are you ready, Mr Gyarden?' he said.

'In a few minutes, sir,' Alf-Gordon said, carefully arranging the case in the order most suitable to his solicitor friends.

'All right, Mr Gyarden. I will precede you,' the old J.P. said, shuffling out.

When the Courts were in session and the Clerk and Deputy Clerk were out of the office, the temporary clerks stopped working. Mona Freeman went into the inner office to chat with Miss Bodden, the typist. Donald Stevenson, who was preparing for bar examinations, began to read a book on Roman Law. Bertram Shaw leaned back in his chair, whistling idly. The other clerks had gone to listen to a case in the Civil Division in which the barrister, Dr Raymond Phillips, leader of the People's Democratic Party, was appearing. Bertram Shaw went over to Ramsay and chatted about the funeral. Then he asked Ramsay to ring Mabel and introduce her to him. 'Don't be a horse-piss, man,' Bertram said to Ramsay by way of arm-twisting persuasion.

Mabel, who worked at the Post Office, had, like Ramsay, gone back to work.

'May I speak to Miss Tull?' Ramsay held the line for a moment.

'Mabel Tull speaking.'

'Mabes?'

'Ramsay! What's wrong?' He telephoned her at work only if something was wrong.

'Nothing. A fellow at the office here want to speak to you.'

'About what?'

'Nothing. Just to meet you, like.'

'Put him on nuh,' Mabel said, sensing Ramsay's embarrassment.

He handed the telephone to Bertram and walked to the other end of the office where Mona was now reading a *True Confessions* magazine. He pretended to be looking through the window but was actually looking surreptitiously at Mona's breasts or what could be seen of them through her low-cut blouse. Ramsay did this at least once a day and Mona pretended that she didn't notice what he was looking at. This was because one morning when they had both arrived at the office before anyone else, Ramsay, almost hypnotically impelled, had slipped his hand into one of the cups of her brassiere and held her breast. She had slapped his face twice very sharply and did not speak to him for days. The incident had been swift, silent and final.

He went back to the telephone and spoke to Mabel again.

'Who is this Bertram?' she asked. 'He don't sound like much!'

'He went to Wolmers,' Ramsay said, for Bertram was listening keenly.

'What he look like?' Mabel asked.

'He went to Wolmers, I said,' Ramsay said, raising his voice slightly.

There was a pause, then Mabel said, 'Oh, I see. Listen Ramsay, I can get a chance to go to England you know. A fellow from Hospital, a Senior Clerk, was telling me that Government giving nursing scholarships next month. Listen, I tell you tonight.' She suddenly shouted into the telephone, 'Some inquisitive naygahs are listening to my conversation! See you tonight.' She hung up.

At eleven o'clock Donald Stevenson came in with a large greasy paper bag full of hot patties, and he, Ramsay and Bertram each ate six patties.

Later in the morning Cyril Hanson telephoned Ramsay. He had been his best friend at the secondary school. He was a remarkable games player, had kept up his games after school and now played regularly for the island's soccer team. He was very extrovert, full of personality and supremely confident in himself. He was sensitive only about his parentage, for it happened that he had been born before his mother married. He was now working as an Education Officer in the Jamaica Improvement Association. The post of Education Officer should have been given to someone with more experience but Cyril had pulled the right strings and had talked his way into it. Ramsay envied him his vitality and confidence.

'Hello, Head,' Cyril greeted him. Ramsay's school nickname was Head, partly because of the size of his domed forehead and partly because he was clever. 'How're you keeping up, old man? Don't get too morose, you know. These things have to happen.'

'I'm taking it easy, man,' Ramsay said.

'You know what I 'phoned you about? Has Capleton's case come on yet?'

'I don't know,' Ramsay said.

'Listen, I was telling Capleton about you last night. He wants you to join the League. I think you should join the League, you know, Head. The trouble is they don't have enough intelligent, educated young men in the movement. Not enough intellectual stiffening.'

'They might send Capleton to jail, you know, on Emergency Regulations!' Ramsay said. A woman's voice broke in. 'Please stop holding up the line!' the voice said.

'Jail? Not a chance,' Cyril said emphatically. 'I was talking to Fernandez last night. No case against Capleton.' Cyril always gave the impression of knowing every important person in Jamaica intimately. It was his chief stock-in-trade.

The woman's voice said, 'Come off the line! It's not you one pay Public Service sixteen shillings a month!'

'Woman, don't be a fool, don't annoy me!' Cyril said sharply. Then the line went dead. Ramsay jiggled the hook but they had been cut off.

Cyril Hanson's highly polished desk in his office at the Jamaica Improvement Association was bare except for a telephone, a desk pad and a photograph of his school hockey team. In the photograph he was elegantly dressed with a loose knotted silk scarf and a school blazer with the collar turned up. He alone smiled in that photograph, his glistening perfect white teeth set off by his light-brown complexion.

There were three bookcases filled with books on sociology and adult education – a legacy from his predecessor. Cyril's work consisted mainly of telephoning people – teachers, civil servants, other welfare workers – and outlining grand and vague plans for lectures, demonstrations and exhibitions in the rural areas. Twice a month for about four days at a time he travelled around the island introducing guest speakers and lecturers to tiny country audiences and giving the same lecture which lasted for exactly fifteen minutes on 'The History of the Jamaica Improvement Association'.

Cyril was an intrepid planner, and he passed for a young man of advanced ideas because whenever he found a new painter or musician who was all the rage in Kingston's intellectual circles he would take him to the remotest parts of the country to show his pictures or to play to bewildered audiences. Cyril's most brilliant idea was to employ a dialect comedian known as Tennis Barrett. Tennis would clown for ten minutes before each lecture and the local branches of the Association sent enthusiastic demands to headquarters for the quick return of 'Mr Cyril Hanson and his band of educators'. The Director of the Improvement Association, Mr Phipps-Help, a retired marine biologist, read these demands with surprise, but had to declare himself satisfied with Hanson's work.

Cyril didn't much mind being cut off from Head Tull for he had other telephone calls to make. First of all he telephoned the office of Dr Raymond Phillips – he knew that Dr Phillips was in court – and left a message inviting Dr Phillips to be a member of the Brains' Trust he was organizing for the annual festival. Then he telephoned Joe Mercer, a clever young Jew who was producing the annual pantomime, to find out how it was going and whether he, Cyril, could give Joe Mercer a write-up in *The Improver*, the Association's monthly magazine. During these telephone conversations he made copious meaningless notes on his desk pad.

A tall wispy typist drifted into Cyril's office and started to look through one of the bookshelves. She wasn't his typist – he didn't have one – but he pretended she was his secretary. In Cyril's world every other woman had a crush on him, but this girl, Ella Shaw, was saucy.

'Lost something, my dear?' Cyril asked.

'Not you,' the girl said carelessly.

'You know, Ella,' Cyril said, 'you're so thin that if you turn sideways I wouldn't see you at all. If you had a little more *embonpoint* I'd take you for my girl-friend, you know.'

'I don't want to catch any of the things you have, Mr Hanson,' she said, and wiggled out of the room.

On her way out she nearly collided with Mr Phipps-Help, the Director. He was a completely bald Englishman, fat, with many chins and a huge belly. On all occasions he wore green corduroy shorts and had not been invited to dinner at King's House since the disastrous evening when he turned up for dinner in a red velvet smoking jacket and green corduroy shorts. The other guests at dinner had been the Officer Commanding H.M. Forces in the Caribbean and the Chief Justice of Trinidad. Mr Phipps-Help had further distinguished himself that evening by having two helpings of each course.

'Hanson!' he said as he entered the office. 'Don't be a clot! You can't send a jazz band to Mahogany Vale. What do you think we are? A ruddy circus?'

'Well, the idea, you see, sir, is this –'

'It's a stupid idea,' Mr Phipps-Help wheezed; he had walked up three flights of stairs. 'Think of another idea!'

When he had gone Cyril stroked his chin and reached for the telephone again. He called up a fellow named Fakhouri who had promised to lend him a car that afternoon. Then he rang up one of the Senior Clerks in the Education Department.

'Hello, Mr Blair? Hanson here! About this Rhodes Scholarship entry, what exactly is the position?'

'The position is that you have sent in an entry,' said Mr Blair enunciating with exaggerated precision, 'and now you wait to see if they call you for an interview. That's all.'

'I don't mean that,' Cyril said. 'I mean the general policy. This is a new era, isn't it, adult suffrage, the "people"? We can't have any colour discrimination these days – isn't that true? The Minister of Education is on the Committee, isn't he?'

'Look, Cyril,' Mr Blair said more intimately. 'I'm just a clerk putting papers together. I don't know anything about policy.'

'What are the other candidates like?' Cyril persisted.

Mr Blair began to say something which Cyril didn't catch. Then he said clearly, 'All these things are confidential.'

'O.K., Blairy,' Cyril said. 'Just keep your ears open and see which way the wind is blowing. See you at Kingston Club tonight.'

At three o'clock in the afternoon one of the clerks came into the Courts Office with the news that Capleton had been acquitted. All day, followers of the People's Progressive League had been hanging around the Courts Building. Once when they started singing one of the League songs, 'We will build Jamaica', the police dispersed them.

The clerks crowded round Alf-Gordon's desk for a postmortem of the case.

'It's a bad judgment,' Alf-Gordon said. 'Fernandez was quoting a lot of bad law. The Appeal Court will never uphold the judgment.'

They were all extremely surprised when Capleton appeared, alone, at the office door and asked which of them was Ramsay Tull. Eustace Capleton was a jet black, squat, professional politician. He was wearing a black funereal suit desecrated by a pink-and-yellow tie that was like a vicious gash down his chest. Medium in height he was almost completely bald with a receding forehead and very bushy eyebrows. Yet he was handsome in two features – in his soft pure eyes and in the way his lips became crooked when he smiled. He did not look dynamic or intellectual. His strength as a politician lay in his priest-like, single-minded fervour for the working-class movement and in his reputation for absolute honesty. He stood shyly at the door as Ramsay approached.

'You Ramsay Tull?' Capleton asked. He spoke with a faint American accent. 'Cyril Hanson tole me about you. You really want to join the League?'

Ramsay was suddenly terrified by the League, as if it were a mystery, like a Masonic Lodge. He said, inaudibly, 'I am a socialist.'

'Sorry to hear your father dead,' Capleton said, resting his arm on Ramsay's shoulder. 'Where you living now?'

'In Vineyard Town. St James' Road.'

'We have a group in Rollington Town. Edgar Bailey running it. I tell you what, come round to my house tomorrow night and meet Edgar and you can join his group. Eighteen Brentford Road, opposite Carib.'

Capleton then walked to Mona Freeman's desk and spoke to her for about three minutes. Then he left the office. As he emerged from the building the P.P.L. followers cheered and sang *The Red Flag.* They set out on a triumphal march, Capleton leading, to the P.P.L. headquarters in Slipe Road.

'Goodnight all,' Mona said.

'I didn't know you knew Capleton,' Alf-Gordon said to her.

'Never met him before in my life,' she answered, swinging through the door.

'Hipsy bitch!' Bertram Shaw said, narrowing his eyes.

They closed up the Court rooms and the large building was silent again. Alf-Gordon and two of the clerks sat around a desk drinking T.T.L. rum and eating patties. They were waiting for Miss Bodden to join them in a hand of bridge. Donald Stevenson asked Ramsay to translate a Latin passage in his Roman Law book.

On the way home, perched on the steps of a tram-car, Ramsay wondered why everybody did not at least confess belief in socialism as everybody did in Christianity, or would it take a thousand years? He thought of the 'people', his cousins and schoolmates in Orange Town village, the labourers, the unemployed, their world and their dictatorship. The idea was cold. Then he thought of the literature of martyrdoms, persecutions and secret meetings – the adolescent romanticism that was fed by a resentment against the values, snobbery and prejudice of the secondary school at which he had been 'educated'. Deeper and more vivid was the fringe of poverty on which his family had lived and the strain of appearances which had shattered his mother's nerves. 'Bourgeois', 'bourgeoisie', were words that warmed him like a singing.

When he got off the tramcar he realized that he had made two mistakes – in tenses – in translating Donald Stevenson's Latin passage and the realization amused him.

II

Eustace Capleton's house on Brentford Road was much more League headquarters than the two P.P.L. offices on Slipe Road. The house was always full of unemployed young men, some of whom resided permanently on the verandah. One of the young men led Ramsay down a dark passage into a brightly lit dining room.

Capleton, in shirt-sleeves, was having a meal and reading a typescript at the same time. There were two other people in the room – Edgar Bailey and, to Ramsay's surprise, Mona Freeman. They were watching Capleton read and eat. Ramsay joined the silent group.

'I'm trying to get Miss Freeman to join the League as my secretary,' he said to Ramsay.

Ramsay couldn't understand it. He looked at Mona but her eyes were blank. With her background, Ramsay thought, she should regard Capleton as a dirty black man. He could not imagine what resentments had led her to Capleton. She sat easily, her hands folded, her elbows resting on the table.

Ramsay thought that Edgar Bailey looked like a real worker. He was tall and thin, dark, with a sharp straight nose. His face was long, defined and angular, like a Modigliani. He was about twenty-four. Before coming secretary to the P.P.L. he had been a stone-mason. Now he wore a suit – an ill-fitting dirty tweed suit – the shabby respectability of a clerical post. The black briefcase into which he put the typescript Capleton had been reading was old and battered.

'I hear you want to join us as a comrade,' Edgar said to Ramsay. 'Don't anybody else from Courts Office want to join? We want as much middle-class as possible.'

Edgar and Capleton smiled at each other and Ramsay felt, as he was to feel again and again, an impenetrable wall separating him from them. He thought, 'We all have different resentments', and then remembered, with a shock, that 'resentments' was one of Cyril Hanson's pet words.

'Many middle-class people would join the League but they 'fraid of lose their jobs,' Edgar said.

'That's not what they 'fraid of,' Capleton said. 'They 'fraid of educated *quarshie!*'

'But it's they put the Merchants in power,' Edgar argued.

Capleton's crooked smile again. 'That's not a Merchants' Party. It's a freak fascist party united against socialism by greed and selfishness. A few merchants buy out the union leaders. Ten thousand pound, I'm telling you.'

'But it looked as if the P.D.P. would win easily,' Ramsay said.

The P.D.P., People's Democratic Party, was a middle-class party with a vaguely socialist leadership and no programme. Before the elections they seemed to have the largest, most articulate following in the island. The P.D.P. won two out of the thirty-two seats in the House of Assembly, thirty seats going to the Merchants' Party who now formed the government under a limited self-governing constitution. The twelve P.P.L. candidates had all lost their fifty pound deposits.

'The leadership of the P.D.P. falls into two categories,' Capleton said. His voice became public, as though he was addressing a large meeting. 'They are either romantic Fabians who read a few pink books at snob schools or unscrupulous careerists, and neither type knows the first thing about organizing a political party. They couldn't even organize a garden party. With the backing they had I coulda won half the seats in the House.'

Capleton stood up, took a bottle of whisky from a cupboard, poured himself a small drink and filled the glass with iced water. Then he replaced the whisky bottle without offering it to anyone.

'You see, this is the dishonesty of the P.D.P., they tell lies about us. We don't want revolution. We have the revolution already. It started in 1938. They say I'm a communist, but you know, Mr Tull, I've never read *Das Kapital*. I don't know any theory. The only theory I know is this. There are two stages, right here in Jamaica. First the overthrow of bourgeois society so we have public ownership. Then every mother's son of us will have to go and do a day's work. What is equality in the first stage? "From each according to his ability." Work, work, work, damn hard work, man. Maybe you'll get more than you put in, maybe you'll get less. For a start it can't be helped. You can't change bourgeois society overnight. You get that, don't you?'

Crap! Ramsay thought, a habit from Marcus, a habit from the debating society; at least the way of putting it is crap.

'Then in the second stage,' Capleton continued, '"From each according to his ability, to each according to his needs". And by god, Tull, a dock-worker with a family of fifteen has greater ability to develop the country and greater needs than you or me. That's all the theory we need. Apart from that, attack the government, attack the constitution, organize the workers, take them away from the unscrupulous union leadership until we win the elections.'

'Behind everything is imperialism,' Edgar said.

'Forget imperialism,' Capleton snapped. 'We don't have any guns or 'planes.'

Why forget imperialism? Ramsay thought. The whole of what Capleton had been saying was unsound half-heard theory, fantastically naïve. Any one of the bright Oxford-trained barristers in the P.D.P. with their 'by the same token' and 'the realities of the facts' could tear Capleton's argument to shreds. But he felt, as Capleton spoke, the power of the man behind the doubtful argument. It wasn't a personal power. It was the romantic strength of a cliché, 'the people', the oppressed, symbolized partially in the ragged hangers-on, some unemployable, who lived on Capleton's verandah. It was the power without which no colonial politician could hope to govern his country independently. Compared with these stubborn immovable boys the Whitmanesque poets and Gauguinesque painters who lovingly studied their own mirrored images in the P.D.P. were the palest shadows.

Mona said she had to go home. Capleton invited her to have a look at the P.P.L. offices in Slipe Road. Edgar said to Ramsay, 'You live in St James' Road, nuh? I'm just off Cumberland Avenue. Come passero!'

In front of Capleton's house, too, the green poinsettia leaves were turning to scarlet.

Edgar and Ramsay walked up to Cross Roads. On the bus Edgar said, 'What I can't understand is why you joining the League. Like me so now, I doan have nothing to lose. What school you went to?'

Ramsay told him.

'That's a P.D.P. school,' Edgar said and smiled. They were silent for a while.

'The League is a kind of outlaw party, you know. They send a van of police to every meeting. There's no future in the League. As you well know you can lose your job in the service if they catch you in the League.'

'I don't care a damn, because I'm living a lie they taught me at school,' Ramsay said. 'My whole school life was a fake!'

'It's like that,' Edgar agreed, believing but not understanding.

The ivy or mock-ivy sucked away the moisture from the Chapel walls and the fabric of the school began to crumble. In the sixth form they couldn't grasp the age of the school. It was too old, too traditional when they measured it against the rapid political development which was in a fever around them. The school with its bourgeois values and in-grown snobbery would crumble, too, like the Chapel walls, the sixth-form socialists said.

Ramsay, fresh from a village, entered the sham world of a private language, a swagger, a contempt for boys from other secondary and elementary schools. The school soon made him aware of the gaps that separated them. They were all complexions, all races – Negro, Indian, European, Chinese, Syrian, Jew, in purity and in endless variations and mixtures. They slept in the same dormitories, ate together, played together but they also learned that the Lincoln-Zephyrs, the Mercedes-Benz, the mountains of tuck had, for the most part, found their way into the hands of the fairer boys in direct proportion to their near-whiteness. The unity, the oneness of the same school yell, was superficial, and the much-vaunted 'great harmony among different races' was an inaccurate interpretation of a very precarious compromise.

This mistaken idea about perfect racial harmony in the island was broadcast in the foreign press by stupid welfare workers, governors' wives who wanted to prove the humanitarianism of their husbands' régime, and unscrupulous novelists (themselves uncomfortably half-way between black and white) who tried to peddle the plausible kink that a new multi-racial civilization was developing in Jamaica.

If you were black and could score a century at cricket or brilliant goals at soccer or topped the form in terminal exams the school of all races cheered you, even worshipped you, but only within the framework of the school's compromise. At the end of term Ramsay struggled with his suitcases to the bus stop, while the fairer boys, with stony, unknowing faces, swished past him in grand cars: the precarious racial harmony ended with the start of the vacation.

And so Ramsay learned in his turn to despise the barefoot street-boys and was scrupulously careful never to use their coarse vivid language. He kept his distance from them just as the white boys did from him, only he was more ruthless in his snobbery and, in his hatred of their menace to his artificial superiority, he was utterly incapable of compromise.

It was nothing new, perhaps, in human life – this seductive training that made Ramsay try to despise and disdain his black country heritage. Only in his last two years at school did the discovery of socialism begin to release him from the intolerable commitment to the perpetuation of a class to which he did not belong.

Behind a board fence three small houses enclosed a quadrangle. Oil-lamps and shadows and the flickering gas-lamp in the street. A stand-pipe and trough in the middle of the yard. A few men who had come in from work stood chatting. There was nothing poetic or sordid or sinister about them. They were just workers.

Edgar Bailey lived with his mother and two young sisters in one of the three houses. Ramsay entered a sitting room, the floor of which was clean and highly polished.

'The ole lady must be gone to prayer-meeting,' Edgar said, as they sat down. He told Ramsay about the Group. 'This Group have about twenty-six regular members, you know.' He showed Ramsay a register. 'The young boys in the area support the League but they doan have a vote. Every now and again we give a free party and about a hundred people will come, mostly P.D.P. that come for the freeness.'

'Where you hold your meetings?' Ramsay asked.

'You know Miss Tillie private school on the Avenue? Every Thursday evening we meet there. Miss Tillie really vote P.D.P. but she is Septy cousin. It's mainly a study group. Socialism, Marxism, Soviet Union, British Labour Party, analysis and application to Jamaica – like that. Sometimes a member will bring in a friend. Since last election ten P.D.P. join us here and the same thing happen all over the corporate area.'

The prospect seemed utterly hopeless to Ramsay. Capleton, the hard-boiled politician, and this meagre young man talking in flat careless tones did not seem to be the fiery socialist leadership he fed his dreams on. He didn't know much about the workers but he knew it would be impossible to persuade the Jamaican, no matter how oppressed, to abandon the wealth of the Merchants' Party or the professional snobbery of the P.D.P. or the shilling-an-hour more of the Trade Union and follow a theory, however sound, put forward by a theadbare leadership.

'I believe in Marxism, and I know it can do everything for this country,' Edgar said. His voice was warmer now and his eyes shone. 'Look at Soviet Russia. It's not fifty years old yet. Counting from the end of N.E.P. it's not even thirty years yet and look at that country today.'

'The history is different, though,' Ramsay argued, not meaning to say that but a slave to the habits of the school debating society.

'Never mind the history,' Edgar said. 'We can apply it right here.'

There was a knock on the side of the house in which Edgar and Ramsay were sitting and a large head appeared in the doorway. It was a well-groomed head, the hair razor-parted on the left and a thin whisper of moustache. Septy Grant came in. He was wearing one of the loudest sports shirts Ramsay had ever seen. The detail motif of the shirt was naked girls leaning against coconut palms, the girls in brilliant red, the palms in blue. The girls' legs on the collar seemed to embrace Septy's neck.

He shook hands with Ramsay without being introduced. He said to Edgar, 'What happen now, genius?' Edgar introduced him as Chairman of the Rollington Town Group of the P.P.L.

'Me and Rupert just get a quart of the thing. Come knock a little, nuh?' Septy said, inviting them to have a drink.

They drank white rum and coconut water on the back porch of the house which Septy shared with his married sister, Druscilla, and her husband, Charlie. Septy was a cabinet-maker and he shared a shop with a partner in Allman Town. He talked delightfully and did not seem to be serious about anything, least of all politics. He was talking about Vera Chen.

'Where you pick up this Vera?' Edgar asked.

'Vera! Hmmm!' Septy sipped his drink. 'Mek I tell you. Mek I tell you the whole story. 'Twas a Tuesday – mek I see – laas' year about three week befo' election. I come home from work the evening an' play a game of domino with Frankie and Rupert here, and Chawlie. Then I cool off, you know, tek a baht an' fix up to go to dis pahty.

'Well, mi dear sah, I jump on mi Raleigh down-handle fix an' I caal roun' Hitchin Street near Race Course deh, to pick up Son-Son. Then we chip down to a hun'red an' forteen an' a hawf Lowah King Street. When we reach there, 'bout hawf-pass nine, the rum was flowing a'ready, man, an' everybody was hitting the roof. You woulda never know that a lickle house like that coulda hole so much people. It was a hinvitation pahty, you know, no gate-crashing or hooligans – everybody deestant. An' the radio-phone have a fit tone, man!

'So mi and Son-Son jus' slip in an' lean up 'gains' the window, jus' moving to the music like an' watching the parangles. I look 'cross the way an' I see a nice hawf-Chiney chile in a half-de-shoulder dress sit down in a chair jus' flicking her toe to the music. I touch Son-Son an' I say to him, "I soon come, sah".'

Septy paused to sip his drink. Rupert slapped himself on the thigh and shouted to Septy, as if he was six miles away, 'Yes! You gone on, master!' Septy was Rupert's idol.

'I walk 'cross the room,' Septy continued, 'an' button up me three-button jacket. That time I have me tie jus' flick over in mi breas' pocket, cool. I use me bes' English an' I say to her, "May I hauve this daunce?" She look 'pon me serious, like she frighten to see me. Then she kind of cut her eye, and twist herself an' say, "Allright". When she stan' up you see, sah, she was pretty enough to break your heart, man! I take her on the floor an' lean over to *encircle*. Joe Liggin's *Honey Dripper* was playing.' Septy hummed a few bars of *Honey Dripper*. 'The chile give me a move, you see! She spread out her arms and bounce as the music lick her – an' she revolve.' He stood up and showed them how the girl 'revolved'. 'I say to miself, "Yes, fahda. We are suwinging tonight!"' Septy stood with his hands on his hips, miming his astonishment. 'I monopolize her for the res' of the night.'

'She pretty, you know,' Rupert said.

'But a barmaid, Septy?' Edgar said. 'She going to rat on you.'

'That's where you wrong, my friend. A Jamaica barmaid is the hardest to get.'

Ramsay remembered a story that Bertram Shaw had told him about a barmaid but he felt it was too sordid and humourless to be told in working-class company. He felt paralysed – first Capleton's steam-rollering, now the aimless drinking and talking in what he had imagined would be an 'intellectual cell' of the League.

They talked about women. Septy drank more quickly than the others and he remembered again.

'I remember when I was in country,' Septy said, 'that time I was a small boy never know nutten. I had a big cousin name Maasa. One evening about dusk him say to me, "I going carry you somewhere, show you something". So we go down to the valley-part of the village where Ole Saul use to live. Ole Saul musta been about sixty but him did still frisky, you see, an' him carry a very large member it was a miracle in the village. So when we go down this-ya night, Maasa an' me creep up beside Ole Saul room – you know in country you jus' have one room is a house. We hear Ole Saul an' a woman name Icilda in the house. So after a little we hear the bed a-go rooku-rooku – ah frighten, you see, is the first time I ever hear a bed soun' like that. Then Icilda bawl out, "Lawd, Ole Saul, ah cyan't *bear* it, sah!" Hear Ole Saul – him have a deep, kinda gruff voice, "Bear it. You big. A gal o' forty can bear anything", *roo*ku-rooku *roo*ku-rooku. I jump an' run, you see. Is kill me think Ole Saul killing Icilda!'

Rupert laughed himself into hiccups. Ramsay looked at Edgar's face and was startled by it – ashen, immobile, almost ghastly in the light from the open tin-lamp. He thought of his father's dead face. Then Edgar talked and a world of bitterness, of oppression, glowed around them.

'Every day it get more and more that I can't wait,' Edgar said. 'Wait for the end of the war, wait for the constitution, wait for the people to change. Sometimes I feel it right here in mi guts that I want to murder every Englishman in Jamaica, I want to mash up every big car that a Jew or a Syrian is driving, I want to burn down the whole of Kingston and start again. But most of all I want to kill every political leader except Capleton. What's the use of constitution? The Merchants' Party is the same as the Tory Party and the P.D.P. is the same as the Labour Party – all imperialist. We are too dyam coward in this country. You sing the *Red Flag* but you think a naygah ever dye that flag red except police baton make mistake and bus' him head? You think any Jamaican want to go prison for other Jamaicans? An' yet you know I hate every other race beside naygah!'

'Hi, man,' Septy said. 'Remember Marcus Garvey, you know. And what about Hitler?'

'Nazism not a racialist movement,' Edgar said. 'It's a capitalist movement. Never mind the propaganda, Goebels or Churchill. They say if Hitler win the war the res' of the world will be enslaved or exterminate. An' what happen? My elder brother, Reggie, join up the R.A.F. in 1940 and get kill over Germany. For what? Is murder, man! You think I could put my backside in Liguanea Club or even my friend here, Tull? We too dyam coward in Jamaica! You think a Jamaican naygah today would fight a real people's war for freedom? We get wutliss now, that's it! You remember the Korymantyn slaves that every slave owner use to fear. Every working-class naygah should be a Korymantyn slave!'

Edgar's thin underfed body had taken on a frightening magnificence and in the flicker and shadow of the light he was a little like an El Greco Christ. He stood up.

'I swear to Almighty God that I would rather die as a Korymantyn slave fighting for freedom than be the richest man under the capitalist system!'

Septy' s voice was cool but not contemptuous when he said, 'Sit down Edgar, man, you're drunk!'

'But *you* wouldn't go to prison for the League though, Septy,' Edgar shouted.

'Me go prison?' Septy asked. 'Me? Wait, mek I tell you something. I not putting myself into that kind of worries, you hear, mi sah! I mean to say, I am ready to do any kind of propaganda work, say election-time, I know a fellow work at Industrial Garage, a good passero of mine, well, we can get a ole Mercury any day carry people to polling station. Today you have Capleton; tomorrow who you have? Me nah go prison for that, Massa!'

'Tomorrow you have the League and the people and poverty and socialism!' Edgar said.

They all started shouting political slogans and swear-words at each other. Ramsay, too, was caught up in the defiance of the rum but he was sober enough to be surprised to hear Septy shouting, after his scornful remarks about going to prison, 'But why mus' the imperialists back me up against a wall? I doan like it! Why mus' they back me up against a wall?'

U-Stass burst in on the shouting. His shirt was torn and he was bleeding from a cut on the cheek. There was no time for horror. The drinkers waited while he caught his breath.

'Some P.D.P. beat me up,' he said. 'Up Elletson Road. About fifteen of them!'

They took short-cuts through back-alleys and yards and came out on Deanery Road at the top end of Elletson Road. As they hurried down Elletson Road they could hear P.D.P. campaign songs coming towards them. These P.D.P. boys were the toughs who hung around lawyers' offices. Their main job in the P.D.P. was to prevent their own meetings from being broken up by Merchants' Party followers and to break up League meetings by throwing stones and starting fights.

There were no preliminaries to this fight, no razors, no stones, no sticks. It was a pure fist fight and Septy led them. Fighting with the easy cunning of the practised street-fighter at a disadvantage in numbers he kept away from clinches. Edgar fought always beside him, under his protection. Ramsay didn't fight at all but danced round the outskirts of the fight. The P.D.P. boys got hold of Rupert and U-Stass. They threw U-Stass into the gutter and later he was taken unconscious to the hospital to be stitched up all over.

A squad of police in a 'prowl' car came upon the fight unexpectedly and everybody scattered. Most of the P.D.P. boys leaped the culvert and climbed the barbed-wire fence into Alpha School grounds. The others ran down Elletson Road with a few policemen chasing them.

For a while, as he dodged along side streets and through backyards, Ramsay sensed Septy and Edgar running beside him. Then he lost them. Still running, and now nearing home, he was crossing an open lot which led into St James' Road. A figure leaped at him from behind a clump of bushes and held him by the shirt-collar. He slipped away but the policeman grabbed him again, this time by the belt so that he was 'draped' by the trousers. Ramsay found himself looking into the astonished face of Power, one of the policemen he knew at the office. He broke from Power and ran, and Power let him go.

When Ramsay reached home the whole thing seemed amusing. How could he write an Information against himself? Only the verandah lights were on. He went into Bobsie's room and began taking off his shoes.

'Is you that, Ramsay?' his mother called from her room. 'Come here, mi son, I want talk to you.'

She switched on the light and lay massive and warm on the big blue-quilted double-bed, her long brownish hair packed into a net, her face round as an apple, the flesh firm and flooded with sleep. The fact of his mother that couldn't grow old. Alice Tull's vital body at fifty-three protested against the inactivity age was forcing on it. She suffered from being too healthy and around her there was the atmosphere of a waste of life. It is a terrible thing for the body to die only by the decree of time, objecting to its death. Ramsay's relationship with his mother was so simple as to be remarkable. She had pampered and spoilt him always but he was too weak to take advantage of her love. He treated her now like a child, now like a secret companion, so that there was no need for any maternal authority in his life. She had confided in Ramsay all her criticism of her husband and her other children and Ramsay knew the deepest places of her loves and hates. His father had been secretly afraid of him.

'Since yo' father die you doan't spend any time with yo' mother,' she said, not as a reprimand but as if it were an interesting point for discussion. Ramsay sat on the bed beside her. 'Ah'm getting to feel very tired these laas' days, you know, Ramsay. The leas' thing I do. Is me heart, ah think!'

'Nothing wrong with your heart, Mama. You jus' too fat, tha's all.'

He lifted her arm and pinched her where it sagged and swung. She squealed and slapped his hand, laughing like a girl.

'What ah'm to do about Bobsie?' she asked.

'Bobsie?'

'He going to hell, yuh know. Not working, every night drunk, oh it's a crosses to bear! You can't talk to him, Ramsay?'

'Chu! As for Bobsie. You know he owe me two pounds. Mek him gwaan, he too wutliss. I doan bother with him now.' He remembered something and took three pounds out of his wallet and gave them to her. She slipped them into the top of her nightgown.

'Your father never leave a thing, except the forty acres in Orange Town and this house,' Mrs Tull said. 'But never mind, all of you educated already. You know today a man came here, was telling me he could make some money for me. Tha's what I call you to tell you about.'

'What man came here?' he asked with the anxious heartbeat the poor get when they hear about money.

'Ramsay, to this time I doan't sure if a man really come or is a spirit. I was tidying the room, you see, today bright day an' a hear fish passing so I call Maud to buy some and I was in the drawing room standing up. And you know sometimes you feel your mind gone somewhere and you doan know you is where you is? Well, like that. Ah stan' up in the drawing room an' the firs' thing happen I smell a smell like when your father dead body did-lay out in the room. Ah never hear the gate open, I never hear the door open but see this man with a big grip stan' up in the sitting room. And he have this dead smell around him!'

She sat up, wide-eyed and excited. 'You know who the man

favour? He was a white man, very white, no colour in his face. You remember Reverend Hibbert brother who did-come from England and die of consumption in Orange Town? The man was the dead image of Reverend Hibbert brother. Ah frighten so till! Me head grow an' grow. Then he say to me – he doan speak like a Englishman or a Jamaican – he say, "Morning, Mrs Tull, I come to help you". Him sit down and tell me every blessed thing about me and your father and the whole family. Him could even tell me how much money your father leave in the bank. Then he show me a lot of papers, but I couldn' read them, son, and he say he have a society, you put in money like a partner, an' after some time you draw out more; like you put in five pound, two months pass and you draw out fifteen pound.'

'You gave him any money?' Ramsay asked. He had authority only over his mother.

'No, son, I doan have no money to give him, but wait, no? I tell him I doan have any money an' he say all right and give me a address on a piece of paper there on the table under the red vase, an' say if I'm in trouble I mus sen' for him. It could be a samfie-man, Ramsay, but why he smell like that, and why he favour Reverend Hibbert brother that's dead, and how he know everything like that?'

Ramsay read on the slip of paper: 'J. Cornelius Alderman, Travelling Salesman, P.O. Box 57, Kingston.'

'Is just a samfie-man, Mama. Plenty of them come down from the States these days.'

'Maybe I would say is something the Lord send me to show me something,' Mrs Tull said, lying on the bed.

'Don't worry your head about it, Mama,' he said in a flat frightened voice.

'Where you eating these days, son? Every evening for the laas' three days I cook yo' supper an' you doan touch it.'

'I'm all right, Mama. I eat in town.'

'I make some pancake for you this evening. They in the blue carrier-top. Go eat, mi son.'

Ramsay turned the light off and went into the dining room.

He took the carrier-top out of the safe, chipped some ice and filled a big glass with water, then sat down at the table eating the warm pancakes with golden syrup. He still felt giddy from the rum and the fight and the running.

He heard the sound of a car stopping at the gate. He stopped chewing and listened. The car door slammed and the car drove away. He still listened and was relieved to hear Mabel striding up the gravel path alone and slamming the front door. It was about ten o'clock.

'Hi, Ramsay! This long time don't see! Tell me nuh, you doan live at this house again?' She was wearing a white flounced blouse tucked into what was then known as a ballerina skirt, in dark blue. Part of the blouse had come loose, her make-up was damaged and she looked somewhat manhandled. She took a small mirror out of her handbag and studied her face in it. Then she sat on the only lounge chair in the dining room, away from the table.

'What 'bout you?' Ramsay asked without looking up. 'How come you come home so early tonight? And you not block-up neither?'

'You know, Ramsay, sometimes I just get fed up with this Jamaica life. The same same thing all the time! Every gawd man you meet want the same thing!' She got up and stood across the table from him with her hands on her hips. 'I look indecent, nuh?'

Ramsay half-grunted, half-laughed. She reached over, took a pancake and doubled it into her mouth.

'Madge and Rosie can't see you these days. Madge pregnant, you know. You will soon be "Uncle Ramsay".' She took another pancake and Ramsay put the carrier-top at his elbow. She suddenly stopped eating and stared at his shirt.

'Is lipstick or blood?'

'Mus' be blood,' Ramsay said, with the indifference that was his part in the games they played. Actually he didn't realize there was blood on his shirt. He wondered how his mother hadn't noticed it.

'Is lipstick,' Mabel said, with a teasing grin. 'It's that bow-legged girl up the road named Sweetness Terrelonge?'

'Sweetness Terrelonge! I doan know anybody named so.'

'Is Sweetness. The albino chile that live next door Sergeant Wilkins. You think I doan know. Mind you carry her down, you know, Ramskin?' Then after a pause, 'You know the facts of life, Ramsay?'

She sat down and they grinned at each other, extremely happy. Mabel was a real person, Ramsay felt, and he couldn't understand why some of his friends at school were ashamed of their sisters.

'I went to Matinée at Carib this evening, you know.' She drank from Ramsay's glass and left a smudge of lipstick on the rim. 'I saw a nice picture about a doctor and a nurse. Van Heflin. You know this nurse was in love with the doctor, but the doctor was married, you see, and he didn't know about it – '

'Until the wife died and then the doctor found out and they lived happily ever after,' he said cutting her short.

'You saw it?'

'Every picture ends like that.'

'Oh, I know, but is the film stars makes the difference,' she said seriously. 'Of course, Mister Know-All, Mister Intelligence! Anyway, it's a nice picture, really class, especially where the wife died. Make me cry.' Ramsay laughed. 'You laugh? Some big men in the theatre were crying.'

Ramsay leaned back and picked his teeth with a split matchstick, then lit a cigarette. He felt very sleepy and wondered what had happened to Septy and Edgar. Maybe the police had caught them.

'By the way,' Mabel said, 'you know who is Cyril Hanson girlfriend? Mona Freeman, and he get there already and everything.'

'How you know?' Ramsay asked, 'you were there?'

'I hear Cyril sure to win Rhodes Scholarship,' Mabel chattered on. 'A man tole me.'

'You sure Cyril didn' tell you?'

'A man work at Education Office tole me, a grey-haired man was at Slipper Wednesday night.'

'You hear everything in Kingston, eh? What happen to the nursing scholarships a man tole you about?'

'Oh, next month they going to advertise them,' Mabel said. 'I should put in for one, eh Ramskin? I fed up with this Jamaica life, you see, but I don't want to leave Aunt Alice. Lawd, is hard for a woman all your children jus' leave you.'

They thought about it for a while. Then Mabel got up, walked round the table, put her hands on Ramsay's shoulders and rubbed her cheek against his. He could smell liquor on her breath.

'Sweetness Terrelonge is your girl-friend, don't it?' Mabel asked with gentle teasing irony. 'You fall in love with her?'

'I don't know her.'

'She said you 'phone her three times and you wouldn' say it was you telephoning. Why you don't get on the hand, Ramskin? Sweetness is a very nice girl, you know, she was two forms behind me at St Hugh's and she don't have any boy-friend. You should take her on, man.' She rubbed her cheek, cat-like, against his and then suddenly pinched him hard in the back and sprang away laughing. He got up to go after her and she warded him off and shouted 'Ramsee! Ramsee!' at the top of her voice.

'You children, stop that noise in there, ah can't *sleep*!' Mrs Tull shouted.

'Yes, Mama,' Mabel said in a small voice. 'All right, Ramsay. Pax,' she whispered. 'Let's frighten Aunt Alice.'

They turned the lights off and made a great noise over going to bed. Ten minutes later when Ramsay had got into bed and was just drifting to sleep Mabel came into his room with a white sheet thrown over her head. He put a sheet over his head and the two childish ghosts tiptoed through the dining room and the small back room and stood at the foot of Mrs Tull's bed. Mabel touched her mother's feet and Mrs Tull started screaming 'Jesus Christ have mercy! Ramsay! Bobsie! oh Lawd Jesus!'

She fumbled for the light switch and as the light came on Mabel fell on the bed shouting with laughter.

'You, you two *foolish* children!'

'You were really frighten, Mama?' Ramsay asked.

Mabel hugged her and she laughed, too, though the pain in her chest from the shock was almost unbearable. But she didn't mention it.

Mabel slept with her that night and Ramsay drifted into a sleep full of dreams of running and Mona Freeman's long Indian hair. He woke up once in the night wondering if he could be a real communist without joining a Communist Party, could you really be a Christian without the discipline of active church membership? He decided half asleep, that it was like being a Scout, you could be a Boy Scout without being a member of a troop.

★ ★ ★

I leaned against a telegraph pole on St James' Road, a half-poet starved of life and love in my seventeenth year, watching across the street the lights in Mabel Tull's room. I thought myself enclosed and invisible in the moonless dark. I had half-met her twenty-one times, I counted daily and over again, on tramcars, magically and suddenly with my secret flaming in the Chinese lantern afternoon of a garden party, and watched her face, half-hidden in a large white hat, at a communion service. She treated me distantly as the small brother of my sister, her schoolmate.

Mabel was the focal point of all the tortured sexual symbolism in the poetry I wrote so I kept up this senseless vigil, waiting for nothing. I thought of her adult world of fast men, fast cars, night clubs and careless laughter, and suddenly felt self-conscious and unbyronic in the gaslight.

A boy I knew at school approached on a bicycle so I walked to the nearest gate, number fifteen, knocked and listened to the dog barking. The boy recognized me and stopped.

'Hi, what you doing 'round here?' he asked.

'Who live in this house, number fifteen?' I asked, obviously embarrassed.

'I don't know,' he said. 'You looking up a chile, nuh?'

I didn't speak but said 'Yes' slyly in my silence. He went away and I returned to my vigil.

It would be easy to visit Ramsay, I thought, but if I did, I would become ordinary again and shed the poetic mantle of the dark and she, too, would be ordinary and perfumed and paralyzing. So there were the lights in Mabel's room and the shadows on the curtains. I thought of the love one could manufacture and write poetry with and found it difficult to concentrate on Mabel, except when a door slammed or someone walked down the path from the Tulls' house to the gate. I tried to believe that if I contemplated her distantly and suffered her father's death, the funeral and my enormous love, I might write the final overwhelming poem – to impress her, for she had read the copy of my poems I had lent to Ramsay.

I was waiting for nothing, perhaps to see Mabel come out of the house, but certainly not to speak to her or have her know I waited, watching her room for nothing. So, after ten minutes, I walked away.

I walked alone at night for the restless days were friendless, but the nightly familiar streets, twisted with thin gaslight and shadows, were dark enough for me to flaunt my loneliness before them. On almost every walk some incident gave me pleasure, or opened an aspect of life to me. There were the usual street scenes – night-higglers of fruit with little tin kerosene lamps, the domino game outside a tailor's shop, the drunks, the laughing women, earthy as mud, who came tumbling out of gateways blown about with coarse joy. I liked particularly to watch barefoot boys in the gutter playing the game of keeping up the pip of an orange in the air with their feet and counting aloud the number of times the pip was played. They often counted to incredible figures, 'a t'ousen an' wan, a t'ousen an' two'.

As I walked up St James' Road I heard the sounds of music and charted them through a maze of streets and alleys. It was a party and there were as many people standing outside the house watching and listening as there were people inside drinking and dancing. The crowd outside didn't want to go in and dance, they only wanted to listen and watch, and I joined them. The late arrivals, well dressed and powdered (including the men), walked through the crowd as if we didn't exist. I saw a chap I knew going in.

'Hi, Fitzy, what happen now?' I shouted to him in the masonic language of Kingston schoolboys. Fitzy was dark with a large head and very soft skin. He was wearing a zoot-suit and carrying two gramophone records under his arm.

'As yuh see it,' he said. 'Yuh not going in?'

'No, man,' I said, 'I jus' passin'. Who giving this party?'

'Is Arabella birthnight party,' he said, dabbing his forehead.

He rode all the way from above Cross Roads on a down-handle fix. I didn't know who Arabella was. He showed me one of the records.

'Joe Liggins' *Honey Dripper*,' he said. 'Yuh know it? Is great eeh? I going mad dem with it.' He was listening to the music and already jigging.

'I see yuh, sah,' he said, and was immediately swallowed into what my envy described as a den of lust and drunkenness. No poet, I thought, should contaminate his talent by trying to escape from it. So I walked away, a poem swimming and dying against the fading sounds of jazz in my mind.

I had sixpence in my pocket so I went into a Chinese soda-fountain on Deanery Road and asked for a malted milk. As I sat at a green table gobbling the drink there was the enormous clangour of a bicycle thrown violently on the ground and Roderick Ashman came in. He leaned the violincello he was carrying against the counter and asked for a glass of milk. I had met Roderick Ashman strangely. One evening as I sat in the gallery of the Ward Theatre waiting for the annual pantomine (it was *Soliday and the Wicked Bird*) to begin, Roderick came along, introduced himself and said he had read a poem of mine in my school magazine. It was a poem that began,

> *The futility of this mêlée*
> *And the lasciviousness of the streets*
> *Mingle with the promiscuity of women*
> *And my dreams of the to-be.*

That poem had been the symbol of my discovery of the thirteen-volume Oxford dictionary and had no real meaning as far as I knew. Roderick interpreted my poem to me and gave it a meaning. He was a bundle of energy and talent – he played the 'cello in the island orchestra – and he could put into words all that I felt about art and poetry. He was a chunky little fellow, unbelievably wise in his spectacles, with a fury of spiked hair. He had a reputation for being 'mad'.

'What you doing out at this time a' night?' he asked me. Why did everybody question my right to be out?

'Going for a walk,' I said. It was after nine.

'Lissen,' he said to me. 'Come and hear some records at K.C. I've got the key to the Music Room.'

We trudged along to K.C. talking poetry and music, Roderick pushing his bicycle with the 'cello balanced on it, and I almost running to keep up with his mighty stride. Then, in a room without lights, I listened to the final statement of longing and unfulfilled desire which was all that classical music meant to me then. Roderick hummed each piece, leaping about and conducting, as his spectacles glistened and flashed in the rays from the streetlights. In the scarcely controllable excitement of the music and the dark I began, in my mind, a poem,

> *This swelling strain of sad 'cellos*
> *Is more colourful and painful*
> *Than a soaring bird*
> *Struggling in high winds.*

After an hour of listening we parted, Roderick for his home and I to continue my walk.

I walked west on North Street, then by the Cathedral into Emerald Road, then into South Camp Road keeping close to the high fence of Kingston Club. Just opposite Alpha Academy I saw a prostitute accosting a man. He was mounted on a bicycle but was resting his left foot on the ground, and the woman leaned over the handle-bar to talk to him. I overheard this conversation:

THE WOMAN: But doan you is Missa Bennit what work at Dadlanis an' was at New Year Dance at Bournmut?

THE MAN: Is not me, you know!

THE WOMAN: Is you same one. Yuh t'ink I forget you. Hmmmm. Then what 'bout de thing? Yuh doan waant a rudeness tonight?

The man looked around nervously. Passing them as quickly and as quietly as I could, I got the impression that the man wanted to say something but was being distracted by what the woman was doing with her hands. Out of the corner of my eye I saw that I knew the man. He was Keith Tulloch. We went to different secondary schools but had played cricket against each other in the Sunlight Cup Competition. He had left school the year before.

Keith overtook me on his bicylcle, got off, and we walked together up South Camp Road.

'Hi, skipper,' he said. 'What you doin' roun' these parts?'

'Hi, Keitsy! What happen now?' I said, using the usual formula.

'Yuh see a woman try to proposition me a while ago, sah? I woulda never do a thing like that. Is not safe, yuh kno'!' Keith was brown, tallish and inclining to corpulence. He began to talk about school cricket. 'Yuh remember the firs' match year-before-laas at Wolmers?

It was a great match, man. How much you get that day?' I said I had made about twenty-five. 'Yuh remember how me an' Sidney hole on at the laas' there, an' hole you people to a draw? I made thirty-nine can't-out, tha' day.' I nodded but did not remember that part of the match. I only remembered dropping two vital catches. Keith and I parted at Merrion Road.

I walked back slowly past Mabel's house but it was in darkness. I didn't care now. I saw myself grandly, a great renowned man of letters receiving her coldly and carelessly in the future that stretched magnificently before me. Then as I turned into my street I felt miserable again and tried to choose the time and form of my own death that would spite her and make her sorry. I turned on the small radio by my bed and listened to a jazz programme until my father shouted to me to turn the radio off and go to sleep.

I walked after rain, choked by the steam rising from the wet asphalt. The nights were darker and very sad then. I had nowhere to go to. No party I had looked forward to, no meeting, no rendezvous had been cancelled and I was free as always to roam the streets. But the damp heavy air weighed on me. As I walked past the wet verandahs and the trees that were still dripping, I felt that the rain had imprisoned me in a room with a book.

One night, a brilliant moony night, as I passed the tramcar Stop outside Palace Theatre, a young man – one of the masters at my school – who was waiting for a tram stopped me. He was Mr Cohen, a maths master who taught us chemistry unwillingly. I remember him in the classroom as a pathetic fugitive figure jeered at by thoughtless boys as the blood oozed from one of his fingers that had been cut when the experiment he was trying to show us failed for the fourth time. I liked Mr Cohen. He looked dreamy and was a hopeless disciplinarian and his hair was unruly like a poet's.

'You weren't born in Jamaica, were you?' he asked me one day.

'No, sir', I said. 'I was born in Nigeria, sir. How did you know, sir?'

'I could tell it from your eyes,' he said, very seriously.

I thought this a very high compliment.

It turned out that Mr Cohen was on his way to the home of Dr and Mrs Raymond Phillips. T. S. Eliot's *The Rock* was going to be read by a choral-speaking group and all the important writers, poets and painters in Jamaica would be there. He invited me to go with him. We went by tramcar to Cross Roads. At Cross Roads we were picked up in a large car in which there were already about ten people. I had to kneel on the floor in the back of the car and could not see where we were going. The talk in the car was about the very private lives (no euphemisms were used, even by the ladies) of certain well-known Jamaican painters. Then they talked about Kafka's novels. No one seemed to notice that I was in the car.

When we arrived at a large house, which I guessed was some-where above Halfway Tree, the performance was about to begin. The guests were seated on the wide verandah in darkness while the choral group stood in the drawing room. With infinite grace, and instinctive pity for my adolescent awkwardness, Mrs Phillips, when I was introduced to her by Mr Cohen, insisted on my sitting next to her. There was nothing I could reply to her brilliant summing-up of the mood and meaning of Eliot's poetry. I was nothing but a shy frightened schoolboy, and all the witty remarks I had carefully planned on my walks with which to triumph on just such an evening escaped me completely.

I was very surprised to find, however, that this poem which had been so lucid and exciting when read in the quiet of my room was boring and opaque in Dr and Mrs Phillips' drawing room. After the Chorus of Unemployed, in which the phrase 'To two women one half pint of bitter ale' had a startling poignancy, my mind went completely dead to the sounds of the droning voices. I tried to withdraw from this public contact with the poetry I enjoyed in private. I was bitter and angry about my awkwardness.

After the reading, the verandah lights were turned on and drinks were served. I was reassured by the trite remarks (in which the word 'philistine' was used frequently) that some of the female guests were making. I spoke to two poets who had been in the sixth form during my first two years at school. One, who wrote very fragile nature poetry, told me that he had been struggling against the influence of T. S. Eliot for years. The other, a metaphysical poet who had set the fashion for 'padding' out poems with philosophical jargon, asked me how was school and did I have a cigarette on me.

I took a glass from a passing tray and drank quickly. The drink was very cold and I hardly tasted it. Someone in the distance shouted, 'Is there any ginger ale in these rums, Roger?' The answer was a diabolical laugh. I had never drunk rum before. I soon felt very peculiar and seemed to be floating.

My light-headedness increased steadily and I drifted towards a group in the centre of which sat Mr Cohen looking sorry for himself. He had not liked the Eliot reading, but was finding it impossible to explain why he didn't to the satisfaction of the sharp wits that were questioning him. They were all laughing at him, and again the word 'philistine' was being frequently used not, it seemed, about Mr Cohen but as a kind of intellectual punctuation. I then did something that surprised me even while I was doing it. I walked into the centre of the group, told Mr Cohen that I was going home and asked him for a cigarette. He seemed surprised but gave me one and lit it for me. I stuck my hands into my pockets and started walking home without wishing anybody goodbye or thanking Mrs Phillips. I walked for what seemed hours before I reached the Constant Spring Road. Then, with the pleasure of my introduction to the world of intellectuals sustaining me, I walked the six miles home.

For weeks after this, going through the nightly familiar streets, I thought only of Rainer Maria Rilke whose poetry Mrs Phillips had said I should read.

III

Cyril Hanson lived with his mother in a large concrete-nog house somewhere in Kencot. Mr Hanson had long ago disappeared, still was alive or had died in South America. For a time, after he left, Myrtle Hanson lived well with two maids, a gardener-boy, a car, a chauffeur, and two Alsatians, but in later years the car had been sold, there was only one maid and no gardener-boy and no Alsatians. Shortly after the start of the war Myrtle Hanson had taken a job as the receptionist in an expensive little guest-house called 'Flamingo Lodge'.

Myrtle Hanson was very light in complexion, and in spite of middle-aged stoutness was still, at forty-three, a very handsome woman with an impressive presence. She had been to school in England until her parents (an Englishman and a Jamaican mulatto woman) were divorced, and she still spoke with a refined drawl. Partly on the strength of this and partly because she was very capable she moved in the upper range of society and had entrée to King's House. She served on numerous church committees at the St Andrew Parish Church (where the Governor worshipped), was an officer in the Jamaica League of Women and something of importance in the Red Cross. She was a normal person and always had a current love affair. Her only peculiarity was that she had a deep distaste for very black people believing, as she stated over and over, that people were more or less 'bad' in proportion to the blackness of their skins.

Her life really centred on Cyril, her only child, but without possessiveness. Far from fostering any inhibitions or complexes in Cyril, she had encouraged him to live a normal male life with many boys to play with innocently when he was small, and many girls to play with, not so innocently, after puberty. Cyril's athletic gifts, however, seemed to keep him sanely balanced.

So the arrangements for Cyril's twentieth birthday party were left to Mrs Hanson. It was a remarkably well-chosen group that was invited to the party. There were four members of the House of Assembly, including the Minister of Health – all members of the Merchants' Party. Then a number of lawyers (most of them connected with the People's Democratic Party) many doctors, including one with a very shady reputation, two Syrian merchants, a number of top civil servants – these and their well-decorated wives. They were the public window-dressing guests. On Cyril's account there were well-known sportsmen and sports promoters, Mr Phipps-Help (who got entangled with some youngish amateur actors and actresses from the Pantomime and did not extricate himself all evening), nearly fifty girls aged between eighteen and twenty-four in all shades from ebony to apple-blossom (but mostly apple-blossom), and Cyril's schoolmates. Ramsay Tull was there, so were Mabel and Rosalie whose husband, Martin Lowe, played billiards occasionally with Cyril at Kingston Club. But the stars of the evening were Dr and Mrs Raymond Phillips.

Dr Raymond Westlake Phillips was one of the most remarkable, and probably the most brilliant, of Jamaicans. It would have been difficult to prove, if challenged, that he was *not* the most brilliant. He was a tall athletic-looking man, of direct planter stock and a conventional background. He was a much-more-than-brown man, though the sepia of a slave grandmother had given him an attractive tan. He had been educated at one of the lesser public schools in England and at Clare College, Cambridge. In his seven years at Cambridge he had taken a double-first in Classics, then a first in the Law Tripos, and then a Ph.D. in Law; he had boxed against Oxford in his second year and won his fight. He had also taken a first and prizes in the Bar finals. Surprisingly enough he had been a comparative failure at the Bar. He was weak as an advocate, too impatient, too hectoring, too sarcastic, but he had a distinctive style of address. He had made a lot of money through large retainers but his brilliance existed outside the court-room, in chambers, in society. Now, at forty-six he was a tyro in politics, learning, but not as fast as he thought he was; a gentleman, a nationalist, a patron of the arts, an owner of race-horses, an accomplished after-dinner speaker. It was a little terrifying for Ramsay Tull to find himself at the same party as Dr Raymond Phillips.

Mrs Cecilia Phillips was decidedly, almost perversely, black, and very beautiful. Not only Myrtle Hanson but every society hostess made her an exception in the usual colour categories. She had been one of the first to win the Jamaica Scholarship for girls. She not only had a clever brain but also was the nearest thing to being a brilliant creative artist who practised no art. Her poetry readings, her *salon*, were famous and very tropical and her influence over budding poets and painters and musicians, especially musicians, was notorious. Again, it was absolutely, intolerably thrilling to Ramsay Tull to be at the same party as Mrs Cecilia Phillips.

The party went well from the start, from the light wines and the Strauss waltzes to the point where only the heavy rummers and the jitterbugging youth were left. The wide front verandah was crowded by nine o'clock and guests were still arriving. Although most of the time Myrtle Hanson was supervising the serving of drink and food in the dining room, she nevertheless knew by a kind of instinct when an important guest had arrived. She moved through the crowd, her lovely evening gown blazing with sequins, and arrived at the top of the verandah stairs just in time to be perfectly delighted that Mr and Mrs So-and-So had come.

Cyril was dressed with the careless elegance that only a light-skinned Jamaican of athletic build who has been to a snob school seems to want to achieve – his fawn-coloured tropical suit was cut to perfection in the modified American fashion of the day and the red chrysanthemum in his lapel was like a blotch of blood or an artificial rose as the light caught it differently. He walked past a group of sportsmen and one of them held him under the arm.

'You should be a sure thing for the Rhodes this year, Cyril,' he said.

'Well, you can never tell you know, Andy,' Cyril said looking very serious. 'It's all in the lap of the gods and the gods don't like favourites.'

The group of sportsmen laughed and said, 'That's damn true, boy; that's damn true!'

Three girls were talking about their insides, over by the three large pots of fern. They were rather more ebony than apple-blossom.

'The week before every Christmas Mama gives me a complete washout, and then just after New Year I take another one. All those rich foods, you know.'

'Well, my dear, *my* mummy doesn't believe in purgatives at all. She says it gives you constipation!'

Five minutes later one of them was saying, 'She had this pain on the Tuesday you see and by Thursday they were operating on her she had a local anaesthetic and they put a screen and she could see them moving about but she couldn't feel anything you see and she didn't know whether they had covered her down there but she only has a small scar about one inch long.' They sipped their drinks with satisfaction.

All this time Dr Raymond Phillips was sipping sherry (he never drank anything stronger) and eating large quantities of turkey salad and discussing a case with one of the younger P.D.P. lawyers. Mrs Phillips had found a poet and they were sitting on cushions on the verandah steps discussing whether or not the creative writer should be *personally* involved in society.

Ramsay asked one of the apple-blossom girls to dance to a dreamy sentimental tune called *Long Ago and Far Away*. The crooner, miserable and hungry for love, sang

> *Long ago and far away*
> *I dreamed a dream one day*
> *And now, that dream is here beside me;*
> *Long ago the spell was cast*

The girl's face was withdrawn and melancholy and Ramsay felt that the soft cool skin and the intoxicating perfume were the guardians of her virginity. He wondered if he could sleep with her but he didn't try anything. It was during this dance that he saw Mona Freeman at the party. They looked at each other with a slight surprise, for Mona had left her job at Courts Office and had become Capleton's secretary about four weeks before. Now that she had left the office Ramsay felt that he could make another attempt at her. He looked around for Capleton but was quite certain that Mrs Hanson could not have committed the lunacy of inviting a man who was palpably black and, in the eyes of most of her guests (even those who did not hold to her view of colour), clearly evil.

The next record was Count Basie's *One O'Clock Jump* and the party was beginning to lose its respectability. The rum had begun to do its good work and the sportsmen and the young girls hurrahed it. A little afraid that things would get too rowdy for the older guests, and remembering the whole purpose of inviting them, Mrs Hanson called for the singing of 'Happy Birthday to You' at eleven o'clock instead of midnight. Then, after a number of fulsome toasts to Cyril's health, Dr Raymond Phillips was asked to say 'something'.

In his witty little speech he praised Cyril generally and praised his remarkable athletic record and then, realizing that he was being too enthusiastic about Cyril, he began to praise Mrs Hanson, glowingly, with a choice of phrase that somewhat startled Mrs Phillips. Then he spoke of the Greek ideal, and the older English Universities and said, inscrutably, that the future of Jamaica belonged to the Cyril Hansons. Then they sang 'Forease a jolly good fay-low' and both Dr Phillips and Cyril kept silent.

It was some time after midnight that Ramsay had his first chance to speak to Cyril.

'Ah, Head, boy, the party's going well, eh?' Cyril said, mopping his forehead. 'Eats and drinks O.K.?'

'Fine, man,' Ramsay said.

'Come and meet the old lady.'

Cyril led him into the dining room where Mrs Hanson was slicing ham on the sideboard.

'Hello, Ramsay,' she said. 'Enjoying yourself?'

'Oh yes, thanks. It's a great party, Mrs Hanson.'

'You don't come around these days, Ramsay, as you used to when you were at school,' Mrs Hanson said. 'Going after the girls, I suppose.'

'Ramsay is a big politician these days, you know, Mummy,' Cyril said winking at Ramsay. 'He's one of the P.P.L. Intellectuals.'

'What?' said Mrs Hanson, genuinely horrified. 'With Capleton? It just isn't respectable. Anyway you're young, you'll grow out of it.'

'Come and meet Dr Phillips before they leave,' Cyril said.

'Why did you tell your mother I'm in the P.P.L.?' Ramsay asked, really getting angry at Cyril's insensitiveness.

'Oh, don't worry about that, man,' Cyril laughed. 'Mummy isn't interested in politics. She just dislikes Capleton because he's so black.'

Ramsay was introduced to Dr Phillips while he was having a discussion with Albert French, one of the young P.D.P. lawyers. French was a white Jamaican, a Rhodes Scholar with the Oxford accent of the 'thirties, the badge so much more clearly defined in the imitator. He stuttered slightly.

'This millennium idea, the communist Utopia or any kind of Utopia, is an idea we must continually reject,' Dr Phillips was saying. 'A chap like Capleton hasn't got the foggiest notion how our economic problems are to be solved. In fact I doubt if he understands what they are.'

'But don't you think, sir, that in the realities of the facts, the people, the broad masses of the people, don't care and never will care about economic problems,' Albert French said mildly. 'I entirely agree that we must be honest but what I mean is that if we *say* we are socialists and *don't* promise any kind of heaven and Capleton comes along with what he assures the people will be the true socialist heaven, don't you think our intellectual honesty might be politically unwise, if you see what I mean?'

'Every form of dishonesty is in the long, even the very long, run, politically unwise,' Dr Phillips said, calmly and firmly. 'But, apart from that our function as socialists is to discredit communism in this country, once and for all.'

Cyril thought this the most suitable point at which to introduce Ramsay, adding, as if it were a joke, that Ramsay was one of the intellectual leaders of the P.P.L. Albert French looked at Ramsay as if he thought Ramsay had crashed the party.

'Are you a communist?' Dr Phillips asked Ramsay.

'Marxist-socialist.'

'The usual dodge,' Albert French murmured.

'I didn't know you were actually a Marxist, Ramsay,' Cyril said with surprise, careful to avoid contamination.

'I don't see how you *can* be any other kind of socialist,' Ramsay said.

'Of course,' Dr Phillips said, 'there must be something in a political creed that can organize as mighty a war-effort as the Soviets have done, but then, by the same token, there must be something in the political creed that has organized the Nazi war-machine. We in the P.D.P. oppose and totally reject *all* totalitarian methods, communist or otherwise, and we are determined that it will never become a political force in this country. All the strength I have will be used to that end!'

Ramsay wondered if he should argue with Dr Phillips for he thought he saw, across the mist of terror that had been created for him by Dr Phillips' personality, an opening for a slight protest. The idea of having argued with this brilliant man appealed to his vanity, and he buttressed his awkwardness by trying to remind himself that he belonged to the class that people like Dr Phillips were either oppressing or misleading. So he said, 'But the methods that any communist in Jamaica wants to use are perfectly legal and constitutional'.

There was a second of shock and then the same weary smile from Dr Phillips and Albert French, the smile perhaps of the intellectual tiger about to pounce. Cyril carefully but belatedly imitated the smile.

'The communists' methods,' Dr Phillips said, 'are not limited to force of arms. I doubt if Capleton himself can use a revolver. Legality within the law of the state, perhaps, but there are higher elementary moral laws, the common, indispensable human values which the communists deny. Falsehood, intrigue, dictatorship, the regimentation of thought and action, these things....'

'But isn't the bourgeois litany of Lincolnian democracy an equal type of regimentation?' Ramsay put in.

'It's useless arguing,' Albert French said. 'That façade of jargon conceals both honesty and thought. Of course, Capleton has never learned to *think*, you know.'

'Yes, but setting aside Capleton,' Ramsay said, 'I was a Marxist before I met Capleton, before I left school even. It's a question of truth. Is there only condemnation for Marxism, nothing whatever to be said for it, even as a kind of opiate religion?'

'You can say,' Cyril said with his quick memory, 'it can offer you a slow death with all the freedoms curtailed and all the decent elemental human values denied. And wouldn't you say, Dr Phillips, that as an economic system communism simply will not work in Jamaica?'

This was precisely what Dr Phillips had said ten minutes earlier. He smiled at Cyril's acuteness and sense of balance, and Ramsay thought how much Dr Phillips and Cyril resembled each other.

'I hope you outgrow this phase,' Dr Phillips said to Ramsay to end the discussion. 'You have some good stuff in you.'

As they walked away Cyril said to Ramsay, 'You know, Head, I don't fully agree with Doc Phillips about communism. To me it's just like early Christianity.'

'Why are you such a dyam sycophant, Cyril?' Ramsay asked. 'What have you got to lose?'

'I've got a hell of a lot to lose, man. You'll see,' Cyril replied without a trace of annoyance. 'In any case, hyprocrisy is the oil that makes the wheels of the world go round.'

'Who said that?' Ramsay asked.

'Hanson said it, man, Hanson said it,' Cyril said truthfully. Ramsay went to the bar which had been set up in a corner of the living room and began to drink rum-and-ginger rapidly, like water. He wanted to get drunk and to hell with everything.

A voice beside him said, 'You're drinking too quickly'. The voice had a transatlantic accent, indeterminate English or American. Ramsay turned and for a moment his head 'grew', as if he had seen a ghost, for the man beside him, a white man, very pale, with the skin of the forehead stretched tight across the bones and almost transparent, looked exactly like his mother's description of her curious visitor. But this man was a priest in cloth, smelling of drink, so Ramsay didn't care.

'A party's for drinking,' Ramsay said bluntly. He looked more closely at the priest and it seemed that they were of about the same age.

'Not "too much",' the priest said, helping himself to more

rum, 'but "too quickly". Americans drink too quickly. Jamaicans drink too much. That is all there is to be said about drinking.'

The sadness of the priest's face was in a world different from the gaiety of his words. Ramsay was quite certain that this priest was the same travelling salesman that had visited his mother. They were alone in the dark alcove where the bar was. It couldn't be, Ramsay knew, but his terror began to rise, perhaps he was completely drunk but he also knew he was sober.

'Are you superstitious?' the priest asked. The question jolted him and the extraordinary experience was over. Often in an evening of logic and drinking something happens which afterwards can only be hazily remembered and never explained, a short passage, the moment of turning the handle of a door, the tiny lace handkerchief found clenched in the fist, the phrase of a tune for ever incomplete with no before or after, or, to look at it another way, something the mind invents but is incapable of explaining. This was Ramsay's experience now. For the priest said, 'You ought to go to Oxford. Any college except Pembroke and Christ Church, will do. You should try for the Chelaram scholarship' – and the priest was gone.

For months afterwards Ramsay knew that his mind had photographed an image from anxiety and wishful thinking and rum.

He searched for Mona and found her at a table with Mabel and three fellows he didn't know. Mona was tipsy and giggling.

'This Ramsay, your brother, is a dark horse, you know,' Mona said to Mabel. 'He tried to rape me one day at Courts Office.'

'Who? Ramsay? He's an old hypocrite, that boy.' Mabel was tight. 'He used to sleep with all the maids we had.'

'Then what about you, Mabel?' one of the men asked. He wasn't drunk and he had a large American car waiting outside.

'Who me?' Mabel asked. 'I do it every other day. What you think it was made for?'

The men laughed in concert, a private lecherous laugh. They were three near-white bank clerks.

Mona got up to dance with Ramsay ('Ramsay is alright. He is a comrade these days,' she said) and they danced to Glenn Miller's *At Last.* Mona lost herself in the melody of the love-hungry ballad, but it was all sex for Ramsay – the close savouring of a goddess's body.

'I hear you sleeping with Capleton,' Ramsay said, tight voice, tight lips. 'Is true?'

'Is a lie!' Mona said.

'Then why you join the P.P.L.?'

'Come to my place tomorrow evening,' Mona whispered. 'I want to see you.'

His priest had gone and it was all too easy. He saw two Mabels dancing and a tiny Cyril in the distance and he knew he was drunk.

They had all gone and Myrtle Hanson sat crumpled and broken at the dining table in the necrobiosis of a dead party. Her maid and the hired maid cleared away the dishes, the dirty glasses. Cyril came in whistling and joyous.

'I'm dead tired, son. This is the last party I'll ever give.' She sighed and her face fell apart like a flower that a cruel boy destroys, petal by lovely petal.

'You know, I think the Rhodes is all right,' Cyril grinned. 'Dr Phillips invited me to tea tomorrow.'

Myrtle Hanson leaned back and assembled her memories. 'Oxford is beautiful in summer,' she said. 'On the river!'

It was just dusk and the turning of sunset on the following day. Ramsay found the number and knocked at a green wooden double-gate that let into the drive of Mona Freeman's house. The house was hidden behind a high untrimmed hibiscus hedge and from the gate he could see only the side of the house and the closed unused garage. A notice at the gate said 'Beware Bad Dogs' and Ramsay kept on knocking but no dogs barked or appeared. So he shouted 'Hold, dawg!' and pushed the gate slightly open. A sash window was pulled up quickly at the side of the house and Mona's voice said, 'Come in nuh! No dog is here!'

He walked up four steps on to a small verandah and then into a sitting room. The house was divided into two identical halves by the sitting room, on each side there were two small bedrooms separated by a bathroom. Behind the sitting room, curtained off, there were the dining room and a small pantry.

Mona talked to him from one of the bedrooms. 'I'll soon come. I was sleeping, you know. You know, I couldn't go work today after the party last night.'

She talked on and Ramsay lost the thread of her chatter as he looked round the sitting room. There were three lounge chairs, a rocking chair, a hard-backed sofa, four coffee tables, a large Westinghouse refrigerator (which was probably there because there was no room for it in the pantry) and a small writing table and chair with a telephone on it.

The telephone rang and the shower in the bathroom was turned on simultaneously. Ramsay answered the 'phone and a male voice asked 'Is Lorna there?'

'Lorna who?' Ramsay asked.

'Lorna Carmichael,' the voice said.

'This is the Freemans' house,' Ramsay said. 'Must be a wrong number.'

'Is that 33183?' the voice asked. It was. The voice said, irritably, 'Then can I speak to Lorna?'

'Hold on,' Ramsay said, and shouted at the bathroom door, 'Somebody want to speak to a Lorna.'

Mona shouted above the noise of the shower, 'She hasn't come from work yet!'

Ramsay couldn't understand why Mona's parents were away and the house deserted.

Mona looked extremely cool and rested when she came in. She had caught her long hair loosely at the back, wore powder but no lipstick. She smelled very nice. Ramsay asked her where her parents were and she said her mother was in the country, at Porus. He asked her who Lorna was, and she said that Lorna shared the house with her and worked at the Colonial Secretary's Office. Then they were silent for a while.

'I was very drunk last night,' Mona said as Ramsay lit a cigarette. 'I don't remember anything I said.'

Ramsay laughed but he knew she was lying. He said, 'I was really tanked up last night. Boy, it was a great party!'

Mona closed her eyes and rocked gently in the rocking chair. Ramsay looked at her body stretched out, thought of sleeping with her and felt a tingling all over but he believed that he was looking at the Mona of the Courts Office and not the Mona of last night's party. He felt that the journey from the sitting room to the bedroom, if it did occur, would be like climbing Blue Mountain Peak. He wanted to put out the cigarette, and Mona brought an ashtray across to him. As she leaned over to place it on the coffee table beside him he saw that she wasn't wearing a brassiere and he could see her breasts plainly pear-shaped with the nipples surprisingly elongated and firm. For a few seconds he didn't breathe but when he glanced at her face as she straightened up slowly she was clearly absorbed in some thinking which had nothing to do with him.

She went through the curtains into the dining room and there was a clatter of glasses. She put her head through the curtains and said, 'What you like? Rum-and-ginger?' She brought a bottle of rum and glasses, took a bottle of ginger ale and some ice-cubes from the refrigerator and they had a drink as the sun sank.

Ramsay, whose experience consisted only of crawling silently into housemaids' beds and of being pulled into bed with indecent laughter by some of Mabel's looser friends, did not know what the next move was. But Mona, whose mind had been firmly made up, was only wondering whether to wait until Lorna got back and was thinking that it didn't matter whether Lorna was there or not except that she might bring in a man with her.

'Why you so quiet, Ramsay?' she asked. 'You always look as if you thinking deep thoughts. Mind you go mad, you know!'

'When this Lorna coming home, eh?' he asked. Mona said she didn't know and they had another drink.

The sun had set some minutes before and it was the last of twilight when Mona went out on the verandah and stood looking into the darkened garden now bordered on the street side by the shadow from the hedge. Ramsay followed her and stood at the door and caught the scent of the jasmine from the garden. He thought it was her perfume. Then he stood behind her and slipped his hands round her waist. She caught his hands in hers and leaned back so suddenly and heavily, pressing her body against his, that he nearly lost his balance. He held her breasts very tightly to hurt her for the lust for her he had lived down every day and she turned and embraced him with a might like a wave of the sea. Then they went into the bedroom.

Afterwards she had another shower and lay in bed perfumed in a négligé. Her voice hardened again and she ordered Ramsay about, to bring her nail-polish from the vanity-set, open or close the window, turn the lampshade this way or that, bring her a drink or more ice. He obeyed without thinking, feeling the security of conquest, until she said, 'Doan pay any attention to what I said about always loving me. It doan mean nutten. I always say that when I'm coming'.

They talked about her life.

'There is this one thing, Ramsay,' she said, after she had told him not to sit beside her on the bed and try to feel her up, 'I'm going to marry a rich man but he must be educated. I mean a rich man like a doctor or a lawyer. These civil servants, because what? They have big cars or so. They are as poor as church mouse, they owe for everything, even the clothes you see them wearing. Of course I have to love the man, but to go out Palisadoes and do it in the back of a car and you don't know what whore he was with last night!'

There were two photographs on the dressing table, her mother and her father. She told Ramsay, in confidence, that her father had once been a prominent civil servant who had been jailed for embezzling government money and that her mother was almost a full Indian. Her father was living in America, she said, but they never heard from him, though he used to send her mother dollars occasionally. She didn't tell Ramsay, however, that she and her two elder brothers and her younger sister had been educated at secondary schools on the money her father had stolen and managed to take with him to America after he came out of prison.

'You know why I'm with Capleton at P.P.L. office now? Oh, I'm not interested in politics. See what happen. They were going to fire me from Courts Office. I failed Senior Cambridge and after I left school I was learning shorthand-typing at Durham school. It was only a man I was sleeping with got me this job temporary at Courts Office.'

'But you couldn't get a job anywhere else, say in a store downtown?' Ramsay asked. 'P.P.L. can't pay you anything.'

'It's not that, you know,' she said. 'Mr Capleton is a very good friend to Daddy. As a matter of fact, Mr Capleton is the one who arranged for him to go to the States, that's all. Ramsay, how you keep yourself so much to yourself. All the boys at Courts Office, Alf-Gordon and the rest of them, know how I got the job and that they were going to fire me.'

When he was going she said, 'You mus' always come and look for me. I like you but you're a little boy. But doan bother to go an' tell Mister Cyril Hanson that I gave you anything!'

Ramsay tried to kiss her on the verandah but just then a car drew up at the gate and Lorna came in. She was very drunk, shook hands with Ramsay without speaking, stumbled through the sitting room knocking over tables without trying to turn the lights on. Mona, whom Ramsay had never heard laugh, gave out a piercing shriek of laughter and shouted to Lorna, 'What happen, chile? You block up?' She left him on the verandah and went in to look after her friend.

Going home Ramsay savoured again every detail of this experience with Mona. To sleep with Mona had been his desire for many months. When he thought of her response to him, he felt, in the one-sidedness of youth, that if he could do this to Mona Freeman there was nothing under the stars he could not do. It was the final test, to probe and prove his manhood and cool a gypsy's lust.

IV

The long stairs to the Gallery of the Ward Theatre gave off a nauseating odour of inadequately disinfected lavatories and rat-bat dung. Cyril had met Ramsay outside the theatre by chance and, though he had a ticket for the Dress Circle, he had decided to sit with Ramsay in 'the gods' to watch the annual pantomime.

'It's more fun slumming,' Cyril said.

Inside, the Gallery was warm with six o'clock lights and the smell was wholesome – soap still sticking behind the ears of scrubbed children, the ironed starch of their clothes, the powder and perfume of mothers and nannies. Even in Jamaica the theatre was religion without responsibility and Ramsay loved to give himself up to the magic world that waited behind the simple raising of a curtain.

In the gallery, as all over the theatre, there were scores of people whom Cyril knew and who knew him. So he went around the Gallery shaking hands and chatting with female elementary schoolteachers who laughed and simpered at whatever it was that he was saying to them; mothers who knew Mrs Hanson; and occasionally schoolmates whose younger brother or sister had laid the penance of a pantomime on them. These schoolmates, also friends of Ramsay, carried on long-distance silent conversations with each other all over the gallery in a language of grins and gestures peculiar to their school.

Cyril spoke to the boy working the coloured moveable spotlight, a thin white boy, with a lugubrious face and perpetual palsy of his nervous hands, who was said to know almost everything about stage-lighting. Then he had a word with a fireman who was there to prevent people from smoking in the theatre. This man was bored by the show and alert to smokers, until the local dialect comedians came on; then it was safe to smoke discreetly. Having established his presence in the gallery, Cyril sat beside Ramsay in the middle front row of the curved balcony, leaned over and waved to friends and others in the Dress Circle, tore his ticket into tiny bits and scattered them floating like confetti over the parquet. The ticket was so small, however, that very few people noticed the symbolic gesture.

The band (a popular dance band augmented by a few long-haired instruments like two violins and an oboe) struck up in the limbo of the pit. They played a Jamaican rhumba and were led officially by a broad-backed, silken-haired, auctioneer-pianist who sat in the centre of the pit, but actually the band took its rhythm from the tightly-tuxedoed backside of the double-bass player. The people in the parquet did their best to out-talk the band.

The house-lights faded but in the Gallery there was still the glow of a late sunset over Kingston harbour.

Curtain; and the scene was set in the courtyard of an old plantation Great House. It was characteristic that in a country in which at least sixty per cent of the people are definitely black, the chorus of singers for the opening number had white faces, or puttied faces struggling to be white; and it was characteristic, too, that the American-trained Jamaican producer had so crowded the stage that the set was visible only when the singers swayed exaggeratedly to the music (a rhumba-ish number composed by a chaste English widow), or when they remembered the positions they should be in, but were not, and shifted abruptly.

The singers were dressed in Jamaican national costume, that is, the women were dressed as market-women, picturesque with bandanna, floral ankle-length clothes bulging at the midriff and the men wore the three-quarter length trousers that slavery and poverty had forced on the Jamaican labourer. The middle-class nationalists were the people who maintained that the working-dress of the depressed working class is the Jamaican national costume, but they themselves would never be seen alive dressed like that (except in pantomime or fancy-dress), nor dead, for to the surviving relatives a corpse in market-women's or labourers' dress would be a disgrace to any decent church.

The leading coloratura soprano came forward to sing the

verse. Cracked and wrinkling middle-age saddened her made-up face and her archness was disgusting, like that of an ageing prostitute.

Cyril became restless because his personality was submerged in the dark. He had been seen at the pantomime, the serious social figure. He remembered now that at school he had once acted in *The Importance of Being Earnest*, produced by four producers including an English amateur-professional (amateur in England, professional in the colonies). He had played Lane, Algernon's butler, and had spoken with a faultless accent.

'The theatre. It's something in the blood, you know, Head,' he whispered to Ramsay. 'I've got it, I think, a kind of flair. In the blood.'

'The only thing you'll get in your blood is gonococci bacteria,' Ramsay also whispered.

Cyril's laughter exploded into the shouts and clapping that greeted the villain of the pantomime. He was an English English-teacher, whose voice, pickled in real rum for a decade, rasped like a nutmeg on a tin grater. His face had been made a fiercer red, he wore a bristling moustache and riding breeches and threatened continually to trip himself up with the long horse-whip he carried. He was intended to look like the cliché villain but he only succeeded in resembling faintly a degenerate Mr Pickwick whose diffidence still lingered in the actor's obvious discomfort and embarrassment when he attempted to sing. This man, Roger Benson, of faint Welsh ancestry, was alleged to be one of the finest amateur actors and producers in Jamaica.

'Good old Roger!' Cyril shouted.

'Good old Roger,' Ramsay said.

The pantomime stopped singing and lost itself in the intricacies of a dark plot further obscured by a badly written script.

In the Ward Theatre's Gallery one hears two plays – the artificial life of the stage and the real life of the people, higglers, idlers, whores, in the neighbouring lane. It is possible after some practice to listen to both plays at the same time, select the more interesting one and concentrate on it. Ramsay couldn't understand why the stage hero, a healthy brown strapper with a goodish tenor voice, should want to win the stage heroine, who in real life was white and consumptive and rich, and had once walked on in an obscure provincial production of *Charley's Aunt* in the north of England eight years before, and on the stage was pale and bloodless, and was overacting. So he listened to the voices of the lane.

'What you think of the old lady?' Cyril asked him, quite loudly.

'Which old lady?' Ramsay asked, starting.

'My old lady, man,' Cyril explained.

'I thought you meant *that* old lady,' Ramsay said pointing to the stage where the heroine was gripping the hero in a hold that was as firm as a half-Nelson.

'Peggy? Peggy's all right,' Cyril said. 'English-trained, you know. But drinks too much.'

'English-trained and smells of gin,' Ramsay thought, remembering the rhythm of a phrase in a book he had read as a child.

'But what you think of my old lady?' Cyril repeated.

'I like your mother,' Ramsay said cautiously. 'She always friendly. Why you ask?'

'Yes, but don't you think she is a social climber?'

This, Ramsay realized, was a new tack of Cyril's. He had been reading a new book.

'Well, she is in upper society,' Ramsay said. 'She knows all the important people. Professionals. King's House.'

'Not that. That's all right. I am talking about the psychological factor. I think she is basically, subconsciously, insecure.'

'We all are,' Ramsay said, though it was unnecessary to be tactful to Cyril's tough skin.

'In general. But she is specifically insecure. Partly over the old man, but there is something else. I'm worried about her, Head. She wakes up in the night crying her heart out the way you are in a nightmare. Every day she cracks up more.'

'What's all this?' Ramsay thought. 'She's probably afraid of getting old,' he said. 'My old lady is the same.'

'It isn't only that. I'll tell you in confidence,' Cyril shouted above the singing, to the gallery at large, 'it's her love affairs. You know she hates very black people. Well, she has fallen for a black man and the conflict is terrible.' After a pause he said, 'We live in an age of neuroses' – to introduce the new word he had found.

The singers departed and a bright stage-night came on. It was the Dance of the Fairies, a children's ballet. The children were all white except for one sweet black girl who it seemed had got into the group by mistake. She was the daughter of an illiterate man who had made a fortune in petrol stations and had decided to buy a ballet education for his daughter. The gallery, being mostly black, was delighted to see this black face among the whites.

They were dancing a dance symbolic of the Good Spirits who drove off the Bad Duppies that were bewitching the heroine. *En points* they entered stage-left and toddled across in single file to the heroine's closed door, then broke off, still toddling, after each had listened with cupped ears at the door, into two groups circling centre-stage first, then meeting in a circle down-stage.

The little black girl forgot her part. She was to toddle, alone, to the door, tap gently thrice, dance a *pas de seul* to bring up the blue lights of Faith and Hope. Twice the band played her cue but she remained in the circle safe from the terror of the spotlight. So a beautiful white girl danced from the centre and led the black girl, now in tears, to the heroine's door and showed her by clear gestures ('Aren't you stupid?', 'Have you forgotten this?') what she should dance.

A flush of shame and anger goose-pimpled over Ramsay's body. The black girl remembered and danced her part and the exorcism was complete. You couldn't, if you were a racialist, accuse the Jamaica Children's Ballet of colour discrimination for a black girl had just danced the leading role. The gallery forgot to cheer when the children went out *en points.*

'That was a disgrace!' Ramsay said angrily.

'It's just another case of calling in the white world to redress the balance of the black,' Cyril said, without sarcasm, and wondering if the verbal trick made sense.

'You don't care though, Cyril. You try to sit on the fence.'

'What is there to care about? One girl forgot her part and another was quick enough to save the situation. You read "colour" into everything; it isn't civilized. Is there any colour-bar in Jamaica? It's a question of poverty, mainly. As a socialist you should know that.'

'Oh, dyam socialism! Socialism don't have anything to do with it,' Ramsay said trying to make three points at once. 'That girl's father is rich enough to buy the whole theatre. Oh, Christ, man. *You* see it one way because you are brown and I see it another way because I'm black. I'm dyam sure that the white woman who trained those children *knew* the girl would forget her part.'

'Ridiculous,' Cyril said shaking his head. 'Don't be unreasonable, man. You are a great character, Head. You resent not being white. That's your great resentment. If you were white, everything would be fine.'

'Crap!' Ramsay said. 'I'm black: I can't *want* to be white. You know what *you* believe. You believe that this little Jamaica with a million and a half will one day be a blind country at your one-eyed man's feet.'

'Jamaica belongs to the half-breed,' Cyril said, with personal assurance. 'Not the blacks or the whites. Look at athletics. The best athletes are half-breeds.'

'George Headley?'

'Exception proves the rule, man,' Cyril said, getting up. 'Let's go have a drink.'

As they walked up the steps to the soft-drinks counter Ramsay said, 'It's your usual bourgeois democracy. We are going to string you up, dangling, in about twenty years' time. In 1966, to be exact.'

'String up what!' Cyril sneered. 'And you 'fraid of your own shadow. You can't even swim, Head!'

They were normal again with nothing to quarrel about.

The next scene was full of stage trickery. The mythical Rolling Calf with brilliant eyes, a head only, floated across the black stage. And the children screamed and wished and didn't wish for the lights to come up.

'What you think of Mona Freeman?' Cyril asked, continuing his catechism.

Ramsay's heart skipped guiltily and he thought of asking, 'Who?' but changed his mind and pretended that he hadn't heard the question.

'Eh?' Cyril said.

'What you say?' Ramsay said, concentrating on the same trick done with strings and luminous paint which he had seen at every pantomime.

'Mona. Freeman. What you think of her as a girl?'

'She's a nice piece of tail,' Ramsay said, preparing to bluff his way through. 'But as Birdy said of McCreary's sister "Be careful, she's throw-y".'

They laughed and Ramsay breathed quite easily.

'I'm wondering,' Cyril went on, 'if she isn't a nymphomaniac?'

'What's that?' Ramsay asked, knowing the word quite well but hoping that the flattery of not knowing might mislead Cyril. At the same time he thought she'd probably told Cyril.

'Wants a man all the time. Wants to do it all the time,' Cyril explained.

'But she's very serious about politics, you know,' Ramsay said, speaking quickly. 'She left the Courts to work with Capleton. Maybe she's lonely or wants to get married, well, I mean, what's really wrong with her? I don't know her well or anything.'

'Also,' Cyril said, 'between you and me, she is a thief. Well anyway tha's what I think. You know, one night I was at her place and I had five–six pounds in my wallet, and when I left, you see, to take the bus, not a striking thing but small change in the thing.'

'Then why you invite her to your party?'

'That's all right. She's just got psychological problems, that's all.'

'The whole thing is a lie,' Ramsay said. 'You just want me to know you slept with her. You always try to tell me in a roundabout fashion.'

'No!' Cyril said. 'As there's a God, Head, it's true. She stole it. I'm tell you, man, I'm sure. You don't think – '

'Then why didn't you ask her for it?'

'Couldn' do that. She wouldn't give me anything again,' Cyril said, and his tone praised his own craftiness.

More plot material on the stage and some goodish bits of light comedy. There was a female impersonator who played a princess, all giggly and rowdy, breaking into a deep baritone for the *double-entendre* remarks and being very saucy with the well-known men in the Dress Circle, talking to them and telling them to meet her back-stage afterwards for 'the thing'. It was very saucy and such clean fun. It occurred to Cyril that if he had sat in the Dress Circle he could have arranged with Joe Mercer, the producer, to have the impersonator, Bobbie Townsend, shout to him and run off the stage with a 'Mr Hanson, hoo-hoo!' lifting up 'her' heavy skirt to show an old-fashioned pair of frilly pantaloons. Then the Children's Ballet tottered through some more ballet, but this time without the black girl.

'But coming back to Mona,' Ramsay said, 'Mabel is a bit like that, you know. Not stealing, but about men. She has a lot of boy-friends.'

'Yes. Mabel. What's she doing these days, Head?'

'Trying to get a nursing scholarship to go to England,' Ramsay said.

'Hey, then, boy, we'll all meet in England, eh?' Cyril said with great and insincere enthusiasm. 'That'll be great, man.'

'How you think I'm going to go?' Ramsay asked. 'You want me to swim for Port Royal?'

'But you bound to get the Chelaram, Head,' Cyril said. 'Or, if not, you can try for the next Rhodes.'

'How you so dyam sure you going to get the Rhodes?' Ramsay asked. He himself was quite sure that Cyril would get the award but he hated his confidence.

'Wait and see,' Cyril said smugly.

'Well I don't like Rhodes, because he was a land-thief,' Ramsay said, 'and I don't like Chelaram, because he is a plain thief.'

'Then why you enter for the Chelaram?' Cyril asked. 'It's immoral for a socialist to accept a capitalist scholarship.'

'Chelaram not a capitalist,' Ramsay said. 'Anyway I don't really blame Chelaram. I blame the historical process. But it's time the common people got back some little amount of the money they put in his shops.'

'If you know what's good for you, Head,' Cyril said seriously, 'you won't talk like that at the interview. If you do that they'll throw you out on your arse.'

Ramsay felt very cosy and warm and revolutionary inside, but he knew exactly what he was going to say at the interview.

'You know,' Cyril said, 'for the Rhodes interview you have to walk down a long corridor and the committee is sitting in a room at the end with the doors open watching you. The way you *walk* down there is very important. It's important how you walk in

Oxford, you know. So what you have to do is, first of all, smile and look straight ahead and as you get near to the room start talking before anybody speaks to you. That's the personality test.'

'Is that a fact?' Ramsay asked, quite bewildered. 'How you know all that?'

'Albert French told me.'

'But what you going to talk about when you walking down the corridor? You not serious! You joking!'

'No, it's a fact,' Cyril said. 'I'll think of something to say when I get there.'

'If they ask me at the Chelaram why I want the scholarship I'll say I want to come back and help build Jamaica,' Ramsay said.

'For God's sake don't say that,' Cyril cautioned. Then after a pause, 'Well, maybe that's O.K. for the Chelaram, but not for the Rhodes. Albert French says tell them the truth. Now, I want to be a soccer "Blue" and I want to go to B.N.C. to study Law. I'll tell them that.'

'What's B.N.C.?' Ramsay asked.

'Brasenose College. That's the sports college.'

'Isn't there a college called Balliol?' He said it with a short 'a'. 'That's where Pressy went, don't it?' Pressy was their nickname for their headmaster.

'Balliol,' Cyril said, to correct Ramsay's pronunciation. 'Very intellectual college.'

The local dialect comedians came on at last. They did a skit on a court case, playing the scene in front of the curtain. Rudolph, the 'feed', was the Judge, and Puss-juck, the real comic, was Clerk of the Courts, Barrister-at-Law, Defendant, Three Policemen, Gentlemen of the Jury, Complainant and Two Witnesses all in one. He leaped about the stage from character to character. The 'case' was an action for slander brought against Alphonso Dothething by Icilda Pipeside.

The 'case' began with the usual cry of the Constable (Puss-juck), 'O Yes! any person or person have an unjust cause or complaint to make before his Anna, Mr Justice Maybe, come forth an' be heard. O Yes! O Yes! Gawd Save the King!'

The Clerk of the Courts (Puss-juck) in an impeccably sepul-chral voice gave the charge to the jury, 'You shall well and truly try and true deliverance make in the issue joined between our Sovereign Lord the King and Alphonso Dothething, the prisoner at the bar' (though no issue had been joined with the King). One of the jury (Puss-juck) asked the Judge, 'My honour, is what that him say going issue, sah?' So Rudolph and Puss-juck then went through a long passage about different kinds of 'issues', playing on words, not always decently. Rudolph spoke very quickly, in a high-pitched voice and was completely incomprehensible except for a few choice words and phrases like 'legality', 'accessories behind the fact', and 'botheration'. In the middle of the argument one of the policemen (Puss-juck) suddenly shouted 'Order in Court!' so loudly that the Judge's spectacles fell off his nose and he went groping around the stage on hands and knees looking for them. At this point, in the laughter that was actually making the Gallery vibrate, Ramsay and Cyril lit cigarettes, carefully cupping the matches in their hands.

In the examination of Alphonso Dothething Puss-juck did a perfect imitation of Dr Raymond Phillips.

'I put it to you,' Barrister Puss-juck said, in the silkiest tones, 'that you referred to Miss Pipeside as an "old fowl".'

'You can put it if you like, Barrister, sah,' Alphonso said, scratching himself immodestly.

'Now be careful, Dothething,' the Barrister warned. 'You are on oath. Did you or did you not call Miss Pipeside an "old fowl"?'

'Me, sah? Me, sah?' Alphonso screamed at the top of his voice, and throwing his head far back. 'Me neva, neva, neva, neva, neva say a thing like that!' Alphonso was in tears. 'Mirrana,' he said to the Judge, 'is what this thing Barrister a-say to me, oh!'

'You may rave and rant till Kingdom come, you cannot escape the question,' Barrister Puss-juck said very coolly. Then he rapped out the question again, 'Did you or did you not call Miss Pipeside an "old fowl"?'

This time there was no outburst from Alphonso. He simply said, very quietly, 'Please Mirrana and Barrister, is because of the flitters why Icilda Pipeside bring this case agains' me.'

They laughed in the Gallery and drowned the 'flitters' story completely, for Jamaican comedians did not wait for laughter to subside. A fat man in the Gallery, a retired schoolteacher, laughed himself almost into hysterics and kept on saying, 'They going kill me, they going kill me! Lord! ah cyann stand it, ah cyaan staaand-it!'

The case turned on the evidence of Alphonso's sweetheart, Matilda Slackness. Matilda (Puss-juck) simpered at everybody and had a short intimate passage of whispering with the Judge, accompanied by the most suggestive gestures. Matilda told of how well Alphonso treated her, very 'bunununus', and stated that Icilda Pipeside was only jealous because Alphonso was her man. 'And, you know, Mirrana, him always on spot, you know. Him name right!' It was the pay-off line. The Judge dismissed the case without calling on the jury and then went out arm-in-arm with Matilda as the drums of the orchestra beat a tattoo.

The pantomime ground down to its dull end. Cyril promised to see Ramsay the following Tuesday as he was leaving for a lecture-tour of the country the next day. He went back-stage to congratulate everybody. The buses and trains were overcrowded so Ramsay walked all the way home along East Queen's Street hearing the city's sounds around him but still smelling the painted world of the pantomime. He kept singing in his mind, to the tune of the *Red Flag*,

> *The poinsettia*
> *Is deepest red*
> *Is deepest red*
> *Is deepest red.*

One afternoon, during the Easter vacation, Ramsay visited Surrey College, his old school, to ask the headmaster to act as his referee for the Chelaram scholarship. Percival G. R. Addison, M.A., B.Litt. (Oxon.), was a white Jamaican, just over fifty, tall, a perfect gentleman, whose face since his wife's death had a permanent, sad, gentle peace about it. He was a considerable historian, a 'first' and a research scholar and he had done notable work on Jamaican history. With childless old age he had become a silent, lonely, almost indrawn, man who never left the school premises, a figure partly of pathos, partly of terror, as he walked round the playing-fields watching games. He was a headmaster of the outmoded type who had no psychological jargon and no large educational ideas. An instinctive judge of character (though he had made some amazing errors), he believed that as long as a boy had brains and was made to study, the official and unofficial organization of the school would knock him into a shape fit to tackle life. In general he was a strict disciplinarian, either eccentric or wise in his insistence on details. For instance, it was, in his eyes, one of the greatest of crimes for a boy not to eat the crust of his bread or for a boy not to hang up his wet clothes in the changing rooms after games. His indignant visits to the changing rooms, followed by two or three scowling prefects, had a kind of religious fervour, rather like Christ cleansing the temple, except that every evening this temple needed cleansing. Generations of Surrey College boys had, as their primary memory of the school, the sunset image of Pressy chasing wet shorts and jerseys. But he had no resentments and was the most unintellectual scholar imaginable.

He taught history only to the sixth form, talking, talking, strong on politics and society, uninterested in economics, always recalling little villages in France he had known as a soldier in the Great War. He was a stimulating teacher, for he encouraged his pupils to be socialists and then baited and trapped them with his wider experience, taking, most of the time, an extreme Tory position. He was fascinated and horrified by the Russian Revolution, enthusiastic about the strikes and emerging working-class movement in Jamaica, but was sharply sardonic about Jamaica's political leaders. It was difficult to tell where Pressy stood in politics. His unorthodox teaching methods had led indirectly to the most concentrated piece of reading ever carried out by a sixth form in Surrey College. Finding it difficult to describe the desolate horror of Nazi concentration camps to his history pupils he lent them E. E. Cummings' war book, *The Enormous Room*. The boys read it and were so intrigued by the elliptical style that they discussed the book with the English master who in turn lent them, 'from the point of view of style', James Joyce's *Ulysses*. All the boys except Rupert Hodgkins, son of the manager of Barclay's Bank, took one look at the length of the book and decided not to read it. Hodgkins read *Ulysses* through in three days and then told his colleagues about the final chapter. There was a scramble for the book in the whole thirty-strong sixth form, science and arts, and, after a month, when the book was returned to him the English master was surprised to find that the last chapter had been carefully, though erratically, punctuated. For most of the science sixth it was the only piece of modern fiction that they read in school.

For Ramsay, to return to this school after an interval of nearly two years was to return to a memory of sensations. The smell of the freshly-mown grass, piled and drying, suggested the dusty asphyxia of fever and the itching of chicken-pox. The smooth bark of the divi-divi trees and the corrugated poinciana pods were days spent in climbing trees and hiding and talking smut and swotting religious knowledge for examinations. And the subdued roar of the water-course behind the school was a complexity of over-eating at Scout camps, stealing mangoes and a drowsy Latin lesson. Sensations as trivial and gratuitous as the universe. It is painful for youth to re-enter, even briefly, the ecstasies and mischances of its childhood. He wanted to turn back.

Pressy was in his study smoking a curved pipe and expecting Ramsay. Ramsay knocked and Pressy said 'Come in, man!' They sat facing each other across the desk, Pressy smoking and Ramsay smiling uncomfortably.

'Hoping to go,' Pressy said. He spoke a kind of shorthand. Ramsay grinned and shuffled his hands.

'What university?' Pressy asked.

'I was hoping to go to Cambridge... or Oxford, sir.'

'History or English?'

'I was thinking of... Philosophy, sir?'

'No Greek, little Latin, man. How?' Pressy pushed back his chair.

'Isn't there a course called "Modern Greats" at Oxford, sir?' Pressy started to say something but Ramsay went on, breathlessly, interrupting him. 'And "Moral Science" at Cambridge...?'

Pressy looked at him in a half-amused way with his thumb resting on the defined space of his moustache. This characteristic gesture usually meant that an interview with Pressy was over. Ramsay felt his eagerly-snatched maturity fall from him like a cloak and he was a schoolboy again. He began to get up, then

97

remembered why he had come. 'Can I use your name as a referee for the Chelaram, sir?'

Pressy seemed not to hear.

'It is better,' Pressy said, his eyes twinkling, and remembering, 'to bear those ills we have, than fly to others that we know not of. In any case what are you going to do with Philosophy in Jamaica?' Again the dividing, conclusive finger. 'You can't come back and spend your time in the Blue Mountains contemplating the nature of ultimate reality. Better to read English or History. You don't *have* to teach.'

The study seemed to fill with smoke as Ramsay waited.

'Oxford and Cambridge, very expensive, man. Why not London? If you're keen on economics – London. Oxford – very expensive.' A pause of finality. 'You may use my name!' Pressy nodded sharply and the interview was over.

Why Pressy discouraging me from studying Philosophy or going to Oxford? Ramsay asked himself bitterly. He walked around the familiar dead school, peering into empty classrooms and feeling certain that Pressy would give him a bad recommendation, dwell on his weak character and incompetence at games. The hurt of the laconic interview pierced him slowly. Because I'm poor, Ramsay thought, he trying to discourage me. 'Well, if it's the last bloody rass thing I do,' Ramsay shouted to himself, 'I'm going to win that scholarship, if it's the last bloody rass thing I do!' Tears of deep humiliation ran down his cheeks. But you know Pressy, Ramsay thought, he's always like that, maybe he was giving you good advice. But look at Cyril, he encourage Cyril for the Rhodes because Cyril is good at games and all this personality-thing and Cyril's mother always coining up and sweet-mouthing Pressy. And Cyril is a fool, just scrape through H.S.C., no distinctions, one 'B'. No colour-prejudice, no *dyam* colour-prejudice! Jesus Christ strike me dead, but I'm going! Ramsay looked with surprise at the vehemence of his clenched fists, and in this desolate visit to the school that had nurtured all his imperfections he felt, acutely and entirely, the loss of his father.

Ramsay stood by the swimming-pool, remembering his terror of drowning and watching the lines of the far mountains he had hiked in. Walking away from the school, past the mock-ivied chapel walls where a well-fed society clergyman had thanked God after confirmation class that he would drink a bottle of iced beer that afternoon, he wondered whether Pressy would be alive when he (Ramsay) opened the school to the sons of all the poor and knifed away this cancer of snobbery.

Two months later Ramsay was interviewed for the Chelaram scholarship. He wore the only decent suit he had, an uncomfortable black suit which reminded him of his father's funeral. His mother supervised his dressing with the same anxious care as when he was going back to school at the start of term. She kept on talking nonsense about the interview but Ramsay was not cruel enough to tell her that she was too ignorant to understand anything about scholarships, for Mrs Tull was only barely able to read and write.

The self-consciousness with which Ramsay began his long walk to the Education Office on East Street gave way, first, to an objectless anger, and then, as he neared the prison-like building, to a desire to turn back and go home and take off the horrible suit. Only his feet carried him forward, for his mind had already turned back and convinced itself that the type of education he was now going to draw a lot for was the bourgeois way; he was no better than Edgar, he told himself, and should share that privation and be free for ever from the lower middle-class tight-rope act. The pathos of his mother's prayers and the nervous anxiety he had developed over his cowardice ('weak in personality', 'no strength of character', were the phrases that always recurred in his school reports) pushed him on. He felt that in attending that interview he had everything that was really himself to lose. It was as far as a boy of nineteen, with no background, could go by way of self-analysis. He was deathly afraid of the interview, and the anger at himself, not recognized, was turned, by the expected shift, to a more abstract indignation and self-pity. So he arrived at the Education Office prepared to be insolent to everybody.

There were ten young men waiting to be interviewed. Two of them had been at school with Ramsay and they began talking in whispers, seated in the dark passage which led to the interviewing room. The conversation was nervous and unfriendly. The other candidates from non-snob schools could hardly conceal their disgust and annoyance at the presence of these Surrey College boys. Ramsay recognized one of the other boys who lived near him on St James' Road and they tried to grin at each other. It was unreal, like two frightened dogs baring their teeth at each other. They waited in this uneasiness for fifteen minutes.

Mr Blair, a greying senior clerk, Secretary to the Interviewing Board, read out the names of the candidates in their order of interview. Ramsay's name came last on the alphabetical list.

Mr Blair said that the result would be announced 'later' and that they need not wait after their individual interviews. When the first candidate returned, full of smiles, the tension eased. He didn't speak to anyone but hurried out, jumped on his bicycle and rode away. The two Surrey College boys wished each other 'good luck' formally, and when they were leaving they also wished Ramsay 'good luck'. When Ramsay was alone in the passage he felt again the impulse to flee and this feeling changed gradually, as before, to anger and self-pity.

He knew by sight only three people on the interviewing board – Dr Raymond Phillips, Kewal Chelaram, elder son of old Chelaram, the Indian merchant, and the Director of Education, Capt. A. G. McGuire, a detribalized Scotsman who spoke with a very English accent. Ramsay thought at first that the Board seemed embarrassed to see him and that they wouldn't ask him any questions. After some whispered consultation, during which Ramsay kept his attention fixed on the glasses of iced water on the large square table, Capt. McGuire 'led' him through the factual parts of his dossier (age, school, exams, etc.) as a lawyer leads a witness. The first real question took him by surprise.

'Yuh seh here, Missa Tull, dat yuh waant to work for Jimayca. Why yuh seh dat?' The questioner was a short, stocky black man wearing rimless spectacles, Mr A. Ebenezer Dyer, an ex-elementary schoolteacher and the Minister of Education in the Merchants' Party government.

'Because –' Ramsay began, then thought of 'social service', thought better of it, nearly said 'self-sacrifice' and in the end said nothing but, remembering Cyril's advice, kept his head up and smiled at nothing.

'Yuh mean yuh want to work for the *peeple* of Jimayca, don't it?' the Minister said to assist him.

'Yes, that's what I meant, sir.'

'Tell me again, now,' the Minister said, enjoying himself hugely. 'Yuh seh you come from country. You ever eat shad?'

'Yes,' Ramsay said, quite confused. The Board laughed. Was it a trick or were they laughing at both of them? Ramsay wondered.

'What you eat it with in country?' the Minister asked and closed his eyes delicately.

'Roast breadfruit,' Ramsay said, and wanted to die because since the day he had entered Surrey College, nine years earlier, he had always denied ever having eaten shad and roast breadfruit, the food of the very poor. The Minister sat back comfortably in the querulous, pointed laughter of the Board and said nothing else for the rest of the interview.

The next questioner was a battle-axe of a woman named Mrs Charles, the terror, though Ramsay didn't know it, of Interviewing Boards in Jamaica. She spoke very mincing and off-key upper-class Jamaican.

'What makes you imagine, young man, that you are fit to read English in a university?' She blinked at him through gold-rimmed spectacles but didn't look like an owl as she had a squarish hatchet-face.

'My headmaster advised me,' Ramsay said, and felt uncomfortable, remembering his interview with 'Pressy', when the Board glanced with surprise at each other.

'But you yourself, what do you feel?' Mrs Charles persisted.

'I feel confident I can do it.' Ramsay could not keep the truculence out of his voice.

'What will you do with an English degree in Jamaica?'

'Teach.'

'But you aren't teaching now, are you?'

No answer for a moment. Then, 'Or journalism.'

'But you aren't working for a newspaper now, are you?'

Ramsay was silent.

'Don't you think, young man,' Mrs Charles said, 'that a degree in Economics would be more useful to Jamaica at this point in Jamaica's history than a degree in English.'

This gave Ramsay the opportunity to deliver his only prepared answer. He spoke with great conviction because as soon as he began to speak he realized that what he was saying was not really relevant to the question.

'Although we need to be concerned about political and economic systems, here as elsewhere, there should always be kept alive the things of the spirit represented in the humanism which has made civilization what it is today. I think that no country, least of all a colony, can progress without some appreciation and understanding of literature and art. To exclude them is to dehumanize society. Although politics and economics are important, the finer things of life are equally important. A degree in Economics or one of the social sciences may be of more use to Jamaica but that is not the way in which I want to contribute.'

He half expected to hear the applause which usually followed this kind of statement in the debating society. He and Cyril had written and rewritten this statement carefully for joint use in their interviews. The ideas had been rehashed from some of Pressy's history class remarks. Mrs Charles pursed her prim lips and fumbled with her handbag.

Dr Phillips asked Ramsay if he had done any voluntary social work and Ramsay said he had 'helped' at Boys' Town and was a founder member of a Consumers' Co-operative in his area. Neither of these things were strictly true. Actually he had often visited Boys' Town to see a friend who worked there, and he had taken over the Co-op. membership held by his mother who was a founder member.

'It is said, you know, Mr Tull,' Mr Kewal Chelaram said, 'that all Surrey College boys are socialists.' The Board laughed, because Kewal Chelaram was himself an old Surrey College boy. 'What do you think of the capitalist system?'

Ramsay thought for a moment. 'In Jamaica, we don't have a capitalist system proper. And private enterprise is a good thing when it keeps down prices.'

'You're dodging the question,' Mr Kewal Chelaram said, with a grin.

'It's a fair answer, Kewal,' Dr Phillips said quietly. And they left it at that.

Finally Capt. McGuire asked Ramsay what Oxford college he had thought of entering and Ramsay said 'Balliol' pronouncing it first with a short 'a', and then correcting himself.

For some days after, the interview seemed a far-fetched daydream, but the two lies Ramsay had told weighed on his conscience.

The People's Democratic Party held its two-day annual conference in the Ward Theatre on a Friday and a Saturday in late April. There were two sessions on each day but only the first session on Friday was open to ordinary P.D.P. members and the public. The seating was arranged in a careful hierarchy – on stage, the officers and the Party Executive; in the parquet, the 'accredited' delegates representing Party Groups throughout the island; in the Dress Circle, ordinary P.D.P. members who could show current membership cards; and in the Gallery, the public.

The theatre was crowded by two o'clock in the afternoon but Dr Phillips had not yet arrived. There were many empty seats in the front row of the stage, for the front line P.D.P. officials always arrived late. Edgar Bailey and Ramsay had been seated in the front row of the Gallery since one o'clock. They had had some difficulty in getting in. They had acquired, through Septy, two P.D.P. membership cards but Edgar was spotted by one of the P.D.P. touts who abused and threatened him. So they dashed to the Gallery before the touts there were alerted. Edgar had been to the public sessions of every P.D.P. conference and he usually sat in the Dress Circle. Once, before he had started speaking regularly on the P.P.L. platform, he had sat calmly in the parquet, passing for a delegate, but had got nothing of value to the P.P.L. from the secret sessions which only boiled down to a plea from the country delegates that the Executive was only in Kingston and had too much power. The Executive's superior smile to this plea suggested that the country delegates were harmless idiots.

But it wasn't a joke slipping into P.D.P. conferences these days now that the P.D.P. had a private paid army of toughs called the Action Group. The Action Group would have thought nothing of taking Edgar and Ramsay up the lane and beating the hell out of them.

Dr Raymond Phillips and Mrs Phillips arrived modestly from back-stage where they may or may not have been since one o'clock, and a light breeze came up to unfurl more distinctly the brilliant scarlet and black banners that festooned the stage – THE PEOPLE FOREVER, ONWARD JAMAICA, THE PDP IS DEMO-CRATIC SOCIALISM, PHILLIPS FOREVER.

When the leader was seated the other front liners came in, also from back-stage, and the chairman for that session opened the conference by asking an insurance agent, one of the party stalwarts who was notorious for his loose sexual life, to offer a prayer for the success of the conference. He offered a ten-minute prayer which began as an address to God, continued as an appeal to the British Colonial Office, became a tongue-lashing for the blind, mis-led electorate and ended as an address to God. The newspapers later reported this prayer as a speech. The chairman called the delegates' roll and Edgar noted in his small black notebook that there were two hundred and forty delegates present.

Edgar and Ramsay had very different attitudes to the conference. Ramsay's was a gentlemen's disagreement with the P.D.P.; in fact, in his early sixth-form days he had been an ardent P.D.P. supporter and like many Jamaican schoolboys who debated seriously, Dr Phillips, with his very imitable style, had been his idol. In spite of his present disenchantment with the P.D.P. he still looked forward to hearing one of Dr Phillips' luscious speeches. Edgar's was a simple raging hostility. He thought Dr Phillips was a bad man messing up the people's movement in the island. He didn't have to prove he was an intellectual by praising Dr Phillips' brain and he would have been glad to hear of his death. Edgar attended P.D.P. conferences in the hope of getting useful material for anti-P.D.P. propaganda.

The chairman was introducing Dr Phillips . . . 'who is none other than that great Jamaican, the leader of the only true people's movement in Jamaica, the man who eight years ago saw a vision of his people and founded the People's Democratic Party, none other than our own Comrade Raymond Westlake Phillips!'

Dr Phillips came to the microphone, the banners waved around him and the theatre was hushed. He began, 'Comrades and friends', and paused. It was the Cambridge voice sweetly but

104

poignantly modulated to the Jamaican accent and the trenchancy of the law courts. The pause was electric and then there burst around Ramsay and Edgar the carefully-touted singing of the *Red Flag*. Dr Phillips stood transfigured.

'He thinks he's Jesus Christ,' Edgar whispered.

'Or Abraham Lincoln,' Ramsay said.

'Comrades and friends, I am reminded of a night, eight years ago today, when a handful of far-sighted men and women, agitated by the lack of direction in the newly-emerged industrial movement, came together to launch the People's Democratic Party. I little thought then – I will be frank – I little thought then that today, we should find it difficult to seat all our delegates in this theatre. (*Cheers.*)

'In our eight years of activity we have played a part – second to none – in shaping the political destiny of this country. We have given this country its first idea of how a democratic political party should be run. And it is the P.D.P. that was instrumental in framing the Constitution we now have – and the fruits of which others are enjoying – which, though limited in execution, has given the vote, finally, once and for all, to every adult in this country. (*Cheers.*)

'We were pledged, at the outset, to lead the progressive forces in this country, and to help raise the standard of life of the common people of this country. We have done that, comrades. The record is there, plain for everyone to see. And I am convinced, that although we failed to win a majority to the new House, when we consider what is happening in the House of Assembly today – (*abortive cheers*) – it is still our duty to pledge ourselves anew to working for the complete emancipation of this country, from the dusty, musty and fusty hands of the Colonial Office! (*Tumultuous cheers.*)

'It is true that the people have spoken. But I believe they have been deceived. It is true that at the last election – the first truly democratic election in this country with universal suffrage, a P.D.P. achievement – it is true, comrades, that we were defeated. I do not wish to open an old wound which I know is already beginning to heal, and the causes for which this conference is going to examine and take immediate steps to put right. (*Cheers.*)

But let me make one remark about the present situation in the House of Assembly – a situation no open-minded and intelligent observer can have failed to notice.'

'He sounds exactly like Sergeant Buzfuz,' Ramsay said to Edgar.

'Like who?' Edgar asked.

Of course, Ramsay thought, Edgar wouldn't know of Sergeant Buzfuz.

'Sergeant Buzfuz,' Ramsay repeated and was surprised when Edgar nodded and laughed.

'It is true,' Dr Phillips continued, 'that if you count heads we are in a minority in the House. But if you count what is *inside* the heads –' Dr Phillips was interrupted by a great burst of laughter, clapping and cheering. When it subsided he said, 'Well, comrades, I see you didn't find that problem difficult to solve.' After a short pause, during which the mike began squeaking and an electrician came in from the wings and tapped it gently, Dr Phillips said, 'I draw comfort – so should you – from that situation.'

Dr Phillips went on to enumerate all the blunders which the Merchants' Party government had made in their six months of office, and he was particularly critical of the government's handling of returning ex-servicemen. He went into details about the Ex-servicemen's Resettlement Scheme which had been put up in the House by one of the two P.D.P. members and rejected by the government. He ended this part of his speech with a glowing tribute to the Jamaican men and women who had so gallantly saved the British Empire – here he corrected himself, the British Commonwealth – from destruction. Edgar noticed that there was a considerable sprinkling of Air Force blue in the Dress Circle and he thought of his brother Reggie, dead, shot down over Germany.

'I am told,' Dr Phillips went on, 'that a rumor has been going the rounds that because of the failure of the party at the last election I intend to retire from politics. Now, such a rumor, though it may emanate from the highest circles in the land, is either malicious or, if I may say so, just plain stupid. I have no intention of retiring from politics. I am not as old as all that!' (*Laughter.*)

He then turned his attention to the other political parties. He spoke with delicate irony about the Merchants' Party but he was much sterner with the P.P.L. He spoke very deliberately.

'I know – (*pause*) – that there are certain tu-pence-hay-penny politicians in this c*ao*ntry – (*pause*) – calling themselves a people's progressive movement – (*pause*) – and inflated with their own unimportance in the usual reversal of values that half-understood communist theory engenders – (*pause*) – a certain tribe of samfie politicians – (*pause; laughter*) – passing as friends of the people – though God have mercy on the people *they* befriend – who are trying to infiltrate into our party; who regard the P.D.P. as a bourgeois nationalist organization to be used. I have told the Executive, and I say it now in open c*ao*nference, that they, or anybody, including myself, will "use" the P.D.P. for their own personal aggrandisement and the furthering of their lunatic and ludicrous schemes *only over my dead body.*' (*Tumultuous cheers.*)

A raucous voice in the Gallery shouted, 'Tell dem, Master! Tell dem!'

'Our greatest hope today,' Dr Phillips continued, 'lies in the new trade union movement which has been formed under the leadership of our stalwart comrade, Willie Monteith. (*Cheers.*) It is the first completely democratic trade union this country has seen and in it is prefigured the writing on the wall for Mannie Small and his corruption. (*Cheers.*) To the F.A.T.U.M. we can apply in a new context the Fabian phrase "the inevitability of gradualness". The F.A.T.U.M. is teaching the workers a new lesson in democratic organization and already Mannie Small is being challenged on the sugar estates because gradually and inevitably the Jamaican worker is gaining a new concept of political honesty. Let us take heart, comrades, and go from this conference convinced that our cause is right and will triumph in the end, and, in god's own good times the people shall call us to lead this country to a new freedom, a new independence!' (*Prolonged applause.*)

The delegates then gave notice of the motions they intended to put forward at the private sessions the next day. There was so much noise in the theatre, however, that only those seated nearest each delegate heard his motion. This didn't matter as the motions had been handed in and circulated to all delegates three weeks before the conference, but it showed the public how democratic the P.D.P. was. While the delegates spoke, press photographers took pictures of Dr Phillips in various attitudes – lounging vacantly in his seat with his legs crossed and stretched out, chatting acutely with Mrs Phillips, leaning forward, affecting to listen to a delegate's inaudible motion, a fist under his chin like Rodin's *Thinker.*

Most of the people in the Gallery left as soon as Dr Phillips had spoken. A group of toughs came into the Gallery distributing pamphlets. Each pamphlet had a photograph and brief biography of Dr Phillips and a brief history of the P.D.P. One of the toughs was Bobsie Tull, Ramsay's brother. Ramsay had seen Bobsie very few times in the last few months, for usually Bobsie was asleep in the morning before Ramsay went to work. Bobsie said he had got a job but he didn't say where and Ramsay didn't enquire. Bobsie was doing political touting for Albert French, the P.D.P. barrister and had joined the P.D.P. Action Group.

The P.D.P. Action Group was the most democratic section of the party. It was classless, bound together by poverty and toughness, and was directed by a solicitor who had been struck off the rolls. The Group was made up of 'ex' and current criminals, drunks, punch-drunks, unemployable secondary school graduates. They picked up enough irregular money from the Oxford-trained P.D.P. lawyers to eat two meals a day and get quite drunk in the evenings. They had the other side of the law protecting them.

They spotted Edgar and crowded him.

'You like the Master speech?' one of the ex-boxers asked in a cracked voice. He had been in the fight at Elletson Road.

'Is a speech,' Edgar said carelessly.

'You know, my frien', ah t'ink you better tek 'way yourself,' the ex-boxer said to Edgar. 'We doan need like you so here.'

'Is my brother that, you know,' Bobsie said to one of the toughs.

'Edgar Bailey?'

'No, the other one.'

'You work at Courts Office, don't it?' a small man asked

Ramsay. Most of his front teeth were gone. He was a legal as well as a political tout and had seen Ramsay at the Courts Office.

'You like the Master speech?' the ex-boxer asked again. They were standing around Edgar and Ramsay who were still sitting in the front row of the Gallery.

'Is a speech,' Edgar said again, his voice angry and hopeless. If he had said anything else they would probably have thrown him into the parquet. Edgar got up.

'Come, Tull!' They let them pass. One of the ex-secondary schoolboys, a weight-lifter, called after them, 'We'll be coming into Vineyard Town area, soon!'

'Come nuh!' Edgar shouted. 'We ready for you. Anytime!'

The street had an afternoon dryness and they walked west-wards. Edgar's thin body seemed to shake off the P.D.P. threats. He would delay but not forget. In a flood of confused sentiment Ramsay felt quite certain of his own poverty and class.

They stopped at a snowball cart and Edgar bought two glasses of snowball and strawberry syrup and they ate with one foot resting on the kerb.

'They think they funny, you know,' Edgar said.

Dr Reginald Kendal was one of the new Jamaicans. He could tell at a glance the pedigree of a horse, a woman or a gun. Five years as a flyer in the R.A.F., from which he had been demobbed early, had added finesse to his natural sexual magnetism and though he wasn't an intellectual he was proof of the proposition, current among art students, that any medical student can pass medical exams and that most do at the second or third try. Even as a student at Edinburgh he never had a problem or a dull day. No matter what the circumstances Reggie Kendal would put his tallish vital figure into an R.A.F. blazer and grey flannels and joke his way into the centre of any company at any pub or hotel in Edinburgh. This was remarkable because, though he was hand-some and charming in a Rabelaisian way, he was black. He was half-Indian with fine soft hair and a straight nose. Kendal's age was a mystery even to his closest friends but he couldn't have been less than thirty-four and he had a little distinguished grey in his very black hair. His success with women had been phenomenal in Edinburgh and was legendary in Jamaica six weeks after his return.

The new Jamaican is quite certain that the country belongs to him and that he is welcome in all society. Kendal made use, consciously, of all he had – a fine appearance, a good war record, the colonial prestige of a Medical degree from Edinburgh. He was cynical about death and women's virtue.

He met Mrs Hanson at a dinner given by Dr Thouless, the surgeon at Central Hospital. Neither Dr Thouless nor his wife could remember having invited him to dinner that evening but when he turned up at ten minutes to eight, in a dinner jacket, they were delighted to see him, Dr and Mrs Thouless being English. Mrs Hanson now lived in perpetual nervous excitement over the possibility of Cyril winning the Rhodes scholarship and she looked her best that night. Her dreams were in England, a vicarious return to an idyllic and superior past that would for ever atone for her desperate social uncertainty. Kendal noted her figure and decided she would do. He drove her home in his Jaguar and found out everything he wanted to know about her, though he was at first under the impression that she was rich.

He called on Mrs Hanson almost every evening, but not for longer than half an hour at a time. At first Mrs Hanson with her attitude to very black skins was extremely uncomfortable about his visits. After a time she managed to excuse him his blackness on the grounds that his hair was straight, and that he had said repeatedly that he would never marry a woman who had to straighten her hair with a hot comb. And Mrs Hanson knew, with the certainty of the weak reformed gambler, that she couldn't escape him. He knew the line to take – England, casual mention of aristocratic names, R.A.F. slang, contempt for the stupidity of the native Jamaican. He won her by formal and foolish chatter about England carefully punctuated with very good *risqué* jokes, for she had been one of the most popular entertainers of English soldiers during and just after the war. They were both too cynical and experienced to be romantic about themselves. One afternoon he simply led her into the bedroom and slept with her. He took her out to a night-club, to the pictures, but nobody paid much attention because Dr Kendal seldom went out with the same woman two nights running. He slept with her at any time of day or night and in any convenient place, because under the aphrodisiac of his very good *risqué* jokes she was always ready for him. For Kendal she was 'bang on' and 'a fine caper'.

But she couldn't organize herself emotionally over this affair. The thing soon lost its artificial fantasy and only the physical pleasure and the fact that he was black remained. She became terrified of his easy mastery. He came when he liked, took her politely, efficiently, but with a suggestion of contempt. Once she tried to quarrel with him about his not answering the telephone when she called, and without a word he got into his car and drove away. After two months she decided she was through.

'I've come to my senses,' she said. 'I don't want to do this any more. I want to stop it.' He had brought her grapes and an expensive bottle of perfume that afternoon.

Kendal was amused. 'Are you kidding?' he asked.

'I'm getting too old for the physical thing, and I'm not in love with you.' Then she added, 'But I like you very much.'

'O.K.,' Kendal said, getting up, 'but it's been fun though, hasn't it?' He laughed lewdly and the laugh jabbed at the remains of her pride.

She looked very old, her eyes drugged and sleepless. 'Are you in love with me?' she asked trying to make her voice laugh lightly and succeeding only in sounding like a B-film actress. They had never used the word 'love' before.

'I don't know about this metaphysical thing, sweetheart,' Kendal said, thinking her tone contemptuous and therefore dropping his normal politeness. 'I just wanted you and took what I wanted. That's all. Especially as you are safe.'

'You black coolie ★★★★!' she said. She always used the word in intercourse. She sounded to Kendal exactly like a cockney prostitute.

'An old bitch like you,' he said, 'you don't think anybody could be in love with you, do you?'

Cyril was used to his mother's affairs – she always recovered from them – but this one broke her up completely. Even the strong hope of Cyril's going to Oxford didn't help much. She took to reading the Bible and going to Evangelist prayer meetings at Halfway Tree. That didn't help. Then she heard that Kendal was going around with Mona Freeman who had been her son's girl-friend at one time. She manufactured out of this a moral justification for wanting Kendal back. She asked Kendal to come and talk to her one afternoon. She begged as proudly as she could.

'Love doesn't matter,' she said, 'but I want you to come back.'

'O.K., fine,' he said.

He was neither surprised nor flattered.

V

They were jitterbugging outside Chen's Radio Shop that Saturday evening. Boysie Chen's shop is on Slipe Road, just below Devon Avenue where the street lamps make a pattern of shadows continually criss-crossed by the headlights of fast cars and faster buses. Right opposite Chen's shop there is the barber's shop; beside the barber's, going towards Cross Roads, there is Mark Andrews, 'Merchant Tailor'; beside Mark Andrews' shop there were the offices (two rooms) of the People's Progressive League. In the evenings most of the boys and unemployed young men around Slipe Road gathered either outside Chen's shop to listen to the music or on the piazza of the People's Progressive League offices.

The boys were jitterbugging to Dizzy Gillespie's music. Two boys were dancing in the pool of light formed by a street lamp and the others stood round in a circle laughing and clapping encouragement. One of the dancers wore ragged blue three-quarter length tropical trousers, a T-shirt and was barefooted. The other, short and muscular, wore short pants, shirt and tie, full-length stockings and boots and danced the female role. They did every step in the jitterbug's repertoire, shifting, shuffling, and following every change of rhythm and phrasing in the music. It was strange that though the street was noisy with motors and horns and people shouting, when you watched the dancers you could hear only Gillespie's music.

Edgar Bailey got off the Papine bus at the stop just below the music and slipped into Chen's shop where there was a soft-drinks counter at the back, partitioned off by a swing door.

'Hi, Vera, this long time doan see,' he said to Vera Chen who served him a drink at the counter. Vera was Septy Grant's girl-friend, a very well-put-together half-Chinese girl. She was wearing a sheath-like shantung silk dress that just managed to contain her hour-glass figure.

They chatted about Septy Grant.

A middle-aged man wearing a green felt hat with a gay feather stuck in the band came in. He was short and paunchy, in shirt sleeves and braces, and his smile was full of gold fillings.

'What 'appen now, comrade!' he said to Edgar. Then to Vera, 'A cool Red Stripe, dear. But Lawd, Vera you looking stocious tonight!' He tipped his hat on to the back of his head, beat his palms on the counter, devoured Vera's back as she bent over the ice-box, and sighed deeply.

George Lannaman ('Skipper G.') was probably the most experienced political tout in Jamaica. He had begun his career in the days of the old Legislative Council and the ten-shilling voter, and many an old councillor owed his seat in the Leg. Co. to Skipper Lannaman's astute and quite unscrupulous campaigning. Then he got into trouble, ran away to Panama and, it seems, Cuba, returned to Jamaica in the late 'thirties, and helped Capleton (who had just then returned from America) to form the island's first trade union. The Workers' Co-operative Union was a small affair with about five hundred members and absolutely no bargaining power and it collapsed after five months. After a while he quarrelled with Capleton and left the W.C.U. to work with Mannie Small, leader of the flourishing Mannie Small Trade Union which was magically transformed into the Merchants' Party and had won the adult-suffrage election. Skipper Lannaman, however, had left Small long before the elections, had rejoined Capleton and helped to found the P.P.L. During the strikes and riots of the late 'thirties Skipper had been imprisoned along with Mannie Small and Capleton (who had temporarily joined hands), and he still had a tricky right shoulder, the result of police batons. He was a tremendous public speaker and had an intense loathing for everything connected with the People's Democratic Party. He was a tout, he agreed, but he touted only for genuine working-class leadership. He had no other trade or profession.

Edgar put his briefcase on the counter and called for another Red Stripe. He said to Skipper G., 'I just coming from Andy up

Hope Road. We was fixing up the statement. I doan't go home since morning, you know.'

Skipper G. took a deep drink, slammed his glass down and said to Edgar in an intense whisper, 'Da's two tings ah never like in politics, da's money an' woman. Money an' woman. One a' dem is boun' to catch you.'

Edgar thought briefly of Mona Freeman and was sure she had no influence on Capleton.

'Capleton and Fitz-Simmonds up at League, now,' Skipper G. said. 'I jus' slip away for a beer. You coming?'

'Yes. I know,' Edgar said and finished his beer.

They went out through the swing door. The boys outside were now dancing slowly, with frequent twirling, to something intricate and weaving by Charlie Parker.

They crossed the street and walked up the piazza steps that led, worn and smooth, to the P.P.L. offices. There were about twenty people on that small piazza, and Edgar and Skipper had to force their way through. It wasn't the usual aimless Saturday evening crowd, for the faces of the men were tense as they argued and gesticulated. And Eustace Capleton's Buick Straight-Eight had been parked outside the offices since five o'clock in the afternoon. It had been rumoured that Capleton was going to be arrested.

On the right-hand wall of the outer office, where Mona Freeman worked at a battered typewriter, Joseph Lowe, the portrait painter, had done a very plastic mural. It was frightening, impressive and depressing. There were two figures looking out of the mural – a black worker with bared torso, who was just beginning a mighty swing with a pick-axe, and a black child grasping the worker's knee with one hand and pointing into the distance with the other. Both figures were much larger than life and were frightening not only because of their tortured bent faces but also because they didn't seem to be exaggerations. You felt, looking at the mural, that this strangely inhuman man, his left foot placed aggressively forward, his body balanced in movement with an orchestration of muscle, would at any moment step into the room swinging his pick-axe. And in the child's face, as the light changed in direction and intensity, you saw the whole shifting range of human suffering. It was impossible to look at that mural without being permanently altered by the memory of its power.

On the other walls, dwarfed by Joseph Lowe's remarkable mural, was the expected wallpapering of political posters. The room was scantily furnished with a bookcase full of large moth-eaten books and thin dusty pamphlets, a green filing cabinet, a bench, a few chairs.

When Edgar and Skipper G. entered the room it was empty, the greater part in shadow, the only illumination being a shaded electric bulb that hung from the ceiling and swayed slightly with every vibration of the floor above. Two young men, Tony and Sam, came in immediately behind Edgar and Skipper G.

'Capleton did-drunk at de meeting on Thursday, yuh kno,' Sam said. 'Ah was on the mike that night.'

'Him dyam careless, man,' Tony, tall, black, finely-boned, said to Skipper G. 'Him dyam careless to say a t'ing like that. Is fifty-fifty now if the police going ban the League or not. An' Capleton careless with League money, too. Mek ah tell you, till we get a nex' leader – '

Skipper G. interrupted him. 'Whey you was 1938 when police bruk upon Capleton head an' keep him in lock-up for two week? Yuh didn't even have teeth yet. Leadah? Next leadah? Unu young bwauy think that because unu read few book Jesus Christ cyaan talk to you? Is which one a' yuh going lead? Only mahga dawg an' monkey woulda follow like you so!'

Tony pointed to the door of Capleton's office (they were all speaking quietly), 'Dat man mus' be li-qui-day-tid!' He enjoyed the word with his eyes and his hands and his tongue. 'We want Edgar to chairman this League. Yuh, Missa Skipper G. Yuh gwine si! Nex' conference Capleton doan get not a vote!'

'Lissen, my friend,' Edgar said, a little disturbed at the thought of leadership and loyal to Capleton, 'Capleton is a good leader an' he's honest. Is just this trouble now. Lissen, is split you trying to split the League, Tony?'

'Hey,' Skipper said. 'Edgar is one of the hardest worker I ever know in politics, but yuh think leadership come so? Who know Edgar? A leader has to has front an' personality an' hexperience.

Politics is a rough game, yuh know. Unu young bwauy dat read about Russia ongle know play-play politics.'

'Skipper,' Tony said, 'from you born you doan do a day's work *yet*, an' still you never hungry neither. You jus' a sponge. You sponge on councillor, you sponge in Panama, now you spongeing on Capleton and the League. You and him jus' two ginal and samfie. Is a wonder unu doan gone prison yet.'

They started shouting imaginative obscenities at each other.

Capleton, followed by a brown-skin lawyer named Fitz-Simmonds and Mona Freeman, came from the inner office and some of the people from the piazza came in. Skipper and Tony, squared up to fight, were being held back by Edgar and Sam.

'What's going on here, Skipper?' Capleton shouted. He was wearing a brightly-patterned Tower Isle shirt in the American fashion and he stood with the muscular alertness of a boxer.

Skipper G. could only blurt out, 'Nuh dis dyam pnya-pnya bwauy yah –'

'Take him out!' Capleton ordered.

Tony freed himself from Edgar's grip and walked from side to side in front of Skipper G. breathing evenly in a temper. He didn't look at Capleton at all. Sam led him to the door.

'Doan mine, Tony,' Sam said, 'every dawg have him day an' every puss him four o'clock.'

'Ah was going buss him head,' Tony remarked to the crowd from the piazza.

'Come inside,' Capleton said to Edgar and Skipper G.

Capleton's office was almost not furnished at all. A large handsome writing desk took up most of the room but the desk was empty except for a desk pad, two fountain pens, a long cylindrical ruler and three glass ashtrays. Capleton sat in a padded swivel-chair, once brown, now an indeterminate grey. There were no bookshelves, no filing cabinets. The walls were white-washed and bare, except the wall facing Capleton's desk on which were hung large poster portraits of Mao Tse-Tung and Marshal Tito. Above the portraits was a framed photograph of Capleton standing on the bonnet of a car addressing a crowd.

Whenever Edgar went into Capleton's office he had mixed feelings. It was heady intoxication to work so near to the dyna-

117

mism of Capleton's glorious vision of the people. But he was uneasy about the comfortable compromises Capleton made – not a betrayal but a tendency to avoid dangerous action by invoking a larger expediency. At close quarters Capleton's overpowering personality convinced Edgar that here was the devoted, unsparing People's Leader, but he was sometimes worried as to whether or not Capleton was more than a shrewd professional politician, a 'ginal' and 'samfie' as Tony said. But then, if your only profession was politics you had to keep on working at it, like Skipper G., without theory or principle, if necessary. Edgar's uneasiness was heightened by the presence of Fitz-Simmonds, the unscrupulous middle-class lawyer who gave the meeting an atmosphere of a gangster's conference.

'Well, look, Fitzy,' Capleton said, worried, 'what is treason? Treason is the express intention to overthrow the authority of the state. Revolution is not treason. Revolution is the intention to redistribute the authority of the state, to take authority from the colonial tyrants, the capitalists and the middle-men and place it in the hands of the people. It's as simple as that. I don't want to overthrow authority, I want to redistribute it.'

'I'm not a theoretical politician, Eustace,' Fitz-Simmonds said. He had large eyes and the rimless glasses he wore made him resemble, vaguely, a frog. 'I'm just a lawyer. Within the meaning of the law, what you said on Thursday night – if they can prove it – is treasonous, Communist Manifesto, or *no* Communist Manifesto.'

'But that's just it,' Capleton pleaded. 'The P.P.L. is not a communist party. Revolution doesn't necessarily mean communism, you know.'

'You can't go on a public platform and talk about the Soviet Union and Mao Tse Tung and liquidation of the capitalists and whatever else and not expect people to think you are a communist,' Fitz-Simmonds said, as if he were talking to a child or the dumbest of witnesses. 'And when you go on to say you have plans to liquidate immediately the Governor and the Colonial Secretary and the Chief Justice (and who else?), and to stick their heads on the flag-pole at King's House, you may be talking nonsense, *but* you have an illiterate mob behind you.'

118

'Of course, it's nonsense,' Capleton said without much conviction. 'Everybody knows is jus' a figure of speech, it's only the figurative heads of those people I was talking about. *You* can prove that in court any day, Fitzy?'

'It wouldn't wash,' Fitz-Simmonds said and lit the cigar Capleton handed him. 'And in any case I'm sticking my neck out to defend the League. They could strike me off the solicitors' roll any time for consorting with criminals.'

The atmosphere became tense when he said this. The others made gestures of horrified protest, but before Fitz-Simmonds could explain what he meant Edgar shouted at him.

'You, Missa Fitz-Simmonds, *you* are the criminal. Everybody know you are the most dishonest lawyer in Jamaica an' if they strike you off it won't be through the League. Who is a criminal here? We doan thief or kill people in this League. But I bet you coulda never explain how come *you* own so much racehorse. An' I bet you coulda never tell how your partner, Andison, get caught for stealing clients' money an' up at Richmond Farm now.'

'God-dyam-it boy,' Fitz-Simmonds said. 'You are dyam impertinent!' Fitz-Simmonds' face flushed and he gripped the arms of his chair. 'What are you? You are nothing but a street boy, coming to me with your dyam facetyness. You get beyond you self now, since these last few days you wearing shoes and can si' down in a chair!'

'Look here, look here, *now!*' Capleton said. 'Hey, take it easy Fitzy, relax, man. I know you don't mean we are criminals Fi –'

'I mean,' Fitz-Simmonds said, 'that if they find you guilty I can get into trouble.'

Edgar still angry, turned to Capleton, 'But him cyaan't come here an' insult the working class. He not insulting me, it's the working class, and look how much money he make outa the League.'

'O.K., O.K.,' Capleton said, smoothly and wearily. 'Cool down, Edgar. Everybody is hot-tempered tonight.' He laughed easily. 'There is no prosecution yet. The important thing is to get the statement in Monday's *Gleaner*. You have the draft, Edgar?' Then to Fitz-Simmonds, who was sulking, 'Take it easy, Fitzy, everybody is excitable tonight.'

Edgar handed the typescript to Capleton who glanced at it, handed it back and told him to read it out. Fitz-Simmonds listened with supreme scorn.

Edgar read: 'The People's Progressive League is an association of workers who aim at bettering the political, economic and social life of the working people in this country by means of discussion groups, lectures, civic education, public meetings and direct political action.

'The P.P.L. is not, and never has been a Communist Party and is in no way affiliated to any international Communist bodies.

'The P.P.L. believes in socialism and accepts the Marxist interpretation of history and the Marxist analysis of modern capitalism.

'The P.P.L. is not a revolutionary organization but an electoral political party accepting and working within the democratic framework. The P.P.L. is the vanguard of the working class, preparing the ground for future transfer of political power in this country entirely into the hands of the working class.

'The P.P.L. is entirely loyal to the British Crown and believes, without reservation, in the Brotherhood of Man and the Father-hood of God.'

He handed the draft back to Capleton.

'You know,' Skipper G. said, 'ah think you better leave out de Marxis' part. If you seh you is a Marxis', den you mus' be a communis'. Is ongle words. You cyaan' fool anybody wid it.'

'But there's a big difference –'

'Look here,' Fitz-Simmonds said, 'maybe you can't *understand*. The Communist Manifesto is a Marxist document. It is also a revolutionary document. Whether you say you are a Marxist or a communist you are still revolutionary. It's the same thing in practice.'

'Well, seeing that's the case,' Edgar said with annoyance at Fitz-Simmonds' assumption that he could give advice about strictly League affairs, 'we doan have any thing to hide, for we are revolutionary, and we're not afraid to admit it.' He looked at Capleton.

'Wait a minute now,' Capleton said, playing with the cylindri-cal ruler. 'We are not afraid. We are a revolutionary Marxist group. But you must consider the facts. The League membership is eight hundred and that eight hundred is all in Kingston here. You see, you can't tell the whole truth today because it will prevent a greater truth from coming in the future. We eight hundred are the leaven in the bread. I've been working in politics for thirty years and people still starving in Trench Town. But I can see a future. You young, Edgar, you mus' wait.'

'If people still starving in Trench Town after thirty years then something is wrong with yuh politics,' Edgar argued. 'Suppose we get self-government tomorrow an' Dominion status, every-thing is going be the same. The catch-as-catch-can politicians like Mannie Small will still get the power. We are preparing the people to tek the power from the politicians when the time come. Tha's why we musn' hide it now. We are a Marxist group for the education of the masses. Marxism is not against the law. We are fighting with ideas, not with guns.'

'No, Edgar, we cyaan't issue that statement,' Capleton de-cided. 'The statement is to prove that we are not communist. The tactics of the moment call for a lie. It can't affect the League work to deny both Marxism and communism.' He felt, but didn't want to say, that the statement might prejudice his case if he was arrested.

'I'm not a politician,' Fitz-Simmonds said largely, 'so I believe that in every country you must have both capital and labour. It's common sense. This League can do a lot of good for Jamaica but it can't change human nature. You people are in a dream. I'll tell you what the real Jamaican temperament is. It's a hurricane temperament. You plant your banana this year, but you expect a hurricane any year, so you don't worry, you don't kill out yourself. If there is no hurricane, fine. If you get a hurricane you just stand by and watch your bananas blown down. You can't do anything about it. You suck your teeth and plant again. But you don't worry, you don't kill out yourself, you don't believe in anything, in any future. As far as the Jamaican worker is con-cerned it's the price of salt-fish *today* that matters, not the price of turkey for the people tomorrow. You can't apply a theory to the Jamaican worker because he is, and always will be, temperamen-tally unstable.'

'Excuse me, Missa Fitz-Simmonds,' Edgar asked bitingly, 'but are you a Jamaican?'

'Of course, I'm a Jamaican, like yourself. Jamaica is a dear little country, but you can't do anything about the people's temperament. They take things too easy.'

'But you are applying your own theory though, Fitzy,' Capleton said. 'No. The theory is very difficult, *I* can tell you. It's the legacy of colonialism. We haven't had enough practice in thinking for ourselves, enough independent thinking to evolve the right theory. But the people are all right, Fitzy.'

An inconclusive silence hung over the meeting.

'O.K.,' Capleton said getting up, 'let's leave it there for tonight. Edgar tomorrow yuh come round to Brentford Road and we can fix up another statement. Bring Andy.'

'Mister Capleton,' Edgar said, remembering Tony at the back of his mind, 'this is the statement that the youth Section of the League feel you should issue – '

'Which "Youth Section"?' Skipper G. asked.

'Yes, which "Youth Section"?' Capleton asked, really surprised.

'I doan mean an actual section,' Edgar said. 'I mean the youth in the League. Well, if you issue anything else we going to split off an' issue our own statement. And don't forget that most of the League is youth.'

'Awright,' Capleton said, soothingly, though his fingers were twitching. 'Come roun' tomorrow an' we talk about it.'

Mona spoke for the first time that evening. She said to Edgar, 'It's a very good statement, Edgar, but it's not right for the time. You don't see?'

Capleton, Fitz-Simmonds and Mona drove off in Capleton's Buick. Edgar and Skipper G. started to walk down Slipe Road. The piazza crowd had gone but the boys were still jitterbugging outside Boysie Chen's shop. Edgar knew that his anger against Fitz-Simmonds' bourgeois cynicism had led him further along the way to revolt against Capleton than he had ever thought of going. And the idea began to grow in his mind that he could lead at least the youth of the League. He saw himself robed in the ragged clothing of the jitterbugging boys and was ashamed of the pathetic respectability of his dirty suit and scraggly string of a tie.

'I'm going to split this League myself, Skipper G.,' Edgar said.

'Hey, you doan mek dat Tony bwauy turn yuh head, Edgar. Yuh too young. Yuh coulda never lead this party.'

'I'm going to do it,' Edgar said, in a faint voice.

They were walking on the pavement, had passed Mark Andrews' tailor shop and were in front of the barber's shop. They didn't notice that there was an unusually large crowd in front of the barber's shop. Then four men suddenly blocked their path – Tony, Sam and two others. As he saw Tony the anger that had been smouldering in Skipper G. blazed again. In spite of his age and paunch Skipper G. was experienced in free fighting and he punched Tony mercilessly although his own left eye was soon swollen. When they closed he gripped Tony in a half-Nelson and forced him to the ground. The boys from Chen's shop came over to watch the fight. They were silent, for their sympathies were all with Tony.

Skipper G. let go of Tony and started to walk down the street through the crowd. In a moment, before anyone noticed it, Tony rushed into the barber's shop and came out with an open razor: Skipper G. felt a thin line, sharp as ice, run across his shoulder. Before he could turn, Tony had slashed through the back of his shirt three or four times. Edgar tried to intervene but Tony brushed him aside, knocking him down and, unintentionally, nicked him on the wrist with the razor. The crowd had increased and was shouting 'Thief!' 'Murder!' 'Police!' In a matter of minutes two policemen arrived and handcuffed Tony but Skipper G. was already bleeding from cuts on his face and hands and all over his chest and back where the shirt had been cut to shreds. Tony walked between the two policemen towards the Cross Roads police station, followed by Edgar and Skipper G. and most of the crowd.

There were about half a dozen boys from Chen's shop who stopped listening to the music as they gazed at the blood on the pavement. One boy, a little older than the rest, was wearing a slouch hat, a zoot-suit with ample chain and brown-and-white shoes. He was called Papa Son.

'Yuh see how the carpie dem handle Tony rough?' one of the boys said. 'Is one thing, you know. Ah neva like tangle wid dem Cross Roads police.'

'Kingston police worse,' Papa Son informed them. 'One day dem cyah me go Sutton Street an' before we *reach* deh dem nearly kill me wid beaten. Hmm. Kingston police!'

'What you did-do, Papa Son?' another boy asked.

'Mi an' a fellow have a argument roun' Mark Lane,' Papa Son said. 'Just me an' de fellow, yuh know. An' two carpie tek me een. Dem say ah was using honseen langwidge.'

'Den wha-happen?'

'Chu. Me no' pay tirty shillings an' go weh!'

They drifted back slowly towards the music that was still blaring outside Chen's radio shop.

Monday's papers carried a P.P.L. statement exactly the same as Edgar's draft and signed 'E. Bailey, General Secretary, Peoples' Progressive League'. Edgar had issued it with Capleton's agreement. The words 'Marxist interpretation' and 'Marxist analysis' had been italicized by the type-setter.

On Tuesday morning, Mannie Small, the Prime Minister, had a consultation with Dr Raymond Phillips. The same morning the Resident Magistrate at Cross Roads found Tony Morgan (undefended) guilty of wounding with intent and sentenced him to six months with hard labour.

On Wednesday morning, Eustace Capleton was arrested at P.P.L. headquarters. He was charged again with 'inciting to riot', and pleaded 'not guilty'. The trial was set for Friday and he was refused bail and allowed no visitors except his lawyers, Charley Fernandez and Fitz-Simmonds.

At the Courts Office Alf-Gordon was happy. He pointed out to Ramsay that the Attorney-General was himself prosecuting in order to secure a conviction and he added, what was common knowledge in Kingston, that Mannie Small had decided to finish his political rival, the man who had suffered with him under the same political batons in 1938. Ramsay had a terse telephone call from Edgar Bailey telling him to come round to the yard that evening but not before nine o'clock.

An old black Ford Mercury was parked outside the yard in

which Edgar and Septy Grant lived. Edgar, Septy and Rupert were sitting on kerosene boxes in the middle of the yard.

'Evening passero,' Septy said. The others said nothing but looked at him closely. Ramsay walked to the stand pipe, drank and splashed water on his face and neck. He felt they were waiting for something and that they didn't want to talk about Capleton. Rupert handed him a bent cigarette and lit it for him. There was no moon and the cigarette tips glowed.

'What happen tonight?' Ramsay asked.

Septy and Rupert looked at Edgar.

'You doan tell him yet?' Septy asked Edgar.

'Tell him on the way,' Edgar said.

Ramsay was excited but he thought the others looked frightened. Then Septy looked at his watch and said to them, 'Come, sah!'

He backed the car, turned in a lane and drove out to Elletson Road. They went across South Camp Road into Allman Town, around Racecourse into East Street, on North Street to Princess Street, south on Princess Street and stopped. No one had spoken on the journey. Edgar got out and walked across to the lane behind King Street.

'O.K.,' he said.

Septy lifted the back seat of the car and took three jerry cans of petrol out of the boot. Edgar took one, gave the other to Ramsay and they carried them to the back of the Excelsior, a dry-goods store owned by a struggling Syrian, which opened on to King Street.

'Stay at the corner an' watch for police,' they told Ramsay. Septy had a key to the huge padlock on the iron sliding gate and he used a large screw-driver to force the lock on the wooden doors. From the corner Ramsay could see the glow of Rupert's cigarette in the car and he heard the parish church clock strike a half hour. The Parade was deathly quiet and the beggars and market-women and country-bus sidemen slept on the pavement in the warm night.

After a few minutes there was a dull muffled thud from the Excelsior. Septy locked the doors and they came running up the lane carrying the empty jerry cans. Rupert had started the car and

Septy drove off smoothly. They drove at sixty along Spanish Town Road, then up Hagley Park Road and, avoiding Halfway Tree, through Constant Spring to Stony Hill Road and stopped where they could see the city spread out below them.

It seemed that the whole of Kingston was on fire. The glow seemed to spread all over the harbour and down-town. It was beautiful to watch.

'The whole rass town on fire!' Rupert said.

'So quick?' Septy wondered. 'It could'n spread so quick.'

'Suppose we bu'n down Kingston, what a hell!' Rupert was in ecstasy. They watched the glow gradually subside and disappear and the city's lights blinking again.

'The brigade must a' put it out,' Ramsay said, and he felt they all hated him for saying it. They dropped Rupert at Halfway Tree, borrowed a bicycle from Andy on Hope Road for Ramsay to ride home on, and Septy and Edgar drove the car over to Molynes Road where its owner lived.

In the daylight it was seen that the Excelsior and two shops beside it on King Street had been completely burnt out, the damage being estimated at £30,000. The pointless protest didn't help Capleton at all. There was talk of arson and nobody connected the fire with the P.P.L. The Attorney-General made skilful use of the verbatim police reports of Capleton's speech and the P.P.L. statement's 'communist avowal'. It was an open-and-shut case and the Attorney-General need not have been so pompous and puffed up. Capleton got six months without hard labour and, because of his age, was sent to Richmond Farm after a moving plea by Fernandez.

Ramsay kept the secret of the fire he had helped to start. At times he wished they had been caught, tried and sent to jail. He thought it would be a greater triumph and more lasting than winning the Chelaram scholarship. He thought this, with tears in his eyes, when the young men who had nothing but their youth and a cancered hope sang *The Red Flag* on Thursday nights on Cumberland Avenue and were one with the poor of the universe.

Mrs Hanson felt that Kendal was ashamed of her. He treated her with careful indifference in public and when he got slightly drunk he called her 'mother'. For a middle-aged illicit affair to leave no nauseous after-taste it must either be a gay triviality or a purifying passion. She knew that she was ridiculous in passion and Kendal, like an unacknowledged conscience, insisted on hurting her into shame, making her helpless and animal. She was gradually losing her self-respect. When she thought of certain things a flush of pleasure and remorse came over her and she feared that Kendal might be using her as bar-room conversation. She was confused, like a teenager, to meet his friends. And, for the first time, she regretted her life, especially her training of Cyril, for at forty her body no longer dictating in undeniable terms, she recalled only horror and disgust in the affairs that had seemed exciting and clever and emancipated. She began to lose the belief in the inalienable right of the healthy body to sin which had allowed her to serve on Church Committees without a qualm. The whole moral structure of her life had gone since meeting Kendal and she knew, coolie hair or no coolie hair, that the present delicious and inescapable evil in her life was due to Kendal's blackness. But she wanted to keep a little of her self-respect.

'Listen,' she said, one evening, 'you don't tell anybody what I do, do you?'

'What do you do?'

'When I'm – '

'Oh, that! No, you do it because you want to do it. I don't mind.'

'I mean I wouldn't like anybody to know that I do things like that. I would go mad.'

'Oh, Gawd! Stop it. Lots of people are like that.'

'It isn't that I'm ashamed or want to help it, you know, or morals or anything.' She was almost crying. 'But if I thought you told *anybody*, anybody at all about it my whole personality would break up, if you see what I mean. It's never been like that before you, it's not that it's bad or anything, but if anybody knew, my personality – '

'Oh, for Gawd's sake, don't start getting metaphysical now!'

'You are a doctor. You only understand the body.' She was crying without tears.

'Well, I haven't troubled your soul, have I? Come on, snap out of it!'

They dressed and he took her driving, at first aimlessly around Kingston. The big smooth purring car, his skill, almost insolent, in handling it, gave her the thrilling illusion of being a frightened virgin. It was safe to ask him now but to put it differently.

'Who was the girl you took to Glass Bucket last Friday?'

'Mona Freeman.' He spoke distinctly and she heard him.

'Whoom did you say?' Her voice fluttered a little on 'say', but she was digging her long beautiful nails into her black leather handbag. He ignored her. She knew all about it but had thought she would have the pleasure of hearing him lie.

It rained suddenly and heavily as they turned into Victoria Avenue. The new Jamaican has a well developed sense of car, especially if he hasn't finished paying for it. Kendal thought of his four new tyres and recent overhaul and he made the Jaguar perform on the slippery Windward Road. Other motorists and the pedestrians sheltering from the rain thought he was drunk. He did two or three controlled skids on the bends in the road, then squeezed between a dray and a bus, actually touching the dray's shaft. Mrs Hanson had lowered herself into the seat and passed quickly from fear to anger.

'Why don't you smash the dyam car, why don't you smash the bloody car and let us finish it right here and now?'

He drove more quietly to the Palisadoes Road and parked by the sea. He was satisfied with the car and he had one of his women with him and the smell of the sea and the lights across the harbour.

'I want to go to the Glass Bucket and have a drink,' she said, very English, with a pathetic air of command, the B-film actress recovering her self-respect.

'You can get down and walk there if you like.' He lit a cigarette, then tried to tune the radio.

'May I have a cigarette, please?' The biting tone of her voice was lost in the wind from the sea.

'Sure.'

It was piano music. She recognized the piece and saw a chance to needle him.

'A Chopin mazurka,' she said, exaggeratedly Mayfair. 'D'you

know, I can still remember the magic of Moisewitch playing that at the Albert Hall before the war, how he made us feel the sadness, the gaiety – '

'Oh, cut out that crap!' he said, switching off the radio.

'Tell me,' she said, tossing her head back, 'tell me about your girl Mona Freeman. She used to be one of Cyril's girls, you know, but he gave her up. She wasn't exactly his type.'

Kendal laughed and told her about Mona Freeman. He gave her every physical detail about his affair with Mona, and added others of his own invention, making sure to insist on Mona's excellence in those things that Mrs Hanson prided herself on. When he was finished she said with a sneer, 'You two black coolies!' He slapped her face, hard.

'Don't use that word to me, you hear,' and beneath the R.A.F. intonation there was a distinct Indian sing-song.

'You're a brute, Reggie!' Her voice was neutral as water, no overtones, and she only rarely allowed herself the intimacy of his Christian name. So he took her. Without realizing it Kendal had parked his car opposite a road junction. The full headlights of a Buick turning into Palisadoes Road shone for a minute on the Jaguar. The people in the front seat of the Buick recognized Dr Kendal's car, saw who was with him and what they were doing. In the next week Kendal broke two dates with her. She was dressed and waiting for two hours, each time. He said he had been busy at the hospital and didn't have time to telephone her.

One evening she had waited an hour for him when the telephone rang. Kendal was at Mona's house and had asked Mona to say he was out of town and not to say she was speaking.

'Hello. Mrs Hanson? This is Mona Freeman speaking.'

'Oh?'

'Dr Kendal is not in a position to see you tonight.'

'Oh? Where is he?'

'At home!' A slight pause. 'That is all, Mrs Hanson. Dr Kendal can't see you tonight.' Mona laughed into the telephone loudly and without amusement and hung up.

Two days later Mrs Hanson drank half a bottle of neat whisky, and, well dressed and badly made up, took a taxi to Twenty-seven Truman Avenue, where Mona lived.

Mona's reaction to Mrs Hanson's cheery stiff-upper-lip greeting was to be as 'common' as possible.

'What happen? You lose your way?' she asked Mrs Hanson. 'I just came to thank you for the telephone call!' Mrs Hanson sat by a window.

'Don't mention,' Mona said. 'Anything else I can do for you?'

'Yes, yes,' Mrs Hanson said. She looked drugged and hysterical. 'You can leave Dr Kendal alone.'

'Hoo-Hoo!' Mona flopped on to the sofa. 'Doan' mek ah laugh-O!'

'He isn't your type really, you know. He's quite a cultured man. You haven't got the background to be the wife of a successful doctor, you know.' She stopped, trying to remember the words, and her patronizing smile hung there a little.

Mona waited for her to continue. It was still hot at five-thirty in the afternoon and the radio played smooth dance music. A butterfly drifted in and settled on the curtain behind Mrs Hanson's head. The deep purple of its wings was like a loose bow on her hair.

'Anyway he's too old for you,' Mrs Hanson said, reasonably and sweetly.

'Then what 'bout you? You ole enough to be his gran'father. Lissen, Mrs Hanson, you mus' be off your head. Reggie don't want an old fowl like you. You see Reggie. Reggie is a Jamaican like me. You think you are a white woman but you neither flesh, fowl, nor good red herring. You think Reggie could really want a St Andrew whore that used to run after the white soldiers in Up-Park Camp? You jus' a poppy show to him!'

She noticed, as if for the first time, as if it were the final word, that Mona did not have to 'straighten' her hair. She knew her affair with Kendal was over.

'You are a coolie,' she said in a tone that was meaningless and desperate.

'Yes, ah'm a coolie. I not ashame of it, but at leas' I know what I am. An' Reggie is a coolie, too. An' he doan *waant* you.' Then she remembered something. 'One thing you know, nobody ever see *me* in a car out on Palisadoes stick up *my* legs in the back seat!'

'Of course, this is very silly,' Mrs Hanson said, recovering her poise. 'You know Dr Kendal is in love with me!'

'He lef' you – '

'He didn't. I told him to go.'

'He lef' you, and you beg him to come back. He doan *waant* you. You suck him to come back!'

Mrs Hanson walked across trembling and hit her on the cheek with the side of a fist. She was angrier and taller than Mona. She beat her with her loosely clenched fists and scratched furrows on her cheeks, but she soon got tired. So Mona simply tore off every stitch of Mrs Hanson's clothes and she stood there with sagging breasts and sagging, ungirdled stomach looking in amazement at her nakedness. She began to whimper, trying to cover herself with the rags of her clothing. 'I can't go out into the street like this? I can't go out into the street like this?'

Mona leaned against the door-post watching her and enjoying an absolute triumph in Mrs Hanson's humiliation but feeling also a little pity, for Mrs Hanson was old enough to be her mother. They listened, standing like that, to an item in the six o'clock news.

'The Chelaram scholarship for 1947 has been awarded to Mr Ramsay Gerald Tull. Mr Tull, who is twenty, was educated at Orange Town elementary school, St Ann, and Surrey College. He passed the higher school certificate examination in 1947 with distinctions in History and English. Mr Tull intends to study for a degree in English.'

They both thought of Cyril. Very politely Mrs Hanson borrowed some of Mona's clothes and was hurt to find that they fitted her. There was nothing more to say, but on the way home she said, over and over, between the loss and the humiliation and the promise of peace at last, 'There is still Cyril, thank God, there is still Cyril.'

She suffered considerably after this, not from the humiliation of the past but from the dead prospect. She was fortunate in not having the habit of self-deception which is the secret of higher education, so she didn't pride herself on her experience. For her life was activity, with or without pleasure or pain, or no activity, which was only pain. And she began to live tonelessly in the moral irrational certainty that Kendal's blackness was the punishment sent her for an irregular life. But still, thank God, there was Cyril.

Cyril used Ramsay's success with an opportunism that was remarkable for its shrewd moderation. He made Ramsay's scholarship a personal public triumph for Cyril Hanson. After all, Ramsay was his friend and he would always have friends who 'did things' to use. So they had lunch at the Myrtle Bank Hotel. It would not be fair to say that he took Ramsay to the hotel simply because he had won the Chelaram scholarship. He had always wanted to take him there but he couldn't do it until Ramsay had achieved something.

The Myrtle Bank Hotel lunch was an impressive performance by Cyril. First he told the *Gleaner* gossip columnist that he was lunching 'Chelaram 47' there, and then he borrowed Fakhouri's Chevrolet. They got to the hotel at eleven so that Cyril could have a swim before lunch. In those days only white youth swam in the Myrtle Bank pool, there was no colour bar but only white youth swam there. Cyril, very physical, joined them. The white boys and girls, cut off from the training in diplomacy the mother country gives, did not know the technique of showing acceptance and contempt in the same gesture. They greeted him (everybody knew Cyril Hanson) and then ignored him. Cyril swam and dived beautifully, comfortable about being ignored and sensing, as he did on these occasions, that he would always triumph as the perpetual exception. During lunch he pointed out to Ramsay that black men who had 'achieved something' were always lunching at the Myrtle Bank, but he didn't add that the whites and very fairs who dined there had achieved only the colour of their skins.

'The thing is for all of us to achieve something and come here,' Cyril said.

'The thing is,' Ramsay said, 'for the government to take over the running of these places.'

'Governments are bad business men,' Cyril said, quoting Pressy.

'Yes,' Ramsay agreed, 'in a capitalist world.'

They drank whisky all through lunch and left the hotel tight and laughing.

They visited Pressy at Surrey College and talked about the school and Oxford and Cyril. Pressy said he had known that Ramsay would take the Chelaram and Ramsay believed him.

The annual festival of the Jamaica Improvement Association consisted of a week of 'exercises' planned by Cyril. He managed to squeeze Ramsay into the programme with a lecture on 'Society and the Individual Conscience'. Cyril was chairman at the lecture and he saw to it that his remarks and Ramsay's lecture were well reported in the *Gleaner*. They were seen at the Glass Bucket 'tripping' what Ramsay called 'the white fantastic'. But it was only when he was with Cyril that he felt the importance, as distinct from the pleasure, of winning a scholarship.

Ramsay spent the evening before Cyril's interview for the Rhodes scholarship at the Hansons' place. Mrs Hanson was extremely nervous because of her fear that Cyril might not win the Rhodes, but not that so much as that Ramsay might leave him in Jamaica. She was tense and brooding and went to bed early.

Cyril made a summary of the personality and character of each of the members of the interviewing committee. (Ramsay was surprised to hear that Dr Phillips was not a member of the committee.) Then he rehearsed all the questions he thought might be asked, most of which were far-fetched. For each question he had a quick, triumphant answer. He got a pencil and paper.

'Now, Ramsay, let's work this thing out. What are the things in my favour? Let's see how it looks on paper.' Ramsay didn't know that this was not only the style but the actual words Mr Phipps-Help always used. 'Let's begin with character and personality.' He wrote: 'Character.'

'Positive,' Ramsay suggested.

'No, better say "aggressive",' Cyril said, writing the word. '"Aggressive" is all right if you have charm as well.' He wrote: *Charm.* 'Right. Social conscience, awareness of other people.'

'That's the J.I.A.,' Ramsay said.

Cyril wrote: *Well-developed sense of responsibility to society.* 'Anything else? Next heading, "Leadership".' He wrote: *Captain of School Cricket, Hockey and Soccer – Captain of All-Schools Soccer – Vice-Captain Kingston Club Soccer.* 'And, of course, the same for games *plus* Senior Cup Cricket and All-Jamaica Soccer. Boy, this is hard work. Let's have a drink.'

While he was fetching the drinks the telephone rang and Ramsay spent five minutes telling Sweetness Terrelonge he couldn't see her that night.

'Now for the academic side.' Cyril chewed the pencil top. He wrote: *Grade I, School Cert., four distinctions including Latin.* 'Latin is very important for Law,' he informed Ramsay. He wrote: *H.S.C., 'B' in History Advanced, 'C' all round.* 'And that's the lot.'

'It's the combination, man. You can't get anybody with a combination like that, man,' Ramsay said.

'The only weak spot is scholastic attainment,' Cyril said, after studying his notes carefully, 'but Pressy will say that I was expected to get distinctions in History and English, and anyway I've got a small distinction in subsidiary Latin. But it's personality, character and physical well being that builds empires. Look, Cecil Rhodes only had a pass degree.'

'What empire you going to build?' Ramsay asked.

'You can build empires without stealing land, you know. It's the same spirit, that's the point.'

'I can see what you mean,' Ramsay said, feeling a little ashamed of his warm sense of his own success. 'Well, you're all set, man.'

'What was the phrase again from the statement?' Cyril asked as if he were preparing for an examination. '"The things of the spirit represented by the humanism which has made civilization what it is today".'

'"*In* the humanism".'

'"In the humanism". And, "to exclude an appreciation and understanding of literature and art is to dehumanize society". I'll try to bring that in somewhere.'

When Ramsay was leaving he begged Cyril to win the scholarship. It was one of the most sincere wishes of his life. Cyril deserved the scholarship. For eight years he had lived as close to Cyril as he would live with any human being.

'I think I'll just bully them into giving it to me,' he said, laughing. 'The aggressive personality. That's the thing for today.'

They shook hands formally.

The next evening at 6.15 Cyril 'phoned Mrs Hanson from

Kings' House where he had been interviewed. All he said was, 'Everything is *all* right!'

Edgar Bailey was born at Twenty Hitchins Street, Allman Town, in 1922. His father was a stone-mason who worked for a firm of contractors during the days and did private jobs for poor people in Allman Town in the afternoons and evenings. He was always in debt but his family never starved and they lived in the house which he had built. Edgar's mother had finished elementary school, passed first and second year pupil teacher examinations, but had failed to get into Shortwood Teacher Training College. She had taught for two years, married Edgar's father and gave up teaching. She had six children of whom Edgar was the fourth. He had been given a decent home life and a strict religious training by his mother.

Edgar's mother was not a remarkable woman in any way. She simply wanted all her children to finish elementary school before learning a trade and 'making life'. Her first two children were girls. They finished school, got married and did dressmaking at home. Reggie Bailey, the first boy, did well at school, was trained at Mico College, and after two years of teaching joined the R.A.F. and was shot down over Germany one night in 1942. He was six years older than Edgar and was twenty-six when he died.

Edgar finished school at fourteen and then for two years, before his father's death, had learned masonry from him. Edgar worked all over Kingston for different contractors and looked after his mother and two younger sisters who were still at school. In 1941 they sold the house at Hitchins Street and moved into a smaller rented house in Rollington Town. Edgar had never known acute poverty or starvation or lack of schooling and he had no desire to be a white-collar worker. But he was frequently unemployed, sometimes for weeks.

He was sixteen in 1938 when the riots began and he didn't understand them until Reggie explained colonialism and imperialism to him. He began to read. He joined the library of the Institute of Jamaica and read all the encyclopaedias, picking up a vague idea of history which he relayed, garbled, to his mates at work. The questions which they asked and he couldn't answer stimulated him to read more. He had never borrowed a book from the library and for months had not bought a book for himself. The first book he bought, for fifteen shillings, was a Webster's dictionary which he took with him to the Institute every evening.

Something began stirring in him and a simple misunderstanding in the Institute gave it shape. He was always one of the last to leave the library when it closed at nine o'clock in the evening. One evening when he was passing the assistant librarian's desk and had said, as usual, 'Good night, miss,' very politely, the assistant librarian, a middle-class Jamaican brown, asked him to follow her upstairs. They went into the director's office.

'I think this is the one, Mr Myers,' the assistant said.

'Let's see that book, young man,' the director said.

Edgar handed him his Webster's dictionary. The director looked at the fly-leaf, then examined each page carefully trying to find an Institute stamp on it. Then he used a magnifying glass to examine Edgar's signature for signs of erasing. He went through the leaves again and handed the book to Edgar. 'This doesn't seem to be our copy, Miss Sharrers,' the director said, and, to Edgar, 'You can go.'

Edgar thought about the incident for some days after and decided that he had been suspected of stealing the library's dictionary not because he always carried a copy with him but because he dressed and looked like a worker, and he came to the conclusion that the Institute library was not intended for people like him. Reggie explained to him that the assistant librarian and the director were, in that instance, the agents of a social and political system which was designed to oppress and destroy him. So he continued to take his Webster's to the library every evening, alert and spoiling for a fight which never came.

He got into politics in a direct way. He was helping to build a mansion for a Syrian merchant on Seymour Avenue, working at the rate of one shilling per hour, eight hours a day, forty-five hours a week, half day on Saturdays. His fellow masons, arguing from the sugar workers' success in getting a wage increase through Mannie Small's union, decided to make an appeal to the contractor to increase their rate to one shilling and sixpence per hour. There were twelve masons and they appointed Edgar, the literate one, as leader of the deputation. Edgar based his appeal entirely on the sugar workers' case and at first was begging, not demanding. The contractor, a black man who had come up by hard work and trickery and meanness, prefaced his withering reply with the words, 'rass cloth!' Edgar then presented some figures he had been preparing. He told the contractor that the Syrian was finding the materials and paying him (the contractor) £2,500 to put up the house in two months; the contractor had hired twelve masons at one shilling per hour which was, for two months' wages, £216; ten carpenters, also at one shilling per hour, was £180; and ten labourers, at three-and-sixpence per day and one shilling on Saturday, was £70; making a total of £466 for labour, so the contractor was making £2,034 profit for the job and he was a dyam thief. He fired Edgar on the spot, although in fact he was making a profit of £3,000, some of Edgar's figures having been guessed.

Edgar got another job shortly after and met a member of the Workers' Co-operative Union which had just been formed by Capleton and Skipper Lannaman. He joined the union and Capleton adopted him immediately he heard about the contractor affair. Edgar learned all the general things that Capleton knew about Marxism, colonialism, imperialism, the capitalist system and strike action, and for about two months he stopped working at his trade to help Capleton and Skipper G. organize three strikes which failed dismally. When the W.C.U. wound up Edgar went back to stone-masonry and began reading again with a new purpose and direction. He learned the *Communist Manifesto* by heart and quoted portions of it in every political discussion he had. When the extension school was started at St George's College, after the war, Edgar attended one of the philosophy classes for a year.

Edgar could not understand Reggie's decision to join the R.A.F. and fight in the war against Germany. Reggie's theoretical arguments were that Germany was threatening democracy and that he had a stake in democracy even as one oppressed by it, that Nazism was anti-Semitic, anti-Negro and anti-communist, and that the Empire stood for something. His personal reasons were more understandable – he wanted the adventure of seeing England and of flying an aeroplane, and he saw shrewdly that if he survived the war he would have a brighter personal future – but he claimed that every bomb he dropped would advance the nigger cause and colonial freedom. His letters were full of this hope and a brisk love for England, a modest enjoyment of fighting and a longing to return to Jamaica. Reggie's life and death proved to Edgar that everything was corrupt in the world around him. His mother, who had never really understood that Reggie might die in this war he hadn't made, came to believe that God was using his death to punish her for some forgotten sin.

Edgar was a foundation member of the People's Progressive League. In 1939, when Capleton broke with Mannie Small, he had taken a small section of the union with him but he could not organize a political party so he went back to the U.S.A. When he returned to Jamaica in 1943 the P.D.P. was four years old and the Mannie Small trade union had complete control of the workers. Capleton collected as many of the old W.C.U. members as he could find and started the P.P.L. with twenty members. He had brought a lot of money and a new flamboyant platform manner from the States. The P.P.L. held weekly meetings in Kingston and St Andrew until the League membership had increased to six hundred. Edgar was an executive member and was put in charge of campaigning in Eastern Kingston.

How the League functioned at all was a puzzle to everybody except the P.D.P. officials. League dues were optional, two shillings per month. Out of this, apparently, Capleton was entitled to a monthly salary of £20, the General Secretary was paid £15 and Capleton's secretary-typist was paid £15; the rest of the money was spent on campaigning. As only about thirty League members ever paid their dues it was perfectly clear to the leaders of the People's Democratic Party that Capleton was sponsored by the American Communist Party and other communist parties beyond, so that he was accused of being in the pay of Moscow at just about the time when Moscow was in danger. The truth was that Capleton ran the P.P.L. in his own way on his own money and the private contributions of a few American friends. Edgar became League Secretary when Andy Maxwell gave up the job.

It was rumoured, after Capleton's imprisonment, that the government intended to ban the League and arrest the executive. This didn't happen. Mannie Small, the Prime Minister, and Dr Phillips were quite satisfied that Capleton was out of the way, because very few left-wing colonial politicians survive a prison sentence. Nevertheless the League membership dwindled and there was a crowd of only about two hundred at the protest meeting in Racecourse. A series of executive meetings was held with Skipper Lannaman in the chair and it was decided that since the League was strongest in Eastern Kingston all public activities should be concentrated there. They gave up the offices in Slipe Road, and Joseph Lowe's aggressive mural now adorned a fried fish shop. And the major decision was that Edgar should run, under the P.P.L. banner, as a candidate in the municipal elections to the Kingston and St Andrew Corporation in July.

A meeting of forty active P.P.L. members was called in Miss Tillie's private school on Cumberland Avenue. Edgar had prepared a detailed map of the electoral area and the work of house-to-house campaigning was distributed – ten houses to each worker. Each had a complete voters' list and a pamphlet with campaign instructions and propaganda written by Edgar and Andy Maxwell. Most of the workers were between the ages of eighteen and twenty-four and almost all of them were unemployed exiles from Capleton's house on Brentford Road. They lived by scuffling and by occasional relief work. Septy Grant and Skipper G. were jointly in charge of the campaign.

After this meeting Edgar, Septy, Andy and Skipper G. met in the yard of Edgar's house to discuss the general future of the P.P.L. Andy suggested that while campaigning for the municipal elections they should send a small group to infiltrate into the P.D.P.

'Never that,' Edgar said. 'The P.D.P. is a sham socialist party. It's based on the middle class and not the workers. And we can't infiltrate into the Merchants because Mannie would smell us straight off.'

'Unu bwauy doan forget that Capleton soon be release, you know,' Skipper G. said. Having no trade Skipper G. was vitally concerned that the League should not disintegrate. 'When Edgar get in the Corporation the League will have a respectable front.'

'Two things we musn' forget,' Edgar told them. 'Firs' of all the middle class can't help us. Yes, you find certain bourgeois elements come to join us because they are dissatisfied about colour or poverty, because they not white enough and they not rich enough. But they can't escape their class. They are their own destruction. Make one of them win £30,000 in Irish sweepstake and they never know the working class exist. But they can't escape the dialectic!' The intoxication of language began to get hold of Edgar.

'The dialectic must ultimately lead to revolution right here in Jamaica,' Andy Maxwell, an unequal rhetorician, said. 'We only need ten men at the right time to make the revolution permanent.'

'They can jack up the system an' 'cotch the system till the man in the moon but they can't escape the dialectic.' Edgar was flying and he chopped with his hands. 'You know what dialectic is? "The immediate, moving in this negative direction, has been submerged in the other, not nothing, as is assumed to be the ordinary result of dialectic: it is the other of the first, the negative of the immediate; thus it is determined in the mediate, contains the determination of the first in itself. Thus the first is preserved and maintained in the process of alteration".'

'Jesus Chris' Awlmighty!' Septy said, scratching himself with pleasure. 'Tell me those language again! Tell me those language again!'

Edgar told him again.

'Now bring it *down* to me, Master, bring it down to *me*!' Septy chanted.

'The system,' Edgar said, on earth again, 'contains its own destruction and its own regeneration.'

Andy and Skipper G. left.

'I think you can win, Edgar,' Septy said. 'I doan think the Merchants will be in this area. *Ef* we work!'

Edgar sat on the steps.

'Don't see Tull these days since he win Chelaram scholarship,' Septy said.

'That's O.K. He can't help us now, anyhow. When he come back if he doan turn a white man by then, we can use him.'

140

VI

Ramsay was twenty in June of that year. His winning of the Chelaram scholarship brought the family together for a while. They had one Sunday dinner together. Mrs Tull, Bobsie, Madge, Rosalie, Ray, Martin, Mabel, Ramsay and even Mrs Tull got a little drunk on port wine.

Mrs Tull was happy enough to start going to church again to pray for her son and be proud of him. Madge and Rosalie knitted socks and sweaters that were too thin anyway and they tried to persuade Ramsay to study law or medicine because teachers don't really make any money. They said he had been given a great opportunity and that he had a great responsibility to his people.

Bobsie was fascinated by Ramsay's cleverness at winning a scholarship without pulling strings; he didn't know it could happen in Jamaica and this must be a record. He tried to persuade Ramsay to forget about all this Marxis' business and look at Albert French, a Oxford man, a real gentleman but a proper socialist who knows that capital and labour must work together. 'All the brains in the island in the P.D.P.,' he told Ramsay. 'Capleton is a criminal jail-bird and that Edgar Bailey never went to school. No educated man could be following a scarecrow like Edgar Bailey.' Bobsie was drunk less often these days and he had more money to spend. 'Anyway,' he warned Ramsay, 'if you keep up this communism in England the Colonial Office will send you back as quick as arse-holes, and by the time you come back P.D.P. will be in power and Doc Phillips is going to illegalize all communist parties.'

Bobsie told him that he had a great opportunity and a great responsibility to the race, but he better study law because there is no money in English. 'And one rass thing you doan better do is marry a white woman,' Bobsie said. 'Look at the leader. He could marry any white woman in England but for his people sake he find a very black girl to marry as an example to his race.'

Only Mabel didn't try to advise him. She had cried when she heard about the scholarship, partly through sentiment and partly because Ramsay was almost her twin. A fortnight after he left the Courts Office Mabel decided she was really going to try for a nursing scholarship. She stopped night-life-ing and joined zoology and chemistry classes at St George's College extension school. But she was still being picked up in large American cars and pulling strings in her own way here and there, even, though no one could prove it, in the Executive Council itself. But she stopped drinking altogether.

In the two months before he left for England Ramsay helped Edgar Bailey in his municipal campaign. The P.P.L. had a lot of funds for campaigning. It had nearly two hundred pounds in hand and Capleton, from prison, sent a personal gift of fifty pounds.

The Merchants' Party was not running a candidate in the Rollington Town Ward and it was a straight fight between the P.D.P. and the P.P.L., that is if you discounted Barrister Murdoch who was running as an independent. Barrister Murdoch was a self-made man who had been an exceptional civil servant in the 'twenties until he resigned in pique for being twice passed over in promotions. Alfred Uriah Murdoch was very black and he decided that he had been discriminated against. He also came to the conclusion that 'they' could not have done this thing to him if he had been learned in the law. So he went to Britain, read for the Bar and returned to be a successful politician in the old legislative council which talked endlessly and was entirely dominated by the Governor. When political parties were formed just before the New Constitution, Barrister Murdoch refused to join any of them, ran as an independent in the universal suffrage elections and lost his deposit. His legal practice dwindled and he was the foremost among those 'starving' barristers with whom the Jamaican Bar was cluttered. He was trying again, on his own and without advisers or supporters, to re-enter politics through the Kingston and St Andrew Corporation. He had chosen Eastern Kingston because the people in that area threw only small stones and not half-bricks. He limited his campaigning to the suburb called Newton Square. The people here were very gentle, voted solidly P.D.P. and never attended political meetings, so that Barrister Murdoch had as his audiences the many children and schoolboys who lived in Newton Square. His theme was himself, a vivid autobiography, who he was, what he had accomplished and what he could do. He took himself very seriously.

Edgar was certain of getting eighty per cent of the Merchants' Party vote and his campaign tactic was to make a distinction between the workers (P.P.L. and Merchants' Party supporters) and the middle class (P.D.P.). He distributed closely reasoned pamphlets on topics like 'Why did the P.D.P. win only two seats in the Assembly?', 'The P.D.P. plan for Starvation', 'You are either a Worker or a Parasite'. Ramsay helped to draft most of these pamphlets. The P.P.L. also, in spite of all the theory against it, campaigned on a basic colour-line realizing that seventy per cent of the electorate was definitely black. The P.D.P. held monster meetings in Rollington Town almost nightly, while Edgar's unemployables conducted a polite house-to-house campaign.

Meanwhile Cyril Hanson 'wound up' his job at the Jamaica Improvement Association and was resting for a few months before going up to Brasenose College, Oxford. He had already begun to move out of Ramsay's sphere, having by then gained fully the freedom of those houses in upper St Andrew into which he had previously *forced* his way, much to their owners' annoyance. He was now going to the beach and the Myrtle Bank pool with apple-blossom girls who had names like Myers, Hopwood, Brandon, Fonseca. He still kept in public view the tri-partite division of himself into 'personality', 'intelligence' and games'. He was one of the chief organizers of the very successful garden party held on the Surrey College playing field in early July, he gave a series of radio broadcasts on 'The Work of the J.I.A. and the Future', and he was playing Senior Cup cricket for Kingston Club. He was always in a hurry, like Chaucer's Sergeant of the Lawe. So that Ramsay had not seen him for some weeks when the two of them were invited to lunch with Dr Phillips at the Jamaica Club.

Dr Phillips arrived just before one o'clock and took them in. He had been in the Appeal Court all morning but looked very fresh and vigorous. They ordered red-peas' soup and sweet cornbread, chicken croquettes, rice-and-peas, candied sweet potatoes and a very soft cornmeal pudding for sweet. Dr Phillips seemed a little irritated that he couldn't be lunching alone. Then he began to give advice.

'You two young chaps have got a great opportunity, a great adventure ahead of you,' he said. 'You are fortunate. The Empire meant one thing at school – of course, an English public school; then another thing during the Great War; and now in recent years an entirely different thing. I was fighting for the Kipling Empire, and then at Cambridge we were disillusioned about the values of democracy – but colonialism wasn't a crime. I still don't think it is a crime. It is the only civilized method by which one advanced civilization can pass its achievements on to backward countries. And if it is true that a nation cannot exist half slave, half free, it is equally true today, especially with the threat of international communism, that the world cannot remain in peace half civilized, half uncivilized. The child must grow up and every parent hates to give up its child, and if the parent cannot be persuaded he must be fought. But it is very difficult to fight against the very things that make you what you are. For instance, it was uncomfortably hot wearing a suit and robes in the Appeal Court this morning, but it is one of those matters in which the form contains the spirit, if you understand me. *You* are fortunate because it is perfectly possible that in your time barristers will plead in the Appeal Court in shirt sleeves, but it is totally impossible in my time. This is a trivial example but you might understand what I mean.'

'I am very much in favour of the traditional aspect of a barrister's robes, sir,' Cyril said. 'We are irrevocably committed to western civilization and all we can hope for is a local democracy equal in every way to the British system. Of course there will be local variations, that's all.'

'What I don't quite understand is how Britain has become a parent to Jamaica,' Ramsay said. He knew his arguments because this had been a favourite sixth-form debating society topic. 'They didn't bring African slaves because the African climate was unsuitable for the slaves. And they didn't enslave Africans because that was a necessary part of their education in civilization. They brought them here for their economic value.'

'Don't allow yourself to be misled by this constant harping on economics that you get from the communists,' Dr Phillips said. 'Of course, slavery is reprehensible but it hasn't been simple anywhere. Take Brazil, for instance – the pattern of slavery there was entirely different. The Brazilian slave could at any time buy himself out of slavery – from the very beginning – and there are instances of negro bishops in the church, during slavery. A whole new pattern of human relationships. We mustn't be too hasty, you know. A fact that is of even greater significance than economics in the breaking up of slave society is sex: miscegenation was ultimately as important as the dethroning of King Sugar.'

It was a beautiful red herring and Cyril, grinning with pleasure, said, 'I hadn't thought of that aspect of slavery, sir. Had you, Ramsay?'

'And the kind of politician who tries to make a moral argument out of slavery,' Dr Phillips said bitterly, 'has evidently forgotten reformers like Wilberforce.'

'There were two kinds of reformers,' Ramsay said. 'There were soft-hearted people, like Mrs Bourne, who in any generation would give their lives rather than see animals suffer, and there were the merchant class. Take Wilberforce. While he was campaigning so vigorously against negro slavery he had English children working in his own factories under conditions worse than slavery.'

'Ah! You don't understand the English!' Dr Phillips said with a condescending laugh. 'That is typical of them. They will contribute millions to an earthquake disaster in Japan and yet be perfectly indifferent to children starving on their own doorsteps. It's part of their greatness. You will see it when you go to England.'

'I don't think it's a mystery,' Ramsay said, trying to hold on to the argument. 'Pressy explained it by saying that Wilberforce and his colleagues wanted a market for their manufactured goods and that while slaves have no purchasing power at all, free men do, no matter how small it is.'

'Who is "Pressy"?' Dr Phillips asked.

'Mr Addison, head of Surrey College,' Cyril explained.

'Oh, Percival! He is a complete cynic. You shouldn't take everything he says seriously, you know.'

They ate in a long silence during which Ramsay's mind tried to find another approach to the slavery question since Dr Phillips would use all his considerable legal skill to rebut any argument he had not thought of first. Ramsay felt envious of both Dr Phillips and Cyril. They were so comfortable, Dr Phillips with his settled status, wealth and clever brain, and Cyril in his newly acquired status and his promise of future wealth. He thought he should study law in order to be their equals, then he thought of Barrister Murdoch and felt guilty as he realized the futility of ambition.

'Why doesn't the P.D.P. have a colour line?' Ramsay asked Dr Phillips. 'Eighty per cent of the people in Jamaica are black.'

Dr Phillips read him a lecture that lasted for nearly fifteen minutes. He said that Jamaica was not simply solving a colour problem but it was proving to the world that a colour problem did not exist. They were rising above anything as petty and vicious as that. There was no black and white distinction in Jamaica and it was mischievous for people to try to invent shade discriminations and shade prejudices which did not exist. Had anyone tried to turn him, Ramsay, out of Jamaica Club? Anything like a colour line in politics would not only disrupt unity, it would make political parties meaningless. Was Ramsay advocating a party for each percentage of negro blood?

'The P.D.P. is a party for all our variations and mixtures, and there is a place in it for the Jamaican of pure English descent and even for the expatriate Englishman if he wants to make Jamaica his home. I don't know which is worse, racialism or communism. And when you get them mixed up you have a compound that is both absurd and pernicious. Of course the P.D.P. is opposed to every form of racial discrimination. But how any intelligent person, in the face of anti-negro feeling in America and anti-semitism in Germany, can try to build a civilized political party based on race, I don't know.'

'I wasn't proposing racialism as a political creed,' Ramsay said lamely, 'but just the fact that the majority of the Merchants' Party supporters are black and the majority of the P.D.P. supporters are brown or near white or white, and there are more blacks in Jamaica than the others.'

'That,' Dr Phillips said in towering anger, 'is not a fact. It is a stupid P.P.L. lie!' Then he began to talk about himself. 'Look at all I have done in these years to foster intelligent progressive political thinking in this country. At every point I have fought unsparingly to rid our country of racial prejudice – and not only on the public platform. My wife has been solely responsible for the literary and artistic awakening which we are seeing in this country and you will find that the people she has inspired are of every complexion from black to white. It grieves me to think that this work is going to be shattered by immature politicians who preach artificial racialism.'

They had coffee and Drambuie.

'You have a serious responsibility to your people,' Dr Phillips told them. 'And if you are going to make use of your opportunity and ability you had better not have a fixed set of ideas when you go to university. Join all the clubs you can, talk to everybody who will talk to you, forget you are a negro and be a human being for three years.'

He got up to go and noticed Ramsay's despair.

'What are you going to read?'

'English.'

'Oh, my wife would like to meet you before you go. Cyril can bring you round.' And then before he drove away he said to Ramsay, 'Don't lose the enthusiasm of your youth but don't become bigoted and embittered!'

'A great man!' Cyril said as Dr Phillips drove away. 'In spite of everything, the saviour of his country!'

'But he don't understan' the communist position, though.'

'Don't be silly, Head. You think there is anything you can understand that a man like Dr Phillips can't understand? You must be crazy.'

Ramsay clipped up his trouser legs and pushed his bicycle up the street to where Cyril had parked Fakhouri's car.

'So you haven't heard from the Colonial Office yet,' Cyril said.

'No, but I should hear soon.'

'So they might send you to London or one of the provincial universities. That would be rough!' Cyril said smugly.

'I doan know,' Ramsay said opposing carelessness to Cyril's cutting superiority. 'Anyway I'm booked to sail on the *Ariguana* on the sixteenth of August. When are you leaving?'

'I have to wait until we play the key match against Lucas at the end of August. By the way, I got a letter from Dr Whitehouse. My tutor.' Cyril said 'Dr Whitehouse' as if he were an old friend.

'What did he say?' Ramsay asked.

'Oh, nothing much. The usual things.' Cyril got into the car and started it. 'I'll ring you later in the week, Head. Watch you!'

Ramsay prepared to make that hazardous and, because it was non-essential, unintelligible, journey from the colonies to the mother country. It was easy to prepare, to be certain for the first time of the spelling of 'woollen', to feel unreal and comic in a three-piece tweed suit with the sun crawling all over you, to be frightened of losing your passport and a steamship ticket more than your life.

But two shadows hung over him. The first was old and had to do with the hands of the living God. He had sworn, dying of fever when he was a boy of eight, in the saddest country evening, the delirious wall full of the clear shapes of devils, that if he lived he would devote his life to God, as his mother had taught him. Or perhaps he had read a story like that later and read the miracle of his own survival into it. And the shadow of a fundamentalist wing of God always covered him, as ludicrous and frightening as a sketch by William Blake, but knowing that he would for ever break his covenant he lived in comfortable terms with his own death. The certainty that he was already dead immunized him and sometimes made him feel indifferent to life. He lived in an internal world of certainty and surprise, now thinking, 'This death, this accident that I am approaching at the corner of North Street and South Camp Road cannot be mine,' and at another time, 'This pleasure, this achievement, this present Mona Freeman, this journey to Britain cannot be mine.' He strived after nothing and his character was permanently twisted in.

The other shadow was new. Everybody told him, till he sang it, that he had won not a scholarship but a responsibility. He was to bear, as a penance for a very good school record, the weight of himself, his family, Surrey College, the whole negro race, black Jamaicans, and all Jamaican children yet unborn and unconceived. A politically conscious colony is always looking out for messiahs and is quick to invent them, so that in a decade it discovers scores of puny messiahs in politics and art and literature. The messiah-makers are a recognizable tribe – over forty, with festered ambition, terrified of the authority of brains or wealth, and religious. This shadow, hanging persistent and inescapable, made him feel like a thief or at least a fraud. Ramsay's reaction to it was the first positive act of 'personality' that he had ever committed in his life, although the act was characteristic in its secrecy. He rebelled against the collective responsibility which was being forced on him for accepting a gift. He refused to take responsibility for other people's envy and lack of intelligence and he refused to take any responsibility for a social system which failed to give his opportunities to all. He insulated himself with a new conceit. 'I am not strong enough to be generous. I must be selfish in order to survive.'

So, through the itching of this conceit and selfishness, his affair with Sweetness Terrelonge became almost a rape. Sweetness Terrelonge had an open face and smooth lips. Her hair was auburn and her eyelashes and eyebrows were ashen so that at a distance she looked almost like an albino. Her whole body was slightly exaggerated – the neck too long, the breasts too heavy for a girl of nineteen, the waist too small, the hips too flat, too wide, the legs bowed. But she had, like an explanation for her body, the attractions of a hoarse voice and a pronounced lisp. He fell in love with Sweetness as he had fallen in love with Mabel's discovery of Sweetness.

Their friendship began with sitting on her verandah in the evening and not turning the light on and letting the darkness shape urgent voices of lust around her and watching the cigarette glow gild his face like a man with a cloak in a film, and hearing, all over their bodies, the other shifting in the chair, and not knowing what the words that were spoken did not mean, and leaving at nine, and kissing and not quite kissing, and going to bed quickly and secretly when he was gone, and walking up to Lucas

Club and back kicking the stones loudly passing her window, and being in love, fresh as a cliché. With all her heart she was knitting him a white sweater. She was a simple girl, grateful that he was there, the perfect wife for a parson.

They went to the botanical gardens at Hope one afternoon. It had rained before dawn and the corners that the sun couldn't reach were still cool. They got off the bus at the main entrance and walked up the tall-treed avenue, weaving, like children, from the paved road to the grass-walk, shy to hold hands in the empty gardens. Ramsay didn't really see the trees or flowers around him because he had walked through Hope Gardens every Sunday of term for eight years. He didn't want to think or over-prepare, so he pointed out gorgeous butterflies to her. Sweetness laughed and said silly things purposely. She thought about the shape of his head and wished he would cut his hair differently and brush it straight back without a parting.

'The Latin name for butterfly is *papilio*,' he said. 'We doan have a Jamaican word for it. As you have firefly and peeny-waughly.'

'You like butterflies?' she asked. He is 'class' at Latin, she thought; she remembered telling Olive Simpson that Ramsay was 'class' at Latin.

At the watercourse they saw a brilliant peacock. Ramsay had seen them all before and he watched Sweetness, plump and alive, her skirt stretched tight as she leaned over the bridge breathing and looking at the pointless water flow and churn.

The main road into the gardens curves just after the watercourse, like the sweep of an arm, displaying a splendid lawn. Palm trees, and little nuts with a yellow sticky pulp around them. They walked into the lily grove that had streams and bridges and a network of paths that had been for Ramsay at eight, and would always be, a little town to be lost and found in. He knew a bench, hidden from the path, where he had carved his name. She thought: *it isn't definitely right to be sittin' here alone, but he's a nice boy, though.*

'I'm sorry an' I'm glad you're going. You are the first boy I've fallen for Rams.' They kissed once, frightened, then serious and lost, then laughing. She moved his hand away and rubbed lipstick from his mouth with her handkerchief.

'We shouldn' do that. Here. Anybody can see,' she said, took his hand and they walked out of the lily grove. *He is a nice boy*, she thought.

People were on the lawn in front of the empty bandstand, and in the refreshment booth. A group of country-school children on excursion clambered on to a truck and went away singing. Two English soldiers smelling of khaki and their race drank Red Stripe beer in tall beaded glasses. He wanted to tell them he was going to England next month. He bought two 'cokes' and she wanted to look into his eyes over the tops of the straws as they do in the films but he was trying to hear what the soldiers were saying. The afternoon sun was wonderfully bright.

Where the gardens end and the mango cultivation begins, where the blue hills seem to be just above you, there was a poinciana tree with a few clumps of aurelia bushes around it. They sat there and could hear the voices distant and coming no nearer.

She refused at first. After a while she sat up abruptly.

'No. You musn' do any of that,' she said. 'We not even engaged!'

'I'm not going to do *that*.'

'An' people might come,' she said though the voices were still distant and coming no nearer. He held her again. *He's a nice boy*, she thought, *but he's trying to do that!*

'Leave me alone!' she shouted, angry and selfish. She jumped up and he grabbed her ankle and they struggled, like trying to wake from a nightmare, like drowning, and he tore her under-wear and it was painful.

'I'm going to marry you when I come back,' he said grudgingly afterwards. 'It isn't anything to cry about.'

'You spoil me now, for ever,' she said, the tenderness coming back into her voice.

Walking out of the gardens, along the shady lane to the top entrance, the apathy left him and he thought she might find a way to come to England while he was there. To go away now would be to break up all the personal assumptions and confidences that his country had given him in nineteen years, to throw away all the preparation for the life he was leaving. In four years this Sweetness would not exist, neither would he, and each would have no personal knowledge of what the other had lost and would be unable to understand what the other had gained. This afternoon, he felt, was the inadequate compensation for all he was losing in going away and his new deliberate irresponsibility told him he was entitled to it. Sweetness thought of her torn clothes which she would keep always to remember him and she felt proud that this thing which she had tried hard not to want had happened. It was too soon to regret.

He found more butterflies and they laughed and held each other.

'Rams,' she said, laughing at the memory of a word-game she had played at school. 'Suppose I get a perhaps child, eh?'

'Cho. Couldn't happen!'

'It couldn't happen just the one time, eh, Rams?'

'Can't!' That was another responsibility he would not take. *He's a nice boy*, she thought.

★ ★ ★

The sixteenth of July, 1947, was celebrated as the first Constitution Day, a public holiday. The people of Jamaica would never forget that day, neither would the followers of the People's Progressive League and the Action Groupers of the People's Democratic Party. For them it was the day of the Battle of Charles Street.

A platform had been erected at the south entrance to Victoria Park, facing King Street, and by ten o'clock the whole of Parade was packed tight. Traffic had been diverted, but only buses were affected because there is very little traffic into King street on a public holiday. The crowd overflowed into King Street as far down as the Commercial Restaurant, and the flower-beds of parish church garden were being crushed by P.D.P. supporters.

It was a day of carefully planned dramatic moments. The ceremony, a thanksgiving ceremony, was due to begin at ten and by a quarter to ten only the Bishop of Jamaica had arrived. He was a black Bishop and got a cheer from the crowd, by mistake, because the word had gone round that Mannie Small, the Prime

Minister, was arriving. The Governor's splendid Austin car drove through Victoria Park and the tight-lipped, handsome, double-fourth-in-Greats representative of the King in his white uniform and medals and plumed white helmet mounted the platform. He was surprised and annoyed that the Prime Minister had not arrived because the colonial practice is that the Governor must arrive last for all public functions. The crowd was restless. Most of the people in the front of the platform were Merchant Party members and they cheered thinly and intermittently as the false news came through that Mannie Small was arriving. The Governor's wife, a tall Spanish-looking woman with a long nose, sharp cheeks, prominent lips and a shapely body somewhat concealed in buoyant yellow organdie, waved her gloved hand in queenly acknowledgement of the cheers.

Mannie Small arrived. The crowd on West Parade began to sway and chant, and bobbing on the waves was the shining bald head of the Prime Minister as he was carried, waving a shining topper, down Princess Street, through the crowd in West Parade and deposited gently on the platform. He wore a morning coat and striped trousers and shook hands formally with everyone on the platform. His appearance on the platform coincided with a tremendous cheer from the P.D.P. supporters in the parish church grounds for Dr Phillips was now visible.

Dr Phillips had sat concealed in the vestry of the parish church since nine that morning. Just before ten he had climbed the two hundred feet to the top of the clock tower and had waited there until Mannie Small arrived. Then he had leaned over the parapet and been recognized by P.D.P. Action Groupers who had been scattered in the crowd and whose job was to recognize Dr Phillips and cheer. The whole crowd, including the platform dignitaries, turned to look at the commanding figure on the top of parish church. It was a brilliant *coup de tour*. He gave the party sign and the applause was deafening. After all it was his day, his Constitution, drafted by the P.D.P., argued into Colonial Office acceptance by the P.D.P. and then appropriated, legally, by Mannie Small. He had the right to be above them and the right to be in the clouds.

The Mayor of Kingston went to the microphone and told the crowd that that day, July sixteenth, was the day chosen by the

153

government to be perpetually and annually celebrated as the first Constitution Day of Jamaica, this lovely isle, so that children to come in their millions would on every sixteenth day of July remember again the great battle fought by the Prime Minister and all thinking Jamaicans for the perpetual freedom of her peoples. He said that July sixteenth happened to be *his* birthday, and he gave them a brief biography of himself and spoke of his long-standing personal friendship with the Prime Minister, Mannie Small. (The Mayor of Kingston, apart from having completed his formal education in the fourth 'book' of elementary school, was also known to drink a magnum of champagne before breakfast every morning.) He stood magnificently, six-foot-three in his robes, and orated about the beauty of the city of Kingston until Mannie Small told him to 'bruk it up' and 'mek de Bishop pray'. The Mayor said that special thanksgiving was due to the Colonial Office who had borne the burdens of the colony of Jamaica for so long. Then he called upon the Bishop of Jamaica to lead them in prayer.

The Bishop of Jamaica, who in 1947 was just over sixty, had in the course of an almost angelic priesthood suffered every kind of slight and indignity from every kind of colonial dignitary of church and state, until the new Jamaica had found a place for him at the top of the ecclesiastical tree. A greying, bushy-haired man, not much more than five feet tall and rather portly, he approached the microphone waddling in bow-legged leggings like a planta-tion busha. The crowd liked his colour and gave him a cheer. Unfortunately his diction was disturbed by a set of false teeth that always misbehaved in the open air when the cathedral walls were no longer there to diffuse his sermons into a meaningless sonor-ity. But he was a good man with a great heart.

The 'unity' which Jamaican clergymen always call for at the start of their prayers is generally understood by the congregation to mean that all present should assist the clergyman by praying themselves, silently, of course, but if you had a good burning phrase like 'Lord Jesus, come!' flaming in your chest it was your business to let it out. And without any difficulty of transition, a political audience becomes, with the words 'Let us unite in prayer', a congregation.

The Bishop gave himself up to inspired literary composition. He thanked God for the bright day and the sky and the shadow of the church tower over the proceedings and for His guiding hand which had led them to the crossroads of independence. He asked that it might be granted to them to realize that the Kingdom of Jamaica was as nothing compared to the Kingdom of Heaven, that the Kingdom of Heaven was 'at hand', that is, an immaterial possibility in a material world; and he asked the Lord to impress on all those gathered present that it was the duty of every Jamaican Christian, to bring together, as one, the Kingdoms of Heaven and Jamaica by ceasing to fornicate and adulterate, by stamping out lying and corruption and the worship of the devil so that they might avoid the wickedness for which Port Royal had been punished and so build Jerusalem on Jamaica's green and pleasant land. AMEN.

The Prime Minister made a short easy speech. He said there was great promise for the future now that political power had passed into the hands of the people. He believed in the Empire and the Commonwealth and knew that under the leadership and guidance of that great mother of nations, Great Britain, Jamaica would grow to become one of the greatest ex-colonies in the history of the world. He intended to be in power for the next twenty years and had no intention of giving up to 'red politicians who are hanging like hyenas over the walls'.

The boos drowned the cheers at the end of his speech.

The Governor did not want to detain them from celebrating this great and memorable day in the quiet of their homes and the family circle but he wanted to speak of two things – slavery and personal insignificance. He said there were still agitators about who tried to use the wrongs done the slaves in the eighteenth century as if they were relevant political arguments today. 'No nation', he said, 'ever progressed by sulking over the injustices of the past. For the errors my country has made, I can assure you, we are heartily ashamed and we are now doing our best to eradicate the memories of those wrongs, not by brooding over the past but by helping your country to advance to a brighter civilized future.' He said that as a Governor he had no personal significance; he represented only the goodwill of the people of England as symbolized in the monarchy. 'I am reminded by his lordship's mention of Port Royal of the verses about that controversial historical figure, Sir Henry Morgan.

> *"You was a flyer, Morgan,*
> *You was the man to crowd*
> *When you was in your flag-ship –*
> *Now you're under a shroud."*

I, too, will soon be under a shroud, but the democratic principle, the avoidance of violence, the ability to compromise on every conceivable issue, will remain the endless heritage of the Jamaican people, a heritage perpetually embodied in this Constitution, the granting of which we celebrate today.'

The Governor drove away through Victoria Park but the crowd did not begin to disperse. They were waiting to march off with their leaders. The Merchants' Party moved first led by Mannie Small who was preceded by a small brass band, two cornets, a trombone, a bass drum and a set of cymbals playing *Onward Christian Soldiers.* They moved in complete disorder along West Parade then up Princess Street towards their party headquarters. The non-party spectators who were mainly in King Street, and had been hoping that a fight would develop between the two marching armies, were disappointed. For it took Dr Phillips nearly five minutes to descend from the clock tower.

Quite suddenly Skipper George Lannaman had climbed a lamp-post just at the corner of Parade and King Street and had started to make a speech to the crowd that was flowing below him like a sea. He wrapped his legs round the post, hung on to it with one hand and used the other hand to emphasize the abuse he was hurling at Mannie Small and Dr Phillips. He wasn't making much sense but he was making a great noise, so that Ramsay Tull, who was standing at the corner of East Parade and Church Street, could hear him distinctly.

A young police corporal ordered Skipper G. to get down.

'Is agains' the law to climb a lamp-pos',' the corporal said.

'This is Corporation lamp-pos',' Skipper G. told him. 'Ah pay mi taxes an' same as I'm entitle to free light at night-time, I'm entitle to climb lamp-pos' in daytime. Not a law go so. Go back a station an' catch fowl-thief. Depot-bwauy!'

'You are disturbing the peace,' the corporal said. The crowd had stopped moving as this was the kind of entertainment they were after.

'You see any peace roun' here to disturb?' Skipper G. asked and the crowd hooted at the corporal.

'Ef you think you bad stay up deh five minutes,' the corporal said moving away. Skipper G. ignored him and turned the crowd's attention to Dr Phillips who had just emerged from the church gate opposite.

'See him there! The Judas of Jamaica! The betrayer of the working-class movement. He makes himself rich off Jamaica criminal and now he trying to play politics. Stop fool the people, barrister, all you want is power to oppress naygah in this country. See him there! The Judas of Jamaica!'

Skipper G.'s harangue was cut short. Five of the Action Group who were flanking Dr Phillips in his slow progress through the crowd rushed at the lamp-post, and Skipper G. descended and disappeared as suddenly as he had climbed.

The P.P.L. boys were in a group at the north corner of East Parade and Church Street, near the fence of Victoria Park. There were about forty of them, waiting idly for the P.D.P. procession to come by. Edgar Bailey and Septy Grant and Andy stood together watching the crowd and looking very sad. The P.D.P. procession came by, about four thousand of them, led by Dr Phillips. It was an excited, shining group. As the vanguard passed, the P.P.L. group started singing *The Red Flag* but Dr Phillips ordered the Action Group to leave the boys alone. The P.P.L. group joined the rear of the procession which moved up East Parade, into East Queen Street on the long march to party headquarters on North Street. The route was East Queen Street, up Duke Street then into North Street to P.D.P. offices next door to the Y.W.C.A. When Ramsay Tull, who had been watching everything from the open land on Church Street, finally caught up with the procession it had already crossed East Street.

The P.P.L. by this time had divided themselves into three groups. The first, of about twenty, led by Septy Grant, ran up East Street into a yard on Charles Street where they had a considerable armament of sticks and half-bricks. The second group, of about ten, also ran ahead but went to Duke Street and waited in the yard of the school opposite the government printery. They built a small brick-heap. The third group, led by Edgar, walked behind the procession taunting and abusing them, and ten members of the Action Group came to the rear to protect their comrades.

The procession swung powerfully into Duke Street, banners flying, colourful and hopeful. There were gathered, among the lawyers, young graduate schoolteachers, elementary schoolteachers, intrepid civil servants, the greater part of Jamaica's political intelligence and none of its shrewdness and selfishness. Dr Phillips was a selfless man who really believed that the formula of moderation could alone give Jamaica a settled but progressive future; and he spent a large portion of his own money on the Democratic Party. These were facts not disputable in the law courts, but if not meaningless at least easily distorted on the political platform. There was a sad innocence about Dr Phillips' thinking in these matters for he could not understand why violence and lies should accompany the most noble occupation a man could adopt, that of leading his people. He marched before the crowd of loyal-to-death followers without the pride or messianic vision of himself that his opponents attributed to him (though he saw the political leader as a melodramatic actor) but taking humbly the shared sacrament of the worship of his followers. He hated the arrogance of youth and he hated to be contradicted. But he did not want to be a dictator.

When the rear of the procession was passing St George's School on Duke Street a half-hearted volley of bricks dropped among them. The Action Groupers spotted the brick-throwers and chased them up the lane behind the school and into Charles Street. Edgar Bailey's group followed them. The brick-throwers turned in the middle of the street and started to fight and immediately Septy's well-armed group came out of the yard in which they had been waiting, and the Action Groupers were completely surrounded just at the time when the P.D.P. procession had turned into North Street and was nearly half a mile away. It was a beautiful, simple and murderous decoy.

It began as a general scrap and the P.D.P. ex-boxers were confidently using their fists. Still enthusiastic from the march and remembering their political hate they abused the P.P.L. Bobsie Tull was the most eloquent and every one of his punches was accompanied by an obscene word. Then the fight stopped as if they had suddenly seen the pointlessness of everything. About twenty other people, stragglers from the procession and a number who had gathered from the yards around, thought the fight was over. They all just stood there in the middle of Charles Street as if wondering what to do next. Then a P.P.L. boy threw a brick.

He threw it five yards and smashed the head of the leading ex-boxer. The blow was surrounded and enclosed by silence. The man was big, six-foot-four at least, a fine torso in a Gene Autry shirt, and the blood from his temple trickled on to the spotless white shirt. He reeled a little as if riding a punch in a forgotten bout and his fingers moved with an absurd delicacy over the raw pulpy spot above his ear. Then the pain of the blow gripped him and he went on his knees, as if praying formally. It was a still moment and the one moment that could be held clearly in the mind of anybody who was in the fight or watching it, this big man on his knees pawing at the stained brick. He picked it up and flung it hard and a P.P.L. boy turned slightly and got it on the hip.

The Action Groupers realized they were surrounded and they wanted to get out and run but they couldn't. The ring of Leaguers closed in. Two Action Groupers tried to rush the enclosure and were pushed back. Then the mood of the fight changed again. One of the ex-boxers panicked and drew a jack-knife and the terror and desperation on his face frightened the P.P.L. boys into the hate and anger a man feels when he must fight for his survival. A knife suddenly drawn in a fight makes the whole thing as personal as one's death.

He never used that knife. Septy Grant's coco-macka stick knocked the knife into the gutter and ripped the flesh of the man's wrist a little. The P.P.L. boys went in with sticks and beat them. It wasn't a fight about politics. They were trying to kill and they weren't thinking about politics at all.

Three Action Groupers ran away before anyone realized it. Then the others ran down the lane and a few bricks were thrown at them. Of the Action Groupers, only Bobsie Tull remained. He couldn't run away because the backs of both knees were swollen with stick blows. He moved like a dog whose back legs have been run over by a car. And still the sticks beat him. He hobbled to a lamp-post and tried to hold on to it with his hands, slipping and trying to grasp, and slipping. They pulled him from the post and he shouted, "Lord God, ah dead!" The sticks still beat him. A few spectators now had enough courage to try to part the fighters, and it was easy because there wasn't any fight left as Bobsie was unconscious. The P.P.L. boys moved off in a body, walking quickly, into Hanover Street then south toward East Queen Street. They threw their sticks into the yards on Hanover Street.

'How your side, Aubrey?'

'Is awright, man, it feel a little stiff, you kno', but, beside that, is awright.'

'Mek ah see it. Wait! Is bleed you bleed?'

'No, from the brick.'

'I think we kill Tull, you know, Septy.'

They passed the Y.M.C.A.

'We have to walk together. They going after us every night!'

'From *dis* hour, boy, I not walking without a knife.'

'Same me, mi son!'

Corner of Hanover Street and East Queen Street.

'What you say we disperse ourselves now?' Septy Grant asked.

Lissen, unu bway,' Edgar Bailey said, 'keep in small-small group, say five or six and if you see them an' they more than you, *run*.'

'Meetin' tonight, Septy?'

'Yes, lissen. Everybody at Edgar house 'bout five o'clock. P.D.P. have a meeting at Cumberland Avenue corner.'

'O.K., passero.'

'O.K., passero.'

'Aubrey what-appen? Yo' side hurtin' you?'

'No, man, is awright. It jus' feel kine a' stiff like.'

They had left Parade only twenty minutes before.

Ramsay had followed the P.D.P. procession as far as the headquarters on North Street. He got frightened at the brick-throwing on Duke Street and thought it safer to stick with the crowd and pretend to be P.D.P. Anyway he liked the excitement of following a procession. It was still remarkable then for a man of Dr Phillips' social standing to lead a mob of people through the streets of Kingston. Ramsay felt it was unwise to be too openly identified with a group as dangerous as the leaderless P.P.L., especially as he was going to another future in Britain. Perhaps Dr Phillips' compromise was sound in the end and he wasn't very sure that privately Phillips was not a Marxist, did not admit Marx's insight, and in any case he could find no book that analysed the materials and problems of colonial movements for freedom. He wrote pamphlets for Edgar Bailey, had lunch with Dr Phillips, sang the *Red Flag* on Thursday evenings at Miss Tillie's school, and would have tea with Mrs Phillips next week. The contradiction was another, more personal, romanticism.

He didn't go into the P.D.P. headquarters because he was afraid that Dr Phillips might recognize him. He turned back at Hanover Street and walked west on North Street towards Steele's bakery where he could buy some of Steele's incredible patties if the shop wasn't closed. He met Skipper G. who told him there had been a fight and that Bobsie was at the Central Hospital. They went to the hospital together and were told that Bobsie was evidently concussed and still unconscious but not badly hurt.

Five days later Bobsie left the hospital to convalesce at home. He had no bitterness about the Charles Street fight. Both Dr Phillips and Albert French had visited him in hospital and he was able to repay Ramsay his two pounds. He said that the Action Group was making a big plan to 'finish' P.P.L. and he was very proud that he alone had not run away from the fight. Mrs Tull took it very calmly. After she knew that Bobsie was not seriously hurt she said that she expected to hear that he had been picked up dead off the street any day at all.

The Municipal elections were held at the end of July. It had been a quiet, almost tame campaign in Eastern Kingston. There were no fights between P.D.P. and P.P.L. followers. A curious rumour had been spread that Mannie Small wanted all Merchants' Party members to vote for Edgar Bailey and the P.P.L. Edgar discredited the rumour until the Merchants' Party M.H.A, said the same thing in the hearing of some P.P.L. boys. Ramsay's theory was that Small was certain of a majority in the K.S.A.C. and was willing to use a P.P.L. victory as propaganda against the

161

P.D.P. Edgar had another interpretation; he thought Small realized the need for working-class solidarity. 'But why didn't Small run his own candidate?' and 'What about the capitalists that are backing Small?'

And the Merchants' supporters turned out in large numbers on election day to vote for Edgar. Septy cruised around in an old Mercury Ford car from booth to booth, talking to voters and estimating, and by three o'clock in the afternoon he announced that Edgar would win. The Merchants' even had agents at the booths who arranged a little multiple voting on the side. Skipper G. was absolutely confident and drunk when the polls closed at six o'clock.

The counting was done at the Municipal offices in Church Street and the first ten boxes gave Edgar a comfortable lead of 250 votes. Just before midnight the P.D.P. candidate overtook Edgar and the last two boxes from Rockfort were: P.D.P. – 106, P.P.L. – 10; P.D.P. – 196, P.P.L. – 5; and the P.D.P. had won by thirty votes. Mr Alfred Uriah Murdoch (Ind.) got three votes, his own, his wife's and his sister's.

Septy, Andy, Edgar, Skipper G. and Vera Chen drove back to Edgar's house in Septy's car. Vera was crying.

'What happen in Rockfort?' Edgar asked, when they were drinking on the porch of Septy's house. 'I jus' doan understand it!'

'Maybe we can appeal, though, you know,' Andy said, hopelessly.

'Don't bother with that,' Skipper G. said.

'Why doan bother with that Skipper?' Septy shouted at him. 'Why? What you know, Skipper?' They looked at Skipper Lannaman. He was wearing a blue tropical suit, a collarless shirt, braces, suede shoes, and a soft felt hat with a feather in the band. Perhaps because of his age, perhaps because he could no longer lean on Capleton, he looked out of place in the group.

'Lissen,' he said talking very rapidly, 'you get yo' full share of vote, Edgar, you get yo' full share of vote. Ah say you can't appeal. You know why you get more than thirty vote? I going tell you, you see. Is I ask Mannie not to run in Rollington ward.'

'You mek a deal with Mannie?' Septy said.

'Ah doan mek a deal,' Skipper G. said. 'Mannie owe Capleton something. He coulda throw away a constituency for it. Unu too young to understan' it.'

'You mean he put Capleton in jail an' then him owe him something?' Andy asked.

'Gawd-Awmighty,' Edgar said, seeing everything. 'Nutten can break up a party like to just lose a election. You couldn' understan' that, you couldn't see that, Skipper?'

'How you mean?' Septy said to Edgar. 'Come again, master, ah not following you.'

'You doan si'!' Edgar said.

Septy and Edgar looked at each other for a full minute.

'You working *wid* Mannie,' Septy said.

'Till Capleton come back,' Skipper G. said. 'Capleton know.'

'You lie, Skipper, you *lie*,' Edgar said.

'You are the worse Judas ever born!'

'P.P.L. finish. You tink a bway like Edgar can feature in politics!' Skipper said. 'P.P.L. finish this same-a night.'

Septy walked stiff-legged and stood over Skipper where he sat on the steps of the porch.

'Leave him,' Edgar said. 'Tony cut him already.'

'Ah go where the workers want me,' Skipper said. He started walking to the gate.

'Tek yo' tail out of here, you wutliss naygah!' Septy said.

Vera Chen looked as if she had grown up only that night. She was very pretty with an olive-smooth skin, distinct cheekbones, slanted eyes and small, milky-white teeth. She must have been more than half Chinese, for her lips were red and when she talked her mouth was like the inside of a pomegranate.

'We lose,' Edgar said, 'but we doan finish yet. We can't finish for we still have poverty and unemployment and colonialism an' a dawg like Skipper Lannaman!'

It was nearly four o'clock in the morning. Andy went with Vera and Septy in the car. Whenever Septy borrowed the car Vera always went everywhere with him.

VII

The Phillips' house had originally been a plantation Great House.
It was hidden away and difficult to find, for though it was only
four miles from Halfway Tree it was 'in the country', and, in a
sense, in another country. You half expected, walking up the wide
circular drive, to see massive bloodhounds bound at you and to
see footmen in livery and carriages and house-slaves and planta-
tion-slaves in white calico near the whitewashed outhouses.

Ramsay turned in from the endless marl road and walked up
the tarred drive. The place was deep in poinciana and the rose
garden, brilliantly in bloom in the centre of the front lawn, was
stylized and artificial and in the very best taste. He saw the stables
on his left and the fine horses he didn't know were fine because
horses were things you rode in the country if you couldn't afford
a car. And there was the incongruous car (instead of a carriage)
parked by the steps to the front verandah – a shiny new Buick
Roadmaster, jet-black and trimmed with silver. He walked by
and smelt the upholstery, sickly-sweet like the seats at the Carib
Theatre. The smell of new cars was one he had not been born to
and he disliked it because it reminded him of asafoetida and feet
with yaws. He glimpsed, on the lawn at the side of the house, a
high thin badminton net.

It was four-fifteen in the afternoon, oppressive and thundery
with one of those tropical mirages where the hills and the clouds
seem to be on top of you because they have shielded the sun. The
verandah was a post-slavery addition but seemed to have the
browning of age hidden by the deliberate creeper which he
thought was honeysuckle. The house seemed specially well kept,
as if a house was not a place for a man to live in but an adornment
to be gathered round him. It seemed incredible to Ramsay that in
tiny Jamaica there could be another distinct world of graceful

dwellings. He felt he might be entering an afternoon in Henry James' *Portrait of a Lady*, and Mrs Phillips would have been delighted to hear of this feeling because her home was planned to trap the visitor into literature.

The male voice he heard in the drawing room, however, was definitely Jamaican. It echoed a little because the room was deep and panelled. Ramsay knocked and somewhere in the gloom Mrs Phillips said, 'Come in, Mr Tull. Did you find your way?'

She was sitting on the largest sofa Ramsay had ever seen, smothered in cushions, and a young man sat on a low chair near the piano. He didn't stop talking when Mrs Phillips greeted Ramsay. He was one of Mrs Phillips' poets, a fair-complexioned man with straight hair. His face was round and quizzical with the eyes sunk far in as in a mask. You remembered his slow, perpetual and slightly sardonic smile, his flat, broad Jamaican accent (which was out of keeping with his hair) and the impression he gave of not listening to what other people said in conversation. His name was Stephen Strachan and he wrote good nationalist verse in the very manner of Walt Whitman and unconvincing love poetry which read like an inaccurate translation of Latin poetry into Elizabethan English. Mrs Phillips had discovered and made him.

'You think, Madonna, I could ever agree to that?' Stephen Strachan was saying when Ramsay sat on the edge of the sofa where Mrs Phillips had patted him an invitation. All the artists and writers under her wing and all the P.D.P. followers and all her servants called Mrs Phillips 'Madonna'. 'So I told him the whole bureaucratic structure stinks with unimaginative pen-pushers like him.'

Mrs Phillips said, 'What I like about you, Stephen, is you've got balls!' Well, she was almost an artist, anyway, and you could see that clearly all over the room. From where he sat Ramsay was looking at a painting of a scene of fishermen catching crabs. To the left of the painting was an enormous box with the loudspeaker extension from the radiogram, but his eyes wandered back to the painting. If you didn't know much about painting you saw three stooping figures, three irregular splashings not as dark as the background which wasn't trees or mountains but a flat ungraded blackness and the light in the picture came from a moon that threw no shadows but silvered the sea-foam in the foreground. It reminded Ramsay of a beach in St Ann. 'I must start learning how to talk about painting,' he thought.

Stephen Strachan told how he abused the civil servant but Ramsay hadn't heard what the civil servant had done.

'Do you write?' Mrs Phillips asked Ramsay abruptly.

He was slow in adjusting to the question for he found himself thinking that the question meant 'Can you write?' Then he thought of lying and finally said, 'No.'

'I've got an itch to write a poem,' Stephen Strachan said, 'but I want a subject, like having an itch to sleep with a woman and not being able to find the woman.'

'Isn't the actual writing more like the *end* of intercourse, a kind of apathy out of which you have to drive yourself, Keats' feeling of lassitude?' Mrs Phillips asked, thinking her way seriously to the heart of the problem. 'The orgasm is the moment the whole poem enters your mind, isn't it, don't you think so Mr Tull?'

It was intended that he should be shocked and he was. Mrs Phillips was not being perverse; she was only being a colonial educated abroad. The situation is that the colonial goes to Britain or America or Europe and copies the attitudes and vocabulary of a certain period then returns to a static society and lives, from then on, in the flavour of an era that Britain or America or Europe has forgotten. A day's fashion becomes permanent and lasts for a lifetime. Mrs Phillips had been in England in the 'twenties. She always began her 'influences' by trying to shock the neophyte into a new type of reality, a one-woman crusade against the entrenched puritan conscience of the Jamaican. But Ramsay had grown up in a tougher world. He wasn't shocked by Mrs Phillips' daring; he was shocked by her relationship with Stephen Strachan which he thought was clearly indicated in the words she used. It was quite the wrong reaction because Mrs Phillips' associations with all her writers and painters and musicians were absolutely pure.

'I don't really know,' Ramsay said.

'Write a poem about the new Buick the party has bought,' she commissioned. 'The modern machine, in what is really a primitive political situation….'

'I could try it,' Stephen said, with the sardonic smile. 'What I like about the car is the way the black sets off the silver.'

'Something symbolic probably,' she said, gently feeding him the idea. 'But you haven't had any tea, Mr Tull – Ramsay, isn't it? We are having coffee, actually, you know, like "coffee-tea" in the country.' She got up and poured the coffee from a long silver pot and did it gracefully and smiled down at him when she handed the cup. She pushed a trolley with two plates of sliced chocolate cake in front of him.

Stephen told a long story about the portrait painter Joseph Lowe. Ramsay didn't follow it because Mrs Phillips and Stephen laughed when certain names were mentioned and left things unsaid, but the story ended with Joseph Lowe compelling a philistine schoolmaster named Barclay to buy pork chops for 'all of them' at Silver Slipper.

'Madonna, I must go,' Stephen said.

'Stephen is going to spend a week at Cinchona,' she told Ramsay, to bring him into the conversation.

They were all three standing with the awkwardness that sometimes follows abrupt decisions to depart. The situation needed a phrase and Mrs Phillips found it. She said, like a benediction, 'The hills. I think the hills will perform their usual magic, Stephen.'

She went into the study adjoining the drawing room and Stephen studied the Picasso above the piano.

'I shan't be a minute, Ramsay, I'm going to take Stephen to Constant Spring Road.' Then the Buick glided away.

He walked around the room looking at things, the radiogram that was about five feet long, the Bechstein, the single row of new books on a low built-in shelf beside the radiogram. Then he peeped into the study which had more books and bookshelves than the Surrey College library. On top of one shelf was a framed photograph of Dr Phillips in army uniform. Then he heard a car enter the drive and he hurried back to the sofa.

It was not Mrs Phillips but her daughter, Patricia. She was dressed for tennis – white shorts and a white long-sleeved jumper. Patricia was handsome and athletic-looking like her father and she had a cool sandalwood complexion. She had been at school in England all during the war and it was only a few months since she had returned to Jamaica. She was nearly eighteen and was doing her last school year at St Andrew's High School for Girls. Ramsay was seeing her for the first time.

'Hullo!' she said. 'Nobody home?' She didn't only sound English, she *was* an English girl.

'Mrs Phillips jus' went out,' Ramsay said, and heard his own very flat voice. She stood over the trolley.

'Choc'late cake! Do you mind if I have my tea? I'm famished!' She sat beside him. 'Are you a painter?'

'No, I'm just here –'

'No, don't tell me. Let me guess. You are a writer!'

'No, I'm Ramsay –'

'Oh, I *know*. You are in politics. No? I give up. Won't you have some coffee?'

He didn't reply till she had poured herself a cup of coffee, put milk and sugar in it and sat down again. It suddenly seemed to him that what he had to say was extremely important.

'I'm Ramsay Tull,' he said. 'I'm going to England next week and Mrs Phillips invited me to tea.'

'Oh, you're the scholarship winner. Aren't you lucky!'

The trouble about a quick English accent, Ramsay realized, is that you can listen to it but you can't talk to it.

'I think this choc'late cake's delicious, don't you?'

The 'don't you' irritated him. Pressy always used it when he wanted you to admit your own criminality or stupidity. He thought of Arnold Bennett's *The Card* and decided to be 'innocent'. She was only a Jamaican girl, for her skin said so.

'Why you talk like that?' he asked her.

She laughed, throwing her head back. 'Oh, I don't know. I just *talk* like that, I suppose.'

'Is your car that outside there?'

'No, it's really Mummy's car, you know, but she's using the Buick today. D'you know, a stupid policeman stopped me this afternoon and wanted to see my driver's licence. Why are Jamaican policemen so *stupid*! I told him it was at home and anyway I had twenty-four hours in which to produce it. He didn't know *that*, of course. But I've got to be more careful, Daddy'll be furious.'

'How you like St Andrew's?'

'Oh, I *hate* it,' Patricia said. 'D'you know, I don't like Jamaica at all. Except the weather, of course. The weather's gorgeous! Anyway I'll only be here until I'm ready to go to Cambridge. I'm going to Girton, you know, where Mummy was. Where are you going?'

'I'm not sure,' Ramsay said.

'Oh, what a pity! Cyril Hanson is going to Oxford. Do you know Cyril?'

'We went to Surrey together.'

'Oh yes, of course, Mummy – or was it Daddy? – said that. Cyril *said* you were going to Oxford.'

'I thought you said you didn't know who I was.'

'Did I? When?'

She stood up and smiled at him in the English way, the lips slightly puckered and the eyes wide open. It struck him that you could learn even a way of smiling from another race. She walked across the room and switched on a tall green-shaded standard lamp. She posed, just for a few seconds, beside the lamp and then went upstairs.

When Mrs Phillips returned Ramsay's first impulse was to go before it became dark. He needed to go now because he did not want to spend the time wishing that she would take him to Constant Spring Road in the Buick. He was uncomfortable because he was afraid that Dr Phillips might come in at any moment and also he thought he heard preparations for dinner somewhere in the background.

Mrs Phillips shifted a lounge chair and sat facing him with her back to the lamp. She talked to him about Stephen Strachan and, in the green light, he felt he was being drawn into a conspiracy. She thought that Stephen had read too much, hadn't assimilated it all and that he ought to write prose because his poetry tended to be lumpy and clogged. The odd thing about Stephen, she said, was that he didn't seem to have any proper 'inspiration' of his own. He only wrote things *she* asked him to write for she only had to say, 'Come, Stephen, write me a poem about this or that,' and he would write some of his best stuff. She wanted to know if Ramsay thought this was odd.

He was preparing himself to say it was time to go when she started talking again.

'The real danger about our artistic awakening is that it's too closely linked to a political awakening. I am afraid that when the political enthusiasm dies the artists will either have to start all over again or die, too. It isn't that they can't observe or are writing political tracts. They have feeling all right, but it's political feeling. Don't you follow?'

'But they will have important historical value,' Ramsay said. It was an adequate phrase which avoided passing judgment.

'Of course, they will have, as you suggest, important historical value.' Ramsay was flattered, as she intended he should be, because she had repeated the phrase he used. 'But what is going to happen to them personally? The artist, surely, is something like a medium with a seance table; the mediocre artist borrows somebody else's table but the great artist builds his own. Stephen has no personal seance table, if you see what I mean. Take away the progressive movement, so that we hear only the Whitman phraseology and not the new urgent Jamaican voice that is striking a new chord today. . . .' She let that hover for a while. 'The painters and sculptors are all right, they can go on for years on technique alone till they have a new experience that will require a significant modification of the technique. But poor Stephen doesn't have the technique. He's only got words, I'm afraid, and he is so very sensitive that you can't talk to him about it.'

Two things irritated him. One was that Mrs Phillips did not talk about his going to England, and the other was that he didn't know just how to go about leaving Mrs Phillips. He remembered reading recently in one of Dr Joad's books that at Oxford and Cambridge you learn how to enter a room and how to leave it.

'You never say anything,' she laughed. 'I have no idea what you are thinking. Perhaps you should write. Why don't you write? You never know. We have things stored in odd corners of our minds.'

Why had she invited him to tea? He had come prepared to talk about himself, about going to England.

'It's very easy to forget Jamaica when you go away,' she said. 'Have you met Patricia?'

'Yes.'

'After eight years in England she simply can't adjust.'

This, Ramsay thought, was the time to go, but she said, 'I think there is *something* going on between Cyril Hanson and Patricia, between ourselves.' The conspiracy again and he moved to the edge of the sofa.

He managed to get up and she said, 'Do you have to go?' On the verandah he saw the flowing lines of the long Buick and the smaller Morris Minor near the stables.

'I think you will be a writer, Ramsay. Oxford will bring that out. Only don't get mixed up in left-wing politics, please. The writer has to keep himself clean. The war against Germany hasn't at all deceived me about the true nature of communism. But you *will* write. I mean, you may become a *writer*. Good-bye, Ramsay, and good luck. Don't forget Jamaica!'

He felt, as they shook hands, that he had always known her. He walked the mile and a half to the Constant Spring Road. He had the feeling that he had spent the afternoon in England.

Mrs Myrtle Hanson sat alone on her verandah. It was raining outside but not heavily now, and she stared into the rain, drowsy from sleep. The sun was still shining in streaks and the showers became small rainbows as she stared. The rain and the stifling smell of freshly dampened dust had disturbed her sleep. She was wearing a yellow tailored housecoat, a yellow splash against the black tiles and the red awning.

The maid brought a tray with buttered toast, cucumber sandwiches, bread and butter, muffins, marmalade, guava jelly and half of a fruit cake. Then she pushed in a trolley with a china teapot and stacked cups and saucers. Mrs Hanson liked to be ready to offer tea if anyone dropped in. With a full meal and all the crockery on the table she didn't feel lonely. But she only nibbled a piece of toast and ate a dry muffin. The hot tea made her sweat and feel cool.

The maid brought her a book and her spectacles from the bedroom and she tried to read the book on her lap and drink tea at the same time. She couldn't concentrate. She closed the book and told the maid to remove the tea things.

The telephone rang. It couldn't be Cyril, he was in Montego Bay, it might be anybody, she thought. She answered and the caller had got the wrong number. She started reading the book again, Emily Brontë's *Wuthering Heights*, and it still rained and she kept looking up and seeing rainbows in the showers. 'I think I'll go and see Marjorie Fenner this evening,' she thought, 'there might be soldiers there but not that, but just *to talk to a human being.*'

The telephone rang again and a Mr Waite wanted to know if she could give a first-aid demonstration to the Girls' Fellowship at St James' Church next Monday at five o'clock.

She told the maid to bring her the decanter and ice cubes. She started drinking and was able to read more steadily. The rain had stopped and the late afternoon was relaxed and passionless. She gradually forgot about Marjorie Fenner and soldiers and ordinary human beings.

It was hot in the room so Reggie Kendal pushed up the sash window as far as it could go. Then he lay back on the bed, put his right foot on the window-sill and smoked a cigarette. Outside there were stars and his Jaguar and puffs of clouds chasing the moon.

'You know Magnus Philibert, the footballer? I did a lovely appendectomy on him this morning,' he said.

'What's that?' she asked.

'Appendicitis. A two-inch cut. Nice job!'

'But how you can *stan'* the sight of blood, Reggie!' Mona said. 'You doctors!' She was very proud of him.

He smoked his cigarette and thought of a girl he knew in Edinburgh. He didn't think of her face or body, just her name, Peggy Ferguson, and the street she lived on.

Mona twisted over to look at the time on the luminous dial of a small travelling clock on the dressing table.

'You know, ever since I've met you I start to use certain big words that I only used to read in books before,' she said.

She had started preparing to become a doctor's wife. She could hold him in bed but she still remembered Mrs Hanson's sneer. Something held herself and Reggie together. It wasn't sex because she felt certain of him now beyond the need for jealousy. It wasn't race, because though they were half-Indian they were both new Jamaicans who were Jamaicans first and anything else afterwards. The time had passed when the word 'coolie', by itself, carried any offensiveness, and it was often used as a term of endearment and a pet-name for people who had no Indian blood. And in her eight years of sexual activity it happened that Mona had never before had a boy-friend with any percentage of Indian blood. Perhaps she had a subconscious racial memory in the matter but she would have truthfully denied consciously wanting to marry him because they were both half-Indians. What mattered was that she liked him very much, he had money, he had a good profession. If she calculated at all, it was along those lines.

Reggie, on the other hand, was more enlightened and perhaps for that reason more consciously race-minded. In Britain he had enjoyed, over his fellow Jamaicans, the privilege of being identified, on sight, with an ancient civilization and culture and, more latterly, with the Indian struggle for independence. But he never set out to pretend he was from India. Sometimes he denied it outright. Sometimes, if there was no possibility of being exposed as a fraud, he would allow the impression to remain. He would say at other times that he was from 'West Indies', hoping that some people would think he meant the western part of India.

In Jamaica, however, there was a still slowly disappearing minority stigma connected with poverty and sugar plantations and lack of education. He was free in Jamaican society but not privileged. He boarded quite happily with a near-white family on Seymour Avenue and everybody liked him. Once or twice, however, he had to use his profession and his charm and his R.A.F. record, with a very firm pressure, to establish his importance. But Mona was only one of his numerous girl-friends and they came from every racial group. He saw her more often than the others because he thought she was extremely attractive. He knew he was going to marry her and he would probably have given that as the reason.

He felt hungry and he remembered that he had promised to have a drink with another doctor that evening but he didn't want to go yet. He turned and could see Mona's hair spread black against the white pillows. A cloud drifted away from the moon and he saw her face now, the concentrated question in her eyes and there were no words to be spoken.

She waited till they were relaxed and affectionate again and then asked him, 'Why you didn' marry a white girl in England?'

'I didn't want to get married,' he said. 'I could have, though; many times!'

Then he remembered his hunger and his appointment.

'I'll take you to "Rainbow" for a sandwich. Come let's get some clothes on!'

The bricks lay on the unlevelled area near the skeleton of the building. The grass was worn away into a path where the labourers carried water from the pipe that had been erected in the adjoining lot. Only the ground immediately around the building had been cleared and the workers had to be careful of 'gallowasps' (half lizard, half snake) and scorpions. It was a large building and there were many carpenters, stone-masons, women breaking stones for the driveway foundation, labourers digging channels for the plumbing, labourers carrying water. They were talking and laughing and sometimes the women sang, 'Go downa 'Manuel Road, fe go bruk rack stone, gal an bway'.

Three men mixed mortar. One man drew slaked lime from a barrel into a watering-can and poured it over the cement. Another poured more cement and the mixture went from dry to very wet to the right consistency. The man mixing with the spade put the mixed mortar on a wooden slab for a labourer to take to the masons at the building. When the man mixing sweated he collected the sweat from his brow on to his curved forefinger and flicked it, palm upwards, into the mortar. It was nice to see him do that.

Edgar Bailey was laying a brick wall. Two end portions of the wall had already been laid and he was working the length of the wall. The line was held taut from a nail in the joint by a piece of worn heavy stone which he had always used and his father had used before him. He picked up some mortar from the large wooden slab on to his mortar-board and slapped the mortar on the wall, then chopped the mortar into little ridges with his trowel. He put a brick into the bed, shoved it into place, tapped

174

it with the handle of the trowel, deftly caught the squeezed mortar on the edge of the trowel and scraped it off against the edge of the brick. It had taken him less than a minute to lay that brick.

He worked quickly and steadily, occasionally stopping to 'plumb' or to stretch his back and massage the end of his spine. He didn't seem important working on the wall in dirty gym shoes and a blue jockey's cap.

When they stopped working at twelve o'clock he bought four salt-fish fritters and a two-pence loaf from the food vendor. They were wrapped in two pieces of old *Gleaner*. After he had eaten he took his can, which was a tall Veedol-oil tin on which a handle had been soldered, bought half-penny shaved-ice and some syrup from the snowball cart and had a long cool drink. Then he bought a big slice of corn pone from the food vendor.

He went and sat down beside the wall he was building, high enough now to give a little shade from the sun. The building was still in the earliest stage. He knew it was to be part of the new University College but he couldn't imagine its ultimate shape and he felt excluded from its social meaning. He took a paper edition of Jack London's *Call of the Wild* from his pocket and started to read.

Ramsay thought he would miss the *Ariguana*. He should have sent his heavy luggage to the wharf the day before but Mrs Tull and Madge and Rosalie were still packing his suitcases at eight o'clock and he was due to go on board at ten. Just after eight his heavy box and four suitcases were loaded on to a handcart to be pushed to the wharf. Then the family got into a taxi and went to the pier. Sweetness Terrelonge was waiting outside the gate to number one pier when they arrived.

Bobsie took charge of the embarkation. He seemed to know all the policemen and customs clerks and security officers and he got passes for Mrs Tull, Madge, Rosalie, Mabel and Sweetness to go on board. The greatest excitement of the morning was the unexpected appearance of Miss Rhona Tull, their cousin from Orange Town. She was wearing a flounced dress of an improbable shade of purple black and her face shone against the sweat and powder as if she had walked all the way from Orange Town.

'Rhona, mi chile,' Mrs Tull said, embracing her. Mrs Tull had been bottling her feelings and Miss Rhona's surprising appearance gave her an outlet. 'But how you come down today, Rhona, and Ramsay sailing to England this morning, you kno', and you do your hair so nice, Rhona!' Mrs Tull began to cry. 'An' you come all the way from Orange Town jus' to see him off, Rhona!' Miss Rhona did not say that she had come up the day before for the annual Jamaica Union of Teachers' conference; she was too glad to get Mrs Tull's warm greeting. So Bobsie got a pass for her, too.

The crowd that had come to see Ramsay off swarmed all over the ship to the annoyance of some of the transit passengers, mostly English civil servants going on leave, and to the delight of the ship's crew who were quite accustomed to 'these people' behaving like that when one of their relatives is 'going to foreign'.

Miss Rhona was amazed at the size of Ramsay's cabin.

'But it small, eeh, Aunt Alice? You could never pitch an' toss as you have a mind!'

The six women and Ramsay crowded into the cabin. He was to share the berth with a Mr Bent, a middle-aged civil servant going to London to do a Devonshire course in colonial administration. Mr Bent, who was not married and had been seen off at nine o'clock by the assistant secretary of his department, did not like the gentle sway of the ship as it lay at anchor and he was lying on his bunk when the Tull family came in. At first they ignored him and he tried to ignore them but he found that difficult because they were advising Ramsay on the best ways to avoid seasickness. Mr Bent saw no point in leaving the cabin. He had just come into it after being upset by the sway of the ship and the smell of the paint.

Miss Rhona, who was very sociable and polite, saw him suddenly.

'Excuse me, sir. You going to England?'

'Yes.'

'Oh, that's very nice. Excuse me, sir, what you' name is?'

'Mister Bent.'

'You relates to Mister Stuart Bent from Middle Quarters?'

'You mean Florence Bent brother?' Mrs Tull asked before Mr

176

Bent could say anything. He shook his head and the six women stood looking at him.

'No,' he said, 'I'm from Trelawny.' He got up and stepped across to Ramsay. 'Well, seeing as we are travelling together,' he said taking Ramsay's hand, 'we better introduce ourselves to each other. I am Mister Emmanuel Bent from audit office. May we be no more strangers!'

Ramsay introduced him to the six women and Mr Bent went out to brave the paint and the gentle ship-sway.

Bobsie led the crowd to the boat-deck. He went into the bar and bought soft drinks for everybody and one hundred English cigarettes for himself as they were cheaper on board.

Ramsay leaned over the railing with Sweetness standing beside him. He could not bring himself to feel he would miss her just as he had failed to feel any grief over his father's death. He knew what he should feel and wanted to feel. He tried to squeeze himself into the emotion, then he tried to drift into it by letting his mind go hazy, but it didn't work. There always obtruded the concrete images of Sweetness, the details of her body, the wide face and the round eyes that he could see clearly without turning to look at her; and he began to panic slightly that the others were deliberately giving him this chance to say good-bye to his 'girl' and that the ship would leave before he would be able to say the necessary things to each of them.

'They say that when the ship is going out of the harbour you can see sharks following it,' Sweetness said. He didn't reply and she said, 'You know that, Ramsay?' He only thought of the initial loneliness because none of his friends would be there. He seemed to be ignoring her, wanting and not wanting them to leave him now.

'I reely love you, Rams,' Sweetness whispered, trying not to cry, 'I'll be waiting for you when you come back here. You must write me, you kno', and tell me every time you wear the sweater.'

'O.K. I'll write regularly,' he said, and knew it was futile to promise away three years of your life. He remembered that he didn't know if she was pregnant and he didn't ask her because he thought, in the talismanic certainty of the wing of God under which he sheltered, that this 'perhaps child', this remote effect, this possibility that would break his mother's heart, this giving of life and death, could not be his.

A few minutes later three chaps from the Courts Office, Alf-Gordon, Donald Stevenson and Bertram Shaw, came on deck. They made him feel irresponsible again.

'All set?' Alf-Gordon asked. He put his hand round Sweetness' shoulder. 'You going to leave Sweetness with me?'

'Cho, you doan have a chancc,' Bertram said. 'Him will her to me long ago.'

She sighed and looked serious.

'How all of you leave the office at the same time?' Ramsay asked.

'We going back right away,' Alf-Gordon said. 'I jus' borrowed Mr Sweeney's car for five minutes.'

'The bar open, Alf,' Donald Stevenson said. 'Come let's have a quick one for the water,' Alf-Gordon said. 'Come nuh, Sweetness! You doan touch the strong?'

In the bar Alf-Gordon said, 'You know, I want you to do something for me when you go to Paris. When you go to Paris' (he lowered his voice so that Sweetness wouldn't hear), 'I want you to catch a nice piece for me, in Pigalle.'

'How you –'

'In Pigalle,' Alf-Gordon said. 'Remember the name, Pigalle.'

'How long you going for?' Bertram asked.

'I don't know. I mightn't come back,' Ramsay said, with the new irresponsibility: then he saw her eyes. 'No, I'm joking. Three years.'

'By that time you just get a fine accent,' Bertram said and added, half to himself, 'Cup o' tie and a sloice o' kyke.' Bertram knew a lot of English soldiers.

They had two more rapid drinks and went away saying good-bye as if they would be seeing him at work next day.

When they had gone he felt very fuzzy from the quick rum and he kissed Sweetness passionately, a minute-long kiss on the open deck. He was happy.

They found the others and Bobsie had a telegram from Cyril. It was addressed to: 'Head Tull, c/o s.s. *Ariguana*'. It read: UNFORT DELAY CAR LACOVIA BON VOYAGE WRITE ON LANDING CYRIL.

The final farewells were full of merriment because Bobsie, determined there should be no tears, started to clown. Mrs Tull said he wasn't giving her a chance to say good-bye to her son properly. She gave Ramsay a bible and repeated all the instructions that she had been giving him over the past month. When they were at the gangway ready to go ashore they discovered that Miss Rhona wasn't with them. Bobsie found her sitting alone in a corner seat of the main lounge, quite tight. Nobody ever found out how Miss Rhona had got tight on the *Ariguana.*

When the ship pulled out of Kingston Harbour and he could no longer see the people standing on the pier he went to the stern of the ship to see if any sharks were following it, but he didn't see any. He watched the land recede and wondered if the whole journey would be as smooth as that. He walked all over the ship until that got boring. After lunch he went back to the cabin and found that Mr Bent was seasick. He went on deck, sat on one of the wooden benches and remembered Mrs Phillips had said he should write. He tried to think of something to write but his mind froze, he felt lonely, and wondered if the whole journey would be lonely. The ship stopped at Bowden and he watched them loading bananas and went to sleep that night hearing the shouts of the banana loaders.

Next day he met English men and women walking the deck. They smiled at him but didn't speak. Then he met the two Trinidadian girls, a tall, beautiful Indian and a Chinese girl. They were going to study nursing in London. It was the first time he had ever met anybody from the other islands. The Indian girl was full of life: she reminded him of Mona but she was taller, darker and altogether more beautiful. The three of them tried to play deck games but they didn't know the rules for scoring. The Indian girl spoke to the deck steward with authority, the nine hundred miles from Trinidad having made her a seasoned traveller. She was slightly affected. But when she came down to dinner that evening, her long hair swept back into a bun, and wearing a stunning evening-gown Ramsay felt proud of her and of himself among the white passengers.

He went ashore at Port Antonio with the two girls and they walked up to the hospital that overlooks the harbour. The girls sometimes spoke *patois* and to the local people they were obviously foreigners. Walking with them Ramsay had the guilty feeling that the sea journey from Kingston to Port Antonio had made him a foreigner. They tried to teach him *patois* words and they laughed at him because he kept on forgetting while they didn't have any difficulty in remembering words and phrases in the Jamaica dialect.

They left Port Antonio at five o'clock, just at sunset, in an orange glow that was the mood for departure. They were really leaving and that truth had a physical quality, a hospital on a hill, labourers on a wharf, the steady turning movement of a ship. He was alone looking over the side when they passed through the narrow channel of the harbour and headed for the open sea. He tried to remember something about 'Albion' in *Childe Harold* but it didn't fit, and he tried Yeats' 'white breast of the dim sea' but the sea was bright green. He thought of Mrs Phillips' warning and tried Claude McKay's 'I have forgotten much but still remember the poinsettia's red, blood-red in warm December', but it didn't fit either because he did not want to know what to remember. He wanted some words that would tell him what to feel.

He was startled by a voice beside him, 'Take a good look, myte, you won't see that shore again for a long toime!' The sailor's face was familiar, very white with the skin stretched tight across the bones and almost transparent. It was the face of the travelling salesman his mother had seen, and of the priest at Cyril Hanson's birthday party. The sailor disappeared into the ship's bow and Ramsay realized that the emotion he wanted to feel was fear. He never saw that sailor again.

On the second day out they passed Cuba, Haiti.

And then the Atlantic.

VIII

JAMAICA 293.

Ten score and ninety-three years ago the English founding fathers Penn and Venables, Admiral and General, William and Robert, crab-ambushed in Hispaniola, came roaring into Kingston Harbour. They found cattle and horses and disease and Aranaldo de Ysassi and negroes, so they stayed.

Sugar.

The minutes of the Council of Barbados for 1693 record an order for the payment of ten guineas to Alice Mills for castrating forty-two negroes according to the sentence of the commissioners for the trial of rebellious negroes.

. . . that these dead shall not have died. . .

Rule Morgan, rule Britannia over the shapely mulatto women kept by the yonge 'Squires for a certain Use.

Tall ships they were that came riding.

Sam Sharpe came riding over the hills of Westmorland on a white horse with a bible and a mouth of eloquence so they hanged him for his slavery in Montego Bay. And he will always ride those hills on a white stallion.

But they got Emancipation, these slaves, they got religion, these niggers, and they got education, these negroes.

We went looking for the negro and we found a peaceful man who wanted a little quiet at night to copulate in, and a little corner in the afternoon to drink and eat in, and a little space of ground and a nice coffin (*that* was very important) to be buried in but he would bust yo' head if you got facety with him.

We went looking for the joyous abandoned negro laughter of Gertrude Stein's imagination and we didn't find it on the beaches, in the slums, in the villages, under the sea or in the air. But one day we met a negro ex-R.A.F. L.A.C. on King Street and he was really laughing with joyous abandoned laughter. All the shoelace boys on the street and some market-women gathered around him in amazement in front of the Cenotaph as he laughed joyously.

'Hi, my fren',' one of the shoelace boys asked, 'is whey you lurn dat big laugh?'

'I learn it in London,' the laugher replied. 'In Piccadilly Circus, man!'

They all went away trying to laugh like the laugher for they thought it was a good joke to laugh like that. That day King Street was full of intense, nervous, bewildered, negro laugh-learners who laughed in the till-then-unknown broad glow of negro sunshine. That day only.

JAMAICA 293.

Our symbol is The Scuffler.

A negro stands by the fence of Hope Gardens, the watercourse behind him. He holds an empty crocus bag in his hand, trailing it on the ground beside him. He has an interesting face, a long nose, a long pointed mouth and his eyes are quick and restless and always smiling. He is five-foot-four, thin but with good calf muscles, wears three-quarter-length trousers and is barefooted. He is looking at the lanes of Bombay mango trees and the mangoes that never turn to more than a deep shade of crimson. The mangoes are Jamaica's and his. He looks far into the walk and listens. It is a sunny afternoon and the overseer is usually around at this time but the mangoes are his as much as the overseer's. Anyway you can't scuffle without danger. He slips through the barbed-wire fence without touch-it. He hides the bag under each tree, climbs the tree, fills his pockets, climbs down and fills the bag. He is under a tree planning his climb when he hears a dog bark and he hears boots crunching the dry twigs and trouser-legs swishing through the high grass. The Scuffler shoulders his bagful of mangoes and climbs miraculously to the very top of the tree and waits. The dog passes and smells only the wind. The overseer passes with his holster and gun, walks as far as the watercourse and continues in another direction patrolling the place. The Scuffler waits, and very quietly continues to fill the bag. After ten minutes he climbs down and walks quickly and almost soundlessly to the fence. When he is near the fence, the overseer, two hundred yards away, hears someone running through the grass and he fires his revolver, aimlessly, three times. The Scuffler calls the schoolboys to a tree near the Gym and sells the mangoes to them at a penny each. When his bag is empty he walks down the school drive whistling easily, bouncing on his right leg as if he was a defective rubber toy. His eyes are still smiling.

Ah came fram Sin' Mary in the bloom of the year when mi mother die. Ah did have a antie live on Slipe Road an' she take me in as a schoolgirl. Ah did frighten o' Kingston yuh see, doze days – even a tramcar ringin' wid a bell down Slipe Road coulda frighten me outa mi sleep. Me antie was a higgler. *You* never know starvation excep' yuh read it in a book. Sometime we couldn' buy a truppance bread or quattie sugar to mix beverage. Ah never forget, one day we was coming from school an' we see a ole man stretch out on the pavement; he never eat for t'ree day. Yuh doan know what starvation is. Me baby fahder was a shoemaker in Hallman Town, an' for two year we never want for nutten. Den rum mash him up. Ah took a work as a domestic in Sin' Andrew but ah coulda nevah keep a work as a domestic – ah'm a facety gal, you kno'. Doze white people?

JAMAICA 293.

A little black man with the peak of his cap pulled low over the left eyebrow is standing at the batsman's end ready to receive. From the bowler's end he is seen to be looking straight, square down the pitch and his pads are six inches clear of the leg stump. The tall bowler runs twenty yards in, smooth run, smooth action, and the ball is overpitched nine inches wide of the off-stump. There is a flurry of legs and dust in the popping crease and the little man plays the ball on the half-volley with wrists like a spring-lock, hard along the ground to the right of square-leg. When the ball hits the boundary board the little man is standing nearly two feet wide of the off-stump, his face is full turned and his body three-quarters turned in the direction the ball has gone. The next ball is about six inches short of a good length. It does something in the air a bit, and then pitches on mid- and off-stumps, swinging in off the pitch and rising. The little man is suddenly six feet tall and the ball seems to wait until he lifts his shoulders and hooks it with a generous voluptuous sweep of the bat. At the moment of impact the sound of the ball on the bat is like a pistol shot. Mid-wicket, a seasoned Test cricketer, doesn't waste his energy chasing the ball and a spectator returns it triumphantly to the bowler. The little man shuffles across to the next ball and lets it hit his pads and trickle down to gully. The next two balls he pushes defensively into the covers and waits, alert for a misfield, a yard outside the crease. The next ball has a lot of work on it, the bowler putting all the swing of his big body into the delivery. The ball fizzes off the pitch and the little man, quickly but without hurrying, moves inside the line of flight and plays with a slight forward movement of the body, dropping his wrists sharply as the ball hits bat. The perfect glide. In a moment the ball hits the boundary board and fine-leg, unable to stop himself, runs into the crowd. OVER.

The little man stands quietly, his right hand clasping his left wrist behind his back and his bat hanging loosely in his left hand. He watches the field being set and notes precisely, to the inch, where each fieldsman is placed. The little black man seems lonely and god-like standing there, for all the fieldsmen are white and the other batsman is a white Trinidadian.

A woman, not more than thirty-five years old, living in The Dungle in a house that was once a motor-car; sent her eight-year-old son to buy her sixpence-worth of cornmeal. It was her last sixpence in the world. The boy knew it was her last sixpence and he wanted to help her. He went to the shop in Jones' Town and returned with the cornmeal and gave her back the sixpence. She was frightened and fit to cry that the boy had returned with sixpence-worth of cornmeal *and* the sixpence.

Meanwhile
in the new Jamaica
there is progress,
in art and literature the *avant garde* sets up the nine-pin
of THE PHILISTINE and neatly knocks it down,
the racial harmony continues and a new multicoloured

civilization and culture emerges from the heads of the
intellectuals,
the British Army at Up-Park Camp keeps peace drinks beer
takes our women,
there is no Enemy
JAMAICA 293.

PART TWO

WITHOUT COMPASSION

I

Cyril Hanson arrived in Oxford two days before the start of term with a rolled umbrella, a yellow briefcase, a flat cloth cap and an Oxford accent. He was met at the station by Ramsay who had been sent to Oxford direct from Avonmouth by the Colonial Office and who had already spent nearly six weeks there. Cyril walked along the platform chatting to a white American; he was saying that he couldn't get over the rolling greenness of England and the well-kept placid bits of river they had seen after Didcot. He saw Ramsay and shouted from twenty yards off, 'Hullo, Ramsay, o' boy!' Ramsay wondered what on earth Cyril was carrying in the large yellow briefcase. The American seemed quite amazed at Cyril's personality, and Ramsay felt cheated because Cyril really looked as if he had been at Oxford for years and was a member of some newly-invented, aggressive race that would ultimately baffle the ethnologist.

Ramsay had learned by subtle indirections from the English people he met before term in non-undergraduate Oxford that a literary negro was an absurdity, a circus dog that had learned a few tricks. He had come there to learn more tricks and to study, as his father had said, everything a white man could do. What he began to doubt was the genuineness of his reactions and whether he had a right to them. There was a point on the journey from Didcot where the train rounded a gentle curve and suddenly Oxford, spires and towers, dreamed up out of the autumn mist like something in a medieval story. That moment had seemed genuine and his, something his whole colonial education had prepared him for. But never again would Oxford seem so lovely. For now, even before the real stresses of a new environment had begun, he was doubting his right to the sense of personal possession he had for the reanimation of the dead

189

past and inert words in a book which a walk around Oxford gave.

In the taxi the American was saying, a little cynically, as it was a grey October day, 'Towery city and branchy between towers.' Ramsay thought that his own flat Jamaican voice was nearer than the American's to the tune of Hopkins' verse but he felt the American had a right to the quotation, a right that was inalienable for the American, but one to be 'given' to him, a black colonial carefully encircled by the limitations of his supposed subhumanity. He told Cyril that he had met a few West Indian and African undergraduates and Cyril replied brusquely that he had not come to Oxford to meet West Indians. Ramsay thought Cyril was trying to show the American how cosmopolitan he was and how superior to himself whose tiny shirt collar and badly-knotted tie and outsize sports-jacket gave him the general air of a stage negro. The American asked Ramsay, politely, what buildings they were passing. Though Ramsay was glad Cyril had come he resented his presence without quite knowing why. The American got out at Balliol.

'Cyril, what's the accent and the flat cap for?' Ramsay asked.

'When in Rome, o' boy, when in Rome!'

Ramsay saw him to his rooms in Brasenose College and then Cyril had to hurry off to Rhodes House.

The most depressing spot in Oxford for Ramsay was the area between the Radcliffe Camera and St Mary the Virgin's and the High. Somewhere *there*, beneath that commanding church tower he should have felt, without architectural accuracy, the Middle Ages' last enchantment and it was precisely there that Ramsay felt his own disenchantment most acutely. Everything depended on 'who' you were, the whole network of money and history that you were, or in his case, perhaps, on *what* he was. His disenchantment had begun on the first morning that he spent in Oxford. He came down to breakfast in his 'digs' in St John's Street. There were three other people at the table, a Gold Coast African who had taken his degree, an African girl and an English undergraduate who was teasing the girl. They were all talking in a friendly way. Then the English chap pointed to the girl.

'She's blushing!' he said. The laughter faltered for a second and so, recovering quickly, the English chap asked, 'But how do you know when you are blushing?' The tone of the question suggested that he really wanted to know.

'You see it in the eyes,' the Gold Coast man said easily and started talking about a Constitutional Commission that was then at work on his country's future. When the English chap had left the African said to Ramsay, 'I didn't want that English boy to get away with anything. He thinks we are fools!'

For some hours that morning he thought over the incident. Did the English chap want to be insulting, could the impotence of his language to describe the girl's reaction for both user and hearer be taken to imply inferiority; if so, why did he accept such a lame answer? Or was it simply a recognition of otherness? Ramsay saw the civility of the African's inadequate reply as the clue to the whole matter, the layers of general distrust under which real feeling was concealed, the negro's only way of grasping civilization. He was disenchanted because he saw that in the general situation of which this incident was a symptom he could be himself only cautiously, deliberately – at any rate the self which his previous education had formed and which should have found its apotheosis in Oxford. The realization came like a flash of conversion, like Paul being converted to the receiving end of persecution. He wrote to his mother and Madge and Mabel that day. He described the climate and the buildings but he couldn't tell them that the only truth he had found was that a negro's only responsibility is to *endure* and in that way he might ultimately become a man. When he told Cyril about the incident Cyril had said, 'What does it matter if you blush red or blue or black, or don't blush at all? You are too sensitive, man. Nobody hates you!'

'It isn't hate or feeling in that sense,' Ramsay said. 'It is a condition of knowing whether or not you are regarded as a man and the fear, that if you are not regarded as a man, you may not be able to prove that you are a man.'

'But I know I'm a man,' Cyril said. 'I doan' have to prove it.'

'You are exceptional, Cyril,' Ramsay said. 'The world, any world, belongs to you.'

The first undergraduate friend Ramsay made was a white

American freshman, in his college, reading English. They shared an immediate and amused dislike of their literature tutor and an inability to worship old stone. Ramsay was grateful to this man because he took it for granted that Ramsay had read and understood a few books before coming to England and that there were things in England to which he had a right to object. He took tea in the American's rooms. One of the people there was a disillusioned American Rhodes Scholar from Nevada and at New College in his second year who advised them about Oxford conversation.

'Always say something surprising,' he told them. 'That's the secret of Oxford conversation. It doesn't matter how preposterous or outrageous or inaccurate what you are saying is, so long as you arrive at a far-fetched conclusion!'

Ramsay went to a few lectures on Chaucer. The lecturer was a delightful man who looked like a country squire with the same epicurean zest for Chaucer that Chaucer's Franklin had for good living. He also went to one lecture on *Beowulf* but the professor had omitted to bring his spectacles and had held his lecture notes two inches from his face. As what he could hear or follow of the professor's lecture was too abstruse, anyway, Ramsay did not return to the other lectures. Going to lectures proved that he was earning his Colonial Office keep and he felt he learned something at every lecture until his literature tutor told him that he could hardly be expected to survive in the rarefied atmosphere of English Literature. It was after Ramsay had read the tutor a bad essay written in front of a dying fire at four in the morning in the drugged mist of too much alcohol and too many unsobering cups of Nescafe – the type of essay his tutor must have heard very often. 'I don't *think* you should be reading English, you know,' his tutor said. 'Probably P.P.E. or Law might be better. We have a black man in this college whom we have switched to a pass degree and he's doing very well now.'

Ramsay insisted that he had come to Oxford to read English and he would read English. But he stopped going to lectures altogether after that. In the mornings he would take his books and notepaper to the new library at the Union, sit in one of the deep chairs in front of one of Oxford's most comfortable fires and gradually go to sleep. He also read a lot of modern fiction on the first floor of the old library. The Union was a kind of paradise that had transcended colour, with its African librarian and Indian treasurer and yet, even there, with the leaves turning brown and falling in Frewin Hall he read:

I could hear women too, and then all of a sudden I began to smell them. 'Niggers,' I whispered. 'Sh-h-h-h,' I whispered.

It always happened that, when he had begun to feel community with a writer and enjoy a book, that contemptuous word and attitude would pull him up short. He read inattentively and got the mistaken idea that Faulkner was a negro-hater.

Then he met Guy Horne and Oxford took on a definite shape. Guy Horne first saw Ramsay as a figure, three minutes before lunch in late November, trying to huddle into itself in the single shaft of sunlight that touched, apologetically, a small area in the first quad.

Guy Horne was a classless Englishman, a product of the war and statistics and evacuated schools and levelling up, a working-class Londoner who had always spoken with an upper-middle-class accent. He had been called up in the R.A.F. just after the end of the war and had spent his National Service in a perpetual 'gloom session' somewhere in the Middle East. He found himself in Oxford with some surprise and immediately developed an unassailable attitude to the place. He saw Oxford as a free activity theatre in which most undergraduates were acting, in the sense of endeavouring after something, truth, a Blue, a Union reputation, a College Club reputation, a First, a coffee society reputation, the O.U.D.S., a Second, a way of making a living afterwards, a reputation for doing nothing or for knowing 'what's going on'. There were a few others who were not actors, and who felt they shouldn't really be there. They were not spectators because the actors themselves were their own audience. They were the outsiders who spent their time watching the others act or being acted to, and recording everything for private viewing but with less discrimination and sensitivity and inertia than a cine-camera. The outsider drifted cheerfully from place to place, not where the acting was most exciting but where it was most amusing. Guy Horne could sit for an hour in the morning in The Cadena, drinking one cup of coffee and listening. He lived, symbolically, out of college in his first year. He was dark-haired, very short, with a bouncy walk, had no distinction whatever and no affectations.

Guy and Ramsay became friends because (if there are ever real reasons for a friendship) they both liked frivolity, for different reasons, and hated living in England, for the same reason. Frivolity was Ramsay's best escape from his racial and political awkwardness; for Guy, frivolity was the only thing worth pursuing for any sake; and they both disliked the English climate. The first thing they spoke about was Oscar Wilde's wit and Guy was the second person in England who automatically credited Ramsay with ever having read and understood any English literature.

The outsider is *not* an outcast. He *is* invited to parties and to coffee after Hall, and in Hall he sits with the liveliest groups, even at the Boat Club table, but nobody ever expects him to throw a party or to want to be sconced. The first thing Ramsay and Guy did was to find the snippet of conversation which best defined Oxford. After listening for nearly two terms they decided that it was:

'Wher' you off to?'

'Going to listen to some Sibelius. Like to come?'

'Lahv it!'

Guy 'outsidered' everywhere. He even went to lectures and tutorials in that spirit. Realizing that their friendship was regarded by the other men in the college as an oddity, Ramsay and Guy became actors for a while. They started entering rooms with obscure Shakespearean conversation. To enter the Common Room loudly with 'I do not know Maecenas. Ask Agrippa', was sure to turn one or two heads away from *The Times*, and going into the bar at 'The George' with, 'If we compose well here, to Parthia,' could stop the fluted faery voice that was relating what 'Nevil' had said.

The success of his friendship with Guy made Ramsay remember Dr Phillips' advice, 'Forget you are a negro and be a human being for three years.' Guy had what he would have described as an essentially 'bash-on' attitude to colour. He knew it was there but he didn't see it and he really liked Ramsay whose mind and emotions were not noticeably different from his. He genuinely despised those white people who were colour-prejudiced and even gave up an incipient friendship with a girl from St Hilda's whom he brought to tea in Ramsay's rooms because she was uneasy and excessively Christian to Ramsay. The first serious moment in his friendship with Guy was, as Guy reported it, the girl's saying that she couldn't possibly bring herself to kiss a negro. Guy's frank bewilderment, and his explanation that the circumstances of the remark had nothing to do with Ramsay personally, saved the friendship. The frivolity continued but was set in a more sombre key. Dr Phillips' remark became an obsession for, setting aside the ignorance and ingrained insularity of a few people, it really began to seem possible in Oxford, especially when he considered Cyril Hanson.

Cyril had become an immediate success in Oxford. He was known in the Union where he spoke occasionally, and professed to put forward the 'balanced colonial viewpoint'. The other West Indians hated him and the West Africans regarded him with contempt but it didn't matter since Cyril didn't mix with them, anyway. He was very well known in his own college – the scouts liked him and the dons were aware of him. In their first year Ramsay saw very little of him: he visited Ramsay only to report news of himself. One afternoon towards the end of their first term Cyril came in to say that he had been chosen to play soccer for the University against Cambridge. He looked so remarkably fit that Ramsay felt he had to make an athletic comment.

'What position?'

'Inner left,' Cyril said, and his accent modulated back to Surrey College.

'Are you playing the "W" formation?' Ramsay said, 'W' formation having been one of Cyril's favourite sixth-form topics.

'Oh, no, the "W" formation is t-terribly out of date, o' boy.' He was Oxford again. 'We're playing four forwards up and one scheming inside man. I am the schemer.'

'Well,' Ramsay said, 'you've got your "Blue".'

'And after that *Vincent's*,' Cyril said. 'I had the secretary to tea t'other day.'

'Mrs Hanson will be very happy.'

'I've cabled her the great news. Oh, by-the-bye, have you heard? The P.D.P. won a by-election in Clarendon. In the *country*, can you imagine that?'

Ramsay couldn't sleep at night trying to understand Cyril's significance. Cyril was so wonderfully integrated that he had even developed a stutter. True, he had been annoyed about Ramsay's tutor's remark and had encouraged Ramsay to do his best in the preliminary examination and 'show that ass', but it was a personal annoyance over a friend's discomfort. So Ramsay began writing a thesis that would clarify his own thinking. He called it, *Is the Negro a Man?*; then changed that to, *Is the Negro whose ancestors were Slaves, a Man?*; then changed it to, *Is (Can) the Negro, whose ancestors were Slaves, (be) a Man?* The first paragraphs read:

> *This is not a philosophical treatise but an attempt to define emotion precisely. It is necessary to say this because our first proposition may, very loosely, be called 'metaphysical'. Our postulate is – Man is a human existence with a purpose that is universally valid, that is, a purpose which any other human being might accept and live towards without denying his true nature.*
>
> *We must anticipate by declaring uncategorically that, historically, the post-slavery Negro cannot have a Christian purpose. This statement will be demonstrated later and is put here merely as a precaution against unnecessary stalling of the discussion.*
>
> *We will try first to answer three simple questions – (1) Was the Negro a Man before Slavery? (2) Was he a Man during Slavery? (3) Is he (can he be) a Man now?*

After writing these three paragraphs he put the treatise aside. He was to rewrite these paragraphs numerous times in his three years at Oxford, changing the phrasing to greater simplicity or greater elaboration, sometimes omitting the second paragraph altogether.

He felt that this treatise was a particularly vital exercise after he found that Guy was completely ignorant about the truth of colonialism. This came out during a discussion they had about the 'college communist'. The college communist, Sydney Bogan, was a young Englishman reading the extremely respectable school of Literae Humaniores. This and the fact that he was not a Jew made it difficult for the guardians of college honour to deal with him, but he was almost an outcast and was treated with bare-teethed civility. He played a fairish game of tennis, good enough to be in the college team that went, together with the cricket team, to play the 'sister' Cambridge college. The practice is for the coach to stop at every pub on the road for drinking and good fellowship. On this journey no one spoke to the Communist at all and he stayed in the coach at each pub. Ramsay spoke to him frequently and had tea with him. He was a mild Marxist, quite undogmatic but with a passionate hatred of the Conservatives who were the ruling faction in the college. He was not a party member and he thought a revolution would be unnecessary in Britain. He had only a sketchy knowledge of colonial politics but Ramsay felt sad and frightened about this man's pariah status, a status which through any remote occurrence, such as the massacre of all the English people in Jamaica, might easily become his.

Guy, whose parents were definitely workers, had voted Labour in the first post-war general election, but he adopted the accepted attitude to the Communist and one day told Ramsay, with great delight, that in the Union the evening before Bogan had been severely heckled when making a very red speech on the motion, 'That this House deplores the colonial policy of the Government.'

'Of course, everybody knows,' Guy said, 'that the colonies are not ready to govern themselves.'

'Why not?' Ramsay asked. 'Don't *you* think I can govern myself?'

'But I don't think of you as a "colonial" in that sense,' Guy said, and could not explain himself further.

Ramsay gave him a lurid and exaggerated account of the horrors of slavery and imperialism. Guy didn't seem to be very interested. At one point he said, 'All right, Ramsay, if you say so I believe you, but I hadn't thought British administration was as bad as all that.' And then later, when Ramsay swung into the fantasy of himself as a reformer, Guy who had a clear grasp of Ramsay's character said, 'You will never be a politician. You aren't crafty enough.' One thing that interested Guy was the account of Empire Day celebrations in the colonies. At first he didn't believe that little black children marched on that day waving little Union Jacks and singing *Rule Britannia*. The whole thing seemed extremely funny and he laughed himself into hiccups and tears; he said the English are crazy. Ramsay, who had been brought up to sing *Rule Britannia* and wave a Union Jack on Empire Day and then had grown to hate doing it saw, for the first time, because of Guy's laughter, that, beneath the insult, the Empire Day situation was extremely comic. That night before going to bed he made a note for use in his treatise:

> *Only something less than a man would willingly wave his oppressor's flag over his own enslavement and sing a song of triumph which implied that he never never never would be anything other than a slave.*

At the end of the Easter term Ramsay wrote a preliminary examination, then called 'Sections', in the subjects *Old English* and *Chaucer*. He prepared for the examination feeling hate for his tutor's remark and fear that his tutor was right. He read, by chance, the one illuminating book on Chaucer which, though it gave no new knowledge, made the poet for ever the personal possession of a remote, dispossessed, twentieth-century negro in a cold curtained Oxford room. It gave his life for a few weeks a complacent sentimentality. Then he wrote the examination and was the only candidate to get a distinction in *Chaucer*: and his language tutor, a kind portly man who expected only .05 per cent of his students to have any academic pretensions, confessed his surprise that Ramsay had very nearly got a distinction in Anglo-Saxon, too, and had written, to one particular question, the best answer the don who marked the papers had ever seen. But the exam results proved nothing to his literature tutor, who 'farmed' him out to other tutors; or to Ramsay, who kept himself pure from lectures for the rest of his time in Oxford.

He decided there was no point in striving for a 'good' degree in a world where he had no place, in using a degree to prove that he was an intelligent existence. He noted, for use in the third section of his treatise (although the first two sections had not yet been written):

> *The white world can accept the Negro only as a myth, a mythical stupidity, a mythical cheerfulness, a mythical unmorality, a mythical sexuality.*

Ramsay joined, feeling he had a right to, the English Club, and the reaction to him was either incredulousness or pity. The secretary of the club, a clever girl from Somerville was initially one of the pitying, but she was more than that; the pity was a sublimated curiosity.

She was pretty with a black-haired gypsy look that was neither Welsh nor Jew, and her full lips disturbed him. She made him talk about his reaction to literature, some genuine quality in her manner forcing him to fight down the consciousness of pity.

'The things I like,' he said, 'give me a sense of floating and completeness at the same time but you never exhaust the book or story even, and it never exhausts you'.

'How very much that sounds like sex,' Marjorie Stannard said. The Myth, Ramsay thought. Or Freud? It always embarrassed him when a girl he didn't know spoke to him about sex in this clinical way without love or personal passion. She didn't have any suspicions about his semi-Puritan conscience, though this would not have altered the Myth, since his was a purely contemplative morality, a way of looking at an action after it had been performed.

She was very attractive in his room now that she wasn't wearing an overcoat or a scholar's gown. There were certain facts that he tried to isolate as meaningless facts – the white blouse, the line of her throat, her breasts, her fine legs towards the fire. He tried to avoid making the sexual assumptions that would link those facts together, for those assumptions belonged to another country and another time, so he plunged on.

'I can name *Tristram Shandy*, *The Heart of Darkness*, *Portrait of a Lady* (Henry James), and *The Brothers Karamazov*. Incidentally, *The Brothers Karamazov* is the best novel I've ever read. I get this sense of floating frequently in poetry but only rarely in fiction. While one is floating one keeps on asking, "How did he manage to conceive the thing?" It's a personal reaction but I could prove that all these books get their power from perfect construction.'

He turned from the fire to which he had spoken the words and tried to remember what stupid thing he had said that could make her look at him so glassily.

'The trouble about Oxford conversation,' she said, 'is that it tends to become so impersonal, as if life was a vast abstraction.' Then, after a pause, 'Do you write, Ramsay, yourself?'

He thought of lying but instead said, 'No', quickly.

She was looking at him and smiling eagerly. That was the cue, as he understood civilized conversation, to introduce another abstraction wrapped in a surprising metaphor. He had just chosen the idea and the metaphor and was beginning to shape the sentence in his mind when she said, 'D'you know, there is something *very* silly that I very much want to do.'

'What's that?'

'I'd like to touch your hair. It *is* silly, isn't it?'

This was genuine, blurted out. She sat on the arm of his chair. 'It is very *soft!*' she said, as if Ramsay might not know, her surprised fingers still trying to believe this softness. 'It's *very* soft.'

He knew that her curiosity went further than that but he resented being humanized from a golliwog into a lover. That way he would have no validity as a person. He shook his head irritably.

'Don't you want me to do that?' she asked.

'No, no, it isn't that.' He could not say what it was and she had been very sympathetic to him. She went back to her chair and they talked about English literature.

'She *did* come here with that Myth in her mind,' he thought, while she was talking. And she thought, 'He is excessively shy and alone in this country and so *much* in need of friendliness.'

He did not go back to the English Club and he refused her invitation to tea. After two terms he did not recognize her at first when she stopped him in the street.

In their first summer term Guy and Ramsay became close friends of the Prince. The Prince was a tall elegant sober young African who had spent a few years at an English public school. He was faintly amused by Oxford and would have been an outsider if he didn't get so many invitations to tea and sherry parties. He was much more initiated into Oxford life than Guy or Ramsay. Once during Eights week, though he hadn't been to the races at all, he was invited to a party on the Christ Church barge. He got out of the Meadows by climbing into Merton Gardens and then he arrived in Ramsay's room with his speech slightly muddled and his usually correct Trilby hat at a rakish angle and he looked generally like a slightly tight ambassador. The Prince was a symbol of what Ramsay would never be. His ancestors had never been colonial slaves and though his country had been conquered in almost equal battle by a European nation it was his own. Ramsay envied him his simplicity of purpose. To the Prince questions of racial discrimination and imperialism, though extremely important, were subordinated to his personal responsibility to return and work for his people. Oxford was only a small part of his preparation for that work. Even his amused progress through the Continent during the vacations fitted in with that purpose. He did not need an abstract treatise. He was this Prince, with this royal tradition behind him, and this commitment for life. He was not pompous and he was extremely witty, especially in his own language. Guy and Ramsay knew that he would one day return in triumph beside his Emperor, as cynical to the deference he would then be given as people were now cynical about his complexion. He was completely a man and proof to Ramsay that slavery and continued domination dehumanized a people for ever. Ramsay was ashamed that he had ever enjoyed the monstrous caricature in Waugh's *Black Mischief.*

Out of his friendship with the Prince and invitations which both he and Cyril received to meet the English Queen, Ramsay got another idea for his treatise. Cyril was much more visible during summer because his cricket was not quite up to university standard. He had played well enough in the trials, though, to be made an Authentic almost immediately. He came in one day to invite Ramsay to a Drake Club dinner. The Drake Club is a collection of Commonwealth undergraduates, mostly Rhodes Scholars, who invite important public men to address them on topics 'affecting' the Empire and Commonwealth. Ramsay had the impression that it was slightly more reactionary than the Conservative Club. Ramsay was in his most sarcastic mood because Cyril evidently thought he would be honoured by the invitation.

'What the hell you joined a club like that for, man?' Ramsay asked. 'What do you do there? Sing *Rule Britannia* after dinner? Weren't you a socialist at one time?'

'Oh, yes. 'Course. But you've got to find out what the other man is thinking.'

'You can read it in the *Telegraph*,' Ramsay pointed out.

'Well, *really*, nothing can happen to you if you have dinner at the Drake Club,' Cyril said, wearily. 'You sit beside Conservatives in Hall, 'ntchu? Come, don't be tiahsome.'

'What you mean "Don't be tiahsome"?'

'That's the way the word is pronounced here, "tiahsome" –'

'I would be contaminated for the rest of my life!' Ramsay shouted.

'My dear Ramsay, you've got some sort of inferiority complex,' Cyril said.

'O.K., O.K. But you don't realize that you and I *are* inferior; it's not a complex, it's a fact,' Ramsay said, to deflate Cyril a little. 'Thank you very much, Cyril, but I cannot come, I have married a wife.'

'Oh, by the way,' Cyril said getting up and striding slowly about the room, 'I'm going to be presented to the Queen on Thursday, at Rhodes House.'

'So am I,' Ramsay said.

'No. I'm perfectly sayrious.'

'So am I. At Goldsmiths' Hall in London on Tuesday.'

'In London, eh?' Cyril said very crestfallen. 'Rather a long way to go just to meet the Queen.'

'You brute! Ah catch you!' Ramsay said, and they burst out laughing. It was the laughter of Jamaica and Surrey College and for a moment they saw themselves, from outside themselves, as two perfectly ludicrous negroes in an Oxford room.

Cyril recovered his poise. 'You really mean that?' he asked.

Ramsay showed him the embossed invitation card.

'Come on, Head, let's go and have a drink.'

They went into 'The Bear' and Ramsay was proud that Cyril was wearing a 'Blue' scarf and knew most of the undergraduates in the pub. Perhaps Cyril represented the only possible compromise.

'Heard from Mrs Phillips,' Cyril said. 'Asked after you.'

'Oh, yes?'

'Pat is going up to Girton next term.'

'Who?' Ramsay asked. He knew quite well who Pat was.

'Patricia Phillips, don't you know?'

'Oh, you mean the "tennis-anyone" girl,' Ramsay said. Oxford had given him the phrase but it seemed spontaneous.

Cyril drank some beer and nodded.

'She's a very good games player, you know.'

'I can think of a few games I'd like to play with her,' Ramsay said. Cyril grinned. It was an extraordinary grin but it wasn't quite right. It looked like the Cheshire Cat's grin drawn by a cubist. Cyril had seen an ex-major who was telling a dirty story grin something like that and he decided to copy it but he hadn't got it quite right. He only looked idiotic. Ramsay remembered how perfectly Patricia had smiled in the English way.

The Queen arrived in Oxford on the next Thursday and Cyril was presented. He wore morning coat, cravat and topper and performed a long-remembered genuflection when the Queen shook hands with him. Ramsay displayed his invitation to Goldsmiths' Hall prominently on his mantelpiece, but he didn't go to London. He was not unimpressed by royalty and ceremonial and he would gladly have gone to meet the Queen of the Netherlands. The trouble was that this Queen was supposed to be *his* Queen and he felt he was a fraud who had no inherent right to be her subject. He added a sentence to his treatise:

The Negro finds it difficult to accept a personal sovereign because a modern sovereign represents a racial memory that the Negro has lost.

The summer term contained certain facts – the sun again, the long twilights, the river, garden productions of Shakespeare, but Ramsay could not recover the enchantment he had lost on the first day. He drifted with Guy from place to place with good appetite as one takes one's pleasure in any university in any country. They hired a gramophone and borrowed classical records and with the curtains drawn, shutting out the sunlight, they argued themselves into believing they were in another world. Guy wrote what can only be called 'smoky' verse and Ramsay, who had no ear for music, tried to learn to read a score. But mostly they drifted about and got bad reports from their tutors at the end of term. Guy went off to Austria and Ramsay stayed in college getting drunk every night with those chaps who had just finished taking their finals or with those who came up later for 'vivas'. Then there was nobody left in college but himself. It was a centreless existence: he wasn't even lonely. He went into 'digs' and spent every day reading fiction in the Union Library until the Union, too, was closed. Then he went to Paris for a week.

He did all that one could do in Paris for a week in the middle of August, the buildings, the shows, the people to be looked at. It was an irritating week. Paris was interesting but nothing happened except that he met a girl from British Guiana he knew at Oxford who asked him if he had a copy of yesterday's *Times*, he was held up and 'frisked' by the police twice very late at night and some whores in Montmartre mistook him for an American and swore at him. When he returned to Oxford there was a letter from Guy Horne waiting for him.

'Dear boy,

I have an excellent idea for a birthday party in your honour next summer. When were you born by the way? We'll have three punts down the river. Punt 1 – Banks of flowers, a chorus of *gypsy* girls singing a Greek ode in French composed by myself. Punt 2 – You, surrounded by very very blonde girls and champagne bottles. Punt 3 – Myself and a be-bop band, playing *Tull's Delight*. Do you think that will get me a fellowship in a cry of dons at All Souls?

I got drunker and drunker and Vienna was lovelier and lovelier.

Seriously though, I have met two wonderful Nigerians at London University library where I go daily (being broke) to read some history. We have lunch together and I am beginning to grasp the colonial problem. What a mess!

I saw the Prince in Paris walking down the Champs-Elysées with *the* most gorgeous piece on that remarkable street.

Don't be depressed, Ramsay. Remember,
>"The Lillie of a Day
>Is fairer farre in May."

You must hold that lily gently in your medieval hand and if you see that kind Lord on the High (but only on the High) *please* give it to him.

"He (you, not the kind Lord) was likely had he been put on, to have proved most royally."

Ever,

Guy.

P.S.– Come to London and see Helpmann's face and les girls!'

Ramsay was not depressed but restless. He did a month's half-hearted reading in the Radcliffe Camera. The year had brought one truth but it could not be transliterated into his treatise. It was the memory of a diminuendo from his week in Paris,

>doucement, bébé, doucement
>you black man, you blaack maaan,
>la bouche, bébé, la bouche!

The apotheosis of the negro. He wrote in his treatise:

>*The Negro is not a man but an inconsistent myth created by himself in the white man's image.*

II

Ramsay was in his second year when the West Indians in Oxford acquired a flat in Beaumont Street. There were about twelve West Indians in Oxford and Ramsay knew eight of them quite well. At that time West Indians in Oxford had not yet begun to make much of the fact that they were 'West Indians' – they met each other as coloured men in a white world unless they came from the same island.

The flat was rented by a Trinidadian and a Grenadan who were third-year law students. It was a ground-floor flat (basement kitchen) with a spacious sitting room, cluttered up with furniture. At whatever time of night or day Ramsay went there at least five West Indians were perfectly at home in the sitting room. Whenever the talk became too noisy the two men in their third year would lock themselves into the little bedroom off the sitting room and try to work.

These men were not names. They were islands. And, contradicting Dr John Donne, each was an island entire of itself. They were Trinidad (1), Barbados (2), Jamaica (2), Bahamas (1), Grenada (1).

Who were these men? What were they like?

They were –

TRINIDAD. *Born:* Port of Spain, 1923. *Educated:* Queen's Royal College, 1934–43; Columbia University, B.A., 1946; The Queen's College, 1946, reading law. *Favourite pastimes:* Arguing about Union Debates and the colour problem in U.S.A. *Personality:* Sardonic wit, elegant dresser, good French accent. *Opinions:* Believed West Indian Federation would be either impossible or unpleasant and that JAMAICA 2 advocated Federation only in the hope of getting a big Federal job. *Complexion:* Black.

BARBADOS 1. *Born:* Speightstoun, 1927. *Educated:* Harrison College (Barbados Scholarship), 1945; Hertford College, 1947, reading law. *Favourite pastime:* Discussing law and cricket. *Opinion:* That everybody except himself was stupid. *Complexion:* Light brown.

BARBADOS 2. *Born:* Bridgetown, 1928. *Educated:* Harrison College (Barbados Scholarship), 1946; Worcester College, 1947 – read law for two terms then switched to English. *Personality:* Charmingly oblivious of other people. *Occupation:* Creative writer. *Publication:* ELEGY FOR OLD ISLANDS (Barbados Advocate Press, 1947). *Opinion:* 'In literature today creative writers, especially those in newly-emergent countries, become immortal during their life-time. I *too* want to be immortal.' *Complexion:* Black.

JAMAICA 1. *Born:* Sligoville, 1920. *Educated:* Sligoville Elementary School; Tutorial College, Kingston, 1933–1938; Keble College, 1946, reading P.P.E. Served in R.A.F., Flying Officer, 1941–46. *Personality:* Rabelaisian. *Favourite swearword:* Small-islander. *Special knowledge:* White women. *Complexion:* Black.

JAMAICA 2. *Born:* Kingston, 1923. *Education:* Halfway Tree Elementary School; Wolmer's Boys' School (Centenary Scholarship), 1941; Toronto University B.A. (Modern Languages), 1945; Jesus College, 1946 – B.Litt. student. *Favourite pastime:* The cinema. *Opinion:* Fanatic advocate of West Indian Federation. *Complexion:* Sambo.

BAHAMAS. Age and early education unknown. St Catherine's Society, 1947, reading P.P.E. L.A.C. R.A.F., 1943–47. *Idiosyncrasy:* A brand new bicycle, licensed, with lights. *Special line:* Economic double-talk. *Complexion:* Black.

GRENADA. *Born:* St George, 1926. *Educated:* St George's Secondary School; University College, 1946, reading law. *Personality:* Gentle, genteel, fascinated by Oxford. *Favourite pastime:* Discussing law with TRINIDAD.

One winter afternoon Ramsay walked into the sitting room of the flat to find all the islands listening to something BARBADOS 2 was reading.

> '"Ro-mance me! Ro-mance me!" Rose Reynolds said as the pole with which I was punting stuck in the mud. "Ro-mance me!" Rose was a stout healthy black Jamaican girl who had come up for a week-end with Fay Grant.
> "Is that a song, 'Romance me'?" Charles Lindsay, my English friend asked.
> We dissolved into laughter and the pole kept sticking in the dissolving mud.'

Ramsay took off his overcoat and asked BARBADOS 2 what he had been reading.

'It's a novel I'm writing,' he said, 'called This Queen of Romance.' He was sitting on the floor near the fire that didn't have much coal on it and he was wearing a white turtle-necked sweater. 'It's symbolic. The point is that Rose Reynolds' "romance" was the thing farthest from Matthew Arnold's mind when he said Oxford was a "queen of romance". When Rose says "romance" she means "sex" and she is therefore the new queen of romance as she explodes in from the negro world to degenerate our ivory-tower sensibilities.'

'What world you belong to?' JAMAICA 1 asked. 'You look kinda black to me.'

'I belong to no world. I am an artist.'

'You're talking crap.' JAMAICA 1 said. 'You read any critics? They'll shot you down in flames, o'boy. And there's nothing looks so stupid as a bare-arsed nigger being shot down in flames.'

They all laughed.

'Don't fool yourself, boy, I'm not writing for any white critics to say my work isn't white,' BARBADOS 2 said. 'I'm writing for negroes to read.'

'So you admit you are a negro,' JAMAICA 1 said.

'Look. I'm a negro. O.K., I'm a negro. But I am a negro outsider. If I'm drunk I laugh at the whole bloody lot of you. If I'm sober I just wonder what it would be like if the world was to explode and God tried again to see if He couldn't make everybody black or everybody white. I am detached.'

'Choh, read on again, man,' Ramsay said.

'Right. Now this is another episode. You see I'm trying to prove that the colour-question can be used as the basis for a new kind of fiction. If the material is really new the treatment will also be new.'

'O.K.,' Trinidad said. 'We've heard the theory. Press on!'

'Right. Two characters, Jamaicans, Mr Popsie Grant and his wife Fay are sent by the Colonial Office to one of those British Council courses in the Cotswolds because they complain that they miss the Blue Mountains very much. Popsie is reading Law at an Inn of Court and Fay works in London. O.K.? Well, at this course they meet an English Duke, the Duke of Clintonshire, who is at the course because he wants to see what the new levelling-up is about, or something like that. Anyway, he is there. He is over seventy and is harmlessly eccentric. He finds the course full of middle-class and working-class people he can't abide and so he makes friends with the Jamaicans, but that is another episode.'

'You don't have a general plan?' Jamaica 2 asked. 'You *should* have a general plan.'

'No, I'm building it up in sections, like a mosaic. Listen.

'The Duke of Clintonshire took his two Jamaican guests to visit one of the stately homes in the neighbourhood. Mr and Mrs Grant were terrified by the two great danes they saw on the white porch and by the liveried footmen who seemed to Mrs Grant to be vaguely connected with the police. As soon as they went in Mrs Grant dodged into the nearest lavatory, locked herself in and stayed there until the Duke and Popsie had gone upstairs and had returned to say that nobody was at home. The Duke said they would try again next morning.

Before leaving the Duke's home next morning Popsie and Fay asked the Duke to make certain to explain exactly who they were. On one occasion the Duke had forgotten they were his guests and had set his own great danes on them.

"But why?" the Duke asked. "You are my guests!"

"But it's kine-a awkward you know, Mr Duke," Fay said.'

'You mean to tell me that this Jamaican woman is so dark that she calls the Duke, "Mister Duke"?' JAMAICA 1 asked. 'That's stupid. You better write another story.'

'There's nothing stupid in that,' TRINIDAD said.

'Don't be insular.'

'"O, yes, of course, quite," the Duke said.

"You know what you can say," Fay plotted. "You can say that Popsie was at Axford University with yo' son Nigel."

"Nigel?" the Duke asked, trying to remember.

"Doan you have a son named Nigel?"

"Hold on!" The Duke consulted a large diary.

"Oh, yes, of course! Nigel died in the war. Silly of me to forget that."

That morning they braved the dogs and footmen and waited at the top of a stately staircase for Lady Bracebottom to receive them. She arrived from a dark corridor in a flurry.

"This is Mrs Grant – the best of my wives," the Duke said. "And this" (pointing to Popsie) "is Phillips, my aunt's cousin. And this (indicating a young lady in immaculate white who was standing near them) "is my brother-in-law's niece, Augustina."

A bewildered Lady Bracebottom found herself shaking hands with her own chambermaid.'

BARBADOS 2 started searching through his folder for another episode.

GRENADA went out to make some tea for himself in the basement kitchen. When he got to the door JAMAICA 2 said, 'You going upstairs? It's not your turn today, fellow.' They all laughed. Someone started to play a Scarlatti sonata on the piano in the flat above, and they were silent for a few minutes looking at the rich walnut panelling of the room and the heavy old damask curtains and hearing this other music that tried to separate them from the selves that they had come together to preserve.

BARBADOS 2 read another episode from his manuscript and they continued playing this game of winter frustration which, beneath the frivolous civilized enquiry, was as earnest as the need to keep warm or to keep sane.

'You've lifted a whole paragraph from Flaubert, isn't it?' JAMAICA 2 asked.

'No. From Dorothy Parker, actually,' BARBADOS 2 admitted. 'But I'm only a negro. I've got to copy.'

'Ah, there you are again,' JAMAICA 1 said. 'You admit you are a negro.'

'I never said I wasn't a negro. I said I do not belong to the negro world. That's a different matter altogether. My point is that I must copy because I'm a good artist and – '

He was interrupted by a crashing sound as if the building was caving in. Above them was a sudden hole in the ceiling and the slippered foot of a young Englishman hung stupidly through the hole. He pulled himself out of the hole and the slipper fell into the room.

'They had a fire last night,' TRINIDAD explained, when they had stopped laughing. 'They had a party and burned a hole in the floor. That man is mad.'

A very red-faced man peered in at the door. He was blond and large with a slight resemblance to Oscar Wilde. Phillip Cooper-Chaundy had 'gone down' from Christ Church two years before but he had only got as far as Beaumont Street. He wasn't a don and he wasn't a writer but he knew a lot of writers.

'I say, I'm t-terribly sorry,' he said speaking directly to TRINIDAD. 'You know, I put a carpet over the place that was burned and then forgot I'd put the carpet there.' He looked at the hole in the ceiling. 'Not much damage, really. I'll get it fixed tomorrow.'

JAMAICA 1 handed him the slipper. 'Good job you didn't come through,' he said.

'Isn't it?' Cooper-Chaundy said and went upstairs to continue playing Scarlatti.

'He isn't a bad chap at all,' BARBADOS 1 said. 'I don't think he's prejudiced at all. Every time he meets me on the street he speaks to me.'

'Oh, you might just as well say our friend upstairs isn't prejudiced either,' TRINIDAD argued, 'and what will that prove?'

'Our friend upstairs' was a woman of about thirty who lived alone in the top flat of the house. All the West Indians, with the exception of Ramsay, BARBADOS 2 and BAHAMAS, knew her well.

She was half Irish, separated from her husband, and was a typist in a solicitor's office.

'The only thing it proves,' JAMAICA 1 said, 'is that in this country we are forced to live immoral lives. That's all.'

'Who's forcing you?' BARBADOS 2 asked.

BAHAMAS had been trying for the last five minutes to get a word in but nobody paid any attention to him. He was a quiet man who never argued; but once in a while he would come out with a statement which, if it was comprehensible, was beyond dispute. He was holding his hand up permanently like a schoolboy asking for permission to speak.

'I'm a communist,' BAHAMAS said, ignoring the laughter that followed TRINIDAD's remark. 'I'm a communist because I am uncivilized and I hate!'

'You are the most civilized man in here,' TRINIDAD said. 'Look at your new bicycle and the fine three-piece suit you are wearing!'

'You don't understand western civilization,' BAHAMAS said. 'It's a matter of techniques. You can't eliminate hate with techniques. Machines have nothing to do with hate. There are two tendencies in the world today – either you make the whole world two-toned and hate-festered or you make the world a colourless red and free. And *that* red is not the colour of blood – it's the colour of a new society. That's another aspect of the dialectic between man and nature. The capitalist machine has conquered nature and now the machines have conquered man. The dominance of the machines is breeding a new man to subdue the machines again, and the new man is a communist and he is both black and white.'

There was a vague air of lunacy in the room while they sorted themselves out.

'Dixisti,' TRINIDAD said, looking profound.

'But a negro is a man,' JAMAICA 2 suggested.

'Only in war-time,' BAHAMAS said, darkly.

'Quite,' TRINIDAD said with his usual air of summing-up. 'But hate is a very untidy sort of emotion.'

'The *type* of the emotion is unimportant,' BAHAMAS said. 'Nothing could be more untidy than that you fellows are carrying on with that woman upstairs.' He had a particular dislike for the woman but he never explained why. He put on his overcoat.

BARBADOS 2 who had been writing all the time said, 'Listen to this. It's the first two sentences of *This Queen of Romance.*

'If you take any group of ten healthy men in a bar anywhere in the West Indies, whether they married or not, within three hours of their leaving that bar one of them will have slept with a woman; within twenty-four hours eight of them will have slept with a woman; and within two days all of them will have slept with a woman. This is known as the West Indian condition.'

'You mustn't write that sort of thing,' TRINIDAD said. 'People might take you seriously and think you are an anthropologist.'

There was a knock on the door. The woman who came in, 'our friend from upstairs', was not particularly pretty at first sight. Her teeth protruded slightly when she talked and her cheek-bones were too high. She was a well-built blonde, inclining to stoutness. She was physically attractive because you could see that she was nearly thirty yet she looked much younger. She said, 'Having a big argument?'

'Hello, Deirdre,' TRINIDAD said. 'Been in long?'

'I went to the pictures,' she said. She sat on the divan between the two Jamaicans.

'What about cooking some supper for us,' TRINIDAD said.

'Sure,' Deirdre said. 'For how many?'

'You think I'm going to feed these clots? For two, of course, my dear Deirdre.' She got up to go. 'Raoul is in the kitchen. Don't start cooking anything with him.'

She turned at the door, stuck out her tongue at him and then laughed, looking very pretty and happy and innocent.

The Jamaicans and BARBADOS 1 left.

'Is her name really Deirdre?' Ramsay asked.

'No, it's "Veronica". I just call her Deirdre, as in Synge,' TRINIDAD said. 'She's full of tragedy.'

'Has she read the play?' BARBADOS 2 asked.

'The part of her that is Irish doesn't read at all,' TRINIDAD said.

TRINIDAD, who was wearing a red smoking-jacket, saw Ramsay

and BARBADOS 2 to the street-door, the perfect host. They stood in the cold and listened to him talking.

'That exploration of romanticism, is an excellent idea,' he said. 'Have you read *Cyrano de Bergerac*? You can't really understand romanticism without it. I'm probably sentimental, you see, but I had a girl who wept just as Roxane does in the balcony scene,

> 'C'est à cause des mots
> Que je dis qu'elle tremble entre les bleus rameaux
> Car vous tremblez, comme une feuille entre les feuilles;
> Car tu trembles! car j'ai senti, que tu le veuilles
> Ou non, le tremblement adoré de ta main
> Descendre tout le long des branches du jasmin
> Oui, je tremble, et je pleure, et je t'aime, et suis tienne
> Et tu m'as enivrée!'

He closed the door softly. TRINIDAD was very good at closing doors softly.

BARBADOS shuffled off to Worcester College and Ramsay stepped into the Oxford night resenting the bite in the air and the gathering fog. He alone, and perhaps BAHAMAS was not integrated. When he got home he made a note for his treatise:

It is remarkable that the Negro ever writes at all. In order to endure he must be cunning and silent. Jazz is a mode of silence.

Ramsay tried to analyse his friendship with Guy Horne. There seemed to be far less compromise in it than could be expected and ideally it should have been a rich friendship from the personal and racial contributions that each brought. But Ramsay regarded it as distinguished by two features, its impermanence and the sense he had of Guy's otherness. Guy for his part took the friendship in his stride but deep in his consciousness there was a slight idealization of Ramsay as a kind of 'dusky potentate' (one of the inventions of the 'twenties; the other is the 'beautiful virile animal'), not in fact (for he knew Ramsay's dispossession), but as a useful fiction which kept his own racial conscience quiet. There was no impersonal reason why Guy should not one day be the Governor of Jamaica and sentence Ramsay to prison as an agitator. This realization led Ramsay back to his desire to smash the system that made him need perpetual explanations for Guy while Guy was quite clear about him; that could turn a gentle harmless person like Guy Horne into a tyrant. Ramsay could see clearly that he was up against something more formidable than economic imperialism, because Guy could use phrases like 'nigger brown' or 'work like a nigger' easily, as if they were dead metaphors. The position that Ramsay was gradually drifting towards, and which he tried to resist, was that 'racism' (which included the consciousness of race) was antagonistic to 'man' and that his education should place him, in any controversy, firmly on the side of man. He tried to resist this position because it seemed to him an excessive, inhuman refinement where, instead of turning the other cheek, you deny that you've been slapped at all. His friendship with Guy became a series of isolated gestures that were fundamentally human, but the gestures had to be made within a carefully constructed world which Guy had almost a genius for constructing. And after each gesture Ramsay wondered just what it was that he had escaped from. The 'world' was made up of bits chipped from European philosophy, music, art, poetry, an esoteric vocabulary, the nice conduct of a clouded cane, of a sherry glass. For Guy these things were not serious: for Ramsay they were serious but had no personal permanence because the background from which he judged them was borrowed.

Ramsay wondered how it was that although all the other West Indians, even, to some extent, Cyril, would have agreed with this statement of his own predicament and would have translated it into their own terms, they had found a satisfactory personal solution. They didn't seem to be drifting, they seemed satisfied with the society at home into which they would fit as lawyers and economists and to which they would add yet another stratum of snobbery. One West Indian who seemed sublimely happy and in no predicament was a man at Lincoln College who would be considered maladjusted in conventional psychology. He was dark brown and he dressed in the 'arty' manner. He kept away completely from all other West Indians. The fact that he was permanently attached to the Experimental Theatre Club gave the impression that he was reading English. Ramsay had met him and been impressed by the soft glaze of his eyes and the softness of his hands. The Beaumont Street West Indians dismissed him as being a homosexual, a condition they would have laughed at in anybody else but which they despised in a coloured man. Yet Ramsay wondered if this man, setting aside inherent qualities, was not much more civilized than the rest of them. This man would always be on the side of humanity in the debate and if he was ever conscious of his colour – if Cockney children ever shouted 'hello, Blackie' at him – he regarded it as a childish habit, like the old habit of shouting 'Beaver' at a man with a beard. For him there would be no lack of continuity. His life had no need of a background against which it could define itself.

Guy's illness in December that year first dissipated the view Ramsay was getting of things and then brought it into sharper focus. A mass radiography campaign discovered that Guy had a spot, about the size of a penny, on one of his lungs. His parents made a great effort and sent him to a sanatorium in Switzerland. Ramsay could not remember ever having been so sad at parting from anyone, his dead father, the rest of his family, Sweetness Terrelonge. Guy wasn't seriously ill – the spot would clear up, with proper treatment, in about six months – but they walked around Oxford that December in infinite gloom. At first the effect on Ramsay was to make him turn his back, despising himself, on the 'racism' which should logically have made him indifferent to Guy's illness, and yet he remembered, with another kind of loathing, those slaves who at emancipation had, out of pure loyalty, remained with their white masters. Guy's illness was the intrusion of seriousness into a frivolous world but that couldn't shatter the world because, in the sense of being some-thing they had faith in, it had not existed and Ramsay was still generally disenchanted. When he focused his attention on the physical aspect of Guy's illness there was obviously no need for sadness, because *there* they were animals together and he could feel only the slight fear that he, too, might have contracted the disease.

The odd thing was that after Guy left for Switzerland at the end of the year Ramsay was merely aware of his absence but did not 'miss' him in the romantic sense of 'feeling incomplete'. The frivolity continued, there were other 'outsiders', and Ramsay realized that Guy was only, and could only be, a charming engineer who taught him how to build worlds which were different from the real world. It was in the real world that they had failed to be humans, the glances on a bus, a waitress's disbelief that Ramsay would be eating the same food as Guy, the unconcealed surprise in those around that Guy and Ramsay, this black, were *actually* discussing Strindberg before the theatre lights went down. He had got from Guy an inverted knowledge of what his father had called 'what a white man can do', and he had learned his delightful lesson against a background of despair. Guy had been neither a catalyst nor even the mildest stimulator.

Ramsay now spent more of his time at Beaumont Street where there was no 'otherness', not even Deirdre, and his real stimulator was the Barbadian who was working steadily on his novel. He didn't see Cyril Hanson often, partly because Cyril was busy playing soccer and then busy visiting Patricia Phillips in Cambridge and then busy eating dinners in London and partly because he had said to Cyril, 'You don't want to change society radically because that way you'd be out of a job. I dislike any profession that is built on human weakness. It smells of the midden.'

He got a letter from Guy.

Dear Boy,

Really, I'm most awfully well (that was sometime a paradox) and I'm improving, as they say. The doctor visits me every day and there are nurses, very unHemingway, if you know what I mean, but my French is doing well.

I miss Oxford and things. How is the Prince?

Honest I'm not an anarchist (or any kind of 'ist') but I shouldn't mind if the whole world were destroyed so long as that would give you an important place in it because you are the most human human being I know. (I wish I could put that into Latin.)

My window looks out on mountains and I think of ski-ing again – a white uncomplicated pure world, graceful silent patterns, an abstract sublime world. Perhaps, perhaps. Isn't the English climate feelthy!

If you are in London look up my parents, won't you, Ramsay?

I read much of the night and should therefore get a good fourth when I come back.

In the meanwhile lay this to thy heart and farewell.

Guy

This letter gave Ramsay a shock. It surprised him that Guy, with whom he had never discussed his predicament or his treatise could have seen so much and he was ashamed that Guy and not he had made this serious gesture of fundamental recognition. He felt that Guy could never be a colonial governor.

Ramsay drifted about now with a new confidence. Beaumont Street nationalism gave him the comforting illusion of belonging to a recognizable, delimiting society and he played with Oxford as a cat plays with a mechanical mouse. At the end of his second year he went to a party in Exeter College. Sometime during the party he found himself facing a girl undergraduate who had an attractive face that was slightly distorted by the effort to look clever and be sophisticated at the same time.

'What're you reading?' she asked.

'English.' The girl looked at him with O-ed eyes and mouth for a moment.

'How very unlikely!' she said.

For the first time he understood 'blind rage'. He felt a small explosion at the back of his head and for a few seconds he couldn't see at all. His muscles tensed to slap that stupid, sardonic face. But he had learned another way. He slipped past the implications of her surprise and went on smoothly to talk about Shelley's *The Cenci*, which he had never read.

'I have just been re-reading *The Cenci*,' he said, and watched the girl's face twitch with annoyance at being out-manoeuvred in undergraduatemanship by this '?'. He talked about *The Cenci* as if it were Oscar Wilde's *Duchess of Padua* which he *had* read. He talked steadily from sentence to sentence for five minutes and the girl couldn't get a word in. And he knew the right moment to leave a sentence unfinished in the air.

'Although what I've been saying is more appropriate to Oscar Wilde than Shelley – '

He turned abruptly from her as if she had never existed and

then started to talk to somebody else. *She has a nerve*, he thought; *she still has to learn that trick even if I do come from the depths of the jungle. Impudent strumpet*, he thought, as the indifferent sherry whirled round his tongue.

THE MONOLOGUE OF SKIP JOHNSON, BAHAMIAN, STUDENT OF POLITICAL ECONOMY.

it must *be* immortalized, man, God-dyam-it, man, it must be *immortalized*, it's like a time I was in the R.A.F. but I'll come to that. You take this independence thing, nobody can *give* you independence, if he can give you he can take it back, if you don't fight for it, it's never yours. As I was saying, in the R.A.F. a man got fresh with me. He was bigger than I and in any case I can't fight at all, ever since I was a boy – and I'll tell you a story about when I was a boy – that *too* must be immortalized, but to come back to this story. They was a big crowd around us, all whites and I squared up to fight, like this, you see, hold the bicycle, like this (oh, never mind the traffic, man, they must wait, my bicycle is a vehicle, isn't it?) and some of the people were trying to hold me back. Man, I was scared stiff, I tell you – but I started to shout, 'I was a boxer once, you know, I was a boxer once,' like this, you know, like this, oh, never *mind* the traffic, man. The man took one look at me and walked away, you have to bluff your way, all the time

you know what I like about this place, it's not the old buildings, you know, it's the way you get into what you never dreamed of before. You know, I recited poetry to music at the Music School, Edith Sitwell. I know you wouldn't believe it, the 'Man from a Far Countree', t-r-e-e,

> *Though I am black and not comely*
> *Though I am black as the darkest trees*
> *I have swarms of gold that will fly like honey-bees*

I got a big hand, man, like a boxer, but when you get a big hand they mean, 'Oh, can he speak English?' To hell with them

but I'm telling you again something else this time, they're bamboozling you, the anti-communist thing, you don't have to be a communist at all to see it. Take this instance now, I put it to my tutor last week and he could only say, '*There* you may be right, Mr Johnson, you *may* be right after all,' he says if I'm lucky I'll get a third – to hell with him. Now you see there is this novelist writing about Soviet propaganda tactics, number one, camouflage of the facts so he gives, as the reason Hitler obviously couldn't beat Russia, the Soviets' own statement that their industrial potential in 1939 was equal to Germany's. Don't you see, why weren't the facts camouflaged that time? It's bamboozling, and again he says the Russian population is twice that of Germany, so Russia had to win, but according to what he himself says that shouldn't matter because half the Soviet population is starving in Siberia. Better read the Bible, man, that's the kind of propaganda I like. Two things in Marx, you know, which are the foundation of political economy, social conflicts are class conflicts and class relationships depend on the methods of production and distribution, that's the most profound and the sweetest thought in the world, and it *will* be immortalized, man, God dyam it, oh, you have a Jamaican conscience. What kind of a Jamaican are you, I've never heard you say 'rass'?

like the time I went to Holland, you know, and I met a Dutch girl who wanted to learn English, you see, and she said the American soldiers used a phrase very frequently and she didn't know what it meant, so I said 'O.K., tell me' and you know what she said, she said, 'Fuck off! Did I say it right? Fuck off!' Just like that. As I'm standing here in Walton Street opposite Ruskin College, it's true

the Colonial Office don't want me to go back to Bahamas, you know, I'm telling you, they think I'm dangerous, they *know* I'm dynamite. You're quite right, *that* must be immortalized. I didn't ask to come here, you know. When I was in London last vac. I went to the Colonial Office and, you know, a man there was trying to persuade me not to go back home after I'm finished. 'Why don't you go up North and take a job in industry?' I said to him, 'When you give me advice like that you are taking on a moral responsibility for life. Can you bear a moral responsibility like that?' and I walked out and left him. But they know I'm going to blow that country up when I get back so they're trying to keep me here, man. The kind of fellow they like is Amar. Take Amar, every day he's horse-riding in North Oxford, in grey flannels, he can't even buy a pair of riding breeches. What's he going to do at home, ride up and down the savannah?

look at that silly woman peeping through the curtains, she never seen two spades walking in the street before? Reminds me of when I was a schoolboy at home, there was a woman who used to be at her window every afternoon when school was over calling in the boys. I went in one afternoon and she started to touch me up, you see, and say, 'Let's see how well you growing up.' I'm telling you, man, I was positively hilarious

Guy returned from Switzerland at the beginning of October and Ramsay was terrified when he saw him at the station. He didn't believe it was Guy Horne, the extremely pale face with the skin stretched tight across the bones and almost transparent. It was a clear day on the platform and he saw Guy's first face long enough to recognize it as the face of the travelling salesmen, the priest, the cockney sailor. Then the face was Guy's again, thinner and paler than before his illness. Ramsay reckoned that the illusion was caused by his failure to remember precisely what Guy had looked like and the trick of his mind which had turned up that dead accusing image. It gave his relationship with Guy a new dimension and they could not recapture the note of frivolity.

TRINIDAD, GRENADA and the two Jamaicans went down and Beaumont Street society broke up. The nationalist certainty he had tried to believe in was gone and he thought of going back to his treatise but there didn't seem to be anything to say. He visited Cyril in his 'digs' more often and he was kept up to date about Cyril's courting of Patricia Phillips. It was very correct, almost eighteenth century. She came over for the week-end of Eights week, he went over for the May Ball, she came over for the Commem. Ball, he always asked her if he could kiss her, he wrote to Mrs Phillips once a month. When Ramsay asked why he was carrying on this minuet, Cyril said he 'had a plan' and he wasn't shaken by Ramsay's guess that Patricia also had *her* plan and was putting it into vigorous operation in Cambridge. Cyril was sure, theoretically, of her chastity.

'You simply can't find a girl of that type in Jamaica,' Cyril said.

'Obviously. She's just an English girl in black face,' Ramsay said.

'That's an offensive thing to say,' Cyril said, extremely annoyed.

'Is it offensive to have a black face? Look at her mother.'

'You said it with a sneer!'

'Yes. I was sneering at her being English, not at her complexion.'

'Oh, she isn't all *that* English. She loves Jamaica. But of course she's highly cultured. Anyway, Jamaica is her home.'

'That's just it!' Ramsay said with a mad triumph. 'That is the very root of every problem we have at home!'

Cyril took his curved pipe from his mouth and looked at Ramsay in a steady unbelief. They were in the same room but in entirely different worlds.

Ramsay met Deirdre one day and she invited him to her flat. He stayed for half an hour before a tutorial and she asked him to come back for a longer visit. He went back the following evening and had supper with her and they sat chatting about nothing whatever for a long time. At about ten o'clock she made some coffee for him before he left and he did not see her again in Oxford. Beaumont Street was the past.

He wrote his finals against a background of progressive jazz, the final discovery, the final excuse, that he *ought* to know more about negro music than English Literature. He could get along better with Dizzy Gillespie and Charley Parker than with Matthew Arnold and Tennyson, a chord on A arpeggioed over G seventh, *dru*piano, *dru*piano *dru*piano dru, dru, a flood of sixteenth notes, miscellanies of notes like ice, triplets, a passing chord, up an octave, down a third, a brief arpeggio, *klook-mop*. Actually Ramsay, who was practically tone deaf, didn't hear the different shades of polytonality but concentrated, more or less accurately, on the drums.

Meanwhile Mabel Tull arrived in England at the end of May to do a course in housecraft. She brought news from another planet. Bobsie was running as P.D.P. candidate for Eastern Kingston in the elections in August; Capleton and Edgar Bailey were still organizing the P.P.L. but nobody took them seriously;

Reggie Kendal, who had married Mona Freeman two years before, had been divorced by Mona in a scandalous case and Kendal had returned to England to do an M.R.C.S.; Sweetness Terrelonge had married Bertram Shaw. Nothing had changed, the place was still the same.

Ramsay walked with Guy on the last afternoon. It was the end of July with an out-of-phase sad light.

'Is it Arnold or Hopkins?' Guy asked.

'Neither. Something in Charley Parker.' End of that street.

'The trouble is you never touch any of this, personally you never change it,' Ramsay said. 'Like a politician dying, a radical politician, with the world the same. It's all pointless.'

'There is nothing to remember, only old stone,' Guy said.

'You've seen me for three years,' Ramsay said. 'Do you think you are more capable, than I am, of ruling me?'

'What do you mean?'

'Do you think I could ever be under your tutelage?'

'God forbid!'

'Well, then leave us alone!'

'Don't spoil the afternoon. This is what I wrote in Schools, "The low standard of living in the colonies depresses our higher standards, disease in the colonies is, actually, a threat to our own health and so on, therefore emancipate the colonies."'

'You poor man,' Ramsay said, 'they gave you a "third" for being a Fabian!' They laughed.

In Beaumont Street they met a tall scare-crowish under-graduate with a face like an aristocratic ghost. He was wearing purple corduroy trousers, a yellow waistcoat, a blue sports-jacket, a long thin red bow-tie. His socks were incredibly green and he owned the street with a marvellous walk, his 'legges casten to and fro', his eyes in a mist. He was met near the Playhouse by a short undistinguished man in a sober grey suit and heavy horn-rimmed spectacles but whose accent was ex-travagant.

'I say, dear boy, wher' you off to?'

'I'm just going to my masseur to have a rub down,' the marvel said.

They let him have the street and the last word.

Ramsay's departure, next morning, was like any other. He felt he had not moved, that his 'education' had been a joke unless education is a series of picaresque adventures loosely held together by the persistent ignorance of the hero. And through it all – the tinsel gaiety, the superficial friendliness, the other-worldliness of art – he had felt always within him the deep irrevocable humiliation of being a negro in a white man's world. But he had reduced his treatise to one sentence:

The Negro is not a myth but a man.

'There needs no ghost, my lord,' his other, cultured mind echoed.

III

Deirdre lived on a London street nameless as any other in the anonymity of fog and the same area gates, and the same tube stations from which you step into the wet night that is always poignant with the lights that prove other people endure, with the faces that are going somewhere anxiously and hear the tube and must catch it, the faces that must end somewhere in sleep sometime, the lonely, to turn left into the fog of her street and find the street-door slightly ajar.

She had a front room on the ground floor. In one corner, away from the street, there was a red screen behind which were a wash-basin, a small gas stove, a waste-paper basket; near the door was a black chest of drawers with her underwear in the top drawer and her blouses in the second drawer. The other drawers were stacked with food. Opposite the fireplace there was a grey-covered sofa which collapsed at night into a small double-bed. Two lounge chairs were by the fireplace, there was a heavy ornate archaic chair by the table with the wireless set and another lounge chair was in the corner nearest the window. Behind the door there was a cloth wardrobe with Deirdre's dresses and coats and above the mantelpiece an oval-shaped mirror distorted your face when you tried to look in it.

Deirdre's real name was Veronica Madden. She had finally divorced her husband and used her maiden name again. She was working as a typist in a bookseller's.

Ramsay first went to that room for a farewell party Trinidad and Barbados 1 gave for themselves. After that he went to see Deirdre occasionally. She asked him not to call her Deirdre any more but Vera, and so he went to see her frequently. But there was no sex, not even a flirtation in the friendship and they were physically unaware of each other. She was holding on to the memory of Beaumont Street and he was the souvenir. He went to see her because she was pleasant and always glad to see him and because he was futilely trying to hide from the Colonial Office who wanted to send him home. They shared that huge joke. He did not think seriously about his visits to Deirdre. He would spin a coin to decide whether to go to the cinema or visit Mabel or visit Deirdre. But once when he didn't go to see her for a week she said she was hurt.

Then they exploded, without warning, into a physical affair. It was eight o'clock one evening. He had been in her room since five in the afternoon and they had run out of talk.

'I don't understand why you haven't been attracted to me, Ramsay,' Deirdre said.

At first he thought it was another conversation, somewhere else, that he was hearing. He looked at her, admitting he had heard her speak, but her face was the same as always, smiling slightly, a face that was too familiar to be pretty.

'I *have* been,' he said. It was unreal like a part he had learned in a play.

'When?'

'I am in love with you. I've always been in love with you.' He didn't know he was acting. 'But you haven't given me any encouragement.'

He was sitting on the sofa and she looked at him from the chair by the fire. Their voices had been quite toneless as if the conversation had been about a new scarf he had bought and not shown to her. She didn't stop looking at him as she walked across to the sofa, kneeled in front of him and kissed him deeply and steadily and slowly.

'Why?' he asked her.

She looked up at him and it was the same familiar face, the front teeth protruding slightly when she smiled, the skin at the corners of her mouth drawn back in two lines. 'I've always wanted to do that,' she said.

They began to reorganize themselves. Each was afraid the other wasn't interested, exactly as if they had been trying to apply the words of a play to real life for the past five minutes. Ramsay's hands got cold and his whole body froze when he remembered 'I am in love with you', and the kiss.

She got up and said she was going to bed, flatly, without inflection, as if forgetting it was early, that this was her bedroom and he was there. He was still frozen, paralysed by the necessity for action and the inability to act without looking stupid. He remembered Beaumont Street and had a momentary fear that she might have found the negro myth to be true. He put that aside quickly because he knew her so well as a friend.

She went behind the screen and he watched her head and arms above the screen as she undressed. She came out in a pale blue nightgown and he moved away from the sofa and watched her convert it into a bed. She got into bed and asked him to turn the light off.

He put on his overcoat and scarf, turned the light off and then sat on the other side of the bed away from her, feeling the same paralysis and anticipating the choking fog and the chill of the street. There was nothing he could ask her and he was quite incapable of leaving.

She said, 'Why don't you lie down for a minute, before you go?'

He felt that she had somehow spoken selflessly, to help him, and he took off his scarf and overcoat and shoes and lay down. She went into his arms and kissed him more passionately than anybody had ever kissed him. He felt something deeper than a thrill – a sort of recognition of a self that had no emotion or sensation for the cold weight was still there at the pit of his stomach.

'I'm frightened,' she said. 'I don't know what it is, but I'm frightened!'

They lay there in the dark of that room into which the street light seemed to press the colour of the fog and talked, trying to build up the relation abstractly. They talked about sex and their experiences and belief in god, anything that would delay personal commitment, hoping they could come later, at the end of the affair perhaps, to the beginning of a flirtation and the lyricism of falling in love. Then he began deliberately and with an effort to detach himself mentally. He told himself that her sudden use of 'darling', her being frightened, even her trembling was a drama-tization of an emotion that had nothing, essentially, to do with him. But he had been caressing her, almost without realizing it. And the whole thing had become real and personal for her.

'I want you to take me! Please take me!' Her voice was intense and controlled. She kept on saying she wanted him to take her.

'You want a man, Vera, you don't want me, you are in love with somebody else and just because you are excited and I am here, you think you want me but you don't really want me, you want a man.' He said that too quickly, as if he wasn't thinking it himself but had been told to say it.

'I want *you* Ramsay.'

'No, you don't.'

He continued to caress her.

'If you aren't going to take me,' she said, 'you better stop what you're doing.'

He had detached all but his body from the situation so that it wasn't Vera there (whom he really liked) but an enemy, someone who had laid this fundamental hold on him before there had been time for tenderness and need, someone he had to win, or lose and win again, by hurting her and then temporarily detaching himself. So he kept on fondling her and she moved into an excitement that made her aware of his presence only, without recognizing him.

She said, in a painful whisper that was completely without tenderness, 'Please take me now, *please.*' Then she said it again, coarsely.

For him it was as if the play had faltered at that moment, someone had muffed a cue. He sat up and began putting on his shoes.

'I'm going home,' he said. 'I don't want to miss the last tube.'

'You can't leave me like this. It's too cruel! Take your clothes off and come to bed.' She had passed the stage of waiting to be possessed and, though she still smouldered and trembled, desire didn't matter to her now. She wasn't hurt but she wanted to rescue something. She didn't want him to go but it didn't matter except that she knew he was wrong. She *was* in love with him.

He put on his overcoat and scarf and she realized that he was really going.

'All right, Ramsay,' she said, 'kiss me goodnight before you go.'

He got the last tube home and he knew that he wanted her but still without being able to believe that he wanted Deirdre and not just a woman.

He spent the next week-end with her and they made love perfectly as if they had always known each other. They were surprised at the agreement of their bodies, as if it were something outside them. They had to cling to the word, the personal name, in that common, precious illusion of the destruction of the flesh. 'The bed is hot enough to roast chestnuts in,' Deirdre said. It wasn't very funny but they needed to laugh themselves into sanity after that violence.

He did not know he was in love with her until she began singing, over and over, a part of a sentimental song they had heard in the film *An American In Paris.* She remembered only a small part of the tune and only a few of the words.

> *The Rockies may crumble, Gibraltar may fall,*
> *Tra-la-la-la-la;*
> *Tra-la-la, our love is here to stay.*

She was not connecting the words of the song with their affair. She simply liked the song and was annoyed that that was all she could remember of it. There was no sentimentality in that snatch of a song on her lips and Ramsay thought of the repeated tune as the tone colour of their intimacy, a stage property that would disappear with the rest of the illusion after the play had ended, a makeshift that would be a dead song afterwards, with no power to recall a mood or an emotion. But during the affair the persistent 'Rockies' and 'Gibraltar' somehow gave him all at once the immature, adolescent emotion that he would have already grown out of if he had spent the three years at home in the safe, understood sexual *milieu* that his birth had made him an accepted part of.

He was very disturbed that Deirdre was white and that, in spite of her race, he could not bring himself to be cynical about the affair. He felt he ought to be cynical about it, because she had known all the boys in the Beaumont Street flat, because there was so much sex in the relationship, because there was nothing remarkable about Deirdre. Instead, in a few weeks he felt the usual confusing mixture of uncertainty, tenderness, anxiety, desire, jealousy, that people feel when they say they are in love. He tried to fight her off by telling her about his affair with Sweetness Terrelonge as if that had been a uniquely negro affair of white sands and jasmine and oleander. He wasn't troubled by the fact that he was lying but by Deirdre's correct assumption that this somewhat artificial situation in a London room was deeper and truer for him than anything had ever been. And there was one thing about Deirdre that made him desperate to fight her off – she had a genuine hatred of white people who were colour-prejudiced and she did not excuse them at all, on any grounds. When he went out with her, to the cinema or to a concert, wherever they had to be a fixed point in a crowd, the only difference between them was the physical fact of skin colour; in every other way they were together in that unspoken, throttled battle. It was a complicated battle because half of the hate and disgust people felt was directed against Deirdre. The battle would have been simpler if Deirdre were negro and it would not have occurred at all if he had stayed at home with Sweetness Terrelonge. Yet when he saw leading negro personalities in England with white wives he had a vague proprietory feeling about Deirdre.

He introduced her to Mabel and Mabel disliked her immediately.

'She's conceited and affected, Ramsay,' Mabel said. 'I don't like her – not at all, Ramsay. She treats you like a little puppy-dog!'

'You don't understand her, Mabes, it's just her manner. And she was nervous meeting you. She's all right, I'm telling you!'

'You don't see the two of you together, like circus fleas. She isn't the type for you. I think this Oxford jus' turn you into a fool!'

'She isn't prejudiced at all,' Ramsay explained.

'What you know about prejudice?' Mabel asked, very annoyed. 'Prejudice isn't to sleep with you, it's to live with you. Don't, for sweet Jesus' sake, doan take that girl home to Jamaica, you hear?'

'I'm not going to *marry* her. You think I want to marry her?'

'Oh, well, then. You were going on so serious. But I still doan like her, though!'

Mabel had changed a lot since coming to England. She thought that England was something to be very serious and very middle-

230

class about. She believed that Ramsay was determined to make a mess of his life, after wasting his time at the university. She wanted Ramsay to stop dodging the Colonial Office and go home. She herself was determined to be a success, working very hard at a housecraft course at Battersea Training College and cutting out men altogether. 'These days,' she said, 'I can't even *hear* a man talking to me unless he put a ring on my finger.'

Ramsay had two pleasant weeks with Guy Horne who had come back from Spain where he had been working in an English bank. He was being transferred to a branch of the bank in South America. They went to the theatre, concerts, cinemas, almost continuously.

The night before Guy left for the Argentine they had a curry dinner in an Indian restaurant in Tottenham Court Road.

'I don't think I'll ever see you again, Guy. You're sure to get caught up in a revolution or something.'

'I could come to Jamaica,' Guy said. 'It isn't far. Anyway we'll meet at a Gaudy, o' boy, a Gaudy, that'll be it!'

'By the way,' Guy said later, 'what are you going to *do*?'

'Teach, I expect. Or write. Or get into politics. Anything. I've got no bright future. I might marry Veronica and get a job here as a navvy.'

'Yes! Why don't you stay here and get a decent job?'

'Don't be silly, Guy. You know what my chances are of getting a "decent job" here.'

They realized their complete separation from the selves they had known for three years, from a past that had died six months before. At Leicester Square station they said a confused good-bye, trying to keep away from the note of finality. Guy sang, 'An airline ticket to romantic places', and talked about 'senoritas', like a bad film.

But the last thing Guy said was, 'Don't stay in this country, Ramsay. Look at me, I'm getting out of it. I don't mean anything abstract like discrimination and prejudice – not abstract, *objective* rather. For yourself. Be a writer. Go back home and get the place in your veins. You don't realize it but you're getting bitter already. It's a hell of a thing for *me* to say, I know, but there you are, I've said it! I'll write you from Buenos Aires. Bye, o'boy. Look up my old people before you leave. I'll tell them you're coming.'

'Have a good time, Guy, and don't forget to write,' was all Ramsay could say.

Ramsay spent the next week writing a short story which he thought interpreted his affair with Deirdre. He called it *The Persistent Face.*

I didn't realize I was being haunted by a face until I met Deirdre, but I knew the face very well long before meeting her. It was the face of a white man, very pale with the skin of the forehead stretched tight across the bones and almost transparent. I saw that face first when I was drunk at a party in Jamaica, but I had known it before from my mother's description of a ghost she had seen and had thought was a travelling salesman. Then I saw the face again, most terrifying, when it was the face of my English friend Guy Horne among the smoke and fog of a railway station. I could not analyse the reasons for the persistence of that face except to guess that it appears when my emotions are in a particular but unanalysable state of confusion. It is also possible that I am crazy but I doubt that.

Deirdre (that's not her real name, but she was part Irish) was a beautiful, well-brought up girl and at that time slightly promiscuous, but with discrimination. I met her when she was living in a flat in Swiss Cottage. Deirdre was inclined to be thin but she dressed cleverly to emphasize her small breasts and pert buttocks. She was lively and friendly and had a trick of personality which kept you talking to her although most of the time she was talking nonsense. That is true; and it is also true that she was intelligent.

A friend of mine from the Bahamas was at that time the boyfriend of a French girl named Therese, a friend of Deirdre's. We all went to Deirdre's place often and then one evening I went alone when Frank, the Bahamian, had made quite certain that Therese wouldn't be there. Deirdre told me easily that she was married but separated from her husband and that she had just ended an affair with a chap named Charles Lindo from Dominica. She wasn't interested in that sort of thing any more but I could come to see her when I liked.

There was something about her that compelled me to go on visiting her and, at first, to go on taking her at her word. She was, for one thing, my first experiment in the proposition that a black man and a white woman can have a completely innocent, non-intellectual friendship. That was only a part of the compulsion. I wavered, every time I saw her, between two images of her – one of unspoilt youth, the other of suffering. I would sit in her flat and watch her sitting there friendly, open, eager to entertain and I would feel guilty that I had ever despised the white races. And connected with the opposed images was an illusion I often had that she sometimes became somebody else.

The proposition was only half proved, however, because we drifted into an affair that asked no questions. It was sentimental and lyrical. I can wrap London around that affair, in memory, and have a perfect dream, especially of the end of summer and the peculiar physical stillness of everything.

Deirdre became the concretization of all the things I had grown up to consider mine and later had come to believe I had borrowed and had no right to. Even her dramatization of eating a meal or having a drink did not seem affected. Even that quick way of smiling directly at you (which I had always distrusted) I now felt was something from a tradition I could never grasp but should consider myself fortunate to be so close to.

There was nothing Deirdre ever said that was memorable, even in its triviality, and I cannot invent things for her to say. For two months she said she loved me and there was nothing to believe or not believe about it. She was a beautiful person. It is a pity I cannot describe her now but I would have to begin with her face and it was her face that ended the affair.

I remember the conversation that preceded the end.

'Look, I'm sorry, but Mr Griffiths doesn't want you to come here any more,' Deirdre said. Mr Griffiths was the landlord.

'Well,' I said.

'Don't you see? I've got to stop seeing you.'

'Why? He isn't your father, is he? What're you saying?'

'Don't make it difficult,' she said. 'I'm through with you!'

'Are you serious?'

'I don't want another nigger, ever. And you're the worst of the lot. Charles was better, at least he didn't moon and slobber, and he could satisfy me!'

'Don't I? You said – '

'If I said anything, it was a lie!'

That is all I can remember distinctly, except my confusion, my uncertainty, as to whether she had lied earlier or was lying then. That mattered to me. I didn't feel indignant that she called me a 'nigger' like that. I had passed beyond niggerness now, because of her, to a kind of mastery of the white world. But she was trying to destroy me by subtly inverting the myth. When a lie ends an affair there can be no discussion.

She told me to leave her flat but I refused to go and actually I am still there now, in her sitting room at six o'clock in the morning, coolly using her writing desk, her pen and her notepaper.

Earlier this evening, after she told me everything was over between us, a white man came in and they went into the bedroom together. Later he came out and went away. I was sitting near the fire and she stood over me laughing. I didn't resent her laughter or her lie or the bitch she was. I didn't think myself a fool or that I had lost my mastery of the things she was. But I looked up and saw her face and I strangled her, and her body is there on the sofa and she is dead. I had to destroy that face. It was the face of the salesman, the priest, the sailor, Guy Horne. It was the face of my blackness and my inferiority and my ambition. It was my own face.

He showed the story to Deirdre who read it through twice and handed it back to him.

'I wonder what happened to your friend from Barbados,' she said. 'The one who used to write stories.'

'Look, don't try that English trick with me,' Ramsay said, unreasonably annoyed. 'Do you like the story or not?'

'Do you expect me to like it?'

'Why not?'

'You know, I wouldn't know if it's good or bad,' Deirdre said. 'But I don't like it. It isn't true in any way at all. I know it isn't about me but it still isn't true. The two things don't fit together, that face and this girl.'

'But suppose it was a true story? Suppose you didn't know I wrote it?'

'Well, I would think the girl deserved what she got if she stopped loving a man because of that,' Deirdre said. She did not like the discussion, any more than the story. Ramsay had recently been trying to hurt her, she thought, by ambiguous innuendoes about her past. She had had to lie considerably and he caught her out once. So she was frightened by the story.

'On the contrary,' Ramsay said, 'I think it's the best grounds for divorce.'

'Actually, you know, Ramsay, I come from a very good family. We were quite rich before the war.' The conversation had become lop-sided, she was accusing him of something and breathing heavily. 'Don't judge me by what I've been doing at Beaumont Street and all that. I've had a hard time, you know. Anyway I don't want to marry you and I don't want to live in Jamaica if that's what the story means.'

'Vera, it hasn't got anything to do with us,' he tried to explain. 'It's just something that might entertain anyone who reads it.'

'I know that, my dear, but I still don't want to marry you.' Her voice had an edge. 'And it isn't because you are black, if that's what the story means.'

'How does all this "marriage" business get into it?' he asked. He was very relieved. 'I am not even working. I've got exactly twenty pounds in the world.'

She got up and poked the fire aimlessly.

'But you're relieved that I don't want to marry you, aren't you?' she said with her back to him. She threw the poker against the grate. 'Oh, I'm fed *up* with this pokey room! Let's go to the pictures!' She strode across the room and flung on her coat and scarf. He thought she was dramatizing again.

They saw a bad film, that was supposed to be funny, about winning the football pools. Through most of the film Deirdre was crying silently, but Ramsay didn't know that. He was wondering, with some anxiety, what he would do when he had spent his money.

Veronica Madden was born in London of very poor parents who were strict and religious. She was educated at a fairly good secondary school and worked as a shorthand-typist in London before the war.

She was thirty-two years old.

Both her parents had died in the blitz and while she was in the

A.T.S. she married a man she had known since childhood. Her in-laws disliked her and while her husband was away on service she went to pieces. She was unfaithful to him and was determined to have a good time at any price. She ended up in a Borstal Institution. When she was discharged she felt she had learned her lesson and she made up her mind to live a good clean life.

She was reconciled with her husband and they tried to make a home together but failed. Her husband drank heavily and was unreliable in every way. One night he beat her with a dog-whip and only the timely appearance of the neighbours saved her from being strangled to death. She left him and subsequently obtained a divorce on the grounds of cruelty.

She went to Oxford in a mood of despair to be as far away as possible from the old environment. She met JAMAICA 1, became his friend and gradually got to know the other West Indians. She began to have fun and enjoy herself with them and thought it was better than the 'good time' she had had before Borstal. She wasn't very promiscuous but would go with any of the boys who pleased her, one lover at a time and faithful to him while her affection lasted – usually about six months. She was amazed at the respect with which the boys treated her, even the ex-lovers, and she came to identify herself with their problems. They had got the top flat at Beaumont Street for her and she was happy for the first time in her life. She had returned to London after the boys left because she felt she had now learned something about tackling life.

Then Ramsay Tull appeared with his concealed helplessness. Long before they became lovers she had fallen in love with him and had wanted to marry him and to go to the West Indies with him. She dreamt about it every day. Those were the only things that she had enough personality left to desire.

She did not tell Ramsay that she had once been in a Borstal Institution.

When Ramsay told her he would be going home the following month, she said, 'Oh, I'm very glad for you! There's no future here, is there? It's the best thing to do!'

Ramsay sorted parcels at Mount Pleasant Post Office during three weeks before Christmas. He didn't like the icy mornings and the dust of mailbags and the cold he caught the first day. The workers were friendly and they seemed to regard him first as a human being and then as a foreigner. Then Waldo joined his section of sorters, Waldo 'the jew-boy', as the two cockney girls called him. The workers in the section had never seen Waldo before but they spoke of him as if he were a well-known criminal. Ramsay had to ask Dolly if she had known Waldo before. Dolly was a heavily-mascaraed blonde of about nineteen who wore a violent shade of lipstick and a violent perfume. She said, through the chewing-gum, 'Naw! 'E's just a dirty jew-boy,' as if Ramsay would understand what that meant.

Waldo was the perfect outcast, the man who knows people don't want him around but who insists on his right to be there, as if he doesn't know that people despise him. He was a short, fleshy-faced young man of twenty-five, always well dressed and neat. He kept up a steady flirtation with Dolly and the other girl and he knew just what points of their vanity to touch. There was, on both sides, a habit of contempt, but, superseding that, there was a sexual habit and Waldo was quite attractive. None of them took the flirtation seriously and when he got to know Waldo better, Ramsay was amazed at the outrageous things he said about Dolly and the other girl: Waldo regarded them as sluts and he knew how much they despised him. Ramsay thought that it would take a negro centuries to achieve Waldo's subtle refinement of racial hate where the harmless, amusing flirtation was a kind of shadow-drawing of the real, desperate, vicious struggle in which the girls had to preserve their racial purity and Waldo had to survive as a self-respecting Jew.

Waldo came in one day with a peace petition which he wanted everybody to sign. The signing of that petition was magical. When Waldo was not in the section – was in other sections trying to persuade workers there to sign – all the workers in Ramsay's section abused Waldo, the Soviet Union, Jews, Communism. But when Waldo returned they agreed with all his arguments and eventually they all signed the petition. He had a story, which took three days to tell, of how he went to a youth festival in Austria. The story was not about the festival itself but about the difficulties English delegates had had in getting to Austria. According to

Waldo they were prevented by the Americans from going through West Germany and the treatment he said they received from American soldiers was exactly the same as the treatment Communist soldiers are reported to give Westerners travelling in Eastern Europe. These stories had a legendary quality and Ramsay couldn't make up his mind whether to believe both or neither. The English delegation eventually got into Austria through France and Italy and Waldo gave the impression that the manoeuvre had been more difficult and more romantic than Hannibal's crossing of the Alps. Waldo was a serious man but was entirely without gloom. He didn't expect to be completely believed because, he said, 'you're fighting against prejudice, propaganda and apathy'. He was distinguished from the hundreds of workers that Ramsay saw in the post office by his clarity of purpose, the signatures on the peace petition being more important to him than his pay packet – a fact which seemed marvellous to Ramsay.

The night of Christmas Eve, Waldo and Ramsay knocked off at the same time and Waldo invited him to a party he knew of that was being given by West Indians. Waldo was surprised that Ramsay did not know any of the West Indians who would be there. They did a pub-crawl by bus and it took them nearly two hours to get to the party.

The party was going well in an ornate Victorian drawing room. Some of the furniture was out of date, the two uncomfortable sofas, the straight-back chairs, the heavy oval dining table, the 1930 model wireless set. The music was coming from a small noisy portable gramophone on the dining table.

Everybody was glad to see Waldo but they were annoyed that Ramsay, a West Indian, had to be introduced to them by Waldo. Almost immediately Ramsay was the target for the wit of a psychology student from Trinidad. He was a burly, squat man with intelligent eyes and he must have been a bully in his youth. He reminded Ramsay of the bullies he had feared at Surrey College.

'You don't look at ease, man,' the psychologist said. 'What happen? You don't approve of the company? Not like home, eh?'

'As a matter of fact,' Ramsay said, 'I'm quite enjoying it.'

"'I'm quite enjoying it,'" the psychologist mimicked. 'Talk natural, man, we're all West Indians here.' Ramsay grinned foolishly. 'Look at this man,' the psychologist said, commanding the room with his booming voice, 'a perfect example of an educated colonial. He doesn't approve of us because we don't measure up to the Jamaican conscience. You used to be a Boy Scout, didn't you?'

'Yes,' Ramsay said. He did not really want to admit it but he had to say something to give the impression that he was at ease. He felt that the people in the room were very much older than he. There were four Trinidadian girls, four girls from Jamaica, two men and two girls from Barbados, one girl from Dominica who was pretty and was studying housecraft, three Jamaican men (one wearing sun-glasses) and an assortment of whites, half of them British, half of them from Europe.

'Let's sing a hymn for him,' the Trinidad psychologist said, to a round of laughter.

Fortunately for Ramsay someone put on Nellie Lutcher's record *Fine Brown Frame* and the psychologist danced to it with a large-eyed Barbadian girl. He danced, with exaggerated indecency, to the sofa, where Ramsay was sitting and said, 'I bet you don't dance like this at Oxford.' The Barbadian girl thought that was very funny.

Ramsay recognized Lorna Carmichael, the girl who used to share a house with Mona Freeman. He wasn't sure it was Lorna because whenever he caught a glimpse of her face it was upside down. She was sitting on the knees of a hefty Swede with her back turned to Ramsay but at intervals she leaned far over backwards, laughing wildly at what the Swede was saying or doing. Ramsay was quite tipsy and he saw Lorna as the one point of familiarity on which he could focus what was left of his soberness. He walked across to her and saw, without embarrassment, that she had been laughing at what the Swede was *doing.*

'Aren't you Lorna Carmichael?' Ramsay asked. The Swede grinned at him and nodded emphatically.

'Yes,' Lorna said. 'Who're you?'

'I'm Ramsay Tull. I used to be a friend of Mona Freeman. I hope I'm not interrupting you.'

'You're not interrupting anything,' Lorna said. He wasn't, for the Swede's hands were extremely busy. 'Oh, Mona had a terrible time with that coolie man, you see. A reely wutliss divorce case. The things he wanted Mona to do!' Lorna squealed and wriggled and turned from Ramsay to pay more attention to what the Swede was doing. Ramsay was sure she had not recognized him.

The door opened and an enormous ebony-coloured man, wearing a duffle-coat, came in with the wind. He was built like a heavyweight boxer but his head was very small. He had been drinking and was not accustomed to being drunk so he was trying to look profound. He had the aggressiveness of an unintelligent man who is trying to become a well-known personality and the childishness of a powerful body that is temporarily paralysed by alcohol. He gurgled when he laughed and when he sang it sounded like a *tremolo* laugh (and he sang often during the evening; he had a powerful baritone which he said could break wine glasses or something). The first thing he did, before speaking to anyone, was to turn off the gramophone and sing a chorus of *Ole Man River*. The girls said he sounded like Paul Robeson. Then he tore a book in two with his powerful hands. Then he saw Ramsay's large head.

'Man, where you get a head like that from?'

'It's a specially sensitive head,' the Trinidad psychologist said grudgingly, as he was now no longer the centre of the party.

The enormous boxer-singer swayed over and caressed Ramsay's head and they were all great friends together. Then he sang a negro spiritual and then announced that he would soon be in films.

'The negro wants a new art form,' the Trinidad psychologist said. 'Any of the existing art forms are already a projection of white sensibility. We can't use them without being apes. You,' he pointed to the enormous one, 'need an entirely new art form.' The singer grinned and tried, unsuccessfully, not to look like an ape.

'There is nothing negro or non-negro about art,' Ramsay said. For a moment he thought he was only thinking, not speaking, but he could hear his voice distinctly echoing through his head. 'Reality is enclosed within a series of transparent integuments.

The thing that art is trying to get at is behind the integuments but it *can* be seen through all those layers of non-reality. The artist is trying to remove those integuments and come to a knowledge of THE THING. With each integument he removes, reality changes shape and meaning and assumes a greater clarity. But when he removes the last integument THE THING has disappeared and there is nothing there. That is the only artistic problem. Only the very greatest artists can remove *all* the integuments but then they usually go mad from getting so close to reality, like Van Gogh. The other artists see THE THING distorted through the integuments but in a lifetime all they can do is to remove two or three of these barriers to truth. This is a universal problem and a specially negro art form is another myth.'

The room swayed a little and then was contained in the splashing of gin in the glass he was holding.

'This man is obviously a sex-starved romantic,' the Trinidad psychologist said. 'These integuments are an abstracted form of layers of flesh. You can see, in this our well-brought-up friend from Jamaica, a perfect example of what Britain can do to a nigger. Go home, young man!'

The girl who danced on the table, Minna Brown, had not been very prominent during the evening. She was a Jamaican girl studying history in London University. She had been in the A.T.S. during the war. She was brown-skinned and very plump. She thought she could dance. She wanted to impress the enormous boxer-singer. It was her flat.

She announced that she was going to do a Row-manian dance. She had been born plumb in the middle of Kingston, on lower Duke Street in fact, but she was going to do a Row-manian dance. She put on a de Falla record that was pulsing and exciting and she danced a swirling rhythmic calypso to it. The enormous boxer thought the dance was wonderful and that Minna would probably get into films, too. Minna had spent a summer in Spain and there she had learned to do Row-manian dances.

Experience is not the things you can remember from the past. That is only a consciousness of existence. Experience is the broken series of moments, only a few in a lifetime, that permanently alter your personality. You do not 'remember' experience

241

since it cannot be detached from your personality. To Ramsay, this party had been an experience. It was a white Christmas and he stood tipsy in the snow and became aware of himself. He was aware of the softness of everything and the sweet stinging of the cold wind on his stretched face. He was aware of being in a world where things happened, people starved, men were fighting in Korea, people were praying, his mother was praying – all struggling, breathing, eating, sleeping, to exist. That was all you could be sure you *had* to do. It didn't matter that it wasn't a black Christmas and that there would never be peace and goodwill. The bells told their story and he thought of the end of that story and of the cliché which Pilate had coined, that you yourself – in any moment of pure perception, of complete self-awareness – are truth. Let them accuse him, standing stupidly there in the snow, of *anything*; it didn't matter, for he found no fault in himself and would wash his black conscience in the white snow. A few seconds after thinking this, he was violently sick against a lamp-post.

IV

I stood in Piccadilly tube station watching people coming up and going down the escalator. I like watching them. I was the only point of complete rest in the tube station. Even the girl in the brilliant green coat standing there absolutely still by the world clock was not at rest. She had the doll-like immobile prettiness that London shop girls have until they smile, and she was imagining her boy miss his tube, come up the escalator, apologize and take her arm to go wherever they were to go. She turned to the clocks that only told her he was half an hour late by the time in any part of the world, and then turned back to help me watch the people going on and off the escalator.

London is the only place I know where you can be dead idle without having to make an excuse, even to yourself. That is why I spent all my vacations there. That, and Mabel Tull.

I met Mabel Tull for the first time in England at a West Indian Students' Union dance at Kensington Town Hall. I didn't know she was in England, and meeting her that night was a little like being blinded by lightning. She was tremendously glad to see me and would not let me out of her sight or let me dance with anybody else that night, and she insisted that I see her home. By this time I was old enough to understand why I had once thought I was in love with her, and to 'know better'. She was physically attractive now in a very precise way, but there was no question of her being in love with me. I found out afterwards that she had been using me at the dance as a shield against a man she had met on the boat who had been pursuing her like, she said, 'a donkey in heat'. Mabel had a completely original line in metaphors. I found out why she had attached herself to me that night only when the man, a tall moony Jamaican, who was studying either English or music in London (I think he was studying music and was greatly 'thrilled' by poetry) accused me of being engaged to Mabel. I wasn't engaged to Mabel. It was more as if we had been married and divorced from each other and now were very

243

good friends. At any rate I preferred that to being her 'younger brother'. Each vac. I went to London, spent long hours chatting with her and having very chaste tea, took her to the theatre, to the Festival Hall, and once, with Ramsay, to Wigmore Hall. She made my position clear to me one day in Kew Gardens.

'I have had a serious obstetrical operation which will result in the complete atrophy of my organs of sensation,' she said. She was extremely desirable that day and the circumstances in which she made that remark gave me the feeling you get when people call flowers by their correct botanical names. Then she added, 'What I've jus' told you is a lie, but you know why I said it.'

At another time she said, 'You are a good boy and very cultured and one day you'll be a great palooka. That's why I like you to visit me.'

So I was at Paddington Station the Thursday morning Ramsay left England, partly to see him off and partly in the hope of being seen off myself by Mabel. I was catching the 11.45 to Oxford.

Only Mabel, Cyril Hanson, who was in London reading for the Bar, and an English girl I didn't know, had come to see Ramsay off. We talked about Jamaica, how lovely the climate was (it was early January in England), that Ramsay would soon be eating salt fish and ackee and roast breadfruit. The English girl laughed very much at everything that was said.

Ramsay talked to me about Orange Town and Surrey College. I come from Mount Horesh, a village about three miles from Orange Town in the St Ann hills, and Ramsay and I had been at Surrey College together. He had been a mild quiet prefect we all liked. I remembered him walking up and down the central driveway of the school, reading Penguin books and musing. He was a brilliant debater whom we looked forward to hearing on Saturday evenings – a mysterious hero who gave a dimension of intellectual depth to the drabness of school life. We were sure he would win a scholarship on 'brains' only, although he did not have any of Cyril Hanson's flamboyance.

Cyril was the games player. If I have ever hated anybody it is Cyril Hanson. He had been a bully of the worst type; even as head boy he carried on a ceaseless campaign of terror which he tried to disguise as a high unselfish morality. That was his force of character, his positive personality. Mark you, he was a good leader, but he gave everything he did an unpleasant flavour of priggishness. For instance, I played on the school cricket team during his second year of captaincy and he wouldn't let me bowl as I wanted to bowl. He gave good advice as a captain but he wrapped up the advice in the sort of morality you hear in confirmation classes so that I wasn't quite sure whether I was bowling to a boy from another school or to the devil himself. By the way, nobody in all my years at Surrey ever read the lesson in Chapel with as much sanctimoniousness as Cyril did. The result of his exhortations to me on the cricket field was that I bowled very badly that year. But he was a sweet soccer player and the best off-break bowler we ever had at Surrey.

When his mother came up to Oxford, during his B.C.L. year he invited me to have tea with them at his digs in Longwall Street. Mrs Hanson still looked young and handsome. One got the impression that she dressed and behaved in a desperate effort to prove to herself that she was getting old. It seemed that she felt it was mortally dangerous for her to think of herself as being young. She was much more likeable than Cyril because more pathetic. She said that England had changed very much since she was a girl there; she said it with a satisfaction which suggested she was now ready to die in peace. I hated Cyril even more when I saw how much his mother worshipped him. I don't suppose I need have been quite so much against Cyril; after all, we were both games players and were in the same college. I took over his rooms in Longwall and I could become very moral about the fact that he went down from Oxford owing his landlady £43 13s. 6d., as she complained to me every day. I didn't think for a moment that he wouldn't pay it all at some time but I thought his unconcern about it characteristic.

We always imagine that people like Cyril Hanson are not conscious of the reaction they produce in other people. On the contrary, I think Cyril calculated with great care. His rolled umbrella, bowler, black coat, clean white collar, B.N.C. tie, briefcase and a copy of *The Times* under his arm, would have been absurd in any other coloured man, but it was right for Cyril. He could be a Tory or a socialist whenever he needed to but he was first *the* Cyril Hanson, Oxford Blue, Barrister-at-Law. He would probably become a great colonial political leader.

Ramsay was different. He belonged to the Surrey College romantic tradition – the brooder, the 'philosophical' mind, the revolutionary. I think this tradition began with the boy who had written, in a school newspaper before the war, a pacifist article that ended, 'I am a communist because I am an atheist and a coward'. The verandahs of Upper St Andrew had buzzed with the scandal and when this 'communist', then an R.A.F. fighter pilot in 1942, was shot down over Spain and only the buttons of his uniform were found, the same verandahs of Upper St Andrew were still buzzing with the scandalous shortage of meat and petrol. My generation had never seen the article and had believed in it only as a legend. Ramsay Tull was our embodiment of that legend.

He was in his last year when I went up to Oxford and he had welcomed me to the University. I thought he would have got a better class than a 'third' and it made me despair a little because he had been so clever at school. I didn't accept the view then current that negroes were debarred from getting 'firsts'. I believe he failed because he was too preoccupied with political thinking. My impression however is Ramsay was *not* a communist at that time. I remember a discussion he had with a Jewish communist named Waldo at the colonial hostel in Hallam Street. Ramsay seemed to have been arguing against the idea of a working-class solidarity that would include both negroes and whites. He was making the fairly valid point that a colonial negro regards being the guest of Buckingham Palace as more valuable than economic independence. Of course it was a cynical one-sided argument, useful only in winning a debating point. Then he said that Marxism should become flexible enough to include the peculiarities of the negro temperament. Waldo said that that was romantic and racialist.

I don't know, myself. I am a little repelled by asceticism. My idea of Paradise is to live in Mount Horesh, plant some banana, rear a few pigs, ride over the small property on a frisky horse every morning, kill a pig and have a big drink-up once a month, play country cricket and write poetry. The only sensation that will keep me living in a town is jazz. I know that Ramsay disliked anything as simple as this, but I don't think he was a communist.

As his train pulled out of the station the English girl who had been so gay stood, with her fists clenched by her side, staring at the train and weeping without control. I had never seen an English person weep like that in public. When the train had gone we looked for her but she had disappeared.

Mabel and Cyril saw me to my train and came into the compartment with me. Cyril made all his bad Oxford jokes which had made him so unpopular in London. Mabel kissed me goodbye and said she was very proud of me but I think she was just beginning to grasp the emotion of Ramsay's departure.

The chap opposite me in the compartment was wearing a Univ. tie and reading a copy of *Mandrake.* I watched the countryside we passed through; had lunch; watched the countryside again, the sticks of winter trees, the pale sky. After Didcot I tried to think of the things Oxford meant, swans on a lake, green ivy, brown ivy, immemorial stone, a piano sonata, voices in Hall, your own life, autumn; *fugaces, labuntur anni.*

The cemetery, just before you pull into Oxford station, was covered over in a romantic shroud of bright snow. I closed the book I had not been reading and started putting my luggage together.

PART THREE

DOWN 'MANUEL ROAD

'Lippy had heard so much piano that he couldn't play piano any more. He only thought piano.'

Duke Ellington

I

Willie Monteith was all but canonized by the People's Democratic Party. He was a thick man with a fleshy nose and heavy hanging lips and, at a glance, he looked foolish. But he had been principally responsible for the P.D.P. landslide in the second general election after the new constitution. Monteith had organized F.A.T.U.M. (Free Amalgamated Trade Union Movement) which had successfully challenged the Mannie Small Trade Union on the sugar estates. He offered the workers an honest government and a middle-class standard of living. It was a resounding victory, but the P.D.P. won through Mannie Small's default.

Small, even after the elections, was fairly strong in the corporate area but he had become careless about party organization and he underestimated the magnetic pull middle-class standards had for the aspiring worker. Any of a number of chances might make a working-class family want to put on the externals of the middle class – one of the children might win a scholarship to a big secondary school, one of the young men might have returned from farm work in the States with a slick variant on the art of scuffling, or it might be sudden fantastic wealth, say a thousand pounds, acquired when a foreign bauxite company bought the family's two acres of red land. They didn't change their accents but they voted P.D.P. Even the civilizing 'mass marriages' created a confusion from which the P.D.P. benefited.

Mannie himself put down the Merchants' Party's failure to the disappearance of his three best organizers. They hadn't really disappeared but had gone off to America with three thousand pounds of the party's funds. Because of the many irregularities that these organizers had been connected with within the party, Mannie did not make any public charge against them. He had enough trouble defending himself from the accusation of corruption especially after the Minister of Education, Mr A. Ebenezer Dyer, had been convicted for embezzling public funds. Mannie began the rearguard action of calling the P.D.P. a communist party. That didn't help, for Dr Phillips had ample proof of his persistent Fabianism. The P.D.P. was returned with a majority of ten in a House of thirty-two members.

One incident had marred the sweetness of the P.D.P. victory. Skipper George Lannaman, who was one of Small's foremost workers, had been killed in a clash between the Action Group and Merchants' supporters returning from a Merchants' Party meeting. The coroner decided Skipper had died of a heart attack but the Merchants' Party propaganda was that the P.D.P. Action Group had murdered him.

Dr Phillips affected to take the office of Prime Minister in his stride. He still kept up his law practice and delegated many of the subjects of the Premier's portfolio to a group of very capable ministers – the Minister of Health had been an insurance agent, a specialist divorce-case solicitor was the Minister of Communications, a former racehorse trainer was the Minister of Education, and a graduate (in poultry farming) of Fisk University was the Minister of Agriculture. And the country was run on the advice of *ad hoc* committees of experts outside the Cabinet. Dr Phillips seemed to lose his enthusiasm for politics now that he had 'brought his country to the threshold of independence'. The monomania and the prophet's mantle which had been necessary to bring his party to power seemed to fall away from him like an old skin and he was brilliantly revealed as an accomplished dilettante. His speeches in the Assembly often had the flippancy and slight tang of contemptuousness you expect in the individualistic after-dinner speech. He could still argue a case but he didn't bother with facts now. He left the facts to Albert French, the Minister of Finance. French depended exclusively on a young civil servant, a graduate of the London School of Economics, who was an expert on graphs. Every speech made in the Assembly by the Hon. Albert French consisted of two parts; the first part was incomprehensibly profound as it was made up of long quotations from *The Review of Economic Statistics,* and the second part was an oversimplified précis of government financial policy prepared by the L.S.E. graduate. It was often said by government back-benchers that the Hon. Albert French had been 'a notable mathematician in his schooldays'.

One of the most prominent members of the House of Assembly was Mr Bobsie Tull, member for Eastern Kingston. He was twenty-nine when elected and he had become quite sober and responsible. He was a typical young colonial politician with a fairly good secondary education, an enthusiastic intelligence, a thorough understanding of the habits and ways of thinking of his people. To these qualities Bobsie added, from his own personality, a gift of the gab, no conscience, little scruple, and a romantic adventurousness. Shortly after Ramsay left for England, Bobsie with two other Action Groupers had joined an oil-tanker and gone to Brazil where they spent three months mostly wandering around the rougher sections of Rio de Janeiro. All they seemed to have learned was how to use a revolver. Bobsie was elected, without lobbying, to the P.D.P. Executive and became Dr Phillips' bodyguard (in the sense that he went everywhere with him) and the unofficial disciplinary officer of the party, skilled and successful in gentle political blackmailing. And he took over sole control of the Action Group and was introducing a stern military discipline into that unit of the party.

Bobsie was the *enfant terrible* of the P.D.P. 'After independence,' he would say, 'we *mus'* have a dictatorship because colonialism is a dictatorship and we jus' taking over the same institution. After independence we mus' have some small fish-head corruption because colonialism is corrupt and we are only taking it over.' Whether the idea was his own or not nobody was sure but he brought it into every speech he made in the Assembly and on the P.D.P. platform. He would say that dictatorial methods and corruption were inevitable in Jamaica, and in the same speech praise the democratic virtues and declare that the P.D.P. was the repository of all political and social freedoms. Dr Phillips repeatedly denied that he had any intention of becoming a dictator and said that Tull's opinion was not party policy; but he denied it gingerly, because Bobsie had a large following in the P.D.P.

Bobsie prospered and was a good representative. He owned a new '51 Chevrolet in which he drove his mother to church every

Sunday. His office on Cumberland Avenue was open for at least two hours every day and he was generous with his money and his car. He would lend his car, free of charge, to anybody in his constituency (P.D.P. or not) to go anywhere in the corporate area, and his regular chauffeur was the same boy from the People's Progressive League, a boy named Aubrey, who had once hurled the devastating brick at the Action Group in the Battle of Charles Street. Bobsie kept in very close touch with his constituency, holding a meeting every Sunday night to explain government policy and his own behaviour in the Assembly. The people in Eastern Kingston loved him.

Dr Phillips devoted most of his energy to the Society for Cultural Advancement. The Society had originally been an *ad hoc* committee formed to co-ordinate activities – painting, drama, music, creative writing, dancing – for an island-wide Festival of the Arts. Mannie Small, who was then Prime Minister, had voted thirty thousand pounds towards the Festival, for Dr Phillips assured him that it was entirely non-political. The Festival was Mrs Phillips' idea and she chose the theme – 'Jamaica Emergent'. At the first meeting of the committee it was decided that a permanent co-ordinating secretary should be appointed and they chose Mr Phipps-Help, at an annual salary of two thousand pounds. On Dr Phillips' promise that the job would become permanent after the Festival, Mr Phipps-Help resigned the directorship of the J.I.A. and a retired British Army officer, Colonel FitzMorris (who was enjoying Mandeville's salubrious climate although Mandeville's mosquitoes were enjoying him) became the director.

'Jamaica Emergent' was a great success. From all over the island thousands of school children walked scores of miles in the sun to sing and elocute at parish capitals. In Kingston there were art exhibitions, concerts of music and dancing and Stephen Strachan, the poet, wrote a tremendous pageant called 'Jamaica Whither?'. The pageant was staged under lights at Sabina Park and consisted of a series of floats that moved round the circumference of the park, playing to each gallery in turn, rather like a miracle play. Each float depicted a scene in Jamaica's history. The prize for the best float was given to Mrs Ursula Reeves' dancing group which danced 'Pocomania'. Mrs Reeves was a large, heavy gym-mistress at the Shortwood Training College and she had seen voodoo dances in Haiti. Her group danced with power and abandon and demonstrated the ability of the negro body to contort itself impossibly. Immediately after the Festival numerous dancing groups were formed all over the island and Mrs Reeves was given a special travelling allowance and a car from S.C.A. funds to go around instructing the country in creative dancing.

The picture of Jamaica which emerged from the Festival was that of a country peopled entirely by politicians and various grades of intellectuals. The ordinary worker was hard to find during the Festival. Sometimes you saw him nailing a platform or running an electric wire, and, once, during an important rendering of a Chopin prelude in the Institute Lecture Hall he was heard hammering on empty oil drums in a backyard in the nearby lane – but, on the whole, he showed very little interest in the Festival. Mrs Phillips said this was a pity because the Jamaican worker is 'so picturesque'.

The S.C.A. was formed a week before the Festival ended. Dr Phillips thought it might eventually become the island's Arts Council, one of his dreams, and though he had great faith in Mr Phipps-Help's organizing ability he considered it best to steer the Society himself. His axiom was that there was nothing immoral or undemocratic about a country having a small cultured élite while the bulk of the population was illiterate. He got some actors together (amateur actors hoping to become professionals) and made a number of instructional films mainly to do with agriculture. The actors looked like actors, not farmers. Nobody was discouraged when the Mobile Film Unit reported that the country people preferred westerns and Charlie Chaplin. The S.C.A. was concerned with higher objectives. By giving work to middle-class amateur actors, musicians and dancers it ensured that the island's cultured élite did not atrophy.

This was still a graceful hospitable country, free to all races, a romantic place on an airway ticket, a place where the rejected from other lands can find asylum and a new importance. If you tried to see it whole you saw it through the eye of the middle-class short-story writer – you saw an unemployed black man facing his hundredth day of unemployment and the starvation of his commonlaw wife; the brown-skin lawyer, well fed, hearty, very sympathetic to the poor; the brown-skin couple (so scandalous, so passionate) copulating on the beach in the very tropical sun, and that black unemployed, hungry man waiting, hearing the sounds of brown-skin copulation, and, inexorably, in the inescapable pressure of economic and social circumstances, he must murder the brown man for a few stray shillings in the brown man's abandoned trousers, he must murder and be vindicated and condemned, but the writer's 'neutrality' must keep him *there*, the unemployed vicious black animal encased in a style made fashionable in Europe or America. The fact is that one night a man took the 'weed', ganja, marijuana, found a couple on the beach who were *not* copulating (the papers said they were singing Catholic hymns) and murdered him and raped her, brutally, and the only pressures he suffered from were the fumes of dope on a diseased brain. That was the 'progressive' instant to induce middle-class pity for the poor, 'the realities of the facts'.

'We mus' still continue,' Edgar Bailey said. 'Dr Phillips and the P.D.P. trying to give the workers freedom in Dr Phillips' way, not the people's way. The workers in this country still support Mannie Small – don't mind they only have twelve members in the House, it's a working-class party. They going turn out the P.D.P. quick sharp. Mannie get corrupt an' too big an' too smart but the people going put him back. You will see!'

'Even if. What *we* to do?' Septy Grant asked.

They were standing on the piazza of the P.P.L. offices on Slipe Road waiting for Capleton and Mannie Small. It was a bright Sunday morning with a breeze blowing up and the dust on the breeze. The patches of asphalt on the road were melting in the sun. Three black girls in white hats and white dresses flared over crinolines turned in from Devon Avenue and were having trouble with the breeze. The street was full of well-dressed people with large Bibles. One drunk was trying to find his way home.

Edgar and Septy sat on the piazza steps.

'Nutten, nutten! Ongle wait,' Edgar said. 'There's gonter be a big buss-up an' only *we* can survive it because we not greedy.

Only the P.P.L. can give the people freedom in the people's way.'

The People's Progressive League had come alive again after Capleton's release and they rented the old offices on Slipe Road. Joseph Lowe's mural continued to dominate the outer office although there were grease stains now over the worker's arms and the child's face. Capleton's prison sentence had been effective P.D.P. propaganda but the youth still clung to the League. The League had no power and no hope of power and for the unemployed boys this 'politics' was a way of scuffling within the law under no discipline except that of withering abuse and defence or attack in street fights. It was impossible to say what these boys believed in. Perhaps they believed only in Edgar Bailey's personality. Capleton's money was finished and American aid was small and infrequent. In the general election eight hundred pounds had been found to put up sixteen candidates all of whom lost their deposits. After a while some of the youth who wanted to work joined Mannie Small's union and jobs were found for them. Even Septy Grant wavered. Then, for a short time, the public became very interested in the League when Mona Freeman started speaking on its platform.

After her divorce from Reggie Kendal, Mona went back to work with Capleton in a mood of personal anger. Her marriage had failed for her at the social level long before she began to be disgusted with what she had said in court had been a gradual physical degeneracy in Kendal. For a time she tried being a respectable prostitute from night club to night club and was briefly notorious and starving. Then Capleton persuaded her to work again in the P.P.L. offices and she started speaking at P.P.L. meetings. She made the same speech every night and it had nothing to do with revolution or socialism or party politics but it was very effective. She explained why she had joined the P.P.L. in the form of a confession, as converted Christians confess at street meetings that previously they had been running down the smooth road to destruction until a voice said, 'weary wanderer, come and listen', and they were saved. Mona said *she* had been running down the middle-class road of destruction until the voice told her where they (the audience) could only be saved.

257

There was nothing in those speeches but there was everything in Mona. She dressed very well and she wrapped her hair in a chiffon scarf and she made an allusion to sex in each of her speeches. She didn't keep scandal out of it but made clear references to the type of life the wives of P.D.P. politicians lived, the facts she said she had gathered when she moved among the upper classes. For two months everybody came to hear the 'coolie gal' and then she fell back into the rhythm of a hopeless, unsupported political party. She had to choose between days in a government office where nothing happened, evenings at night clubs with other women's husbands, bored Sundays of brokenness, days of intrigue and scandal, and meaningless political slogans, dependence on Capleton and the fragile hope of entering one day a glorious kingdom. She was another of the condemned and lost.

Edgar and Septy waited at the P.P.L. offices until Capleton's Buick drove up. In the car were Capleton, Mannie Small and an assistant permanent secretary in the Ministry of Education. Capleton was old and thin and his face was always in pain from the severe gastritis he suffered from after his prison sentence. He knew, in his every word and gesture, that he had failed, but not as the colonial educated understand failure in terms of passing examinations; what he wanted to achieve was identical with the idea he had for a workers' socialist government in the island. As long as that idea did not lose its urgency for him he saw his failure as a chance-determined thing, as a man may fail to produce children. He would have carried on the League with ten members.

They sat round the table in Capleton's office.

'Well, Edgar, what you say to the proposition?' Mannie began without preliminaries.

'The League can join with you,' Edgar said. 'On a condition!'

'Awright,' Mannie said. 'Let's start somewhere else an' come to that. Ah catching up with Willie in Clarendon, ah'm there every day an' hour the House not sitting but, you know what, the P.D.P. having money behind them today, big money, you have some young Syrians today with big money an' big ideas.'

'You have money,' Edgar said. 'You know laas' week I was at the corner of Church Street and Eas' Street an' Mr Capleton drive past in his car, and a man stood up there say, "Tha's the only honest politician we have here in Jamaica, Capleton!" I know the man. He's a P.D.P.'

'Look,' Mannie said, 'you people not in politics, you know. You doan have no following, you never win an election, you doan have a trade union. Is play-play politics this, you know. But you *could* be in politics!'

'O.K.,' Edgar said, 'argument done!'

The civil servant was a 'progressive', self-made man. He had been educated at Central Branch Elementary School and Mico College and had been teaching in elementary schools until Wolsey Hall helped him to a London external pass degree. He went into the Education Office as an Education Officer, got a grant from Mannie Small's government to spend ten months in England and just before the Merchants' Party were turned out of office he had been made an assistant permanent secretary. He was unusual for a civil servant. He was remarkably efficient at his job, lived well within his income and was afraid of nobody – he was legendary among teachers for his intelligence, efficiency and courage. He was unusual as a man because he was one of the few people who consistently said what he was thinking, not what he had selected from his own thinking and modified by what other people said and what he thought they were thinking. For this reason he very often didn't make sense in conversation. So he began talking from nowhere.

'You notice how everybody is afraid to work,' he said, 'to do the thing for the thing? You mus' show this, you mus' show that, you mus' prove this. Nobody can work for work. Even Jesus Christ was trying to prove something, tha's why he was a man and not God. All of you say you fighting against imperialism. That could be a thing for the thing, better than Christ for he ran away from imperialism. But that would be work. *I* want the Englishman who is head of my department to clear out so that I can become permanent secretary of Education for I have the brain and the experience. And the only man who can move that Englishman from here is Mannie Small.'

'You fighting imperialism, Mannie?' Capleton asked.

'What you mean? Yes, I'm the workers' representative.'

'We can never see it the same,' Edgar said. 'How you manage to fight imperialism with imperialists' money?'

'Look,' the civil servant said to Edgar, 'you use too much abstraction, man, and you heading either for jail or the lunatic asylum. You want to get the Englishman out but you can't get him out because he's been fucking your women for centuries. Life not pretty, don't try to pretty-pretty it up. Mr Capleton here is dying right now and when you see him stretch out you come and tell me if he's pretty. You trying to pretty-up everything. Of course, Mannie use the people money and he was Prime Minister for four years *and* we nearly ruling ourselves. You caan' get the Englishman out of your blood and you can't get him out of your economy but you can get him out of the civil service and the government. Don't pretty-pretty up the thing with abstractions, man. I want to head that department.'

'Awright,' Mannie said, 'to come back again, sixty-five pound a month, a union car you can use all the time. I doan want the League and I doan want any of this Marxis' thing. Workers, capitalists, anti-P.D.P., anti-Willie Monteith, and me. I let you have this, too, you can say anything but doan use the words.'

'Let's put it back this way,' Capleton said. He looked very tired. 'You get Edgar with the union, Mannie, straight against F.A.T.U.M., no politics, just the people.'

'You so sure you have the workers,' Edgar said to Mannie. 'O.K., then. Employ another organizer. You have a job, Mannie? You can work at any trade? I'm a mason, you know.'

Capleton came alive for the last time in his political career. He could gamble on anything now. He had seen a red dream get mixed up with a black dream in the States and he had suffered both disillusions and he thought he was dying though the doctor said he'd be all right soon.

'This is the very last proposition, Mannie, take it or leave it,' he said. 'I will start the W.C.U. again on the estates, only splintering, sucking F.A.T.U.M. but not troubling you; but on the socialist line. After a while we have a vote around and when W.C.U. and your union together have a clear majority we merge with you and withdraw. That's the last proposition.'

'In other words,' Mannie said, 'you train them and turn them loose on me, don't it? I doan want it. I only want Edgar Bailey.'

'Take it or leave it, Mannie,' Capleton said. 'No training. No infiltration. Only working-class solidarity. I don't have any more use for power, only work, as my friend here was saying.'

The meeting broke up and they went from Capleton's darkened offices into the bright street. There had been no decision and nobody had known what anybody else, except the civil servant, had been thinking. Septy Grant might have been thinking about the discussion or he might have been thinking about Vera Chen, but he knew that Capleton would revive that union, the Worker's Co-operative Union, and that he was really offering Mannie nothing.

The drunk who had passed up the street earlier hadn't found his home but had found the back entrance to another bar. He saw the politicians getting into their car and his mind heaved with an idea. He held Capleton's shirt. 'You know what, Capleton, I'm a rass red!' the drunk said and smiled a fixed charming smile at Capleton. He continued down Slipe Road telling the world he was a 'rass red'.

Capleton's W.C.U. was unbelievably successful. A free independent trade union of dock-workers joined with him and he also organized among the municipal council workers. W.C.U.'s presence created an initial confusion on the sugar estates because Mannie did not dare to attack them. After a year a straw vote showed that F.A.T.U.M. had fifty per cent, Mannie Small Trade Union forty per cent, and W.C.U. ten per cent. It was only after the vote that Edgar and Septy Grant (who had given up his cabinet-maker's job to help with the campaign) discovered that Capleton had organized the W.C.U. on money that he got from Small. But they kept Capleton's senseless word and disbanded the W.C U. on the sugar plantations after the vote, returned to Kingston and tried to keep the League alive. Capleton's doctor diagnosed gastric ulcers which he tried to treat without surgery.

II

This island was a place of long monotonous hills and sealed-off villages in the hills, a few where a man, long-known and out of exile, could enter and draw his soul around him.

To enter the village, walking, you crossed a simple bridge of planks and wooden rails over which the village 'warner' one morning prophesied death and destruction and in the evening a truck full of drunken innocents fell from that bridge thirty feet to the dry river-bed. You crossed the bridge carefully remembering not death but the presentiment of death the old toothless woman could smell on her blood. Then a steep gravel road to the sharp turn and the village gate. The river was there, a spring, a trickle waiting for drought, the sweet water you sucked through green pimento leaves; that perfumed water, your first sensuous thrill, taken for thirst but for ever, in memory, the sacrament of belonging. The road to the village was rock, unblastable, unfertilizing rock, rock, the deep trees up and down the hillside that the road was a line across. Just at the entrance before the first turning it was dark and cool in spite of its place near the sun. The gate you opened to the village was the gate of your own astonishment at the tensions under which you had lived for twenty years away from yourself. Your village is always open and has many closed gates.

The expected things you believe have changed assure you of your identity, and the simplification objects press on you make you realize the extent of your exile. The corn still growing as you round the first turning, on stony ground (so that religious ripples start and you anticipate the old church) is still corn growing. And the other trees, especially the pimento and the white dots of its blossoms you knew you could never forget and had forgotten; mango, coconut, sweet-sop, sour-sop, custard-apple, star-apple, not as trees, shapes for a painter, beautiful things (trees like that for you now in Cézanne) but as the tactility of your boyish hunger.

You can shed nothing passing this stone wall laid by hands that can never lose their hardness or their grace and you cannot wish you had those hands because you have chosen the way of non-identification. It is the first houses that shock you. They wait to trap you into simplicity so with your city habit you prepare to close yourself like the shame-a-lady fern your feet are kicking into modesty. You knew, you knew and should not have come back to the smells of the marl path, of the uneven floor polished with green bush and plain bees' wax, of the green smoke that told you as a child that your dinner wasn't ready and you would be late to play ball. You know that rocking-chair with a bump on the backward swing, you know that chipped enamel mug, you know the giant Bible and the copybook names in it. Again, from the city, it is the village people you want to avoid for they link you to objects with a simplicity that breaks down twenty years of certainties and velleities and labyrinths of tentative selves.

The gate you *must* enter was green, the lower hinge had gone and you had to lift it gently away from you brushing the tip of the large ageless rock. Sunflowers, large and yellow, dominated the garden where nobody bothered with the roses now, and in the circular rock-beds Josephs' Coats and the red spongy Cat's Tail lapped each other carelessly and rich. To touch again for belief there were the galvanized tank, the pomegranate tree, and the sugarcane root.

There were forty-eight steps forming approximately an inverted 'T' to the verandah of the house. The same uniform green bush and wax-polish smells were there and the small rooms that were not your memories any more, as when you woke up in a strange country in the dark and felt briefly at the tail-end of sleep one of these rooms shaping itself and losing its shape around you. Now they were your personality. The impulse was to go higher, through the house and climb, past the barbecues, up into the coffee grove, steeply, breathless at the end of your last journey, towards the top of the hill and the giddy biblical church.

On its steps you commanded the village and the island and the truth. Every village story you had read was the story of this village, every church, every garden. You had never left them. From this tabernacle step a variety of colours returned and you saw that the island was a purple-grey between the green of the trees and the afternoon of the sun. A valley flowed away from you, all the way down the St Ann red clay across the placenames of saviours, Sturge, Buxton, Wilberforce, across the Christian messages of Mount Zion and Salem, to the sea. The sea stood up straight in a curve of the bay ten miles across your need to remember how small the island was, how small you were; the sea that locked you in and made you a warm realized thing. Looking at the sea there, through this window of half-return, *that* was life, the breakers you could not hear, the soft white stitches where the waves turn over, the miracle of the myth-enduring sea.

The sea's wash was controlled, answered, and soft as the ship slowed to take the pilot on board at about three o'clock in the morning. Ramsay went on deck and saw the unbelievable island stretched out in that special Palisadoes' before-day half-light. He could make out the shapes of other ships and fishing boats and he saw Kingston lit up with the new assurance of a real city. The ship waited for something and he walked along the deck towards the Captain's bridge trying to see, in the dark, places he knew he would not recognize. But it was home, and, until he landed, something to return to. He forced himself to think he remembered the special quality of the warmth around the island, the special smell of the breeze.

He saw the pilot and was surprised that it was an old friend, Pilot Collins, who had been the chairman of his mother's Co-operative Group. He shouted to him.

'Wait! Is you?' Collins said coming to the top of the bridge-stairs. 'Glad to see you back. Soon take you in to see the folks. How England?'

'Fine, man. Fine!' Ramsay said eager to fall again into the Jamaican accent and idiom and sensing the social pressure that required it.

'Well, Jamaica doan change much, you know,' Collins said, 'but we going on steady, you know.'

'You don't race out again to be the first pilot at the ship?' Ramsay asked.

'No, we have a union now. Is better like that.'

'So everything is changed, eh?' Ramsay said. He felt disappointed; he had looked forward to seeing pilots' boats racing out to the ship.

'Anyway,' Collins said, 'when you get in the wharf the boys will still dive for coins. They doan change that yet.' He said it sharply and though Ramsay had had no real relationship with him he thought it strange that he could not recognize the sharpness as one of the tones of Collins' voice.

'Come round the house when you have time, man,' Collins said. 'Glad to have you back. Miss Alice will be please.'

And for the first time since he began the journey Ramsay felt he was not a foreigner.

Voices brought the sun up, voices with the earth in them, the dialect in free cadenzas coming up to the ship in waves like a rehearsed concert. It seemed to Ramsay that those voices had no relation to poverty and hunger and dispossession. That was the thought with which he grasped his return and it lasted for a minute only.

The tourists threw coins over the side and the boys dived and came up with the coins held in their grinless teeth. Then Ramsay established his abstract identity and went ashore. They were all there, his mother, Madge, Rosalie, Ray, Martin and Bobsie. He was older now, frightened of his earlier adolescence, and he found that he could not break the habit of four years of lovelessness to plunge into this new warmth that had always been there unrecognized. They took him with a simple family joy but they placed him in a context that had nothing to do with love. He was a fact of status, of achievement to be added to their own lives and dreams and importance. He was the triumph of the colour of their skins.

He said good-bye to the Welshman, manager of a banana plantation in St Mary, who drank with him every day of the journey. He heard the cadenced careless tones of his own voice and sensed the satisfaction ripple through his family. That was another fact. He had moved from one milieu of cautiousness to another. At twenty-three, a man, he would never know himself. The self-knowledge he had learned in England had not prepared him for simple human relationships, and he felt a confused compassion and self-pity as his mother held him, the lost one, and cried.

Bobsie and Ramsay fell into a quick instinctive understanding that had not been there before. Bobsie was dressed splendidly, the M.H.A., the ruler, getting a cheerful deference from the steamship officials, the customs officers and the police. He had time for pride but none for sentiment.

'You fix up with a job yet, ole man?' he asked Ramsay.

'No. But the government will find one for me, I expect.'

'I am the government, you know, Ramsay!' Bobsie said.

For Ramsay, this was an extremely complicated remark. It was one of those moments when tone and fact and intention are so mixed up that the mind which is trying to understand the remark races through four or five different attitudes in a few seconds. Ramsay had never congratulated Bobsie on winning the election, he had not shown he was proud of his brother; his own education, in certain circumstances, was insignificant compared with political power; he should *depend* on Bobsie; and Bobsie was afraid that, politically, Ramsay might still be where he was before he went away.

'Today black man is really ruling the country. Not like in Mannie Small time,' Bobsie added.

They put the luggage into Bobsie's car and Ramsay sat in front and Mrs Tull sat in the back seat. He told her about the sea journey and the things he was longing to eat.

'Listen, Ramsay,' Bobsie said, 'in Jamaica today you have to look out for yourself, you know. Is not scuffling, is work, you understand me? But Jamaicans wicked to each other. Nobody not going to help you, excep' you own family, you understand me?'

'It was always like that,' Ramsay said.

'Listen,' Bobsie said. He paused, leaned his head slightly to one side, frowned into the windscreen and kept his mouth open for a little before he spoke again. 'You want a headmastership?'

'Me?'

'Yes.'

'Headmastership of a secondary school?' Ramsay said.

'Not in town, you know,' Bobsie explained, 'in the country. In St Ann.'

'What school is that?'

'It's a private school,' Bobsie said. 'If you teach in a Kingston school as an ordinary teacher you get what? About five hundred pound, don't it? I can get you this school for eight hundred and fifty pound. You come from Oxford. The man there now don't even pass intermediate.'

'But I don't have any experience,' Ramsay said. 'I've never taught in my life.' He was being too subjective and was slow to understand what Bobsie was getting at.

'Never mind that,' Bobsie said, the cool samfie man, 'if you want the school I can get it for you. It's not a government school, but I know the man who own the school. I have him –' Bobsie took his hand off the steering-wheel and made a gesture of holding somebody by the neck. 'I can get it for you in a week.'

'But suppose the government don't want me to teach in a private school,' Ramsay argued. 'Anyway the whole idea is fantastic!'

'You should really think of it, Ramsay,' his mother said, very slowly. 'Is a really *good* opportunity.'

Bobsie drove on easily, with a sad smile. He knew that all Ramsay had was 'education', but he was his brother.

'You say is fantastic?' he said speaking softly, cynically. 'I could make you headmaster of Surrey College if I wanted. You don't understand what happening in this country today. I tell you black man is really ruling!'

Bobsie was not boasting. He knew perfectly well that he couldn't make Ramsay headmaster of Surrey College but he wished he could be challenged to try the pressures and threats that might work in that fantasy of corruption.

Ramsay needed in the first few months to learn a new land-scape and he met the intellectuals. They smelt of a new era of intelligent moderate nationalism but Dr Phillips' myth was beginning to lose its unifying force. Too many had been left in victory with only tired emotions.

There was a little bar near Cross Roads where the P.D.P. intellectuals gathered. It was the enclosed part of the first-floor verandah of a night club and was lit by a single unshaded bulb. The bar was a four-feet square opening above a half-door that had a wide ledge on it. There were two small tables and some very ragged canvas chairs in the enclosure. There were no shelves of bottles where the barman stood. He was in a tiny passageway and behind him a door was kept closed on the gambling den. When you ordered a drink the barman ducked under his half of the ledge; you heard him wash a glass in a bucket and you heard him pouring the drink but you never saw the bottle or the brand of rum.

The group that met there was dominated by Stephen Strachan. He was at last in rebellion against Mrs Phillips and nationalism, maintaining that the rest of the world had found and lost nationalism three hundred years before Jamaica. His new poetic theme was the futility of using skin-colour tension as a basis for art since colour either as a sanction for contempt or a standard of excellence was gradually disappearing in the West Indies.

One weird night they had been discussing the barring of a well-known West Indian politician from a hotel in Nassau.

'The only thing that will satisfy a goddam naygah is for God to make him white,' Stephen said, very drunk. 'What him want in those people's country? He belong there?'

'Don't be a damn fool, Stephen,' somebody said.

Stephen took a scrap of paper from his shirt pocket and seemed to be reading them a poem,

> 'Here we are turning
> black into white
> white into black
> a controlled contriving . . . '

There was nothing written on the scrap of paper and they were all drunk.

'Colour is very important man,' Ramsay said. 'They've been turning black into white in America since God was a boy and look at it today. South Africa, everywhere something. Oh, damn it! All art is useless unless it makes people want to change something or change themselves. Anyway you can't turn black into white; no matter what you do you are only turning white into black!'

'Then why did you marry a white woman?' Stephen asked him and the others laughed.

'I'm not married,' Ramsay said, searching his mind for an

allegorical meaning. They knew he wasn't married but they laughed at him just the same.

'Nobody can dictate my theme,' Stephen said, sobering up. 'If I see the old Greek legend of Persephone being relived in East Queen Street then I am free to use it as plot, structure, everything. Look here, don't talk communist balls to me, man! I am Stephen Strachan the poet and I know all the arguments for and against the nationalization of art. You are talking Marxist fart, man!'

He got back the city's pace extended now by the social upheaval of his education and he went into rooms that he had previously seen only through windows. Bobsie's political importance frequently placed him in awkward situations where he wasn't sure why he had been asked into those rooms. For nearly a year he moved on the fringe of the fringe of the outer King's House circle, among drinkers who assumed that the P.D.P. might, if it got into the wrong hands, go too far in a socialist direction, among cocktail parties that talked about 'West Indian culture' as if it were someone who had only just left the room, musical recitals at homes well in from the roads in areas of St Andrew he would still be humiliated to walk in during the day. He kept as far from the People's Progressive League as possible. He had tea with Mrs Phillips occasionally and read her two prose poems he had written on the basis of a painting of market-women by Joseph Lowe. She was very enthusiastic about them and took them from him with a vague promise of publication. She had something new to say about art each time, some new metaphor that could say only the one eternal sayable thing.

'I always think of the artist as a kind of village idiot or saint – much the same thing – who is chosen to take objects out of a lucky dip and explain them. Some of the objects may not need explaining to the crowd around him, only taking out and showing. Selection is no more calculated than dipping your hand into a closed bag, is it? Style is only the patter, the things you say when you are showing the objects around, and, of course, the manner, the way you use your hands.'

But there was no illumination. The room had changed and was lighter now; instead of a Picasso it was a Matisse, instead of fishermen catching crabs it was an abstraction of sunlight and hills by Juanita Hernandez. Mrs Phillips seemed twenty years older but the silver coffee service remained young and the fine elegant horses marked time delicately in the stables. Every time he entered the room he felt that the house had stopped, the end of an era before the era had begun. She was quite powerless to make him a writer.

She told him that Cyril and Patricia would soon be formally engaged and they talked about the certainty of Cyril's success. He felt a sudden need to catch, in talk, some of that future glory and he told Mrs Phillips pointless sentimental stories about what Cyril and he had done and said at Surrey College. In colonial bourgeois society people are not themselves but what other bigger or more eccentric people have said to them or shared with them. Whenever Ramsay now left her, Mrs Phillips drove him in her Morris Minor the six miles home to the house on St James' Road which had been repainted in green and white.

Mrs Hanson was quite frank about the material comforts she was looking forward to when Cyril returned. She still looked young and handsome in a late maturity. Ramsay visited her often because she phoned him nearly every day and insisted on his coming to see her. They talked about Cyril and Oxford and her visit to England and her loneliness.

Ramsay had reached the point of hoping for something to happen in his life and after each visit he resented the thin relationship and the waste of time. But he, too, began to feel that there would be something apocalyptic about Cyril's return and, what was more, he was flattered that he had the memories of England that Mrs Hanson's talk stirred although he did not particularly want to remember those things. She had preserved her youth, or her childishness, and age touched her only in her inability to remember that Ramsay's mother was still alive. It was a little strange that this annoyed him because in that society it was not at all remarkable that neither Mrs Phillips nor Mrs Hanson had met or wanted to meet Mrs Tull.

Ramsay had refused Bobsie's offer of the headmastership in St Ann and he had taken a job at Hampstead School in Kingston. The headmaster was an old man, past retiring age, bald, very black and a devout Christian. But for pressure from the Education

Office he would probably not have employed Ramsay. Ramsay joined the staff in the middle of the term and the school really needed a teacher for Religious Knowledge. After their first interview Mr Byfield was quite sure Ramsay was an atheist, although he *said* he was a Christian. During their discussion Ramsay had tried to define his position by saying, 'We both believe in God, but we don't believe in the same God.' Mr Byfield, who was a no-nonsense Baptist and had learned his religion direct from the missionaries regarded Ramsay's attitude only as a youthful attempt to be different, and he gave him a time-table two-thirds of which was Religious Knowledge. Mr Byfield advised Ramsay to teach it as literature without dogma. He did this thoroughly and, as there was no set curriculum, he merely ranged all over the Bible reading with the boys the passages *he* thought were of interest. The only remarkable thing about Hampstead School was the number of boys whose parents wanted them to have extra lessons in English. Mr Byfield told him firmly that he should never give extra lessons free but charge at least five shillings an hour. It was not of importance to Mr Byfield that most of the parents were very poor and that their children were being taught English badly in the classroom. It was a black boys' school and had a deep 'English' complex and it was an ancient staff room joke that English was a 'foreign language' at Hampstead School.

The staff was completely Jamaican and aggressively religious. There were four graduates – Mr Byfield, Mr Stewart who taught mathematics, Miss Smith who had been at 'school' in Pennsylvania and taught geography, and Ramsay. Four of the other eight teachers had been trained as elementary schoolteachers at Mico College and the other four were boys who had just left school. They were all Baptists and they thought of themselves and the school as being underprivileged.

Ramsay became the centre of a network of tensions in that staff room. It was exactly like a play. Mr Stewart, nearly fifty, was an old boy of the school and had only just missed winning an island scholarship; then, twenty years later, after he had taken an external degree of London University, he just missed getting a government grant to do a Teacher's Diploma in England. When he found out that Ramsay had been at Surrey College he told him that he would have been given that government grant had he (Mr Stewart) been teaching at Surrey. He found a way of saying that accusingly to Ramsay once every day. Miss Smith resented two things about Ramsay – the settled status of his degree and the number of telephone calls he got from very insistent female voices. She was in her middle thirties, wore tailored suits and managed to preserve that very cosmetic American look of the negro fashion-plate. She talked about America as if it were the Kingdom of Heaven and she talked about the Kingdom of Heaven as if it were, of course, at hand; at the same time she tried to carry on an astral flirtation with Ramsay on the basis of his many telephone calls. But she never lost the chance of pointing out how incomplete and lacking in *fullness* the English system of university education was. She played the organ at morning assembly and her pupils got very good results in geography examinations.

The Mico-trained teachers who were extremely efficient at their jobs were quite annoyed that Ramsay really knew only one subject and they thought he was lazy and too mild with the boys because every minor crisis which occurred in the school, such as the late ringing of bells, was traced to Ramsay's neglect or forgetfulness. But they joined with him in a mysterious village bond of irony at Miss Smith's sophistication. The four boys on the staff were not at all pleased about Ramsay's apparent igno-rance of games and spent a lot of time explaining the finer points of cricket and football and recounting epic games they had played for Hampstead against other schools. At the same time they greatly admired Ramsay. They regarded him, this man who looked like them and had gone all those thousands of miles to study, as a prophet – a prophet without a message, or to whom the message had not yet been given. They were very willing to do his duty or take his preparation periods for him. Ramsay never got bored with staff room conversation and regarded himself as a *punctum indifferens.* He was still waiting for something to happen to him.

The first thing that 'happened' was trivial. He arrived at school drunk one morning after spending the night at Stephen Strachan's house drinking and listening to a writer named Sandy Brown complaining that certain 'philistines' had refused to put on a play he had written because it had a strong socialist theme. He had come to school by taxi straight from Stephen's house at the bottom of Mountain View Avenue. Apart from persistent blinking and an unusually affectionate manner there was nothing peculiar about his behaviour. But he made the mistake of singing too vigorously in assembly. Mr Stewart had a consultation with Mr Byfield immediately after assembly.

Ramsay discovered that if he sat at the desk in the classroom he started falling asleep and that when he walked around the room the hot stuffy air made him dizzy. So he took his class to the far end of the playing-field and they were not heard of again until the lunch break. By that time Ramsay had had two hours' sleep in the grass and his class of eleven-year-olds had climbed the mango trees and the guinep trees in the adjoining garden, had had many fights among themselves and then had improvised a game of cricket with limes and bats made from coconut boughs. Ramsay returned to the staff room and found a silence which suggested that a prayer meeting was in progress. Mr Byfield was there and he summoned Ramsay to his study.

'Well, Mr Tull,' he said, 'I mus' tell you that I take a very serious view of what happened this morning. If you were sick you should certainly stay at home.'

'I wasn't sick,' Ramsay said, with the clarity that sometimes follows a drunken sleep. 'I was drunk.'

'Well, Mr Tull, this is a religious institution, you know, and we don't tolerate that kind of thing here, If it occurs again I shall have to inform the Board.'

'The who?' Ramsay asked. The fog had began to creep back.

'The Board of Governors of the school. They wouldn' be pleased at all.'

'I'm terribly sorry about what happened,' Ramsay said in his best manner. 'It won't happen again.'

'You know, Mr Tull, we Baptists are not against a little wine, as St Paul says, in moderation. But a teacher is an example. A teacher is a beacon light. Don't let it happen again!'

Ramsay returned to the staff room and told the younger

teachers fantastic tales about his drunken escapades, none of which were true. Nobody, not even the boys just from school, had any sympathy for the devil's work of drink and another tension developed. The incident had more serious consequences. Both Mr Stewart and Miss Smith told members of the Board about it and Ramsay was 'discussed' at the next Board meeting. And the assistant permanent secretary in the Education Office gave him a stern friendly warning. Then Mr Byfield, who had been teaching English throughout the school for twenty-five years, gave half of his classes to Ramsay and taught religious knowledge himself.

He began to settle into a lotus-land pattern of life where there were no disillusionments to be a martyr about, and no anger to sharpen life to a burning point of futility. It was an easy comfortable life. The disease he had felt at nineteen he now explained to himself as an adolescent twitch which he had rationalized into a social and political deprivation. He now had money, Bobsie had money, his mother was comfortable and he could go with assurance into any house anywhere. There was drink and there were the arguments of the people that circled around Stephen Strachan. Alf-Gordon and Bertram Shaw from the Courts Office were regular members of the gambling group in the night club at Cross Roads, and though he didn't gamble he drank with them often and they went on week-end trips to do more drinking in the country. And there were girls that were fresh and old in their experience who gave him back his four lost years and asked for nothing in return.

Every week Edgar Bailey 'phoned him and asked him to help, in an unspecified way, with the P.P.L. He told Edgar that he was still trying to assess the political situation fully and was trying to decide whether political activity of the P.P.L. variety had any meaning when there was no possibility of getting any political power. He made an adroit delaying argument by condemning the P.D.P. government in Edgar's terms while at the same time accusing the P.P.L. of selling out to Mannie Small. He did not want to say that he was very comfortable visiting Mrs Phillips and reading short stories to her and drinking with Stephen Strachan and going to British Council sponsored classical records concerts in St Andrew mansions. And there was something priest-like and frightening about Edgar's dedication, a hard moral core which he had not noticed in the earlier years.

He tried to judge his experience and his life and he came to the conclusion that he was a neutral point only with a habit of observing. Not entirely neutral, though, because he recognized a chameleon quality in the way he adopted the manners around him in an easy contradiction from Alf-Gordon to Mrs Phillips. His original terror of responsibility now seemed to him unfounded. All he needed to be was conformist, with a streak of difference based on his visit to England. He tried to live hard and one day noticed signs of an approaching nervous breakdown. It was a buzzing sound in the back of his head. Ramsay had had two nervous breakdowns when he was at school, each accompanied by a disgusting rash all over his body that gradually dried and flaked off. The school doctor never told him the diagnosis of the rash but only asked him if he had had any 'connections with women'. During his second term at Hampstead School the buzzing and the rash came on and he was forced to give up drinking and to spend three weeks in bed. The doctor only said that he was 'run down'.

He recovered in time, however, to attend the year's intellectual high-spot sponsored by the Society for Cultural Advancement. He received a gold-embossed invitation to be present at a lecture on 'Culture-Persistence Patterns in the Stratifications of Leadership among West Indian Red Ants'. The lecturer, Dr Marmadoskovski, a distinguished American '-ist', had been doing field work in the Caribbean for three years. He was a short thin man with a large bald head and large ludicrous hands like something out of Jean Vigo.

The lecture was delivered on a lawn in East King's House Road, one of the most stately lawns in Jamaica, brilliantly floodlit that night. The audience was made up of the 'intelligentsia' (a word they liked to see in the newspapers) and they came together with the self-consciousness and courage of people who are afraid that they might be told the truth about themselves. They shared a terror of the West Indian red ant – a mysterious species which had begun to appear in small numbers throughout the Caribbean and had begun to assume leadership of the other common black ants.

Dr Marmadoskovski was a brilliant man and he lectured logically and coherently for two hours without notes. His articulation was not disturbed by the gum he was chewing.

He explained, with the help of a blackboard, his general methodology and the relative importance he gave to theory, empiricism, retentions, survivals and syncretisms. Then he attacked, academically, the inadequate methodology of his friends, Popsicle and Fudge, who had worked in the Caribbean field some years before him. Dr Marmadoskovski said that he had expected to find, judging from previous research, not the common black ant but the long-suffering negro ant which is inclined 'to flight rather than fight' but it seemed true, as Popsicle and Fudge had asserted, that this species existed, oddly enough, only in Europe. West Indian ants, on the whole, suggested to him a physical and ideological equalitarianism, a fact that Fudge, in particular, tended to overlook. The bulk of West Indian ants live in minimal communities and make their nests, consisting of a single or two or three chambers, in the ground: this was interesting but not nearly so important as the indisputable truth that the eyes of the worker ant are, with a few exceptions, poorly developed or even absent. Both these facts accounted for the predominant leadership of the newly arrived red ant which had evidently come into the islands on the ships that brought soldiers to deal with the riots of 1938. He did not accept Popsicle's view that under certain circumstances a black ant might become a red ant.

'I am prepared to assert,' Dr Marmadoskovski said, 'that, in spite of the views of Popsicle and Fudge, there is conscious leadership and apparent intelligence among West Indian red ants. And the term I have coined for this leadership is "flagratic leadership", in the Pauline sense that it is better to marry than to burn.'

He went on with St Paul for a while, then he mentioned the flagellation of monks in Tibet, then he touched on the Kinsey reports, but he wasn't taking his audience with him. It was only when he came back to St Paul and mentioned *en passant* an interesting anthropological specimen, named Doris, that he had met in the field (Hanover Street) that the audience realized he was being whimsical. They laughed smugly at his wit. Then he distinguished four types of flagratic leadership in ascending order of importance: (1) flagratic leadership with a bad smell; (2) flagratic leadership with no smell; (3) flagratic leadership without intelligence; (4) flagratic leadership with intelligence.

The real message of his lecture, however, was that the West Indian red ant was either entirely *sui generis* or originated in Europe. There was no evidence of any African origin as in the case of the common black ant and he discredited all the conclusions in that direction that Popsicle and Fudge, particularly Fudge, had come to. He was firm about this because he saw that if any connection were established with the African ant then, even theoretically, there would be serious consequences for the structure of West Indian cultural society. The flagratic leadership with a bad smell was trying to maintain that African culture patterns were part of their techniques of biting and living in trees, and Fudge had given credence to this view. What was wrong was Popsicle and Fudge's methodology and Dr Marmadoskovski ended his lecture with a sentence fifteen minutes long which began, 'We must distinguish between specific and general attributions, real or assumed, appearance or reality, and since in the works of Popsicle and Fudge we find only a vague methodology ultimately lacking in specificity….'

After the lecture Mrs Phillips introduced Ramsay to Dr Cecil Woodbine, the headmaster of a secondary school in the country. Dr Woodbine was a zoologist by training and had identified himself completely with the nationalist movement. They discussed Dr Marmadoskovski's lecture.

'Really brilliant, *I think*,' Dr Woodbine said. '"Flagratic leadership". Do you know, it reminds me of one of Huxley's novels where a poet thought the word "carminative" was *so* beautiful till he discovered it meant "wind-expelling" – tee-hee! Yes. But "flagratic" – that explains such a lot, doesn't it?'

Then he invited Ramsay to a summer conference he was organizing for July.

'It's a kind of rest cure, you know,' Dr Woodbine said, 'with a strong intellectual undertone. I'm quite sure that as a writer you'll find it stimulating.' Dr Woodbine narrowed his eyes confidentially. 'Just come and *observe*, you know, and help with the discussions. We have to rough it a bit, but you'll get some good country air. I'll send you a note about it later.'

Dr Woodbine's letter of invitation asked Ramsay to help with a short-story writing group and promised him a week in the country with free board and lodging.

III

Ramsay arrived at Hillview Secondary School on the afternoon of the first day of the conference. To these hills come office-sore members of the middle class with intellectual leanings and private frustrations, once a year, to be intelligent together and to master economics, painting, politics and drama and to solve all the problems of the West Indies, in a week. Ramsay was billeted in a dormitory between an effeminate English landscape painter (no exhibitions) whose complexion was ashen, like leather gone bad, and a thick-set Jamaican portrait painter (ten exhibitions).

The portrait painter was laying out a pair of mauve pyjamas on his bed.

'This is the only pair of pyjamas my wife lets me show in public,' he said. Then he laughed with such a tremendous shout that Ramsay looked round the room in astonishment to see if there was some other cause for the painter's amusement.

'I'm sure I've seen you before,' the English painter said, with an Etonian lisp. 'Were you here last year?'

'No,' Ramsay said, 'I've never been to one of these conferences. There was a British Council course in Cambridge –'

'They are very good – very relaxing,' the portrait painter said, grinning widely. Ramsay remembered his name: he was Joseph Lowe. Lowe's fingers were squat and thick for an artist but the whole hand was sensitive. 'You can have a very good time, you kno', if you bring yo'own spirits,' he said, and laughed again, a bellowing asthmatic noise.

'I'm helping with the painting,' the old Etonian said. 'Teach people to paint in a week.'

'Everybody in the middle class wants to be a painter. It's kind of fashionable,' Lowe said, in a voice that was half-affected. 'But you meet real interesting people.'

They waited for Ramsay to say who he was.

'I'm a kind of writer,' he said in an unconvincing way.

'You know Charley Miller, then? The journalist. He's here, too,' Lowe said, and waited for further identification.

'Charley Miller. Oh, yes?' Ramsay said. He had never met Charley Miller.

Lowe puffed at his cigarette, pouting like a girl. 'At the Highgate Conference in 1944 we had a wonderful time. Good country weather, yo' kno'. I'd like to buy a house in Highgate.'

'What really happens at these conferences?' Ramsay asked the Etonian when Lowe had gone.

The landscape painter was wearing only a large white towel and a broad sun hat. 'Everything's done in study groups. In the mornings things like economics, social science, politics; in the afternoons, interest groups in painting, drama, dancing and so on – that's where *we* come in; in the evenings dull lectures by distinguished bods. The theme this year is "our social problems". It's very interesting. Do excuse me. I'm going to have a bath before dinner.'

Ramsay was left alone to the dank walls of the dormitory and the tank dripping near the window. He was tired after the car journey from Kingston and there was nothing to think.

On the way down to dinner Ramsay looked at the setting of Hillview School – a landscape of hills in a patchwork of red earth and green grass. All round the buildings, which were spread out on the peaks of four hills, there were brilliant flowers and charming rockeries and a few domestic servants to give a human interest to the amateur painters' splashings.

He queued for his cafeteria dinner and as he moved along by the square green tables he overheard the dominant themes of conversation.

'Do you know so-and-so?' 'I'm a nationalist, not in culture but in politics,' and chiefly, by implication, 'I am very intelligent and by coming to this conference I am contributing to the nationhood of my country.'

He shared a table with three young men uncomfortably well-dressed in jackets and ties while everybody else was trying to look summery in sports shirts and slacks. They ate rapidly and in silence and did not fit in with the bright chatter at the other tables.

Then one of them said, 'These people happy, boy!'

'Are you taking the course?' Ramsay asked them.

'We are all painters, sir. This is Robert French, this is Ferdinand Walters and this' – pointing to himself – 'is Oswald Campbell.'

'It's a good thing like this for people from every walk of life to come together and discuss our problems,' French said.

'But what happen after the discussion?' Walters said. 'Nutten. They not doing *nutten* for Jamaica!'

'Well, if it come to that,' French said, 'what *you* doing for *your* country then?'

'Ah'm paintin' for my country –'

'But,' Ramsay interrupted, 'it's only people like these who have four square meals a day that can afford to look at painting in this country. Painting is important, must be kept up, but bread and butter come first.'

'Lissen, master,' Oswald Campbell said, 'I doan have any butter for *my* bread and I doan know where the nex' meal coming from, an' when it come it not square. But I am bound to paint, and ah doan care whether the Governor or quarshie look at my stuff!'

'But you belong to the working class,' Ramsay said. 'You should paint for your people, not for these people here.'

'That's like politics, like communism,' Walters said, 'but everybody is a working class, even the capitalist. Is the money-man is *my* enemy. He's sucking my blood and will burst with it. Are you a comrade?'

'I just hate the middle class,' Ramsay said, not knowing whether Walters meant P.D.P. or P.P.L. comradeship.

'But is your class, though,' Campbell said. 'I am a sign-painter for a living. I doan eat good food like this every day, but that's not because I am a working class. If I was a dock worker I would earn even eighteen pound a week. But ah'm a painter, an' that is my class.'

Ramsay felt that the painters were shutting themselves away from his accent and his clothes.

'These people not doing any good,' Walters said, 'but maybe they not doing any harm, either. They jus' on holiday an' what's wrong with that, eh, sah?'

The conversation went dead.

Juanita Hernandez came into the dining room late and made a good entrance. She was tall, Spanish-looking and famous as a cold beauty and an abstract painter in miniature. From the way she did her hair into a bun with a tail, from the black stole she wore over her bare shoulders, and from the size of her bust Ramsay realized that she must be intelligent. He thought that if he got a chance to speak to her he might discover that she was beautiful as well.

On the second night of the conference Ramsay had dinner with Juanita Hernandez and Lilly Page.

'You are a writer, aren't you?' Lilly Page asked. 'Working-class stuff, eh?'

'You can call it that,' Ramsay said, looking at Juanita's profile, particularly the fixed half-smile.

'I'm a writer, too,' Lilly said breathlessly. She was fair in complexion and had twilight hair. Her perfume was fighting an uneven, losing battle against Juanita's. 'I'm a lowbrow journalist. Reely, I'm helping Charley Miller report the conference. Of course, like everybody else, my secret ambition is to write THE West Indian novel.'

'You have twenty clear years ahead of you. It won't be written before then,' Ramsay said.

Ramsay was still trying to find out what the conference was about. He had got into a drinking session with Joseph Lowe and two other painters the night before, sinfully, because alcohol was forbidden at the conference. He got awake just before lunch the next day and before he was fully sensible Dr Woodbine had taken him to a classroom and announced to the six ladies there that Mr Ramsay Tull was going to help them with short-story writing. In his confusion all Ramsay could think of was the composition classes he gave at Hampstead School, so he talked about the 'organization of material', that is, 'a beginning, a middle and an end', and set the six ladies a school certificate composition to write, 'A Day by the Sea'. They wrote with great application and afterwards he collected their scripts. Having put their souls on paper for him the ladies became very shy of Ramsay. He was sure he had not got the point of the conference and he had walked round the school in a deep gloom until dinner.

'That's the Englishwoman I was telling you about,' Lilly Page said to Juanita.

'Isn't she thin!' Juanita sneered.

'There is only one painting I like,' Ramsay said, it was his stock lie about painting. 'It's a Degas – a woman, Mlle. Maupin. I saw it ten years ago for two minutes in a magazine and it has haunted me ever since.'

Neither Lilly nor Juanita seemed to think this was strange. 'What do you think of Federation?' Lilly asked, as if the word had an improper meaning.

'That's right! Let's federate!' A small thin intense-looking middle-aged young man in spectacles and an American jacket grinned over them. 'What you kids up to? Having fun? How's the painting going, Juanita?' Then, to Ramsay, 'I'm Charley Miller. Take it easy, boy!'

Juanita, Lilly and Charley chatted for a while about people whom Ramsay did not recognize from pet-names and shortened Christian names but whose scandals were familiar. When Juanita spoke her eyebrows arched into question-marks of particular innocence. Charley Miller was the whirlwind character of the conference: in a moment he was gone.

'Let's have a drink in the town,' Ramsay suggested.

'That's against the rules,' Lilly said, in an English sing-song.

'When I drink,' Juanita said, giggling, 'I behave like one of the Foolish Virgins.'

'How did she behave?' Ramsay asked.

'It's in the Bible,' Juanita said, sharply, and looked as if a pass had been made at her.

'Somebody painted a picture called *The Foolish Virgins*,' Lilly said.

'It must have been Rubens,' Ramsay suggested, and he thought that this remark gave him the right to laugh for the first time since the conference began. He guffawed like Joseph Lowe, and the other people in the dining room looked at him and tried to smile down their disgust.

At 11.00 p.m. on the third night of the conference, Juanita Hernandez ran round the school grounds wearing only a white chiffon night-gown. Those who saw her were quite certain she was not a ghost. Earlier, in the afternoon, there had been a fight between the English landscape painter and Joseph Lowe. Neither of them knew how to fight and the landscape painter got a black eye by running into Lowe's elbow and Lowe got two nasty bites on his hand. But immediately after dinner Lowe and the landscape painter went around arm-in-arm singing *Jesus, lover of my soul*, and *Go down, Moses*.

The distinguished lecturer on the fourth night of the conference was a middle-aged and rather fat civil servant who had done an M.A. in statistics at a mid-Western American university in six months. He read out all the figures and percentages connected with illegitimacy in Jamaica and the conference was horrified. After the lecture the question-time consisted of long homilies about the virtues of decent family life, until Joseph Lowe spoke.

'The chief cause of illegitimacy in Jamaica is the number of unlighted streets,' Lowe said. 'If the government would light all the streets there would be less illegitimacy in this country.'

'But what about the country parts?' a lady welfare officer asked.

Dr Woodbine, the chairman, agreed that the country parts presented a serious obstacle to Mr Lowe's suggestion but he thought that a possible solution might be to impose a curfew in the country.

The lecturer said that, well, the administrative problems involved in a curfew throughout the island would be immense.

'And what about the freedom of the individual?' someone shouted. Another voice squeaked in reply, 'There's *too much* freedom as it is!' The squeaky voice was Mrs Woodbine's.

Dr Woodbine then said that he knew how interesting the subject was but it would help everyone if ladies and gentlemen addressed the chair, formally. In *that* way they would all be able to hear the interesting thoughts so many of them had on this most important subject.

Ramsay got up. 'Mr Chairman, there is nothing wrong with illegitimacy. I am illegitimate myself.'

Those ladies in the audience who were fair enough in complexion to blush did so; the others looked distastefully at Ramsay and then looked away quickly.

'My father was a shoemaker,' Ramsay continued, 'my mother was a dressmaker and my aunt planted yam and coco and rode a donkey to market every Saturday. And they were the most honest, God-fearing people you would find anywhere. What about the economic aspect of the thing? How can a labourer support a family of ten? There is a woman in my village who has had eight children by five different fathers all of whom support her. Those eight children are the best-dressed and best-fed children in the village and very well-behaved, too. If she was married to one of the fathers any children they had would be starving to death. And, in any case, one of those children might become Prime Minister of Jamaica.'

Ramsay sat down in the kind of silence that precedes the playing of the National Anthem.

'Of course,' Dr Woodbine said, 'there is something to be said for Mr Tull's point of view. That is why illegitimacy is *such* an important problem. It might help, however, to channelize our thinking if we divided our discussion into four aspects – the individual aspect, the family aspect, the community aspect and the national aspect.'

The discussion never took place. Mr Allbourne, the headmaster of the Hillview Elementary School, who had been detailed to move the vote of thanks at a pre-arranged signal from Dr Woodbine, got his signals wrong and immediately began, in a pulpit voice, 'It is not often that we are graced by the presence of such a distinguished visitor. . . .'

Five minutes later he reached his peroration. 'In this fair isle of ours, with its perennial springs and its evergreen hills. . . .'

By that time Ramsay and the painters had gone.

On the afternoon of the fifth day of the conference Ramsay set his short-story group the exercise of writing the imagined memoirs of the eucalyptus tree in Dr Woodbine's garden and went into the common room for a smoke. He found Lilly Page there collapsed in an armchair. There was no one else in the room and Ramsay thought her perfume, which filled the room, smelt very much like brandy.

'Why don't you cut out this working-class stuff and write something readable?' she asked. 'You don't really believe in it.

Probably you're working something out of your system, though. Everybody here's working something out of their system. Like me. I've just seen the only man I ever loved walk out of my life, the second only man, anyway.' She lit a cigarette and tried to fan the smoke away from her face. 'I just had a drink with Joseph Lowe. He's crazy. You know what he's doing? He's painting three different scenes, one on top of the other, on the same canvas! Anyway, I like Hillview. It's lovely for a week – cool, pretty, well laid out, lots of fresh air.'

She stopped to breathe and Ramsay said,

'There were times we regretted
The summer palaces on slopes, the terraces
And the silken girls bringing sherbet.'

'That's lovely,' Lilly said. 'Did you write it? You know, I think I see what you feel about the working class. What I hate most is the number of children not going to school. Actually, you know, they've made me secretary of the Education study group.'

'You should be a socialist,' Ramsay said.

'I can't,' Lilly said seriously. 'I'm going to America next year to work my way through college. It's easy. Juanita was in America. Do you like her?' She stood up and yawned. 'Dancing practice! I am the Awakening of Spring,' she said, tottering to the door.

At the concert on the fifth night of the conference the Drama group presented a play called 'Spirit of the West Indies'. The play had been arranged on the group playmaking principle. It was set in London and Jamaica and the décor had been painted by the Painting group. Blue skyscrapers were set against London's skyline and the Jamaican set was full of angular donkeys and market-women. Ramsay played the part of Boysie Smith, the Jamaican social science student in London who is fired with a nationalist zeal. The crisis of the play was reached when Boysie had to choose between marrying his English girl-friend, Rosemary, and returning to his native land to work for his people. The dialogue at this point was unforgettable.

'(ROSEMARY and BOYSIE embracing under Eros in Piccadilly Circus. It is snowing.)

ROSEMARY: I love you, Boysie, and will go to the ends of the earth with you.

BOYSIE (looking into the middle distance): You wouldn't fit into our life. There are no theatres, no symphony concerts, no continental films in my country. No! I must go back alone to the little village in St Mary where the pimento blooms every year.'

In the last scene Boysie returned to his village in St Mary where a curry-goat feed was held in his honour. The final curtain came down on a scene of general merriment and the singing of the calypso, 'Spirit of the West Indies'. The singing was led by a slightly tipsy Joseph Lowe who played the part of Boysie's uncle, Amos. The words of the calypso had been specially written for the play by the English landscape painter. The chorus went,

> 'Ru - le Britannia
> Britannia rule the seas,
> But the one thing you can never change
> Is the spirit … of the West In - dees.'

The concert ended with the Dancing group doing a ballet devised by Mrs Ursula Reeves, and called *Awakening*. The music was by Sibelius and Mozart and the set had been painted by the professional painters to look like a tropical Garden of Eden. The keynote of Mrs Reeves' choreography was 'elevation'. The curtain rose in semi-darkness on reposing bodies strewn about the stage. A thin pencil of light from the wings wavered, then settled on one of the bodies. Lilly Page's body arose gracefully and danced the Awakening of Spring. Then Summer, Autumn and Winter were awakened in turn. The fishes, the birds, the animals, the plants awoke. But there were still two bodies in repose on the stage. They awoke with the bringing up of the floodlights – Adam, danced by Charley Miller, short, with prominent ribs, and Eve, danced by Mrs Reeves, tall and in full bloom. The traditional biblical origin of the human race appeared to be reversed and the dance of Adam and Eve looked like a *pas de deux* between an elephant and an Indian fakir. The concert proved that almost every member of the conference had imbibed some culture during the week. At the party which followed the concert everybody, including the Reverend John Devon in an outlandish sports shirt, sang and bounced to the 'Spirit of the West Indies' calypso.

Next morning, just before leaving Hillview, Ramsay went to say good-bye and thank you to Dr and Mrs Woodbine. He met Lilly outside the Art room. She was wearing a fragile white hat and was made up as pale as death. She joined Ramsay and as they walked together to Dr Woodbine's house he noticed that she was walking unsteadily.

Dr Woodbine stood beaming at the top of the steps leading to the verandah.

'So glad you enjoyed it,' he said to Ramsay. 'I hope you'll come again next year.'

Lilly made her way forward, hand outstretched and articulating faultlessly, 'Thank you, Dr Woodbine, for a very stimulating week.' For some reason she mistook one of the pillars of the verandah for Dr Woodbine, slipped on the steps and fell, head first, into a bed of roses, lacerating her face among the thorns of her several loves.

Ramsay thought the time had come for action when Edgar Bailey asked him to sit on the P.P.L. platform at a protest meeting about the government's refusal to allow a Jamaican national who had lived for nearly twenty years in the Soviet Union to land in Jamaica. It was not a case which aroused much civic indignation in the island and the P.P.L. protest meeting did not even arouse the political indignation of the P.D.P. Action Group. But there were security police among the five hundred people at the corner of Princess Street and Parade and they took shorthand notes of the speeches. Ramsay did not speak that night, mainly out of cowardice, and his indignation at himself drove him into a fury at the persecution of communists.

His presence on the P.P.L. platform had been noted pointedly in the newspaper, and Mr Byfield suggested to him in a heart-to-heart talk that he should leave politics alone. Mr Byfield was interested neither in the freedom of the individual nor the practice in Great Britain: he warned Ramsay that *in Jamaica* for a young man to start getting mixed up in politics was the surest way of wrecking his career as a teacher. Ramsay was the first to sign the P.P.L. petition to the Prime Minister and, three days later, Bobsie informed him, in confidence, that the police had started a file about him.

Only a small part of Ramsay's decision to work with the P.P.L. was due to socialist conviction. In fact he knew very little about Marxism, less, in a way, than he had known at school, and he still had a very firm racialist attitude. His principal motivation was a sudden, fanatical belief that the Jamaican middle class should be destroyed. He could not define 'middle class', except negatively as all the people who were not working-class members of the Mannie Small Union and the P.D.P. He told himself that he had (but he had not) come to this decision *before* Mrs Phillips had cut him dead at an S.C.A. exhibition of painting at the Institute and Stephen Strachan had written a cutting article, clearly directed against Ramsay, about 'woolly intellectual negroes'. Ramsay smelt with satisfaction, a whiff of persecution.

The P.P.L. had been expanding. Their membership was now large enough for them to open a second office in Mark Lane. This was a large room in a house next door to a brothel. Edgar Bailey used that room as a lending library and lecture room for P.P.L. members in lower Kingston. Edgar's single-mindedness had hardened to a lack of awareness about anything outside of politics. It was as if his whole literacy was what he knew about Marxism and communism and what was going on in the politics of the island. He told Ramsay that he was wasting time writing stories for the middle class to read and he warned Ramsay that he better not join the P.P.L. to satisfy his 'conscience'. He (Edgar) could have his arse shot off or he could be thrown in prison any day or night, and it wasn't a joke. There was a marked tension between them.

'You doan have a hope in hell of *ever* getting point five per cent of political power in this country,' Ramsay said.

'I have a hope,' Edgar said. 'You mean that *you* doan have a hope. Look here, we doan intend to get into power jus' like that.

We're going to get hold of Mannie Small Union. You know we had it perfect last year?'

'What happened then? Why you stopped?'

'Firs' of all, the old man *promise* Mannie something,' Edgar said. 'O.K., we break into F.A.T.U.M. Then next thing was this, Capleton was using Merchant money – *we* was using Merchant money an' I never know a thing.'

'He let you down!'

'He's an old man, he's dying, you know. Cancer. O.K., we could mess up Mannie bad but the old man is a dying man. Maybe he lose his hope and he know Mannie have the workers. When you dying like that you can't kill your brother, you know.'

'I don't understand a word,' Ramsay said.

'You wouldn' understand!'

'Capleton, you say, could have got the workers from Mannie, but Capleton is a dying man and Mannie is his brother?' Ramsay said. 'And you still have this great hope. I thought *I* was romantic!'

'Romantic? What you mean?'

'Feeling.'

'Feeling? You think I or Capleton or anybody could be working like this, come day come night, for nutten if we didn' have feeling?' Edgar asked. 'Somehow you doan belong with the workers. I doan care how much degree you have. You doan *belong* with us.'

'But this isn't politics, the League,' Ramsay said, 'not real politics.'

'Right now,' Edgar said, with a resentful refusal to follow Ramsay into any abstract discussion, 'there are five Marxist workers in Mannie's Union. I train them myself. That is all. The whole of the Dock Workers' Union is Marxist. That is all. We will *see* politics, when we *see* politics. That is all.'

They worked together, however, understanding the reality of a wall between them that had nothing directly to do with politics or 'isms'. Edgar felt that Ramsay was too subtly attached to the things he was supposed to be against – his education had shown him one face of the white moon, and he had been connected with P.D.P. values at two levels, of intellect and family, through Mrs Phillips and his brother Bobsie. Capleton and Edgar used him as living propaganda against P.D.P. values, realizing how dangerous to them Ramsay's twisted personality might make this propaganda. Capleton, with unusual sophistication, always referred to Ramsay as their 'Number one risk'.

Ramsay's identification with the League came, not through his attendance at P.P.L. meetings but through a rag of a weekly paper called *The Worker*, which he edited. There was very little to edit. Of the four quarto pages, two were written entirely by Edgar Bailey, one by Capleton and the fourth consisted mainly of Group and Union news. Ramsay contributed one column with the cliché title, 'As I See It', corrected the spelling and paragraphing of Capleton's and Edgar's pages and supervised Mona Freeman's typing of the manuscript. *The Worker* was execrably printed by a small press in which Capleton had shares. Only the security police seemed to read it, although every issue contained something libellous. It had a brief moment of prominence when Ramsay, now thoroughly exasperated at being ignored, wrote a very seditious article which included caricatures of the Governor and Dr Phillips. Ramsay and Edgar were summoned to the office of the Commissioner of Police and warned; the Commissioner said that the only reason why they were not being arrested was that the people who might take *The Worker* seriously could not read, anyway. Then he added, quite casually, 'Sooner or later, we are going to close down *The Worker and* the P.P.L.' The Commissioner was a burly jovial type who played an excellent game of polo and had been in Kenya for ten years. He regretted having to arrest people and having to pry into their private affairs.

The security police slipped up when they allowed Edgar Bailey to be issued with a passport. They understood that he had been invited to attend a T.U.C. conference for colonial trade unionists in London and Edgar had letters to prove that he had been invited. Actually he was only passing through London on his way to a world youth festival in Rumania. Edgar's asceticism made it seem that he was going on a religious pilgrimage. He made it clear that he was attending the festival to see other people who were working, without despair, in equally hopeless circumstances. The other members of the P.P.L. executive who knew where Edgar was going were very excited. Though they didn't believe this, their emotional attitude to Edgar's journey was as if he were going to bring back a transforming wand. Edgar only said, very coolly, 'I not going to heaven, you know. Jesus Christ not in Rumania!'

Edgar handed over a considerable part of his League work to Ramsay, while Andy Maxwell took over the union work and the underground liaison with Small's Union. There were two consequences for Ramsay. First, he had to read up a great deal about Marxism, not out of interest but because Edgar had been giving a 'course' on Marxism-Leninism to about ten workers at the Mark Lane office. Ramsay continued the course, being always only two lessons ahead of his pitifully trusting pupils. He got a great glow of admiration for Edgar when he realized what Edgar had been doing in this course. The ten workers were only just able to read and Edgar had, somehow, been trying to reduce every abstraction to Jamaican terms and parallels and all the parallels were, theoretically, far-fetched. But these ten workers believed that they were, historically, in exactly the same position as pre-Soviet Russia. The questions they asked after each of Ramsay's paraphrases implied that, and they presented a blank wall of disbelief to every subtle distinction he thought he was cleverly drawing. He came to admire not Edgar's astuteness – it was *not* astute – but his courage in reducing this complicated colonial experience so simply to dispossession, the right to something, and some kind of force as the only means of regaining possession. And where Edgar had evidently integrated Marxism into the set he was showing the workers, Ramsay could see it only as a sombre and unrelated background.

The second consequence of Edgar's departure was that Ramsay began to work closely with Mona Freeman. After her brief Joan of Arc period on the P.P.L. platform Mona had decided against starvation and was working in Fitz-Simmonds' office as a typist. Fitz-Simmonds' motive in employing Mona was never clear. It could hardly have been immoral, because Mrs Fitz-Simmonds worked in his office as cashier and general supervisor and she kept a very strict check on his movements. He might have done it as a favour to Capleton, or through a sentimental memory of Mona's father whom he had unsuccessfully defended for embezzlement nearly twenty years before and whose case had given him his first prominence as a lawyer. Whatever the real reason was, he had employed her against the firm opposition of his wife, a very fair and unattractive woman who frequently had tea within earshot of King's House. Mrs Fitz-Simmonds disliked Mona's telephone calls and the passes every solicitor and articled clerk and solicitor's clerk who came to see Fitz-Simmonds made at her and she paid Mona her weekly wages with marked reluctance and distaste. She knew that Mona didn't care a damn about her, and that Mona knew, and didn't care, that she had been trying to persuade her husband to fire her.

Mona preserved a simple loyalty and gratitude to Capleton and still 'believed' in the P.P.L. as the only thing that had meaning outside of her own sensations and pleasures. Every afternoon on her way home from work she stopped at the Slipe Road office and did whatever typing there was to be done. Usually there was nothing to do except the manuscript of *The Worker*, but when Ramsay took over from Edgar the quantity of work increased. Ramsay found he was unable to achieve any real community of feeling and thinking with the real workers in the P.P.L. and he decided that his principal tactic should be an assault, in writing, on the middle class. For about half of his teaching day he set his classes 'composition' or 'silent reading' while he wrote long circular letters to supposedly 'progressive' middle-class people asking for strange donations, and support. Very few of the letters were answered. He produced one successful concert to raise funds to help the relatives of the Jamaican from the Soviet Union who had been refused entry to his country. The concert, which was built around the comedian Tennis Barrett, was well attended (about a hundred and fifty people), and the takings amounted to nearly fifteen pounds. So Ramsay gave up drinking and women and worked very late at night on P.P.L. business with the excited devotion which comes when a young man imagines that his life has, at last, found a centre.

And the tensions in the Hampstead School staff room increased to the point where nobody spoke to Ramsay. Arising out of a controversy in the leading daily newspaper he had written a letter condemning denominational schools and missionaries and the missionary spirit and suggesting that *all* schools should be taken over by the government. It was an airy letter that took no account of hard economic facts but it contained some very casual remarks about Christianity. The staff room silences were a puzzle, until Mr Byfield told him that the Board was very displeased with the letter and thought he might have a bad effect on the morals of the school. Mr Byfield had assured the Board that Ramsay was a good teacher who 'contributed' to the school, and that he would give the usual warning. Then a month later Ramsay got a letter from Mr Byfield telling him that his 'appointment with the school had been terminated' because the Board had discovered that he was living in an 'immoral relationship' with a woman.

Ramsay and Mona were living together at Mona's house. The affair began with a controlled leisurely excitement and the understanding that they were going to marry each other. They did not marry immediately because neither of them could see that a church could add anything new to the relationship. They thought that the pattern of their lives would remain the same – working at their jobs during the day, working at the P.P.L. offices in the evenings and then going home to sleep with each other. And Mrs Tull accepted the relationship. At first she was worried about Ramsay's career until he convinced her he would marry Mona. Then she told him that, in country simplicity, she had been living unmarried with his father for two years before Bobsie was born. He felt he was on solid working-class ground threatened only by the objections that Madge and Rosalie made, and the letter from Mabel which told him he would let down himself and the family if they did not marry immediately. But he had a week of panic over losing his job because he had been secure in his insulation from poverty.

Bobsie promised to get a job for him in the private school he seemed to control in St Ann. Ramsay knew that Bobsie was trying to get him away from P.P.L. work and absolutely refused to take the job if it was offered. Bobsie paid no attention to the refusal and opened negotiations with the owner of the school. His negotiations with Mr Dawkins, who owned the Steadfast Secondary School near St Ann's Bay, consisted of threats to Mr Dawkins' business, his school and his life. Bobsie spent a week in St Ann's Bay threatening Mr Dawkins. There was no mystery about Bobsie's hold over Mr Dawkins. He knew things about Mr Dawkins and had enough documentary proof to send Dawkins to jail for ten years at least. But Mr Dawkins was useful to the P.D.P.: he was respected in St Ann and needed to give the P.D.P. his support. He told Bobsie he would 'think about' employing Ramsay and then he went off to complain to Dr Phillips about Bobsie's threats.

Dr Phillips called Bobsie to an interview at the Premier's office, not because he had any sympathy for Dawkins (he knew Dawkins was a rogue) but because for the last three months Bobsie had been practically running the P.D.P.. It was a ticklish interview because of Bobsie's popularity within the party and his barely concealed ambition to get a ministership. Dr Phillips spoke about Caesar's wife and suspicion and the P.D.P. record for absolute public honesty.

'But listen, Doc,' Bobsie said, 'Dawkins is a thief, you know. He's a criminal that could be in jail.'

'Well,' Dr Phillips said, 'if you have any evidence –'

'He made over one thousand pounds in a racket over farm workers' tickets and the same thing in Enfield land settlement,' Bobsie said. 'I have the papers right now in my car.'

'Well,' Dr Phillips said, 'if you have any *evidence* against Dawkins you should give it to the police.'

'If Dawkins go to prison you lose every seat in St Ann!'

Dr Phillips sighed, caught between two immoralities.

'Now look, Bobsie, I want you to reflect on two things,' he said. He was tired at the end of a long day and in the air-conditioned room his voice had a faintly antiseptic tonelessness. 'First of all, Dawkins has been to see me. If you go on with this pressure our enemies can make out either that I condone it or cannot lead my own party.'

'Dawkins will utter narra a word, Doc,' Bobsie said.

'Something might come out and neither you nor I can risk it,' Dr Phillips said. 'And the second thing is you are trying to get a job for your brother. That suggests favouritism, but that's not half so dangerous as the fact that your brother is working with a communist organization. Both Mannie and Capleton could make capital out of that. The fact is, Bobsie, I don't like it and you must give up any attempt to force Dawkins to employ your brother. Do you see the position?'

'O.K., Doc,' Bobsie said. 'I won't trouble Dawkins, as you say. But do you know how much small-small corruption put the People's Democratic Party into power today?'

'I don't want to know anything about *that*,' Dr Phillips said. 'If I knew I would dissolve the party.'

'If you were to dissolve the party,' Bobsie said, 'I would put it together again.' They looked at each other carefully. Bobsie added, 'I'll leave Dawkins alone, but, you know, Doc, small-small corruption is an essential part of colonial politics!'

Two weeks later Bobsie was made a Minister without Portfolio attached to the Prime Minister's office.

Ramsay advertised in the *Daily Gleaner* that he was a B.A. Honours of Oxford University and that he coached students in English for school certificate, higher school certificate, matriculation, intermediate and finals. Mona added the words 'fees moderate' to the advertisement because fees are always moderate in *Gleaner* advertisements. After a month he had got enough pupils to make an average of six pounds per week. He felt completely justified in every way.

Capleton's illness had definitely been diagnosed as cancer and he was confined to bed and wasted away with acute pain. He tried to run the P.P.L. from his bed and every day he had a consultation with Ramsay. They decided not to hold any street meetings until Edgar returned and Capleton usually had no orders to give except requests to see union executives. He had little philosophy to offer Ramsay, but he repeated his regret that he had had to split with Mannie Small. All along he thought he would die before Edgar returned and he begged Ramsay to persuade Edgar to disband the League and join with Mannie, the last stage of hopelessness. Sometimes, as he watched his body wasting from nearly 200 lb. to 140, he wept with pain and regret. He had been born a Catholic but he refused to agree with Mona that a priest should visit him. His own hell, he said, had come in the fires in his stomach and the fact that he must die and leave the working class without a Marxist leadership.

Mona and Ramsay were very happy for the next three months and decided to put the marriage off as Capleton was so ill. What was left of Ramsay's social and religious conscience was touched when his sister Mabel wrote from England that she was engaged to marry an American negro composer who had come to London to work on a musical. She was childishly enthusiastic about going to live permanently in America and conjured up, with a few phrases from their childhood, the private world of innocence they had shared together. At every moment of the day the thought of Mabel being happily married gave him a pleasurable sense of security.

Bobsie, now with the authority of a minister, did not lose his affection for Ramsay and he did not lose his sense of superiority.

'You mean to say,' he said to Ramsay, 'you go all the way to Oxford an' you come back an' you cyan even drive a motocyar. Is a goddam shame, man! I'll send the cyar round every evening an' make Aubrey teach you to drive.'

After two confused lessons Ramsay gave up and Mona decided to learn instead. She smashed both front fenders, both back light-assemblies and, inexplicably, the roof of the car, and got her driving licence in two weeks.

Cyril Hanson returned to Jamaica, late in August, exactly five years after he had left. He had become much more serious and told Ramsay that once he had settled down and got married he would go into politics. He immediately started getting into shape for the football season and made his arrival known at Kingston Club where he was again asked to lead the senior league XI. He started his practice as a barrister with the goodwill of those solicitors who were members of Kingston Club and he worked very hard at his briefs, for he had promised Patricia that he would save two thousand pounds before she came out in the following summer.

Ramsay asked him to write a series of articles for *The Worker* on his experiences in Britain. Cyril said that was easily the most fantastic suggestion he had ever heard: Ramsay should realize he had to keep himself clean before deciding one way or the other in politics.

IV

Tango lango, lango lay
In Bucharest for my holiday,
Tango lay lay lay
Tango lango lango-lay.

Look de enjoyment we had for the time
Look de luxury superfine
Tango lay lay lay
Tango lango lango-lay.

This is the sort of society
We are striving for universally,
Tango lay lay lay
Tango lango lango-lay.

Edgar you go now and tell the res'
About our days in Buchares',
Tango lay lay lay
Tango lango lango-lay.

Edgar came back from Bucharest singing this calypso. The West Indian youth at the festival had sung it as their contribution to a concert of national music. Edgar returned with a deeper patience and a new relaxation. Nothing he said about the festival, about a society that belonged to the worker, about those youthful voices raised in a universal massive hope, was so important as the personal joy which the memory of that calypso released in him. He had become aware that the term 'fullness of life' was not a mere negation of poverty, a bourgeois excuse, but a civilized condition of which every Jamaican worker was, in himself, capable. His visit to Bucharest had moved him into an assurance of equality, into a feeling that his own *recognition* of equality made him equal to anybody. The change was hardly noticeable, for Edgar was still a serious single-minded man whose pleasures like drink, food, women, seemed somehow outside the range of personal articulation.

The hope the P.P.L. executive might have had that Edgar would return with a transforming wand soon disappeared. Now he had a new status: he was the actual leader of the P.P.L. and in the new confidence he paid no attention to Capleton's advice, and, over the dismissal of a municipal council labourer, called out half the corporation workers for two days. He told Capleton that there had never been enough 'agitation' in the P.P.L.

Mona, to Ramsay's annoyance, had an open admiration for Edgar. It had always been there (Edgar's Bucharest trip gave it only an added dimension) but Ramsay had not noticed it before. His hostility to Edgar's leadership now made him sensitive to Mona's attitude. One remark that Edgar made two days after he returned threw Ramsay right back into the reaction a snob-school and a university education fostered. They were talking about European communists and Ramsay was boasting about the English communists he had met.

'Since you were so much with the party,' Edgar said, 'why you didn' go to Berlin two years ago?'

He could have ignored the question or explained it away but Mona had jeered at him and called him a coward.

'And I bet if you even went you would refuse to march,' she said, and her understanding with Edgar was complete. They talked about things they had done together in the League, while Ramsay was in England, with a deliberate obliqueness.

So Ramsay began a senseless campaign against Edgar's leadership of the League, but the campaign was directed not at Edgar but at Mona. Mona had the peculiar mixture of *naïveté,* strength of character and sense of insecurity to become completely vicious when she was threatened. The League was the only 'good thing' in her life, the only importance she had had outside of the triumphs of her body over some men. And she felt that Ramsay's contempt of Edgar included her. She defended Edgar, sticking to Ramsay's two most vulnerable points – that Edgar had never been mixed-up about his class and that he was a natural leader. Yet, in each quarrel, she would channel Ramsay's fury into sex, like a showman with a marionette, while her eyes and her prehensile body expressed a quite contradictory terror of losing him. That is all there was to Mona. The sexual trick worked every time because they were both afraid to admit that they understood each other.

Neither of them dared to admit that Ramsay's jealousy was sexual, for Mona was afraid of the truth of her past and Ramsay was deeply in love with her. The quarrel over Edgar very soon shifted from Marxism and the League, though they used the words and the incidents: it did not really matter to Ramsay, at the final level, whether Edgar was a bona fide worker or a better leader. Edgar was the block to his power over Mona, a power he needed because he knew how desperately he leaned on her, while for Mona, Edgar, without any feeling attached to him, was her right not to be considered a whore by the man she was in love with.

She began to make very open advances to Edgar, always and only when Ramsay was there. It was her way of proving that she had no personal interest in Edgar. So Ramsay and Mona developed a pattern of daily behaviour which was, serious discussions with Edgar about League matters while Mona flirted with Edgar, a tremendous quarrel afterwards, and then the inevitable reconciliation. This bizarre pattern lasted for about two weeks, until Edgar asked Mona to marry him.

It was during one of the weekly meetings at the Mark Lane office and Ramsay was giving a lecture on *The Russian Revolution.* His lecture was a simplified version of an article in the *Encyclopaedia Britannica:* the workers listening to the lecture would, in any case, never read the *Encyclopaedia Britannica.* Mona and Edgar were sitting at the back of the room.

'That man Tull not good for you, you know,' Edgar said. It was the first time that Edgar had ever mentioned Mona's private life, and the remark took her by surprise. And over the past month she had lost the instinct to tell him he was being 'dyam fast'.

'Why?' she asked.

'He's too erratic,' Edgar said. 'Him doan know what he is, him doan know where him come from.' There was a pause. 'Lissen, don't be surprise. I would like to marry you.'

Mona was surprised that she didn't burst out laughing.

'To mi heart,' Edgar said. 'I'm dead serious!'

'There's nothing like that, Edgar,' Mona said. 'Nothing like that. You are a friend, you see, and we working for the same thing. But – that's my man up there. You know how it is.'

'One day you going be sorry,' Edgar said, and the only feeling in his voice was anger. 'Forget what ah said jus' now. The day you are sorry you can remember it.'

That evening Mona and Ramsay ate a supper of patties and ice-cream they bought on the way home. There was no more point in flirting with Edgar and she was willing to agree with Ramsay about everything.

'You better hurry up and marry me, Ramsay,' she said. 'Somebody else want to marry me.'

'How?'

'Edgar ask me to marry him tonight.'

'That's as if the gardener-boy should ask you to marry him,' Ramsay said. He didn't believe her. Mona had expected every kind of explosion but not *that* remark. It happened that her first sexual experience had been with a gardener-boy.

'It was good tonight, you know,' Mona said. 'The people were very interested.'

'Oh. It's a waste of time. It doesn't do any good at all.'

She went to bed and he sat up over a pile of typescripts of his finished and unfinished stories. He read them for an hour until he had made himself believe that Mona had been Edgar's girl-friend while he was in England and he was quite sure that she would tell him that tonight.

Mona wasn't sleeping. 'Why you don't come to bed, eh?' she called and Ramsay did not answer. A few moments later she could smell something burning and she came out to see Ramsay sitting over the flaming pile of his stories.

'Why you doing that?' she asked.

'Nothing.'

He watched her pour a glass of water over the flames and begin, with the desperate concentration a woman has when she is bewildered, to tear off the burnt edges of the papers and put them into a kind of order. Then they went to bed, simply, as if all that Ramsay had wanted was that gesture of concern. It was the first trivial act in the break-up of his character.

He was sullen and abstract at breakfast next morning. He had ignored her completely in the night and was ignoring her now. She wanted to flatter him with the echo of things he had told her and at the same time to hurt him.

'We'll both be good communists,' she said. 'We can use the revolution for our own purposes.'

'What the *hell* do you know about revolution or communism or anything?' Ramsay screamed. 'You are a fool. The only thing you know is to jump into bed with the next man!'

He sprung up and smashed the porcelain milk jug against the wall behind her. Mona didn't stop looking at him. Her fright was all in her hands which were clawing senselessly at the folds of the housecoat she was wearing.

'I'm just joking,' she said.

'You're not joking. It's Edgar Bailey. You think I didn't see you whispering to him all the time I was talking last night? Eh?'

'You jealous of Edgar? You should be. He's a real worker, not messed up with this bourgeois culture. All these books!'

She was echoing Edgar now and they both knew it.

'O.K.,' Ramsay said. 'I'm leaving right now. You can get Edgar to come and live with you if you like. It wouldn' be the first time.'

He went into the bedroom and started packing his clothes into a ridiculously small suitcase. He had rehearsed the general out-line of the scene frequently in imagination but he had never thought of the props. Mona leaned on the door and watched him trying to pack.

'You need a week to pack what you have here,' she said, hoping that her refusal to gesticulate would make him stay.

'You can have the books,' Ramsay said.

'Sure. I'll read them.'

When he was ready to go she stood in front of him, with all the contempt her body could show.

'You can leave this house,' she said, 'but you'll come back to me. You *have* to come back. I'm not asking you to come back, I'm not asking you to stay; you *have* to come back!'

'You will see!'

'And you know another thing, Ramsay,' Mona said, 'I won't have anybody else – '

'You can have the whole-a Kingston!'

'– I'll wait till you come back, because you're *going* to come back.'

And that was the limit of her cynicism. She tried to grab the suitcase from him.

'But where you think you going, Ramsay? You must be mad!'

He walked to the verandah.

'Anywhere. I can't starve in Jamaica.'

'You see plenty people starving in Jamaica,' Mona said. 'Who you think you are? Gawd Almighty?'

'You can take in Edgar,' he said. 'He's starving.'

She stood on the verandah and watched him go. Then he turned back at the gate. She couldn't stand the humiliation of his coming back and she started to cry with a nervous energy from so far down that it sounded as if she was vomiting. But he had only come back to fetch his briefcase and she had stopped crying when he came out again. Later in the morning she telephoned Mrs Tull from her office and heard that Ramsay had left his things with her and gone into town.

He walked all the way from St James' Road to Mark Lane, bareheaded in the sun, and the buzzing in the back of his head began again softly and at long intervals. He was going to resign from the League and he needed the stimulus of a drink to bring himself to do it and to withstand the lack of surprise there would be in Edgar, so he stopped in a bar on East Queen Street and had three quick rums.

Edgar was alone in the Mark Lane office packing some books and papers together, but Ramsay in his fury didn't notice that Edgar was packing.

'That was a very good lecture, last night, comrade,' Edgar said. 'We must plan another series soon.' Far from showing surprise at seeing Ramsay at that time of the morning, he seemed to expect him.

'I'm resigning from the League,' Ramsay said. 'Today.'

'Why? What happen?' Edgar asked.

'I don't believe in this business any more,' Ramsay said.

'It's not a church,' Edgar said irritably. 'You want something to happen and you join the League to try and make it happen. Nobody ask you to believe anything. How you can "believe" in poverty?'

'Not belief then, faith,' Ramsay said. 'Belief is the intellectual agreement to an abstract proposition and faith is a disposition to act as if the proposition was true.'

'Doan bother with the big ideas, ole man,' Edgar said. 'I went to school but I didn' go to university. What you saying not important but is important I should understand you. Use simple language, man.'

Ramsay realized that he wasn't getting anywhere near to annoying Edgar.

'The villifiers, the slanderers, the most intolerant people in the world are communists,' Ramsay said.

'Doan try to propagandize me,' Edgar said. 'What's eating you?'

'This League is just boy scout Marxism.'

'You confusing yourself, Tull,' Edgar said. 'I can wait and I can hope. *You* will turn any which way. Nex' thing you'll say you're not a negro if it suit you. You can shout all you want but there'll be a real revolution right here in Jamaica. I'll be alive, you'll be alive. We'll see what will happen. Right now it doan matter at all if you leave the League.'

'You might jus' as well hope for the Second Coming,' Ramsay said. 'Anyway, I'm not really doing anything useful in the League.'

'You shouldn' leave yet,' Edgar said and sat on a bench by the window and looked into the street. 'They arrest me this morning. I thought you knew.'

'For what?'

'Subversive literature. They search mi house this morning. The Commissioner himself. I'm on bail till Thursday.'

'What they found?' Ramsay asked, the romance creeping back over him.

'Two papers from Czechoslovakia.'

'We have to do something right away,' Ramsay said. He half-hoped Edgar would be sent to jail. 'We'll march. A demonstration!'

'If I do that they'll change the charge to inciting,' Edgar said. 'The Commissioner told me. Fitz-Simmonds says I can get off with a fifty pound fine, but we doan have a penny and Capleton only have his car.'

This, at last, was the moment for the useful self-centred action. They sat down and planned the demonstration and the banners to be used. Ramsay spoke as if he was going to 'save' Edgar. Septy Grant and Andy Maxwell who had just heard the news came in, and Ramsay, giving orders at last, detailed them to round up as many P.P.L. boys as possible to meet at Slipe Road the next morning, Wednesday. Then he went off to Cyril Hanson's chambers to borrow fifty pounds.

Just before he left the Mark Lane office a woman named Florence, from the brothel next door, came in. She was a tall, heavy black girl, with wide nostrils, thick lips and perfect white teeth. She dragged her feet in a pair of men's shoes, broken down at the heel but her walk was not slovenly.

'What you do, Edgar?' she asked. 'What they arrest you for?'

'Some papers I had,' Edgar said.

Florence looked at him, not understanding, and asked Ramsay, 'What he do? What they arrest him for?'

'Every country have laws,' Edgar explained to her, 'that say you musn' read certain papers because you will make trouble if you read them.'

'But they coudn' arres' you for *dat*!' Florence said, and then asked, confidentially, 'You do something else Edgar?'

'No.'

'They arres' you because of the League, don't it?' She walked across and put her hand on Edgar's shoulder. She was tall and quite old and could almost have been his mother. She said, 'Ef is the League they arrest you for, tomorrow I will *march*!'

'You see that woman, Florence,' Edgar said, when she had gone, 'she's one of the bes' workers in Jamaica, at her trade. Every ship come into Kingston Harbour hear her name. You never have not a revolution in this country without Florence in it.'

'Who asked her to march?' Ramsay asked, resenting Edgar's pointed disregard of his new authority. 'She isn't in the League?'

'You mus' always have the women like Florence on your side, Tull,' Edgar said. 'You can trust her more than you can trust yourself.'

Cyril's chambers were on the third floor of a building near the corner of Church Street and Tower Street and when Ramsay turned into Church Street Cyril spotted him. He had no work to do and had been watching the people and the traffic in Church Street for the past hour. He knew that Ramsay was coming to see him, so he summoned his typist and began dictating a letter to a firm of solicitors.

Ramsay burst in without knocking and Cyril, who was pacing the room in the middle of a sentence, smiled at Ramsay and held up his hand for silence. Ramsay ignored the signal.

'This is urgent, Cyril,' Ramsay said, the man of action at last. Cyril sent away his typist. 'I want to borrow fifty pounds, right away.'

'Have a seat, Ramsay,' Cyril said, professionally. 'What d'you want it for? Or is that private?'

'I want it to pay a fine for Edgar Bailey, tomorrow. Look, Cyril, I'll sign a promissory note to pay you back in a month's time, with interest if you like, but please lend me fifty pounds. Now.'

Cyril leaned back in his swivel chair.

'It's the banned publications case, isn't it?'

'Yes,' Ramsay said. 'They arrested him this morning.'

'I heard about it from Fitz-Simmonds,' Cyril said. 'Bad case; he has to plead "guilty". No, Ramsay, I can't see my way clear to lending you fifty pounds.'

'You haven't got it?'

'Oh, I have it all right,' Cyril said. 'But I don't *approve*, you see.'

'You would lend it to me if you didn't know what I was going to use it for?'

'In the law,' Cyril said, with a stern emphasis, 'when we receive information we don't go in for speculation or moral niceties about what we would have done if we hadn't received the information.'

'Well, lend me fifty pounds as a friend,' Ramsay said.

'Of course, you and I went to school together and all that, but –'

'Don't preach a sermon.'

'Wait. We are friends and all that *but* I have a certain responsibility to my conscience. I cannot, even indirectly, support a thing

I don't believe in. You know, Ramsay, working with the P.P.L. you are letting down Surrey College and Oxford, and getting fired for immorality is letting down Surrey College and Oxford again, letting down your essential humanity, man.'

'Oh, to hell with Surrey and Oxford and humanity,' Ramsay said. 'What's more inhuman than this banned publications law?'

'Moral standards must be upheld in every country, Head, *you* know that,' Cyril said. 'You have a serious responsibility to this country. You won a scholarship.'

'At the moment Edgar Bailey is my responsibility,' Ramsay said. He thought there was still a chance of getting the money from Cyril.

'Your irresponsibility, you mean,' Cyril said, picked up a brief and affected to read it as if Ramsay wasn't there.

Ramsay leaned over, took the brief from Cyril, closed it and dropped it into a tray.

'Do you realize, Cyril,' Ramsay said with an incipient madness behind his eyes, 'that I can give orders to have your car smashed and burned this evening when you are driving home from work? Do you realize I can do that?'

'I think you've got a touch of schizophrenia,' Cyril said. 'Or you're just over-excited. Anyway, I'm sorry. I can't lend you the money.'

'Cyril, you are the perfect prefect,' Ramsay said, and the sarcasm was forced because of the hollow feeling of having failed in the first man-of-action stunt. 'But we are still friends.' He shook hands with Cyril and held his hand, 'I can say you are my friend, the Fraud, and you will die a fraud's death!'

Cyril laughed a queer unconvincing laugh as Ramsay went out. Then he telephoned Dr Phillips and told him he thought something, probably dangerous, was brewing in the P.P.L. Dr Phillips 'phoned the Commissioner of Police and then sent for Bobsie Tull who was in the Assembly.

Ramsay's stooped abstracted figure drifted aimlessly around lower Kingston for two hours, drifting between excitement and the certainty of failure. He walked to Fitz-Simmonds' office intending to go in and impress Mona with the new leadership he had assumed. But he changed his mind when he remembered how deeply, with a perfect right, she would be affected by the news about Edgar. He walked around trying to concentrate on objects, to keep his feeling from becoming thought. At the corner of Tower Street and King Street a man got in step with him.

'Hi, Missa Ramsay, you doan remember me, sah?'

It was Scuffler, a man who used to sell them stolen mangoes at school. He wore a T-shirt, green khaki trousers and dirty tennis-shoes and he watched Ramsay sideways with a subtle smile.

'Scuffler!' Ramsay said, 'What you know?'

'Ah doan see you since you come back,' Scuffler said, bouncing in his walk and watching Ramsay. He waited, but Ramsay said nothing. 'Ah not on the old lines again, you know, sah.'

Ramsay stopped and forced Scuffler's presence into his consciousness. 'What you doing these days, then?' They walked on.

'Reely,' Scuffler said, 'I'm working at Kingston Club. On the grounds. But life hard, Missa Ramsay. You cyan' scuffle *nutten* these days. Ah see Missa Cyril allatime. Him doing fine as a barrister. Ah hear 'im in court allatime.'

Scuffler knew his man. They waited to cross King Street near parish church.

'You remember Mervyn, use to scuffle with me?' Scuffler asked. 'Him tole me d'other day you going to get a big headmastership soon. Is true, Missa Ramsay?'

Ramsay gave him a shilling and crossed the street.

'Gawd watch over you, Missa Ramsay,' he said, flipped the coin into the air, caught it in both hands, blew on it, slipped it into his pocket in one smooth unbroken action.

The coincidences of the day troubled Ramsay. His father, his mother, would have believed in them and he had a feeling that he had reached the end of his reprieve from God's judgment. Action only oversimplified his dilemma. He could only go back to Mona if Edgar was sent to jail, if the powerless authority became his, and yet he needed to make the smug compassionate gesture of paying Edgar's fine. There was no mental conflict, no struggle between principle and desire; Marxism and the emancipation of black people had not got *that* far down into his consciousness. There were only desire and self-regard and existence. He was sick with the buzzing at the back of his head and the occasional blurring of his vision.

They worked late that night at P.P.L. headquarters preparing for the demonstration. The hard core of the League were there working in a grim excitement. They worked on the banners, got in a hand-press and printed hundreds of leaflets and had a long tense argument over the itinerary of the march. Septy drove around Kingston in Capleton's car and announced the demonstration on the loudspeaker. Andy Maxwell went with him and collected signatures for a petition. At about nine o'clock Mona came in to tell Edgar she would be in the march and to find out when it was starting. She didn't look at Ramsay at all. Then the singing started and Edgar taught them the Bucharest calypso,

> *'This is the kind of society*
> *We are striving for universally,*
> *Tango lay lay lay*
> *Tango lango lango lay.'*

They sang for the fun of it. Backward people don't sing to keep their spirits up.

Cyril went straight to Kingston Club after work that day. He practised soccer vigorously, had a shower, went upstairs and joined three young men at a table on the verandah. They were John Fonseca, a Kingston solicitor, Dick Hopwood, who did not work but was loosely attached to horse-racing, and Tony Myers, an insurance agent.

'Hi, Cyril,' Dick Hopwood said, 'how's the knee?'

'It felt all right,' Cyril said. 'I've got to go easy on it, though.'

'What-you drinking, Cyril?' Tony Myers asked.

'I hope you'll be O.K. for Friday.'

'I think so, Dick. Just squash, Tony.'

Tony snapped his fingers and the steward, Alley, came across from the bar. He was a young man, not more than twenty, very neatly dressed in a white shell-jacket and a black bow-tie. He leaned over with extreme deference to listen to Tony's order.

'I think there's a little political trouble brewing in town,' Cyril said. 'A chap in the People's Progressive League is before the court on Thursday.'

'For what?'

'Banned publications, you know, communist papers.'

'All these small-time Reds should be thrown in jail.'

'Horse-whip them, man,' Tony Myers said.

'I think they're planning a march or something,' Cyril said. He remembered the lunacy in Ramsay's eyes.

In the quick sunset they watched the shadow of the pavilion lengthening on the green smooth grass. They felt themselves secure and unmolestable.

Alley put the drinks on the table – two double scotches, a brandy and ginger, and an orange squash. He watched Tony's white fingers grip the pencil and sign the bill.

'I hear there's a big march on in town tomorrow, Alley,' Dick Hopwood said, glancing at Cyril.

'Yes, sir,' Alley said, crisply and correctly. 'A loudspeaker van pass-through announcing it this evening.'

'Are you going to march, Alley?' John Fonseca asked.

'I not in that, sir,' Alley said with a deprecating laugh. 'It's mostly hooligans playing this kind of politics today. They doan have nutten to do, they not working.' He picked up the empty glasses and shuffled back to the bar.

'Now you take a boy like Alley,' Myers said. 'He's got the right attitude. We treat him well here, he knows his place and he's happy. Every one of those Reds should be put against a wall and shot.'

'If they want to march,' Cyril said, as indifferently as possible, 'they have a right to, as long as they don't molest anybody or damage property.'

'Look, all this class thing is bull,' John Fonseca said. 'Alley's grandfather could have been my grandfather, too, you know. He slept with a mulatto and produced my father and he slept with a black slave and produced Alley's father. It's only a chance that Alley is serving me drinks. No matter what system you have, life is a chance.'

Alley stood at the bar talking to Scottie, the barman. Scottie was about fifty and had once been the best 'googlie' bowler in Jamaica until his eyes went bad and he couldn't hold his return catches. He was illiterate and the management of the Club, recognizing his services to cricket, gave him the barman's job.

'Them boy going march to rass tomorrow,' Alley said, quietly, out of the corner of his mouth. 'I going *march* with them, man!'

'P.P.L., nuh?' Scottie said. He nodded towards the drinkers, 'If they ever fine out, you lose your job same time!'

'Is a big march, you know, sah,' Alley grinned. 'Every worker in it.'

'You can march,' Scottie said. 'You young.'

'About two tousand. An' singing,' Alley said.

It was dark now and they could see the street-lights on South Camp Road and watch the headlights of comfortable cars swing into the north entrance to the Club. It seemed to Cyril that he was safest here with the high solid walls around and the voices downstairs laughing with the carelessness of money. It was silly, of course, and Ramsay was obviously going mad. Actually he was feeling a throbbing in his knee and he ought to go home to bed. The situation with Ramsay wasn't frightening, it was just fantastic.

Fonseca, Hopwood and Myers had been together at an exclusive school called Epsom College. When they ran out of conversation they tried to keep alive the importance of trivial incidents in their schooldays.

'You remember Fritz Gould before he was a prefect?' John Fonseca asked.

Myers and Hopwood spluttered with laughter.

'In prep –' Tony Myers said, and could hardly breathe for laughing.

Cyril had not heard this joke before, and after they subsided into giggling John Fonseca explained that Fritz Gould used to slip out of prep to smoke, by walking backwards while watching the prefect in charge carefully; if the prefect looked up before Fritz Gould got out Fritz would start walking *forwards* and pretend to be going to the prefect's desk. It was very funny and Alley, who did not hear the joke, laughed discreetly in subtle deference.

Fonseca ordered another round of drinks to celebrate Fritz Gould's cleverness.

'There is a lot of social reconstruction needed in Jamaica,' Cyril said. 'The situation is quite explosive.'

The Epsom College boys looked silently into their drinks. Perhaps what Cyril said was true but it was in bad taste to mention it over a drink in Kingston Club. Cyril was a wonderful chap but he had not played on the same lawns with them as children or been to the same birthday parties. For them a man who can play a brilliant game of soccer but cannot ride a horse has a kind of moral inadequacy that can easily make him a socialist.

John Fonseca asked Cyril to go to Glass Bucket with them, but he wanted to rest his knee for Friday's match. As Alley watched the three cars drive away, Cyril's in the middle, he said to himself, 'Is going be a rass march!'

By nine o'clock on Thursday morning there was a crowd of five hundred people blocking the traffic on Slipe Road outside the P.P.L. offices. It was an orderly crowd because many of them were uncertain about the precise reason for the march. In order to get such a large crowd together Septy had told them, variously, that it was an unemployment march, a freedom-from-hunger march, a cost-of-living march. He told them they were going to 'march on Dr Phillips', and the more politically conscious workers in the Merchants' Party were always willing to do that.

While the crowd waited outside, there was a discussion in the office as to whether Edgar Bailey should be in the demonstration. Ramsay became suddenly prominent in the discussion and he spoke with great clarity and fundamental cowardice. If Edgar was in the demonstration, Ramsay argued, the police would arrest him, as the Commissioner had threatened, and there would almost certainly be violence and bloodshed. Edgar said he didn't care about being arrested and that some bloodshed would help the cause. Nobody agreed with him. In this slight indecision Ramsay grabbed the largest banner and stepped out on to the piazza. He was greeted by a tremendous, dazzling shout from the crowd, and the song 'We will build Jamaica' was raised.

The banner Ramsay was carrying was a jet black cloth, ten feet by four on which the words, WE DEMAND FREEDOM OF THOUGHT, had been spelled out in large red letters. Two eight-foot poles supported the banner. There were three other smaller banners: DOWN WITH P.D.P. FASCISM, NO CASE AGAINST BAI-

LEY, and WHO KILLED SKIPPER G.? It was this last banner that made the crowd a mob and they started chanting, 'Who killed Skipper G.?' Ramsay had never faced a mob like this before and standing above them on the piazza the sound and movement intoxicated and frightened him.

Septy Grant took hold of the other pole of the largest banner and stepped off with Ramsay leading the mob down Slipe Road. They kept fairly consistently to the right side of the street marching grimly to the chanted rhythm. Just below Torrington Bridge they sang *The Red Flag* pitched, uncannily, at just the right key for shouting and the grimness gave way to a sweeping joy. They sang hymns like *Onward Christian Soldiers*, and *Glory be to God, He sets me free*, and marching songs like *John Brown's Body*. About a hundred schoolchildren joined the procession on the way for the singing.

The intention was to march into the grounds of the National Assembly, present the petition peacefully to Dr Phillips and then disperse.

But as the demonstrators turned into Duke Street they faced a small group of P.D.P. Action Groupers. The Action Group went for the banners and a fight started but had hardly begun properly before the police came in with batons and the Action Group disappeared. The detachment of fifty police had little difficulty in dispersing the mob. There was a lot of pulling about and trampling but the only person hurt by the police, absurdly, was Ramsay Tull. He had gone to argue with a police sergeant that the demonstration was peaceful, and while he was shouting to the sergeant part of the crowd rushed the sergeant, and his baton, quite accidentally, hit Ramsay a sharp blow on the back of the head. He didn't fall, and he didn't lose consciousness fully but from that moment he had only a blurred awareness of place and time and people. For a while there on Duke Street he had a heightened visual sensation of the mob as an animated painting and he remembered afterwards the angle of the sunlight on the trampled banners. But he did not know that it was Mona who took him to his mother's home although he spoke to her quite lucidly on the way.

For three days he lay in bed with a nervous fever. He woke up and was fed by a blurred outline that he recognized only as his mother's voice and her presence. And he knew, in its gentle stillness, the presence of the doctor. But his mind, completely will-less, closed itself from Mona. She spent hours watching him sleep but could make no contact with him. In a nightly delirium he spoke the same words over and over – *car tu trembles, car j'ai senti, que tu le veuilles ou non le tremblement adoré de ta main descendre tout le long des branches du jasmin you black man you blaackmaaan, la bouche doucement la bouche bébé bloody bawdy flagratic leadership, remorseless, lecherous, treacherous flagratic leadership, O explanatory Word, oui, je tremble et je pleure et je t'aime et suis tienne et tu m'as enivrée.* Then he would laugh a long applauding laugh and start over again and again until he fell into a sweaty sleep. Mrs Tull was frightened the first time she heard the clear words that had no meaning for her. Then she accepted a miracle. She believed that Ramsay had seen a vision and was speaking in one of the pentecostal tongues that had descended on the apostles.

On the fourth day of his illness he recognized the doctor. He was a white man, very pale with his skin stretched tight and transparent against the forehead and the cheekbones. He sat on the bed and Ramsay knew there was no escape. The daylight outside was violet and the stillness made him know he must confess.

'I am very ill,' he said to the doctor.

'Yes,' the doctor said.

'I have wasted my talent.'

'Yes.'

'I am a wonderful person and I feel that the world has ignored me.'

'Yes,' the doctor said, and checked Ramsay's pulse.

'I am psycho-neurotic. I shall be a mental cripple for life.'

The doctor did not answer.

'But I shall not die.'

'No.'

'I am a man, doctor, a man! I mean, *still* a man!'

'Yes,' the doctor said, muttering to himself *in secreto.* The stethoscope seemed to Ramsay to be crucified around the doctor's neck.

'There is no mercy, then?'

'None.'

'Forgiveness?'

'There is forgiveness.' The doctor's face swung away from Ramsay like a large white hanging lamp.

'I shall go to the hills,' Ramsay said and added, without purpose, 'finally'.

'You shall go,' the doctor said, now only a shape near the door. 'You will find peace and be healed. You will not remember me.'

When the doctor had gone Ramsay laughed for a long time and rode to a joyous sleep.

He woke up and saw Mona sitting by the bed watching him. He tried to remember why she was there and why her smile seemed to apologize for something.

'Mona! What's the matter?' he asked.

'Lawd, Ramsay, every day I come here and sit down and watch you like a baby sleeping and you don't know me, Ramsay; the doctor say you getting better and can soon move.'

'Is Edgar gone to prison?' Ramsay asked. He had had a dream about Edgar. 'Eh?'

'No,' Mona said, 'he paid the fine. Everything is all right. Forget about that, you need to res' your brain.'

He tried hard to put the pieces together, wondered who had paid the fine. He looked at Mona again and saw that she loved him.

'I've been sad sad, Ramsay,' she said. 'I packed up your things and give them to Aunt Alice. I miss you all the time, at night I doan have anybody to cling to an' I feel sad.'

'Where they got the money to pay the fine?' he shouted.

'Septy sold Capleton car,' she said, understanding that Ramsay had lost for ever to Edgar all but herself. 'Capleton is very very poorly.'

'But what's happening?' he asked. 'Any protest meetings? Any *meetings* I say!' He was shouting. 'Has Edgar called a meeting?'

'Don't hackle up yourself about the League, Ramsay,' she pleaded. 'You mean to kill out yourself for nutten? No, not that, but you not strong enough yet.'

He lay back and was quieter and he heard the buzzing sound

starting again in the back of his head. It was the worst kind of failure.

'I'm going to the country,' he said. 'To Orange Town till I feel better. It's this buzzing in the back of my head like a machine running down –'

'You know what,' she said, 'I'm going come with you after Capleton, well, you know. Aunt Alice said I should come.'

He felt annoyed with Mona, for nothing, for his need of her and his inability to modify the very thing he needed. He wanted to tell her that he would die now, that the will which had kept him alive was gone; it was nonsense but he wanted to communicate that nonsense. If she could love him through the confusion, in those terms, not love him, and *only* love him, until he died. Christ, he really *was* going mad. All those books.

'You were right,' he said. 'All those books have messed me up.'

'No, no, Ramsay, I only said it to hurt you. What do *I* know?' she said. 'You should stop this politics and make life.'

'That's the way you want me? Cyril Hanson and Reggie Kendal and all the men you slept with, to drive a big car and go to King's House?'

She cried, not with the shame and regret he wanted her to feel but because it was simply sad; he was young and destroyed and feeble and she wanted him.

'I want you any which way,' she said, quietly. 'For I love you, and may God never make me love another man who can torment himself like you.' She put her hand on his forehead and he closed his eyes around his first understanding of physical weakness, the sensation of her presence that went down to the root of every nerve, and the escape of impotence.

The next day he got a letter from Mabel telling him the date of her marriage. She wrote about her fiancé, Homer Bryce, with a giggling accent that was unlike her. She advised Ramsay to give up the political joke and get serious about life. She didn't think Mona Freeman was good for him but he should either stop living with her or marry her. She reminded Ramsay that he was only twenty-four and outlined a plan for him to come to America when she had settled there and do a Ph.D. And he should take good care of Aunt Alice.

V

Dr Phillips was interrupted only once when he introduced the Bill in the Assembly to make illegal, in Jamaica, communism, Marxism and all forms of political parties whose basic creeds advocate violence and totalitarianism. This was because the Opposition did not share his sense of the urgency of the situation and because his own party knew that the Bill was being passed to refute the suggestion made by an American journalist that the P.D.P. was a communist party in disguise.

Dr Phillips said, 'In bringing this measure before the House we are not trying to wash from our hands something which has never contaminated them.' Mannie Small interrupted with, 'Then why did the Minister of Commerce and Industries say he is a Marxist?'

'I am not surprised,' Dr Phillips said in measured easy tones, 'that the leader of the Opposition is innocent of political under-standing. We are a socialist party but we do not derive from Karl Marx. I am bringing this measure before the House to protect the leader of the Opposition from his own political *naïveté*.

'The features of communism which my government, like all the governments of the free world, deplores are that total author-ity over every aspect of life, philosophy, art, science, with no room for another opinion, that whole fantastic fabric supported by a sinister secret police with its instruments of torture and concentration camps.

'We will have no part of that in this island and my government considers it its duty to protect the people from this criminal political theory.

'Members of the House may consider that in the realities of the facts the possibility of a physical and violent overthrow of the democratically constituted government of this country is extremely remote. But bear in mind that in, perhaps, ten years we will no longer have the protecting sheltering wing of Great Britain. And once communism takes root here and begins to spread (and the disciplined communist has extraordinary powers of patience and tenacity) when we become a Dominion it may need only a little force to overthrow the democratic institutions in this country. This Bill is a safeguard against the future. It is true that today we have on the whole only gadfly nuisances and underfed hooligans but there are also a very few who show signs of giving themselves over to the regimented fanaticism of that dangerous ideology, and, I am afraid, they have some influence among the more irresponsible workers. I would remind the House that it needs only a few men to upset, in a moment, the work of years.

'In this Bill the government is not admitting any present fears. Far from it. But no matter how well we govern, no matter how much prosperity we spread among the people, there will always be agitators to find faults enough to stir up those elements who, under a realistic socialist system, must have less than others. One day it may happen (I shall be dead then) that this country will have to choose between peaceful inequality, with all the democratic freedoms intact, and a tyranny which gives to the leaders of a single party equal opportunities for vandalism, theft and murder. But only a lunatic would attempt to prophesy in a world that is changing its physical and intellectual shape so rapidly and so unexpectedly. All we can do is to try, while admitting fallibility, to read the present aright. It is our duty, we believe, to keep communist ideas out of this country, *now*. We already have a law covering subversive literature. I shall, very shortly, bring before this House a measure which will make it difficult for any Jamaican to travel to a communist country, and which will make it impossible for *anyone*, Jamaican or otherwise, to travel from a communist country to Jamaica.

'We have here a cosmopolitan, multiracial society in which all colours and races mix with full social and political equality – an example to the world. The only colour that we will not admit freely into this society is red.

'Mr Speaker, sir, I beg to move.'

Dr Phillips' speech was given full coverage in the foreign press and the part of the American Fleet that was exercising in the Caribbean continued its slick manoeuvres.

Eustace Capleton lay dying with four people at his bedside – Edgar Bailey, Andy Maxwell, a Catholic priest who gave him extreme unction, and Mona Freeman. He was a wizened old man. In the heat he had thrown off the sheets and they could see on his body, where the skin and the bone were one, little lumps of flesh, under the skin, that had resisted the suck of cancer. Again and again he tried to vomit but couldn't and he threw himself across the bed feebly trying to batter away the pain in his stomach. Mona held his head and fed him a glass of water. He brought it up again with relief and then lay back on the pillows, waiting.

For the past two days he had lost interest in politics and people. He spoke only to tell of the pain and to ask for water. The images and thoughts he had were related only to physical suffering. The watchers all wished for him to die.

At three o'clock the doctor came in and told them it would soon be over. He waited with them for an hour then went away on his rounds promising to return later. Capleton slept and Mona hoped he would die sleeping.

He woke up and started shouting for Skipper George Lannaman.

'Where Skipper G.? Skipper G.! Edgar, call Skipper G., I want to tell him something.'

'Skipper G. gone long time,' Andy said.

'No! Skipper G. not dead,' Capleton shouted. 'Who say him dead? Who kill him?'

'He'll soon be here,' Edgar said. 'I send for him already. He'll soon be here.'

Then Capleton went to sleep again and his breathing was sharp and painful and the lumps of flesh on his stomach quivered independently each time he breathed. He woke up again and called for Skipper G. and then he fell back and his body stiffened, but he was still breathing.

It is believed that just between life and death the dying man's soul travels into the spirit world for a while and sees a glorious vision, the kingdoms of the world in one universal glance and the portals of the kingdom of Heaven. When his soul returns he dies.

When Eustace Capleton's soul 'travelled' he found himself looking down into a clearing in a huge forest. No day had ever been so bright, no leaves so brilliantly green, but there were no shadows from the trees. Light drums began, led by the rhythm of a metal gong and above the drums Capleton heard women's voices singing a sad resolute song about death. They sang, 'Death, you are strong but, as for today, we are ready to meet you.' The sounds came slowly into the clearing and he saw women in black robes and black headcloths singing and dancing. Suddenly a girl of thirteen, garlanded from the waist up with strings of beads, bracelets on her wrists and ankles, and her hair plaited tight and shining, danced in the centre of the clearing surrounded by the women. She mimed the challenge to death and when she threw her head back in defiance Capleton saw her face clearly and recognized, without astonishment, that it was his mother's face. He had moved into a region where there was no more pain and he laughed, with the women, at the triviality of death.

The people who had been watching the ecstasy on Capleton's face heard, not a laugh, but the last rattle of breath in his throat. Watching him Mona swayed dizzily and had to hold on to the bed-post to steady herself. Andy telephoned the undertaker.

'Right now, I not sure o' nutten,' Edgar said, sadly, to Andy. 'I only sure I'm a naygah an' I'm poor. An' you know what, Andy, some which way, they will *always* beat us like this.'

After Capleton's funeral Mona wrote to Ramsay.

Dear Ramsay, my darling,

I hope you are keeping fine. Capleton died on Tuesday and we buried him yesterday. It was a nice funeral. *People*, you see, Ramsay and *cars*, about fifty cars. I just cry all the time from he died until last night, I never knew I would stop crying. When they were letting down the coffin Septy Grant raised Red Flag, it was like the biggest hymn. I just couldn't stop crying, he was a father to me you know, Ramsay.

But he died good. When he was travelling, you see, his face was so shining he's gone to Jesus I'm sure. We are packing up his things and what we can sell we will sell and Fitz-Simmonds is looking after everything.

I am coming to Orange Town as soon as poss. to look after you until you get better. I'm tired, working and looking after Capleton just wear me out but in the next two weeks I'll be with you.

Cyril Hanson 'phoned to ask for you. He said he wanted to invite you to the wedding so I told him where you are. It's going to be a big wedding, I know the girl making Pat Phillips' dress.

Look after yourself well until I come, you hear? Please give Aunt Alice my love.

Lots of love

from

Mona

P.S. – Please excuse errors. – M.

Edgar kept the People's Progressive League going for a while, working quietly and well within the law. The Slipe Road offices were closed again and headquarters transferred to the room in Mark Lane. Then he bought a small station-wagon for the League and the security police became suspicious when they found out that he had paid six hundred pounds cash for the car. The League held no street-meetings now, for Edgar was concentrating on keeping the spirit alive in a handful of dedicated workers. He kept in close touch with the Mannie Small Trade Union and visited the sugar estates regularly even after Mannie Small had warned him off. But his main work was in Kingston among the dock workers and in the evening lectures he gave.

He had just finished a lecture on 'The Necessity for the total Emancipation of the Peoples of Africa', which had consisted only of statistics illustrating economic exploitation. The ten workers who had listened to him were gone and he was closing up the room when the police came in. There was the Assistant Commissioner in uniform and another security man, in plain clothes, both English. A sergeant and two corporals, Jamaicans, all armed, followed them. And then Bobsie Tull, Minister of Justice, came in.

Edgar heard the warrant for his arrest and heard about the Governor's emergency powers under which he could be detained indefinitely without trial, and he heard that a letter, addressed to him, with a banknote for two hundred pounds, had been intercepted in the post. The letter and banknote were from an international youth organization which gave 'instructions' as to how the money should be used.

'You finish, Edgar,' Bobsie said.

'Why you come?' Edgar asked him. 'You are a policeman?'

'I come to tell you that you finish,' Bobsie said. 'P.P.L. finish at last.'

The policeman said they were ready to take Edgar.

'I have a mother,' Edgar said, 'to look after. And two sisters – '

'Don't worry,' Bobsie assured him, 'they'll be well taken care of. They're in my constituency. Let's go to the station, Edgar. Fitz-Simmonds is there, I 'phoned him. He say you finish this time.'

They allowed him to lock up the room.

Outside, he said to Bobsie, with a tight smile, 'Every day you lose and lose and lose but one day you will win.'

'You used to win all the time,' Bobsie said, as Edgar stepped into the police car and sat between the two corporals. 'You remember Charles Street, Edgar?'

Edgar was in a good mood on the drive to the station. He sang the Bucharest calypso through twice and then offered to teach it to the corporals.

'Look, my frien',' the older corporal said, 'you in the bigges' trouble any Jimaycan ever in. Don't play the haass!'

The wedding of Cyril Hanson to Patricia Phillips in the Surrey College chapel was comparatively simple. As he waited for his bride Cyril's attention was focused on a plaque dedicated to the memory of the school's first headmaster, the Reverend Edward Trevor. He remembered the day, fifteen years before, when he had sat for the first time on that same front pew, a new boy, and had tried to puzzle out the plaque's Latin inscription, *Iustum et tenacem propositi virum*, 'the man of firm and just resolve'. He had come back triumphantly to that perfection while Ramsay Tull, who had puzzled out the quotation with him, had failed.

The guests were seated in a careful hierarchy of colour – John

Fonseca and Tony Myers were the ushers – the whitest in the front pews, the brown in the middle and then a gradual darkening which ended in the back stalls with some black games-playing students from the University College whose brilliant scarlet blazers gave them the terrifying distinction of the unjustly damned. Only Mrs Phillips, who sat beside Mrs Hanson in the second row, disturbed that aesthetic arrangement.

Patricia was a vision of loveliness with her lightly pained English smile.

Mr and Mrs Cyril Hanson emerged from the chapel and walked to their car under an archway of hockey sticks and cricket bats held by the university students and the younger members of Kingston Club.

The reception was on the lawn of the Phillips' house and 'Sylvia Surrey', reporting the 'wedding of the year' in her daily society column, wrote an inspired description of the richness and quantity of the food and drink consumed, the richness and potentiality of middle-class experience.

VI

During an intermission I was up in the little gallery where the band plays in the Club Havana telling the boys in the band that I thought they hadn't quite made it with Tadd Dameron's *Good Bait*, Dizzie Gillespie version. I was rather drunk, actually. The part I was quarrelling about was the second chorus where the theme is played again by the tenor sax and Gillespie's trumpet (muted, I think; anyway I was telling the boys it was muted) comes in over the theme at an interval that makes it sound (if you listen carefully) as if the trumpet is playing in one key and the sax in another. The Club Havana band in their version had omitted the trumpet solo and had therefore lost a whole dimension of the music. I can't play any instrument so I was trying to *sing* the trumpet *obbligato* over the chords Marimba, the pianist, was playing. The trumpeter got it straight off and they said they would try *Good Bait* again later in the night.

Marimba and I were coming down the stairs to have a drink when I saw Mona Freeman come in and walk across the pool of moonlight on the dance-floor to a table in the shadows away from the lights. She was with Herman Belnavis, a tall brown-skin chap I knew slightly, who worked at the audit office and drove a large American car.

I wanted to ask Mona about Ramsay, because I was going to spend three weeks of the summer vac. with my Aunt Queenie in Mount Horesh which is about three miles, across Antrim Hill, from Orange Town and I could walk across to Orange Town and visit Ramsay. I had not been to Mount Horesh for fifteen years and I had to see Aunt Queenie again before she died. She was a wonderful woman. She used to tell me that she had been born a slave (though that could not have been true) and she had in her seventy years never been farther from Mount Horesh than the six miles to Brown's Town. All the time I was in England she sent me at least two pounds every month and sometimes, during the pimento season, as much as fifteen pounds. She was my only aunt and I was her only nephew.

I bought Marimba a drink and walked over to Mona's table. She was happier to see me than Herman was.

'Hi!' Mona said. 'I always see you hanging around night clubs but I never see you with a girl. What happen? You doan function right?'

'Love me or leave me,' I said, American style. Herman was annoyed that I sat down and helped myself to the bottle of rum he had bought. I did not look at him at all but applied a gentle social pressure with my Oxford voice. 'Actually, I'm a kind of unofficial critic for the bands in the clubs.'

'You don't think you should set a better example to the boys you teach in school?' Herman asked, but I didn't go away.

'How is Ramsay?' I asked Mona. 'Is it true that he is going off his head?'

'You see Jamaica malice,' she said. 'It's either T.B. or syphilis or mental asylum. Nothing is *wrong* with Ramsay's head. He's just tired, that's all.'

They went off to dance to a calypso. I was out of love with calypsoes at that time, unreasonably rejecting all calypsoes be-cause I was irritated by the dedicated, sanctified American bleep voice, the New Folk Music. Anyway I was not sure that my attitude had not been formed by jealousy of Mabel Tull's Ameri-can, who 'composed' some of this stuff. I thought of Mabel and Ramsay. Ramsay was a failure but not because he was a Marxist. I do not think he was really a Marxist any more than I was a bop musician; I just liked the sounds bop musicians make and he liked the sounds Marxists make. For Mabel, success was the supreme moral excellence, even illicit sexual success in bed. That is not cynicism. You could not be cynical about Mabel: she was too secure. But in spite of that security, some place some time, in the long run, oh *damn* Mabel! What still held me to the calypso was the bodies of the women dancing to it, 'le visage si triste et le derrière si gai' and the shadows of their bodies under the moon. There was a naked brutality about the way those shadows involved you, abstractly, in lust. I ordered a cup of hot coffee, drank it quickly, drank a small shot of neat rum and settled into a fixed state of beyond-drunkenness.

At about two o'clock I suggested to Mona and Herman that we move on to Bournemouth Club and see what was happening there. Herman was very friendly now and when I complimented him on the skill with which he backed his large car into a small space when he was turning he was very pleased.

It was quiet at Bournemouth Club. Only a few people were there dancing to a five-piece band – piano, bass, drums, guitar and a muted trumpet. They were playing relaxed jazz, wrapping their sleepy souls around it, *Lullaby of Birdland*. I danced with Mona who knew just how to take this music, slowly, behind the beat, getting inside the sound and the rhythm and letting the thing take you around. As she danced she smiled to herself – just that smile, there. A cool breeze was coming up from the sea and it tickled and caressed the back of my neck. I could see the tall glass of very cold rum and ginger waiting for me at the table. I felt *good*. I thought I was really living.

> *'De lever*
> *de pulley*
> *de wheel an' de axle,*
> *de inclined plane,*
> *de wedge an' de screw.*
> *De lever*
> *de pulley....'*

I heard the school-children chanting this as I walked up Chapel Hill into Mount Horesh. I was preceded by a small boy who carried my suitcase on his head. This happened because the taxi-driver who brought me in from Brown's Town said that Chapel Hill was too steep for his car. I was struggling up the hill with the suitcase when a small boy ran out from a cocoa farm and, without my asking him to, put the suitcase on his head. The people I met on the road or who saw me from their yards all gave me two greetings; first, the polite crisp 'Morning' given to a stranger and then, with recognition, the ecstatic, 'Laaawd! Is Cousin Joshie son, come back to Mount Horesh!' I drank coconut water and was kissed, by old ladies I could not remember, in four different yards before I got to Aunt Queenie's house.

Aunt Queenie stood at the front door of her little four-roomed house waiting to receive me. She was tall, stately and unwrinkled in her seventy-five years and she was dressed, as I had always remembered her, in a black headcloth, gold bangles on her wrists and the sweeping Victorian skirt just covering her strong bare toes.

'What a way you grow! The Lord preserve you an' keep you till you come back to yo' Aunt Queenie a big man. God is good, though!' she said, with tears in her eyes.

'Yes, Aunt Queenie,' I said. 'I'm glad to see you.'

She showed me over the little house, then took me into the yard to see the pimento drying on her small barbecue, then she showed me the two pigs and the donkey and the three goats she was rearing. And with childish pride she put on, for me to see, a pair of round gold-rimmed spectacles she had got recently as her eyesight was failing. She made me very comfortable. Aunt Queenie would not have deigned to apologize for the discomfort I might feel after fifteen years away from village life, on that hard bed in that tiny room. As far as she was concerned I was her blood and no amount of 'education' could change that.

I walked around the village, met all my relatives and my old school friends and in the evenings went to the ball-ground in Antrim property to practise cricket with the village team. For breakfast I had bammy or roasted bananas and salt fish fried in coconut oil; for dinner I had calaloo soup or thick red peas soup with bits of pork floating in it, salt fish and ackee, or stewed beef, boiled bananas, flakey afoo yam or roasted yellow yam; for supper, usually fried pork, fried plantain, roasted breadfruit, crackers and a large mug of mint tea, all cooked by Aunt Queenie. After supper I took a lantern and went to one yard or another to listen to the stories, but when there was a ninth night wake the whole village went to the mourners' yard and sat around singing hymns and drinking hot coffee until early in the morning.

The small boy who had carried my suitcase was Wilfred Anguin, about nine years old, the son of my second cousin, Theresa Anguin. Cousin Theresa asked me to take the boy to

Kingston, send him to school there and look after him generally. As Theresa had seven other children I had to agree, and every morning before school and every afternoon he came to do jobs and errands for me. I taught him how to clean my shoes and he made a sling-shot for me and sometimes early in the mornings we went bird-shooting, mostly cling-clings but occasionally we got some pitcharies. One evening I asked him to tell me a story and he told the perfect story no writer could ever write.

Once when Anancy was a little boy he was going on an' him see Ping-Wing bramble wid a rat. Him fight Ping-Wing take 'way the rat so carry it hang it up in the kitchen. When him was gawn Granny come een an' eat off the rat. When Anancy come back him cyan fine the rat. Him say, 'Come, come Granny give me me rat, me rat come from Ping-Wing, Ping-Wing juk me han', me han' come from God.' Granny say, 'Ah cyan't give you back the rat because ah heat it off but take dis knife.'

Anancy go awn until him see a man was cutting cane without a knife. Him say, 'Man, how come you cuttin' cane widout a knife an' I have knife?' The man take Anancy knife start cut the cane an' bruk the knife.

Anancy say, 'Come come man give me mi knife mi knife come from Granny Granny eat mi rat mi rat come from Ping-Wing Ping-Wing juk mi han' mi han' come from God.'

The man say, 'Ah cyan't give you back yo' knife for it break. But tek dis grass.'

Anancy go awn until him see cow eatin' dirt. Him say, 'How you eatin' dirt an' I have grass?'

The cow tek the grass eat it off.

Anancy say, 'Come come cow give me mi grass mi grass come from man man bruk mi knife mi knife come from Granny Granny eat mi rat mi rat come from Ping-Wing Ping-Wing juk mi han' mi han' come from God.'

Cow say, 'Well, a cyan't give you back you' grass but tek dis milk.'

Anancy go on till him see a woman giving her baby black tea. Him say, 'How you giving you' baby black tea an' I have milk?'

The woman tek the milk give it to baby, baby drink it off.

Anancy say, 'Come come woman give me mi milk mi milk come

from cow cow eat mi grass mi grass come from man man bruk mi knife mi knife come from Granny Granny eat mi rat mi rat come from Ping-Wing Ping-Wing juk mi han' mi han' come from God.'

The woman say 'Ah cyan't give you back you' milk but tek dis blue.'

Anancy go awn till him see a woman washing clothes widout blue. Him say, 'How you washing clothes widout blue, an' I have blue?'

The woman tek the blue, use it off.

Anancy say, 'Come come woman give me mi blue mi blue come from woman woman drink mi milk mi milk come from cow cow eat mi grass mi grass come from man man bruk mi knife mi knife come from Granny Granny eat mi rat mi rat come from Ping-Wing Ping-Wing juk mi han' mi han' come from God.'

The woman say, 'Ah cyan't give you back you' blue but tek dis fish.'

Anancy go awn, him see a tar stump blazin' fire widout anyt'ing on it. Him say, 'How you blazin' fire widout fish, an' I have fish?'

Him throw the fish on the tar stump. When it cook Anancy try to pull off the fish but it cyan' come off the tar stump.

De fish stay there till it burn up.

Anancy say, 'Come come tar 'tump give me mi fish mi fish come from woman woman use mi blue mi blue come from woman woman drink mi milk mi milk come from cow cow eat mi grass mi grass come from man man bruk mi knife mi knife come from Granny Granny eat mi rat mi rat come from Ping-Wing Ping-Wing juk mi han' mi han' come from God.'

Tar stump no speak.

Anancy lick him wid him lef' hand. Lef han' fasten. Him lick him wid him right han'. Right han' fasten. Him kick him wid him lef' foot, lef' foot fasten. Him kick him wid him right foot. Right foot fasten. Him buck him wid him head. Head fasten.

Hear Anancy:

> 'Who say no, do no harm
> Amen to glory,
> Cananana Poh.'

Jack mandora me no choose none.

I lay on my back in the little coffee-grove behind Chen's shop. Midday, and the mastering sun strong on this hillside village, lazy as the flicked leaves, the drift clouds and the sleepy dogs. It was August and the pimento perfume came to me on a light breeze. I could hear the children singing on their way home from the river. Mount Horesh. I remembered, with a sweet feeling in my stomach, that at night, 'Over there,' the storyteller would say, 'at the lights of Runaway Bay, the fishermen and the slaves' duppies in white baptismal dress.'

I was a god again, drunk on the mead of the land, and massive with the sun chanting in my veins. And so, flooded with the bright clarity of my acceptance, I held this lovely wayward island, starkly, in my arms.

ABOUT THE AUTHOR

Neville Dawes was born in Nigeria in 1926, but grew up in rural Jamaica. He studied for an MA at Oxford (Oriel College), taught in Jamaica, Ghana and Guyana, and was later appointed Director of the Institute of Jamaica. He wrote two novels, *The Last Enchantment* and *Interim* and a critical work, *Prolegomena to West Indian Literature*.

CARIBBEAN MODERN CLASSICS

Spring 2009 titles

Jan R. Carew
Black Midas
Introduction: Kwame Dawes
ISBN: 9781845230951; pp. 272; 23 May 2009; £8.99

This is the bawdy, Eldoradean epic of the legendary 'Ocean Shark' who makes and loses fortunes as a pork-knocker in the gold and diamond fields of Guyana, discovering that there are sharks with far sharper teeth in the city. *Black Midas* was first published in 1958.

Jan R. Carew
The Wild Coast
Introduction: Jeremy Poynting
ISBN: 9781845231101; pp. 240; 23 May 2009; £8.99

First published in 1958, this is the coming-of-age story of a sickly city child, sent away to the remote Berbice village of Tarlogie. Here he must find himself, make sense of Guyana's diverse cultural inheritances and come to terms with a wild nature disturbingly red in tooth and claw.

Neville Dawes
The Last Enchantment
Introduction: Kwame Dawes
ISBN: 9781845231170; pp. 332; 27 April 2009; £9.99

This penetrating and often satirical exploration of the search for self in a world divided by colour and class is set in the context of the radical hopes of Jamaican nationalist politics in the early 1950s. First published in 1960, the novel asks many pertinent questions about the Jamaica of today.

Wilson Harris
Heartland
Introduction: Michael Mitchell
ISBN: 9781845230968; pp. 104; 23 May 2009; £7.99

First published in 1964, this visionary narrative tracks one man's psychic disintegration in the aloneness of the forests of the Guyanese interior, making a powerful ecological statement about man's place in the 'invisible chain of being', in which nature is a no less active presence.

Edgar Mittelholzer
Corentyne Thunder
Introduction: Juanita Cox
ISBN: 9781845231118; pp. 242; 27 April 2009; £8.99

This pioneering work of West Indian fiction, first published in 1941, is not merely an acute portrayal of the rural Indo-Guyanese world, but a work of literary ambition that creates a symphonic relationship between its characters and the vast openness of the Corentyne coast.

Andrew Salkey
Escape to an Autumn Pavement
Introduction: Thomas Glave
ISBN: 9781845230982; pp. 220; 23 May 2009; £8.99

This brave and remarkable novel, set in London at the end of the 1950s, and published in 1960, catches its 'brown' Jamaican narrator on the cusp between black and white, between exiled Jamaican and an incipent black Londoner, and between heterosexual and homosexual desires.

Denis Williams
Other Leopards
Introduction: Victor Ramraj
ISBN: 9781845230678; pp. 216; 23 May 2009; £8.99

Lionel Froad is a Guyanese working on an archeological survey in the mythical Jokhara in the horn of Africa. There he hopes to rediscover the self he calls 'Lobo', his alter ego from 'ancestral times', which he thinks slumbers behind his cultivated mask. First published in 1963, this is one of the most important Caribbean novels of the past fifty years.

Denis Williams
The Third Temptation
Introduction: Victor Ramraj
ISBN: 9781845231163; pp. 108; 23 May 2009; £7.99

A young man is killed in a traffic accident at a Welsh seaside resort. Around this incident, Williams, drawing inspiration from the *Nouveau Roman*, creates a reality that is both rich and problematic. Whilst he brings to the novel a Caribbean eye, Williams makes an important statement about refusing any restrictive boundaries for Caribbean fiction. The novel was first published in 1968.

Roger Mais
The Hills Were Joyful Together
Introduction: tba
ISBN: 9781845231002; pp. 272; October 2009; £8.99

Unflinchingly realistic in its portrayal of the wretched lives of Kingston's urban poor, this is a novel of prophetic rage. First published in 1953, it is both a work of tragic vision and a major contribution to the evolution of an autonomous Caribbean literary aesthetic.

Edgar Mittelholzer
A Morning at the Office
Introduction: Raymond Ramcharitar
ISBN: 978184523; pp. 208; October 2009; £8.99

First published in 1950, this is one of the Caribbean's foundational novels in its bold attempt to portray a whole society in miniature. A genial satire on human follies and the pretensions of colour and class, this novel brings several ingenious touches to its mode of narration.

Edgar Mittelholzer
Shadows Move Among Them
Introduction: tba
ISBN: 9781845230913; pp. 320; December 2009; £9.99

In part a satire on the Eldoradean dream, in part an exploration of the possibilities of escape from the discontents of civilisation, Mittelholzer's 1951 novel of the Reverend Harmston's attempt to set up a utopian commune dedicated to 'Hard work, frank love and wholesome play' has some eerie 'pre-echoes' of the fate of Jonestown in 1979.

Edgar Mittelholzer
The Life and Death of Sylvia
Introduction: Juanita Cox
ISBN: 9781845231200; pp. 318; December 2009, £9.99

In 1930s' Georgetown, a young woman on her own is vulnerable prey, and when Sylvia Russell finds she cannot square her struggle for economic survival and her integrity, she hurtles towards a wilfully early death. Mittelholzer's novel of 1953 is a richly inward portrayal of a woman who finds inner salvation through the act of writing.

Elma Napier
A Flying Fish Whispered
Introduction: Evelyn O'Callaghan
ISBN: 9781845231026; pp. 248; February 2010; £8.99

With one of the most delightfully feisty women characters in Caribbean fiction and prose that sings, Elma Napier's 1938 Dominican novel is a major rediscovery, not least for its imaginative exploration of different kinds of Caribbeans, in particular the polarity between plot and plantation that Napier sees in a distinctly gendered way.

Orlando Patterson
The Children of Sisyphus
Introduction: Geoffrey Philp
ISBN: 9781845230944; pp. 288; November 2009; £9.99

This is a brutally poetic book that brings to the characters who live on Kingston's 'dungle' an intensity that invests them with tragic depth. In Patterson's existentialist novel, first published in 1964, dignity comes with a stoic awareness of the absurdity of life and the shedding of false illusions, whether of salvation or of a mythical African return.

V.S. Reid
New Day
Introduction: tba
ISBN: 9781845230906, pp. 360; November 2009, £9.99

First published in 1949, this historical novel focuses on defining moments of Jamaica's nationhood, from the Morant Bay rebellion of 1865, to the dawn of self-government in 1944. *New Day* pioneers the creation of a distinctively Jamaican literary language of narration.

Garth St. Omer
A Room on the Hill
Introduction: John Robert Lee
ISBN: 9781845230937; pp. 210; September 2009; £8.99

A friend's suicide and his profound alienation in a St Lucia still slumbering in colonial mimicry and the straitjacket of a reactionary Catholic church drive John Lestrade into a state of internal exile. First published in 1968, St. Omer's meticulously crafted novel is a pioneering exploration of the inner Caribbean man.

Austin C. Clarke, *The Survivors of the Crossing*
Austin C. Clarke, *Amongst Thistles and Thorns*
O.R. Dathorne, *The Scholar Man*
O.R. Dathorne, *Dumplings in the Soup*
Neville Dawes, *Interim*
Wilson Harris, *The Eye of the Scarecrow*
Wilson Harris, *The Sleepers of Roraima*
Wilson Harris, *Tumatumari*
Wilson Harris, *Ascent to Omai*
Wilson Harris, *The Age of the Rainmakers*
Marion Patrick Jones, *Panbeat*
Marion Patrick Jones, *Jouvert Morning*
Earl Lovelace, *Whilst Gods Are Falling*
Roger Mais, *Black Lightning*
Edgar Mittelholzer, *Children of Kaywana*
Edgar Mittelholzer, *The Harrowing of Hubertus*
Edgar Mittelholzer, *Kaywana Blood*
Edgar Mittelholzer, *My Bones and My Flute*
Edgar Mittelholzer, *A Swarthy Boy*
Orlando Patterson, *An Absence of Ruins*
V.S. Reid, *The Leopard* (North America only)
Garth St. Omer, *Shades of Grey*
Andrew Salkey, *The Late Emancipation of Jerry Stover*
and more…

All Peepal Tree titles are available from the website
www.peepaltreepress.com
with a money back guarantee, secure credit card ordering
and fast delivery throughout the world at cost or less.

Peepal Tree Press is the home of challenging and inspiring literature
from the Caribbean and Black Britain. Visit www.peepaltreepress.com
to read sample poems and reviews, discover new authors, established
names and access a wealth of information.

Contact us at:
Peepal Tree Press, 17 King's Avenue, Leeds LS6 1QS, UK
Tel: +44 (0) 113 2451703 E-mail: contact@peepaltreepress.com